M000204565

RED RIVER ROAD

ALSO BY ANNA DOWNES

The Safe Place

The Shadow House

RED RIVER ROAD

A Novel

ANNA DOWNES

MINOTAUR
BOOKS
NEW YORK

This is a work of fiction. All of the characters, organizations, and events portrayed in this novel are either products of the author's imagination or are used fictitiously.

First published in the United States by Minotaur Books, an imprint of St. Martin's Publishing Group

RED RIVER ROAD. Copyright © 2024 by Anna Downes. All rights reserved. Printed in the United States of America. For information, address St. Martin's Publishing Group, 120 Broadway, New York, NY 10271.

All emojis designed by OpenMoji – the open-source emoji and icon project. License: CC BY-SA 4.0

www.minotaurbooks.com

Designed by Omar Chapa

Library of Congress Cataloging-in-Publication Data

Names: Downes, Anna, author.
Title: Red River Road : a novel / Anna Downes.
Description: First U.S. edition. | New York : Minotaur Books, 2024.
Identifiers: LCCN 2024007542 | ISBN 9781250868015 (hardcover) |
    ISBN 9781250868022 (ebook)
Subjects: LCSH: Sisters—Fiction. | Missing persons—Fiction. |
    Self-realization in women—Fiction. | Australia—Fiction. |
    LCGFT: Thrillers (Fiction) | Psychological fiction. | Novels.
Classification: LCC PR6104.O896 R44 2024 | DDC 823/.92—dc23/
    eng/20240216
LC record available at https://lccn.loc.gov/2024007542

Our books may be purchased in bulk for promotional, educational, or business use. Please contact your local bookseller or the Macmillan Corporate and Premium Sales Department at 1-800-221-7945, extension 5442, or by email at MacmillanSpecialMarkets@macmillan.com.

Originally published in Australia by Affirm Press

First U.S. Edition: 2024

10 9 8 7 6 5 4 3 2 1

For my sister Lucy.

And solo female travelers everywhere.

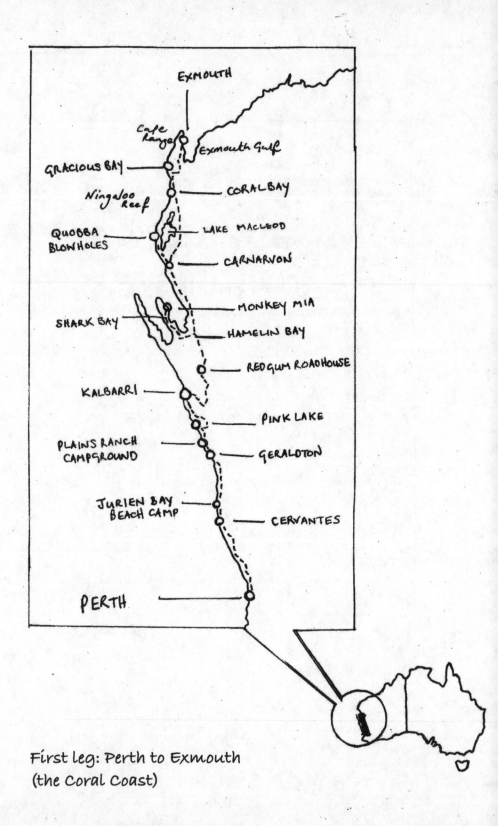

EXMOUTH

Cape
Range

Exmouth Gulf

GRACIOUS BAY

CORAL BAY

Ningaloo
Reef

LAKE MACLEOD

QUOBBA
BLOWHOLES

CARNARVON

MONKEY MIA

SHARK BAY

HAMELIN BAY

RED GUM ROADHOUSE

KALBARRI

PINK LAKE

PLAINS RANCH
CAMPGROUND

GERALDTON

JURIEN BAY
BEACH CAMP

CERVANTES

PERTH

First leg: Perth to Exmouth
(the Coral Coast)

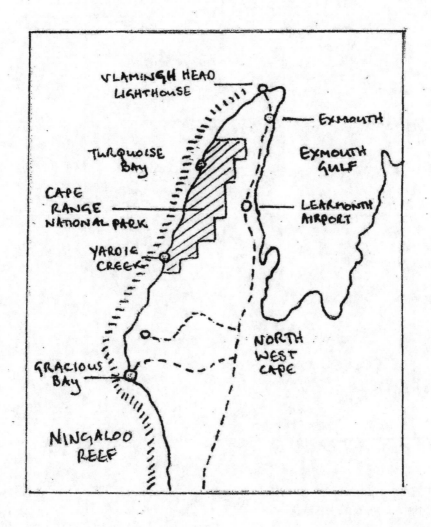

Ningaloo - can't wait!

"Take care of yourself!" screamed the White Queen, seizing Alice's hair with both her hands. "Something's going to happen!"

And then (as Alice afterwards described it), all sorts of things happened in a moment.

LEWIS CARROLL
Through the Looking Glass: chapter IX
—"Queen Alice"

RED RIVER ROAD

Liked by **goodnightpetergraham** and **others**

pheebsinwonderland Hi everyone! I'm Phoebe and I'm a travel addict and vanlifer about to take me, myself, and I off on an adventure of a lifetime: THE BIG LAP OF AUSTRALIA! Only two more sleeps to go. And before you ask: no, I'm not scared. The first thing people say when I tell them I'm traveling alone is "BE CAREFUL"—and don't even get me started on my parents' response. But the world is full of magic, and solo travel offers way more rewards than risks—it's just that the bad stories get told more often than the good. (Sidenote: according to my astrology chart, planetary alignment this year will bring significant transformations and challenges but also *opportunities* and *growth*—how's that for a good sign?!) So I want to explore this beautiful country and share my experiences with you so that hopefully you, and others, won't be afraid to do the same. Please join me as I travel an entire loop of Australia, starting and ending in Perth. Check out my photos, keep up with my posts, and hit me with your own travel tips! There's no advice I trust more than word of mouth. See you on the road! Love and light, Pheebs x

PS: If you're still worried, see my list of TOP TWENTY SAFETY TIPS as compiled from various travel blogs and websites. I hereby swear I will plaster this list on the wall of my van and follow its advice every day so help me god. Happy now, Mum? 😄

(Image descriptions: 1. A long-haired girl wearing denim shorts and a bikini top stands on a dusty red road facing a beautiful sunset. A white van is parked to one side, fairy lights twinkling through the open side door. The road twists and winds like a river over the sprawling desert landscape toward the horizon. 2. A handwritten list of safety travel tips written on an A4 piece of lined notebook paper entitled The Solo Travel Safety Gospel According to Phoebe.)

#solofemaletravel #thosewhowander #vanlife #biglap #australia #lifegoals #chooseyourownadventure #vijasolo #travelgirls #wanderlust

View all 32 comments

mountainlady333 Love this so much, so inspiring ☺♡

itmekezzybee Welcome to #LapLife honey, we're one big happy family!

saltyhair_sandytoess: Hi Pheebs! If you don't have a 4WD, there are some great beaches you can access with only a 2WD if you're interested in off-grid? Absolute beachfront camping, and totally free. I'll DM you the details.

lonewanderer66 Take care of yourself, Phoebe. It's more dangerous out there than you think.

14 May

CHAPTER ONE

Katy

I've made a mistake.

I know it as soon as I catch my head lolling, my eyelids drifting shut. With a sharp inhale, I sit up straight and tighten my grip on the wheel. I blink and the road swims back into focus. Dusty asphalt passes beneath me like fast-running water, the broken white line shining in the twin beams of my headlights. On both sides, red dirt fades to black.

My heart starts to race. *Did I just fall asleep?* I check the speedometer: I'm almost twenty over the limit. *Goddamn.* Swiping a hand across my clammy brow, my foot finds the brake and the van slows down.

The evening is quiet, no other vehicles but mine, but it feels like a close call. I could easily have veered off the road and hit a tree, or collided with a passing kangaroo; I could've smashed into an actual person. I can just imagine what Phoebe would say if she were here. *Are you insane, babe? Tap into your wisdom and pull over. Don't you know anything about how to keep yourself safe?* Oh, the irony.

The horizon to the west is striped with gold. Night has fallen so fast. Surely the sky was still bright just minutes ago?

I keep going. It might not be safe to drive after dark, but stopping overnight on the side of the road isn't an option either. And I can't turn back. I had a good reason for leaving in a hurry . . . didn't I?

I think back. Why did I leave again? I'd been at a campsite. There'd been a guy. I hadn't felt comfortable. And when you're uncomfortable, you leave. Travel 101. But what specifically had made me feel that way? I can't quite remember, the details are blurry—which isn't unusual for me, I can't always pinpoint the reasons behind my feelings. But then I steer sharply around a sudden pothole and something rolls into my foot, cracking me on the ankle. Reaching down, I pull an almost-empty wine bottle from the footwell. *Oh.* The dregs slosh against the cap and my stomach churns with it. *Oh, no.* I run my tongue around my mouth and taste blackberries and tannin. The realization hits me like a sandbag: I'm not just tired. I'm drunk.

Skin crawling with shame, I wedge the bottle between my seat and the door, its glass neck poking out like a little person with something to say. *No.* I glare at it. *You pipe down.* I don't want to hear from any of its full friends in the back either, though I can already hear them calling. Look at me, can't even get through my first full day on the road without a booze-fueled drama of my own making.

I can only guess what *really* happened back there—a friendly camper had tried to make conversation and I freaked out, overreacted, and got behind the wheel despite having had too much to drink. Wouldn't be the first time.

Reaching for a bottle of water wedged in the cup holder, I twist off the top and scull half in one go, gulping down the lukewarm liquid as if it will wash all the bad feeling away.

I keep going and going. The sky grows darker; the stripe of gold turns pink then purple. I check the GPS. My next stop is just under two hours away, by which time it'll be fully dark. I have a booking but not until tomorrow. Maybe if I call ahead, they'll let me check in early? I reach for my phone, but freeze as a light winks in the wing mirror. Headlights. A car, catching up on the road behind me.

Slowly, I return my hand to the wheel. *One elephant, two elephant, three elephant, four.* I check the mirror again. The light disappears as I round a bend, then reappears as the car does the same. *Relax. It's a road. Other vehicles are normal.* Still, I continue to keep watch.

I turn on the radio. A local station is playing some sleazy saxophone number, very early '90s. The song fades out and is replaced by a news jingle. "And now for today's headlines," says the reporter. "The family of missing solo traveler Vivi Green put pressure on police to extend their search to the Cape Range National Park after a—"

I turn it off again. The air around me suddenly feels hot and sticky. I switch on the air con and the soft whirr of the fan joins the engine's white noise. I shift in my seat. The twin pinpricks behind me look like eyes, getting closer and closer. They're also, I realize, moving. Zigzagging from side to side. I squint into the rearview mirror, watching through the dark tunnel of the van's interior as the car crosses into the oncoming lane then slides back in line with me.

Something's not right. I put my foot down and speed up as much as I dare, but when I check my mirrors again the car has kept pace. A glance back at the speedometer tells me I can't go any faster, I'm back over the limit, so I change tactic, slowing down to let the driver overtake. But the vehicle slows with me and hovers right on my tail, swerving and swinging, swerving and swinging.

Spotting an upcoming side road, I signal left and brake, giving the driver plenty of opportunity to pass. But the car accelerates, growing ever larger in the mirror, and it's not signaling, it's not overtaking, it's coming straight at me, and it's going to hit me—

At the very last minute I wrench the wheel, sending my van into the gravel well before the turning. My wheels kick up a cloud of dust and the car shoots past in a streak of light and sound. I crane my neck as it passes, trying to get eyes on the driver, the registration plate, but all I see is darkened windows and the boxy outline of a military-style camper.

Coming to a complete stop, I sit in the dark with the engine idling, hardly daring to breathe, half expecting the headlights to circle back, wondering what I'll do if that happens. But the taillights disappear and the road is empty once more. I kick myself for not stopping much earlier, for setting off so late in the first place, for failing to "tap into" my "wisdom."

Trembling, I urge the van forward, turning onto the side road and rolling along a short distance before killing the engine. I take my hands off the wheel, lean back against the headrest, and cover my face with my hands. I'm so jacked I can feel my heartbeat in my eyeballs.

At the same time, collapse is creeping in like a tide. The long drive, the hypervigilance, the alcohol, the car that ran me off the road—the combination hits me like a narcotic cocktail and fatigue takes over. My eyes start to close.

It's so quiet. I have to rest. I need to sleep. I start to drift . . .

I wake to the muffled sound of rustling grass and snapping twigs.

My eyes fly open and I stare out through the windscreen, studying the shadows beyond. On the surface, nothing has changed. I'm still in the van, still parked on the side road, it's still dark outside. But in my bones I know that something is different.

I click on the interior lights then hit the switch for the LEDs in the back. Their dim glow spills from the windows and illuminates the patch of dirt around the van but not much more.

Then I catch movement to my right. The wave of a branch in the wind? A prowling animal? I press my face against the window, cup my hands to the glass. Maybe I imagined it. But no, there it is again, a kind of disturbance, a wrinkle on the surface of the night. Somewhere out there, something is moving.

I know I should stay put, that it's much safer inside the van than out, but I can't help myself, I'm already pushing the door open and stepping out onto the cold ground. From what I can see, the road is narrower than I first thought, little more than a mud track through a tangle of scrub, probably leading to a farm or rural estate. I have no interest in following it though; the last thing I need right now is some creepy old house. I turn instead to face the highway but I can't even see it anymore. It's like I've traveled miles into the wilderness instead of just a few yards.

Gradually I become aware of soft sounds hovering in the air like drag-onflies. Bugs, leaves, breeze, frogs. Human sounds too. *Breath huff, sole slap, stone skitter.*

"Hello?"

Drawing my phone from my pocket, I activate the torch. The beam is too weak to penetrate much more than the shadows at my feet, but up ahead I swear I can see someone. My heart sputters. *Yes.* Up ahead, standing on the track. A woman. Wearing yellow.

"Phoebe?"

I inhale and a sweet, familiar scent fills my nose.

"Pheebs? Is that you?"

It defies all rationality and logic but I'm convinced it's her. She's here. Sticking to the trail and holding my phone out in front, I take a step for-ward, then another and another. I pick up my pace and leave the van be-hind. Trees tower above me like tall humans, their trunks smooth and rumpled like folds of skin. Somewhere nearby, water is trickling. The hori-zon is swollen with hills, coal-black against a vast star-speckled sky.

Finally, I stop. I can't see her anymore, can't hear her. "Phoebe?"

The track is empty. Red dirt has become sand, the trees replaced by sea grass. The ocean is close.

"Please," I whisper, shivering. "Please come back." But there's no one here but me, no other voices or beating hearts. I was wrong. She isn't here. I am alone.

Suddenly I can't breathe. I can't remember her face—her *real* face, not the one in photos and videos but the real flesh and bone of her. Eye-lashes, freckles, hair, scars. The crinkle of her forehead, the lines at the corners of her mouth. They're all slipping away like sand through my fingers. I'm starting to forget.

Bending forward with my hands on my knees—*Brace! Brace!*—I make a list.

She liked to eat apples in the car, and always left the shriveled brown cores in the cupholder.

Her pet peeve was noisy eaters.

For no reason at all, she never drank the last few centimeters of any drink.

She preferred bobby pins to hair ties and liked to customize them with colorful nail polish. When it was sunny they glittered in her hair like jewels.

People often told her she could "light up a room," and it was true.

Slowly, slowly, my breath returns to normal. I wipe my eyes with the back of my hand. I'm being such a baby. But I'm here, aren't I? I made it. And I have a job to do.

Following the track back the way I came, I return to the van, climb in and tuck myself behind the wheel. Hello again, square one.

In the end I decide that pushing on is the lesser evil. Wherever I am, either something is off or I'm seeing things, and neither problem will be solved by darkness and solitude. I'm much better off finding the next campsite and the company of other people. At least I've had a power nap.

Starting the engine, I turn the van around and follow the track back to the highway.

At first, it's just a feeling. An inexplicable pressure shift, like a descent into deep water. I can't put my finger on it, but as soon as the tires hit the tarmac I can tell that something is wrong.

Frowning, I study my mirrors, searching for headlights, but there are no speeding cars this time. I check the wings again, my eyes jumping from the road ahead to the road behind and back again. Nothing. But then my attention snags.

I adjust the rearview so I can see the van's interior, angling it down toward the floor of the van then up and around the sides—and then I see it: a ripple, like the sheets are breathing, like the van itself is alive.

Next, I hear a soft *hah-huh, hah-huh,* an echo of my own breath. I inhale and hear it again. I exhale to a second whoosh of expelled air. My stomach flips: that feeling when the roller coaster starts to drop.

The bedsheets *are* breathing. The blanket is a weird shape, all bunched to one side. The mattress is lumpy.

It hits me like an electric shock.

I'm not alone.

CHAPTER TWO

Beth

Of all the decisions Beth Randall has made in her life, sneaking into a stranger's van and hiding in their bed is surely one of the worst.

As she listens to the sounds of the driver—a woman?—opening the door and taking her place behind the wheel, Beth presses herself into the mattress as if she might somehow be able to disappear inside it. As the engine turns over, she starts to sweat. And as the van begins to move, all her thoughts curdle into a single clear certainty: *This is how I'm going to die.*

Obviously it's her own fault. What had she been thinking, trapping herself like this? Had she learned nothing from the last year? But she'd had no other choice! She'd been running for so long her feet were bleeding, her legs were cement, and every breath was a bellyful of fire. *Keep going,* she'd told herself over and over. *Weak fucking bitch, don't you dare stop now.* Every step was sending shockwaves from the soles of her feet to the top of her skull, reigniting the pain of each fresh injury.

At first the camper had appeared as just a warm glow in the dark. A lantern? A campfire? No—a van, tucked away on a side road with all its lights on; a HiAce, she realized on closer inspection, the kind of immaculate conversion you saw everywhere now.

"Hello?" she called as she approached—or tried to call, but her voice was little more than a rasp. "Anyone home?" She didn't want to startle the driver, knew full well how people can react when they're scared. No answer.

The van's white exterior was covered with red dirt and mud splashes. A peek through the windows revealed a cute but chaotic space: fairy lights and cushions, cupboards and drawers, a sink and a fridge; a neat little seat and a bed with the sheets turned back as if someone had just recently climbed out. Towels draped over the counter, discarded clothes, a snow drift of snack wrappers and crumpled paper banked up in one corner. No driver, though.

And then a noise cut through the quiet: the faint rumble of an engine on the highway. She spun around to see headlights in the distance. *Shit.* Without thinking, she pulled hard on the side door of the van, almost passing out with relief when she found it unlocked. Sliding it open, she slithered through the gap and dragged it shut again before flattening herself on the floor.

Breathless, she waited with her cheek pressed against the fibers of a striped mat, one half of her brain focused on the immediate threat, the other wondering about keys. What were the chances the driver had left them behind? Could it possibly be as easy as that? But the car outside was getting louder, the headlights closer. *Fuck.* She glanced around her, up at the windows, the shining fairy lights. The van was like a beacon, and all anyone had to do was peek through the windows just as she'd done and that would be it: game over. Where was the switch?

Then she stiffened. Footsteps. Someone was coming. Pulse racing, she clambered onto the bed, tugged the blankets over her body and curled up into a tight ball. It had seemed like a good idea at the time, but maybe it would've been better to keep running? Hindsight is such a bitch.

As Beth feels the HiAce swing back onto the highway, she lies as still as she can, her body bruised like rotting fruit, her throat burning. There's a lump on her head, high up on the left side, and all her muscles are screaming. Frantically, she runs through all possible ways to handle the situation—because however it happens she will be discovered, and then what?

It's actually a relief when the answer comes quick. After just a few minutes, the driver spots Beth in the mirror and quite rightly loses her shit. Piercing noise fills the van, half words yelled at full volume, *wha the get ow who ah how the fuh,* and Beth gives herself up, throwing back the sheets and raising her hands in surrender, *no please it's okay don't be scared,* but the driver is already freaking out.

The van veers in all directions, swinging from one lane to the other before hurtling off the asphalt completely. Every panel and bolt rattles as the wheels bounce over cracked, uneven ground; Beth is tossed sideways and loses her grip on the mattress, eventually sliding right off the end and landing on the floor with a thump. The driver screams and the van swerves again, so violently this time that Beth is thrown against the kitchen counter where she cracks her head on a cupboard door—and down she goes again as the van skids, teetering briefly on two wheels before somehow righting itself and coming to a juddery stop.

Wasting not even a second, the driver yanks the handbrake, tears the keys from the ignition and throws herself out into the night, leaving Beth alone in the back. "Mother *fuck,*" she mutters, and hauls herself up to sitting. Her left eye is pulsating like it might explode and there's something very wrong with her shoulder. "Ow." She presses her fingers to her eyebrow and they come away slick with blood. "Oh, great. Fucking perfect."

She peers out the window. The van has stopped at a dangerous angle, its hood sticking out into the northbound lane, the rear nestled into a shrub. The driver hasn't gone far; Beth can still hear her yelling hysterically somewhere in the dark. It's all *get out, get the hell out of my van, go away, leave me alone,* over and over and over. She needs to shut up or she'll attract attention.

Pulling herself up on the counter, Beth gets to her feet. Blood slides from her temple to her chin and she wipes it away, smoothing back her hair, her mind shifting so seamlessly into self-preservation mode that she's barely aware it's happening. Her body is used to making necessary adjustments; her mind has mastered the pivot.

Straightening up, she slides opens the door and steps out.

On the road some distance away, the driver—rake thin, short hair, baggy T-shirt—is shifting nervously from one foot to the other and brandishing something in the air. "Stay where you are," she shrieks. "I have a gun."

Liar, Beth thinks, but chooses not to call the woman's bluff. Instead, she plays along, reaching for the sky while searching for the right words. *Not the truth. Anything but the truth.*

"I'm sorry," she calls out—or tries to. Her neck and throat hurt so much, it's hard to keep her voice steady. She swallows and it burns like acid. "Please, I need help."

The woman does not back down. Every muscle is poised for attack. She's not a fighter though, Beth can see that. She's shaking. And the thing in her hand is way too small to be a gun. It's a key. Beth eyes it hungrily.

"I'm not dangerous," she continues. "I promise. I was trying to get away, I needed help, and I saw your van. I didn't mean to scare you, it was an accident. Please believe me."

The driver looks around, clearly hoping to see another car or a truck, a passing stranger on whom she can off-load this unthinkable situation—and who can blame her? Beth could be anyone: a drug addict, an escaped convict, a psych patient on the run. She watches as the woman pivots on the spot, both hands pressed to her cheeks. Whoever she is, she's obviously not great in a crisis, just wants all this to go away—but she's conflicted too. Torn. Some part of her wants to help.

Acting fast, Beth drops to the ground as if all her bones have dissolved. She thinks of home and the tears come quick. The driver shuffles forward, and Beth cries harder. *That's it,* she thinks. *Come on, just a little further.* The woman edges closer still, the key glinting in her hand. It wouldn't take much, just a firm push, a swift snatch-and-grab, and she could be gone in seconds . . .

But then the driver stops just out of reach. She folds her arms and crouches down. "Hey," she croons, lowering herself into Beth's eyeline. "Don't cry." Her tone is suddenly gentle, the hysteria replaced by something more controlled. "What's your name?"

Beth looks up, wary of this change. Her name . . . she goes by so many these days, it's hard to keep track. "Lily," she replies, plucking one from her head like a rabbit from a hat.

"Lily," the woman repeats, meeting her gaze with what appears to be deep sadness. "Okay. It's all right. I believe you. I can help." Standing up again, she puts the key in her pocket and holds out a hand. "Let's get you inside. I'll drive you to a hospital."

Beth's stomach lurches. That's the very last place she should go. "Oh. No. That's kind of you, but I'm fine."

"To the police, then."

"Really, I'm fine."

"But you said you needed help."

Beth doesn't know what to say. What excuse can she possibly give?

The driver frowns. "Well, I have to take you somewhere. You can't stay here."

Beth stares out into the darkness. It's true, she can't. And stealing the van would only help in the short term. *Okay, change of plan.*

"Can I . . . come with you?" she asks. "Just wherever you're going? I won't be any trouble, I promise. I just need to clean myself up, get my head together."

The driver tilts her head, regarding Beth with a mix of suspicion and pity—and something else, something unreadable.

"Please. Just for the night. I can't think straight. I just need to rest."

The woman considers this. "All right," she says finally. "Just for the night. We'll decide what to do in the morning."

Beth wipes her eyes with the back of one hand. "Thank you."

"Come on. We can talk on the way."

Beth allows herself to be hoisted to her feet and guided into the van. Safely installed in the passenger seat, she clicks the seat belt into place and braces herself for a deluge of questions, all variants on *what happened to you?* Once again, she contemplates answering with the truth. But she couldn't even if she wanted to. Because the real question is not *what* but *who.*

CHAPTER THREE

Wyatt

Wyatt Cleary is sick.

Just a virus, the local doctor said. *Rest and fluids, back to normal in no time.* But it's been three weeks now and he's still laid up on the sofa with headaches, fever, and a racing heart. Not only that, his eyes are sore too, his appetite is patchy, and despite feeling exhausted he can't sleep.

The bright side is that he's been excused from schoolwork, which Dad says is fine, because at fifteen years old he's already learned all he needs to know and he's going to work for the family business anyway. Doesn't matter that Wyatt has little to no interest in landscaping or plants in general, that's just what's on the cards—and it's not like he has other options. *Can't make a living watching movies,* Dad always says. *'Specially not the ones you like.* Which is true. But for now, thanks to the flu or whatever it is, he can watch as many as he likes.

Right now, for example, he's deep into one of his favorites, an absolute classic. A boy and two girls are off on a road trip; the highway twists and turns as they head into the wild unknown. Wyatt lies on his side, eyes glued to the screen, happy to surrender to the suck of the story . . .

Thud. Shuffle. Thump.

He doesn't react immediately; he's become used to the Noises. The walls of his house have been talking to him for what feels like forever, but he supposes if he really thinks about it he can pinpoint the exact day they started.

He was eleven years old. A summer Sunday, too hot to play or even go to the beach, so he and Lucas had been watching TV. Shirts off, curtains closed, fan on full blast, just the way they liked it. Dad hadn't been there; he would've been nearby of course, out back somewhere, pulling up the garden, clearing the weeds, sweating in the burning sun (*Can't let the weather win, a man's gotta do what needs to be done*), but not close enough to supervise. If he had been, they never would've been watching one of Lucas's movies.

Anyway, there they both were, Lucas on the sofa with his feet up on the coffee table, Wyatt on the floor hugging his knees to his chest, when Wyatt's focus was broken by strange sounds: muffled thuds and scuffles, like the scutter of vermin in a cardboard box. Sitting up, he looked around the room, but besides him and Lucas it was empty.

He turned back to the TV, but seconds later he heard it again: *scuffle-thump-tap*. This time he swiveled right round and scanned the floor, the ceiling, the windows. The Noises were coming from right behind him, he was sure of it.

"What's wrong with you?" Lucas said. "Why can't you sit still?"

Thump-thump-shuffle.

"Did you hear that?" Wyatt said in lieu of an answer.

"Nah."

Getting to his feet, he edged toward the bookcase. "There's something moving around."

"Possum in the roof," Lucas drawled, his eyes still glued to the screen. "Or a snake. Dad found a ringed brown up there the other day."

Wyatt trailed his fingers over the dusty shelves, touching each picture frame in turn: *one, two, three, four.* Sometimes this helped when things felt off.

Thump.

Whoa. He'd felt that one in his chest, in the soles of his feet. How could Lucas not hear it? It didn't sound like an animal. He placed a hand on the wall to the left of the shelving. It felt warm. Stepping closer, he pressed his ear to the wallpaper. The gyprock was humming like a beehive. And the more he listened, the more the humming started to sound like whispers, overlapping sighs and murmurs, or perhaps the rustle of material, delicate fabric caught between fingers, thread moving against thread against thread—

"Wyatt." Lucas was staring at him from the couch. "Y'all right, bud?"

Startled, Wyatt stepped away from the wall. "Yeah."

"What's up?"

"Nothing."

"You hungry?"

"Nah."

"Thirsty?"

"Nah."

"Sit down then."

That was the first time, but it hadn't been the last.

And now here they are again.

Blocking out the Noises as best he can, Wyatt stretches his aching limbs out on the sofa and, just like he had that day, loses himself in the movie. Onscreen, the three backpackers are staring down into a giant crater, oblivious of the horrific fate awaiting them deep in the outback.

Boring, he thinks, and skips forward to the best bit. He's less interested in the setup, doesn't care about the preamble. He likes it when the action ramps up. He likes it when they run.

Liked by **trailinghappytales** and **others**

pheebsinwonderland Well it's only day 1 of the Big Lap but I have already fallen hard for WA. I set off from Perth at sunrise and drove 200km north on the Indian Ocean Drive to Cervantes, stopping off here and there on the way. The landscape was wild: so many trees at first, all different kinds, and then all these massive rocks like chunks of polystyrene, and huge sand dunes that just pop up out of nowhere like bubbles in pizza dough. Took a detour to check out the Pinnacles Desert (a stretch of natural limestone pillars that apparently formed 25,000 years ago) which was totally breathtaking and kind of eerie, like being on Mars. I grabbed lunch at Cervantes (shout-out to the awesome little seafood place near the beach whose name I did not clock, sorry), and then it was back on the road for a slow 300km crawl with many more detours down unmarked side roads to stunning little beaches (Green Head, I'm looking at you!).
Putting the day to bed with some van-cooked food at the delightful #PlainsRanchCampground just past Geraldton, and sending out gratitude for a great start. No job, no responsibilities, no stress— just me, the van, and the big wide world. Gotta love #vanlife!

(Image descriptions: Eight different images of the route from Perth to Cervantes. 1. The road out of Perth as viewed through the windscreen of a campervan. 2. A clump of squat, tufty trees that look like the trolls in *Frozen*. 3. A massive white sand dune rising out of tangled green scrub as if God has dropped his ice cream. 4. The silhouette of a woman on a seaweed-strewn beach, stretched by late afternoon light to an improbable height. 5. The limestone monoliths of the Pinnacles Desert, backlit by a sunset sky. 6. & 7. A woman with long hair successfully feeds half an apple to a reluctant horse, then

celebrates with disproportionate excitement. 8. A campervan at night, parked next to a paddock and lit from the
inside.)

#roadtrippin #cervantes #yanchepnationalpark #pinnaclesdesert
#wanderlust #hungryhorse #eattheapplenotme

View all 32 comments

turnaroundthesun66: Love this! How good is WA?

paperscissorsmountain: Karijini! You have to go, it's AMAZING!

goodnightpetergraham: If you're heading up to Kalbarri, there's a
great café on the waterfront, opposite the memorial. And don't
miss Hutt Lagoon on the way!

ginabobeena: The wildflowers at Lesueur National Park are gorge.
Also the sea lions at Jurien Bay.

lonewanderer66: Your photos are beautiful, do you sell prints?

16 May

CHAPTER FOUR

Katy

I open my eyes and light fills my vision. I flinch—my head is still full of twin beams and asphalt, echoes of a fast-fading dream—but it's just the sun at my window, startlingly bright and already warm. I must have slept late.

Sounds creep in at the edges of my awareness: the clink of glass, a baby's wail, and a faint tinkly tune like a child's music box. I fling an arm over my face then roll onto my side. My guts are churning, my head throbbing. I lightly press a hand to my forehead and it feels clammy. I think of stress balls and wet clay and wonder if my fingers have left little dents in the surface of my skin.

Then I remember. Last night. Lily.

The air inside the van suddenly feels charged: thicker than usual and tinged with an unfamiliar smell. I stare at the partition wall, listening out for movement in the cab. Is she still asleep? What time is it? Sitting up I reach for my phone. 11:41. *Huh.* I almost never wake up this late. I throw off the sheets and grab yesterday's T-shirt from the floor. Nudging a curtain aside, I peek out the window at white fencing, terra-cotta paddocks and horses meandering under a huge blue sky. Beyond them is a long single-story building like a Mexican hacienda: white stucco walls, a red clay-tiled roof, and a large sign that says PLAINS RANCH CAMPGROUND. The sun is nearing its highest point.

Turning back, I survey the chaos of my van. My clothes are every-where, the towels are damp and grainy with sand, and the floor is littered with receipts, shopping lists, business cards, and crumpled tourist flyers; they must've fallen from one of the drawers during the confusion of last night. There are marks too, smears of blood and dirt, further evidence of Lily's surprise arrival.

I get out of bed and peek through the hole in the partition, expecting to find my stowaway snoozing in the passenger seat, but aside from the pillow and blanket I'd given her, the cab is empty. The towel, toothpaste, and clothes are gone too, which indicates she's gone for a shower—but who knows? Again, I look out the window, scanning the campsite, but she's not anywhere nearby, and I realize I have no idea where she might've gone, what she'd be most likely to do. Besides her name, I know nothing about her at all.

Last night, after we'd got back in the van and set off driving, Lily had pretty much shut down. Her teeth were chattering and she was shaking all over, so I put on the heat and passed her a jumper. Literally seconds later she was fast asleep. She was in her twenties, I decided, early-to-mid. Pretty but not beautiful, short but not petite. Wavy shoulder-length hair, freckled shoulders, piano hands, bitten nails. The dry salted skin of a sea-soned traveler. Her right ear bore three silver hoops and around her left wrist was a delicate string of green sea glass. If it weren't for the state she was in, she'd look just like every other vanlifer on the road.

Her cotton T-shirt dress was filthy, the charcoal-gray material streaked with dust and unidentifiable stains, and one seam was split to the hip. Her feet were bare and blistered, her toes black with dirt. No bag, no wallet, no keys, no jacket. Her forehead was bleeding, her knees were grazed, and a rash of purple bruises dotted her neck and collarbones. She looked wild, a creature fresh from hell—and yet there was something angelic about her too.

Was I doing the right thing? I had no information about who she was or where she'd come from, and I was hardly the right person to play nurse; I could barely look after myself. But this total stranger was hurt, and she was alone. And suddenly it wasn't Lily sleeping next to me but Phoebe, lost and hurt and in desperate need of help, and I knew that it didn't matter if my choice was right or wrong. I couldn't leave her. I wouldn't.

An hour or so later we arrived at Plains Ranch and, having successfully organized an after-hours check-in en route, I steered the van through the darkened rows of caravans and tents to my spot. My first thought was to tend to Lily's wounds, but not even a few gentle nudges would wake her up, so I grabbed the quilt and a pillow from my bed and tucked them around her as best I could. I placed a clean towel, shower gel, and toothpaste on the driver's seat ready for the morning, along with a clean singlet and a pair of boardshorts I pulled from the back of a drawer. Then I locked up and went to bed myself.

Now it all seems like a dream: blurry, and highly unlikely. Also inconvenient, and more than a little scary. Good intentions aside, I'm starting to feel like I've made yet another huge mistake.

I watch from the window as other campers move around outside, packing down, packing up, washing dishes, making lunch. Under the awning of a camper trailer, a gray nomad in a fishing hat sweeps dirt from a mat. Over to the right, a man in a straw hat cranks up his barbecue, and farther along, a family of four balance plates of sandwiches on their knees. Delicious smells begin to waft, and my stomach growls. Assuming she's still around, Lily will need to eat soon, too.

I go to check my cupboards, but every surface is so crammed with clutter I can't even think about food preparation. How is everything so chaotic after just thirty-six hours? This was not the plan.

Starting with the bed, I shake out the blanket, straighten the sheets and put the pillows back in their places. I collect the rubbish from the floor, then gather the towels and clothes and put them in a bag ready to be washed. I beat the rug, sweep out the sand, wipe down the benchtop and polish the windows. I go through the cupboards, making a list of all the food I don't yet have and the supplies I'll soon need to replenish.

Finally, I separate the receipts and flyers from the rest of the rubbish and stack them in a neat pile—and as I do, a card slips from my fingers and flutters to the floor. I bend to pick it up. It's a business card, given to me by Detective Dust, the lead investigator assigned to Phoebe's disappearance. Big man, gruff voice, head like a potato. I feel the coarse surface of his palm as he pressed the card into my hand: *If you need anything, don't hesitate to get in touch.* Words that meant nothing once the case was closed.

I turn the card over. The edges are soft with age, the phone number faded but still legible. I wasn't planning on contacting him yet, and maybe not at all, but the little white square falling to the floor right at that moment feels like some kind of sign, like when a tarot card jumps from the pack. I should at least let him know I'm here.

I dial the number, and after just three rings the call connects. "This is Dust." His voice is surprisingly chipper. But then the line hisses with static and I lose him. "Hello?" I say, clutching the phone with both hands. "Hello, can you hear me?"

". . . unable to get to the phone right now, but if you leave your name and number . . ."

Frustration flares in my chest, brief but bright. I wait for the beep. "Detective, it's Katy Sweeney. Um. I hope you can hear me, the line's not great—anyway, I, uh, just wanted to tell you that I'm here in WA, and it's been more than a year now, so . . . well, if you could call me back that'd be great. And . . . that's it, I guess. Okay, bye."

Hanging up, I toss my phone on the bed and cast a doleful eye over my newly clean van. The cushions are back in place, the pillows are plumped, and the patterned throw is artfully arranged. In the kitchen area, the splashback is gleaming, the spice rack is organized, and each individual leaf of my artificial plant is completely dust-free. I've even given the fairy lights a wipe. Everything is back to how it was, how Phoebe would've liked it. I can relax.

But I don't. Because even though the van looks like Phoebe's, it isn't. I've tried to copy her style and taste, hoping it would help, but it doesn't. Nothing will change the fact that she's gone. And as much as I'd like it to, no amount of dusting and polishing will bring her back.

Sitting on the edge of the bed, I pick at my cuticles. My hands are gross, my nails almost as ragged and dry as Lily's. My knuckles are gnarled like burrs on a tree. Phoebe's were much prettier—though of course she'd hated them. *They're fat and stumpy,* she'd say. *They look like paws.* I thought that was funny. *If yours are paws,* I would reply, *then mine are claws.* That always made her laugh.

The memory of Phoebe's giggle in my head is so unexpectedly vivid that I make an actual noise: half laugh, half sob. I close my eyes, desperate to hang on to the laugh, but it's already sinking out of reach, back to wherever my mind hides these things. And then it's gone; I can't hear her anymore.

The grief hits me like a slap of cold water. It does that sometimes, catches me off guard, still hurts like it's new, usually when I least expect it. It's just a few seconds but in the moment it feels endless, like being trapped under ice.

Unlocking my phone, I pull up Phoebe's Instagram account. **pheebsinwonderland**. 477 posts, 2,837 followers, 692 following. Solo Female Traveler 🌏. Nothing but awe, wonder, and epic adventure. Blog coming soon! And there she is: caramel hair, deep brown eyes, and a bow-shaped mouth stretched wide in a dizzying smile. Photo after photo after photo. My eyes roam the grid, and I start to feel better.

The account is bright and beautiful. Each square is a window into a different world and Phoebe is the sun. I scroll to the first post of her Big Lap trip and drink in the image. With her glowing tan and favorite yellow bikini, she looks like a shooting star fallen to earth. It's how I think she would want to be remembered: free but grounded, and always moving forward. The accessibility description reads like a poem.

The next image shows a map of her intended trip—a single loop around the edge of the country traveling mainly on Highway 1, a route of around 14,500 kilometers linking almost every mainland state and territory capital—with subsequent tiles detailing each "leg." Phoebe had chosen to kick off with the diverse 1200-kilometer stretch from Perth to Ningaloo, known as the Coral Coast. According to the caption, this journey has everything: beautiful beaches, cliffs and gorges, outback stations, marine parks, and a diverse range of landscapes. Apparently Perth is also the perfect place to pick up a van beforehand then sell afterward before flying to Indonesia. I don't click into this post much; I hate being reminded of how few of her plans she actually got to see out.

Another thing I don't like are the comments. Beneath each entry are a handful of remarks from readers, random people who think they knew her just because they had travel in common. *We travelers are like one happy family,* someone wrote under one post. It made me want to write back and explain what the word "family" means. Actually, it made me want to scream. Now I avoid reading them. I don't like what they do to my heart.

I move on to another picture, one of many sunset shots where Phoebe is walking away from the camera into a blaze of light and color. I reach out to touch the screen, trace her silhouette with the tip of my finger, and a knot forms at the base of my throat. For a long time, these posts have been precious to me. They represent my last link to her, the only real connection I have left. I also hate them because they symbolize the reason she's gone: if she hadn't gone traveling on her own and been sucked into the world of "influencing," she would still be here. But she's not. And now that *I'm* here instead, treading the same path, the Insta account has become so much more. It's now my anchor and rudder, map, and compass. It's even more special than ever.

I stare at the pictures, willing each tiny version of Phoebe to come alive and look at me, but in almost all the shots her back is turned or she's half submerged by shadow or backlit by the sun. This isn't because she was self-conscious or shy—no one could ever have described her as either—but because that was her trademark aesthetic: she liked to let the scenery speak for itself. She said it was her point of difference, the thing that set her apart from all the cookie-cutter influencers with their filters and fakery and uniform dewy make-up. She didn't want her looks to be the focus. And they aren't—but her energy still radiates from the pictures, undeniably vital. Even when she was actively trying not to be the center of attention, she couldn't help but be just that.

Despite their beauty though, I can't help but see the darkness. Until I find her, Phoebe's photos will never be anything but portraits of disconnection and isolation, unnamed danger forever lurking just out of shot.

The captions are always chirpy, though. I try to lay the words of the Plains Ranch post over my own recent experience. The same departure from Perth, the acquisition of as similar a van as I could possibly find. Same route, same landscape, same pit stop for lunch. But the two versions don't match as closely as I thought they would. Admittedly I've only just started, but so far moving alone in the world does not feel especially peaceful or liberating to me, and the scenery is only breathtaking in the sense that my chest feels tight. I look at the expanse of sky, the rolling plains, the open road, and where there should be a thrill of excitement there's just grim determination. Phoebe is alive, I know she is. And I will find her, even if it kills me.

My phone buzzes with a text from Mum. You okay?

I roll my eyes: I only messaged her yesterday. But then I feel bad for making her worry, because of course she's worried. I dash off a quick reply—all good, nothing much to report, love you—and return to Instagram.

I want so badly to understand how Phoebe felt while she was here. I want to retrace her steps, stand in her shoes, see the world through her eyes . . . because how else will I ever find answers? When everyone else has given up, when the search has been called off and a dead end declared, what else can I do but go hunt for them myself? Or am I supposed to sit at home and just hope that new evidence shows up? Pray for a new witness to come forward? Trust that it will all just "work out"? *Sometimes there are no answers, sweetie,* my mother is fond of saying. *Sometimes we just have to let go.* But I don't accept that. I can't.

I think of the campers outside all going about their business: eating, drinking, showering, shedding hair, spreading germs, chatting to their neighbors, using their phones, spending their money, smearing their fingerprints on everything they touch. I stare at the floor and know that even though I've cleaned and tidied, remnants of Lily's blood still linger on the vinyl, soaked into the cracks. In fact, the van is already full of her—hair, skin, scent, saliva—and I know for sure that my instinct is right.

People do not just vanish. There is no "thin air," no "without a trace." Everyone leaves traces; you just have to find them. And if you can't, it's because you're not looking in the right place.

CHAPTER FIVE

Beth

In the farthest of six slightly dubious-looking shower stalls, Beth stands with her eyes closed as the scalding stream of water pounds against her scalp and turns her skin pink.

Her whole body hurts. Every muscle is so tight and tender she can barely move. She winces as the water flows over the cut on her forehead, her bruised neck and grazed knees, counting the places where her flesh has risen like bread. There are fewer marks than she'd expected, especially around her throat, but in a way it's not surprising. Some people know exactly how to inflict pain without leaving evidence, like it's a class taught in school.

She pumps cheap soap from the dispenser on the wall and rubs it hard into her skin, trying to permeate what feels like a thousand layers of grit and dirt and sweat. The water at her feet runs orangey-brown, a cocktail of filth, and she thinks about where it's all come from, all the unfamiliar surfaces her body has come into contact with over the last few days, weeks, and months, and all the ways she has been changed by them, blunted and sculpted into a whole new shape like a shell on a shore.

Placing her hands on the wall in front of her, she hangs her head.

Grief and fear and regret and misery wrap themselves around her organs and squeeze.

Different day, different campsite.

She sits by a pool, hardback notebook spread open on her lap, making notes as usual. The silence of the early morning has been filled with the scream of zips, the thunk of car doors, and a shit ton of rowdy laughter coming from over near the deep end. Three girls and five guys are plowing their way through a carton of beer, chucking each other into the water and cracking jokes at max volume. But Beth doesn't mind. It's comforting. Nostalgic. Normal people having normal fun on their normal holiday.

She returns to her journal. It started out as just a way to keep tabs but it's much more than that now: a collection of stories, observations bottled and corked for later consumption. Writing them calms her down, reading them cheers her up. Site number four, *she writes.* Married couple, no kids, straitlaced, young pros? *She taps her pen against her teeth, then returns the nib to the paper.* Six and seven: middle-aged guys trip, beer and dude talk, out early, back late.

And on it goes. On site eleven, a toddler's bid for freedom is thwarted by a sleepy-eyed mother. On fourteen, two teens play on their phones while munching bowls of cereal. The curtains of an Apollo rental twitch then fall still.

Beth notes that the couple in the Airstream haven't stirred yet. She eyes the caravan's shiny exterior, curved roof, and solar panels. Flashy fuckers. They'll be feeling dusty after all the top-end gin they put away at dinner. But they'll be up soon if they still want to catch that midday swell. She studies the windows, watching for movement.

"Hey," someone says. "Want one of these?"

She looks down. In the pool, a good-looking surfy type with chiseled deltoids is holding two frosty bottles of beer aloft in his tanned hands.

She points at her chest. "Who, me?"

He grins. "Yeah, you." He's cute. His gaze is direct, his smile curious, and for a moment she's tempted to return both. "What's your name?"

"My name?" She pouts at the guy in the pool, feigning diffidence. What is it this week? "Eliza."

"Eliza." The guy nods approvingly. "I like it."

She repeats the name in her head a few times, just to make sure. Eliza, Eliza. *South Australian driver's license, Adelaide address. Childcare manager, exercise enthusiast. She feels her body adjust accordingly, a subtle but necessary shift. She has to embody this person, allow her to take over. Next week it'll be something different, but on this day, in this place, she is* Eliza, Eliza, Eliza.

The guy in the pool flirts for a little longer, but as "Eliza," Beth is not allowed to reciprocate. Eventually he gets the hint and swims away, but not before leaving one of the beers at her feet as a "gift"—which she accepts only when his back is turned, swiping it from the ground and swiftly downing half the bottle in just a few gulps. The buzz hits her fast, and briefly "Eliza" is close to okay. But then the person she is deep inside remembers the day ahead and all the things she has to do, and the illusion dissipates.

She flicks back through her notebook, skimming the previous entries and jotting down a couple more lines about the Airstream couple before dropping her pen into her lap and stretching out her legs. Draining her beer, she places the bottle on the ground and stares over the pool fence at the campground beyond. A woman is walking back from the shower block, long legs striding over the grass, arms swinging freely, silky hair flying out behind her. She is tanned and fresh and lithe. She wears basically no clothes and seems fine with it.

"Eliza" watches, observing the woman's bouncy gait, her upbeat rhythm. "Eliza" imagines peeling the pretty woman's skin from her glorious body and slipping into it like a dress. "Eliza" wonders how it might feel against her own bones.

And then her body goes cold as a shadow falls across her face.

"Found you," says a voice.

Turning the heat up as far as it will go, Beth focuses hard on the pound of the water, the hiss and splash as it hits the tiles, but try as it might her body cannot fight the ensuing avalanche of sense memories: the spike and sting of gravel, the sway of the van in motion, the terrifying screams of the driver . . . Christ alive, what the fuck had she been thinking? No wonder the poor woman had been terrified.

Guilt twisting in her gut, she rubs soap into her hair and the suds flow over her neck and back like a waterfall. She doesn't want to lie, not now and not ever again, but what else is she supposed to do? She has no money, no phone, no identity documents, no transport, no friends or family. There's no avoiding some kind of explanation, but honesty will only make things worse.

Found you.

No, the truth is not an option. And it's not necessary anyway. Things are finally working out. Or she is alive, at least—and if she wants to stay that way she needs to come up with a decent cover story.

Milky liquid spills over her cupped palms and splashes onto the tiles below. She washes gravel from her grazes and mud from her skin, and as the filth sluices away an idea begins to form. She considers it, waiting patiently for it to take shape. A voice rises up in her head, clear as a bell. *Be confident. And quick.* And a plan slides into place.

She mulls it over, checking for flaws. Why not? She's done it before, she can do it again. It doesn't even need to be wholly convincing. Just enough to buy her some time.

Ignoring the nagging dread in the pit of her stomach, Beth turns off the tap, dries herself with the borrowed towel, and changes into the clean clothes her rescuer had so thoughtfully provided. She steps out of the stall and her reflection greets her in the row of mirrors. She still looks like hell, yesterday's events still scored deep into her body, but the shower has at least washed the worst of it away.

"You're a solo female traveler," she whispers to the woman in the glass. "And your name is Lily."

Lily, Lily, Lily.

CHAPTER SIX

Katy

"I like your van," Lily says, wincing a little as I dab Betadine into the cut on her head. The wind has picked up so we're sheltering inside with the door closed. "Did you convert it yourself?"

I glance at the L-shaped kitchenette, my hand still hovering at her brow, cotton wool pinched between forefinger and thumb. Now that I've tidied up, the beauty of the conversion is on full display. Timber benchtop, tiled splashback, steel sink, queen bed. There's a decent amount of storage (a clever configuration of units beneath the mattress, pullout boxes that double as seats, cabinets and drawers in the kitchen, and a whole panel of bulkheads around the ceiling) as well as a foldout dining table and even a showerhead attached to the water tank via a long silver hose. But I can't take credit.

"I got it secondhand," I tell her. "A guy in Perth. He's a builder, did it all himself. Gave me the longest tour on FaceTime before I bought it, and another in person when I picked it up."

"Well, it's nice. Pretty."

"Thanks." *Pretty* feels like the wrong word, but I guess I know what she means. Not every build goes so far as tongue-and-groove paneling, linen curtains, and scatter cushions.

I go back to dabbing. "Hold still, nearly done." The wound is looking better and the swelling has gone down, but I'm still concerned about infection.

When I'm sure as I can be that it's clean, I apply a Band-Aid, then pass Lily a tube of arnica cream and a couple of ibuprofen before returning my bulging first aid kit to the cupboard under the sink. Then while she tends to her bruises, I set up the stove and make tea.

"Thank you," Lily says when I hand her a mug. "And sorry again for putting you through all this, you're being incredibly kind. I don't know if I'd have done the same myself. Weird girl shows up in the back of your van? I'm surprised you're not halfway to Darwin by now."

I shrug. "You needed help."

She smiles. Without all the blood and dirt I can see her face more clearly: round and innocent with delicate features. Her figure is fuller than mine—my clothes are a tighter fit on her than on me—but she has a way of making herself look petite. In fact, with her crossed legs and arms wrapped tight around her middle, she reminds me of a vacuum-wrapped parcel, shrunk to the smallest size to take up as little space as possible.

We lapse into silence again. Outside, the wind buffets the van. A horse nickers, and another brays. Seconds later, a kookaburra answers with a cackle.

Lily takes a sip of tea, wincing as she swallows. "You must be waiting for an explanation." Her voice is soft and husky, and she has a habit of lightly touching her throat as if attempting to manually summon more sound.

"Whenever you're ready."

"Well, I was traveling, obviously. Doing the loop thing. The Lap. A long-held bucket list item. I had a camper, much smaller than this one. I wasn't really sticking to a schedule though. Just exploring."

"Alone?"

She nods.

"Is that an American accent?"

"Illinois."

"How long are you in Australia?"

She makes a face: *how long is a piece of string?* "I was looking for this place I'd heard about, some natural sundial. I took what I thought was the correct turn but I guess I got lost. Suddenly I was in the middle of nowhere with no GPS signal and no sense of direction. It was weird. Like, I'm usually a human compass." She pauses, frowning. "Anyway, it was getting dark so I decided to pull in for the night. I had a bite to eat, read for a while. And then I heard noises outside."

My turn to frown. "Noises?"

"Yeah. A sort of tapping. You know like how stones sound when you kick them?"

Goose bumps erupt all over my skin. *Breath huff, sole slap, stone skitter.*

"I went to take a look, thought maybe it was other travelers looking for the same spot. But . . ." Lily's hands are shaking. She puts her tea on the table. "I couldn't see anyone, so I walked around a little. It was quiet; the noises had stopped. The sun was going down, the sky was pretty. Everything seemed to be fine." She closes her eyes. "And then there was another noise: louder, closer. I felt something brush against me. Then someone grabbed me. Right here." She touches her neck again.

"And then . . . I don't know. The next thing I remember is lying on the ground in the dirt, and it's night, and I don't recognize anything, and my van is gone and all my belongings, my phone, passport, my fucking shoes, everything." Her face crumples and she starts to cry. "I looked and looked but I couldn't see the van anywhere. I had no idea what had happened, where I was, what to do. So I just got up and started walking."

I fetch some paper towel and hand her the whole roll. She tears off a sheet and wipes her face.

"I was walking awhile, I think. And then I saw your van, just sitting there in the dark. And the lights were on, and it looked warm and safe, and I was so scared that all I could think to do was get in and lie down." She looks up at me. "I'm so sorry. I wasn't thinking, I must've been in shock. I just didn't know what else to do." She presses the paper towel to her eyes.

I take a minute to think. *Alone, attacked by something unseen, no clues as to what or who, all belongings gone . . .* I feel dizzy, light-headed. "Are you sure you don't want me to take you to a hospital?"

"No." Lily says it quickly and firmly, swiping the tissue under her nose. "I just need a ride back up north. I have friends in Broome. I'll go find them and take it from there."

"Okay. Do you want to call them first?"

"What?"

"Your friends. You can borrow my phone, let them know what's happening."

"No, I . . . well, I guess I could, but . . ." Lily looks away then back at me and sighs. "Ugh, okay, you got me. There are no friends. I just need a cash job and a cheap place to stay, just while I figure things out—but like, under the radar. Broome is a good place to do that."

"Why under the radar?"

"Because I'm actually not supposed to be here. In Australia. I'm traveling illegally. Without a visa." She hangs her head. "I'm not proud—and believe it or not, I didn't do it on purpose, things just ended up like that. Anyway, that's why I can't go to the police. If I do, they'll send me back to the States."

"And that would be a bad thing?"

"Yes," she says, looking me right in the eye. "A very bad thing."

Again, I don't know what to say. *Illegal.* Thoughts crowd my head—possible responses, reasons, solutions—but none seem right. Instead, I stare down at my knees, my bare toes, the floor of the van. There's an insect by my right foot: a grasshopper, green as a leaf, with sharply angled back legs and long antennae. I fix my attention on it. *How did you get in here?* For some reason its presence feels like a good omen. I decide it's a girl.

"You know what's weird?" Lily says. "I just realized I never even asked you your name."

A rush of anxiety. *I didn't tell her my name? We really* are *strangers, what are we doing?* Suddenly I want to be alone so badly I could scream.

But the grasshopper at my feet tilts her tiny alien head and looks up, waving her antennae as if to say, *don't worry, everything will be okay.*

"Katy," I say. "Katy Sweeney. Pleased to meet you."

Lily smiles at the formality. "Same."

Another lull. I check back in with the grasshopper, hoping for further reassurance, but she's not there anymore. My little green friend has gone. I feel strangely abandoned.

Once Lily is all patched up, I make us a breakfast of yogurt and granola that we eat at the foldout table like we're interviewing for a job—though which of us is the employer and which the candidate, I can't tell.

Lily takes small, almost furtive bites as if at any moment someone might cuff her round the ear and tell her to stop. "So, where are you from?" she asks.

"Sydney. Dulwich Hill. Do you know it?"

"No. I've only been to Sydney once and that was just to see the Opera House."

"Ah."

"And you're a teacher."

"Sorry?"

She points at my chest. "That's a school shirt, right? What year do you teach?"

I glance down at my wrinkled polo shirt and the embroidered emblem of Marita Heights Primary School. A blush creeps up my neck. Why am I wearing a work shirt? I look like I'm leading an excursion or on my lunch break. "It varies."

"It's term time now, though, right? Schools aren't yet on vacation?"

I nod, thinking about my classroom, all the little tables with pots of pencils in the center of each one, and wonder what my students would be doing right at that moment. I'd been gone no time at all but already they felt a world away. "I'm on long service leave."

"Wow. Teachers get good benefits here, hey?"

"Oh, sure. Heaps." Reports flash through my mind. Parent-teacher meetings, lesson plans, staff-room politics, bus duty, fundraisers, costume days, NAPLAN, swimming carnivals, and permission notes. The long hot summer stretch, all those weeks of empty days with nothing to fill them. So many benefits.

"So how long have you been traveling solo?"

I count the hours. "Not long."

"And what made you want to start?"

"Actually, I didn't. Not really."

Lily waits for me to expand, and my first instinct is to get up, open the door, and throw myself out. I don't want to tell her anything. But isn't this exactly why I came here? To talk to people? Ask questions? Breathing deep, I dig my phone from my pocket, bring up Phoebe's Instagram and pick one of the few pictures where you can see her whole face. I turn the screen around and Lily leans forward.

"Who's that?" she says. "Your sister?"

I feel a smile tug at the corners of my mouth. "How can you tell?"

"The eyes. And there's something around the mouth."

I take a look. She's right about the eyes, but I don't know about the mouth. Cameras very rarely point in my direction and when they do I smile with my mouth closed. But the resemblances are so few it feels nice to have one acknowledged, even if I don't quite agree. Instinctively I run a hand over my short hair, wishing it were long like hers.

"Her name's Phoebe," I say. "This time last year she was traveling alone, driving this same route along the Coral Coast. The intention was to complete the entire Big Lap, but she never made it out of the state. Just three weeks after she set off from Perth, she completely disappeared and she hasn't been seen since. Even her van is gone, all her belongings, everything. It was like the ground had just swallowed her up."

I sense rather than see Lily's reaction. I can't look at her. If I do, I'll cry.

"Nobody knows what happened. There was an investigation but they couldn't find anything. No clues, no evidence, no witnesses, no suspects. And then just recently, they closed the case and everyone gave up. I guess with nothing to go on, it's hard for some people to keep the hope alive.

Not me, though. I *know* she's still out there. I feel it. So, I'm following in her footsteps, tracing her journey from beginning to end, right to the place she went missing."

"Jesus," Lily says eventually. "That's awful. I'm so sorry."

Awful. Yes. Sliding my phone back into my pocket, I meet her pitying gaze and rebuff it with a firm jut of my chin. "Either I'll find her, or I'll find what happened to her. And I'm not going home until I do."

Lily drains her tea and rinses her mug at the sink. "Where was she last seen, if you don't mind me asking?"

"Ningaloo. A servo just south of Exmouth has security footage of her filling up around mid-afternoon on June third. That same day, she posted on Instagram saying that she was on her way to hike the gorges at Karijini, and that's the last she wrote."

"She never made it to the gorges?"

"Not as far as we know."

"Shit." Turning to face me, Lily leans against the cabinets. "Ningaloo to Karijini? Man, that's a long drive; five hundred clicks, give or take. They couldn't narrow it down?"

"Apparently not."

"And there were no suspects at all? No sightings, no calls from potential witnesses?"

"No one."

Lily tugs at one ear. "I don't understand. She must've met people along the way. Are you sure *nobody* came forward?"

I rein in my mounting frustration but she reads it anyway.

"Sorry," she says quickly. "Of course you're sure. I don't mean to drag you through it all again. It's just . . . wow, that's some mystery."

I stare out of the window. A couple of campers walk by with a bucket stacked with dishes. A woman carrying towels and a wash bag herds her two small children to the shower block. Beyond the sandy paddocks, orange dirt becomes grasslands become a blanket of rolling green hills.

Lily clears her throat. "Listen," she says. "This is just an idea and please feel totally free to say no, but . . . is there any chance I can come with you?"

I blink. "Where?"

"To look for Phoebe." Her eyes are wide and pleading. "Ningaloo, or Karijini, or wherever you end up. I know it's a long way, but I can be super quiet and respectful of your space, and I'm totally fine to keep sleeping in the cab. I was just thinking, y'know, I'm heading north, you're going that way anyway, and maybe I could help you find her." She shrugs helplessly. "Two heads are better than one, right?"

"Oh." I'm taken aback. Share the van? With a law-breaking stranger? For another eight hundred kilometers? "Um . . ."

"I'm a good person," Lily cuts in earnestly. "And I'm smart, all evidence to the contrary. I'm clean and tidy, I can cook but don't eat much, and I promise that as soon as I get myself sorted I'll pay you back every cent of what I owe."

I chew my lip. My brain ticks. I suspect Lily is not being completely honest, even after the confession about her visa. There's something off about why she's avoiding the authorities—and why, when she's in such a desperate position, would she not want to go home to the States? But, I realize, I can't let her go now. I'm already too invested. I want to know what happened to her. I want to help. Most of all, meeting her feels like a sign. Serendipity. It can't just be coincidence that, while searching for the reason Phoebe went missing along with her van and all her belongings, I find a solo female traveler who was mysteriously attacked and robbed of her van and belongings. It has to be the universe throwing me a line.

"Please?" Lily's eyes are shiny with tears. "I have nowhere else to go."

I open my mouth to speak, answer at the ready—

Tap, tap, tap.

Startled, I spin around.

Tap, tappity, tap, tap.

"Hello?" says a male voice. "Anyone home?"

My eyes fly to the door. Someone is outside.

CHAPTER SEVEN

Beth

Tap, tap, tap.

Beth stiffens.

Tap, tappity, tap, tap.

"Hello? Anyone home?"

The voice is muffled, distorted by the wind.

Found you.

Her pulse rattles like windows in a storm.

Katy leans over her to peek between the curtains, then goes to the door and slides it open just a crack. "Yes?"

"Oh, hi!" says the person at the door. "Sorry, I wasn't sure if you—"

The voice is not familiar. Beth exhales slowly.

Katy steps all the way outside and closes the door behind her. Alone in the van, Beth pinches the bridge of her nose. Her story seems to be holding up, but she's already drained by the effort it takes to playact *and* stay vigilant at the same time. And did she really just beg a complete stranger to take her in? What is she, a Dickensian orphan? At what point did her life go from plain old shit to a straight-up nightmare?

Fussing with the Band-Aid over her eyebrow, she checks her story for holes. *Traveling . . . sundial . . . lost . . . noises.* So far, so plausible. The visa thing works as a great reason why neither police nor hospital are options, and the accent lends another level of disguise. It was a risk, taking a punt on Katy's ethics like that, but it seems to have washed.

It's not all lies, though.

Someone grabbed me.

My van is gone and all my belongings, my phone, passport, my fucking shoes, everything.

I had no idea where I was, what to do.

Without warning, her guts heave. She gets up and hangs over the sink, already panicking about what she'll say when Katy comes back and finds the place reeking of vomit . . . but nothing happens, and the contents of her stomach remain safely on the inside.

Straightening up again, she stares blankly through the window at a post so crowded with hand-painted signs it looks like a hat stand. *Stables. Farmstay. Reception. Swimming pool. Camp kitchen. Toilets.* She can still hear Katy talking to her visitor through the door at her back, but otherwise the campsite is settling into a post-lunch hush. Plains Ranch is quirky; not her favorite kind of place to stay (she'd much rather a resort-style holiday park with big bathrooms, hairdryers, and a regular cleaning schedule) but it is the kind she's grown used to: rustic but reputable, charming in a low-key sort of way. Busy but not too busy, cheap but not too cheap.

A vintage Viscount caravan stands on the neighboring pitch, empty wine and beer bottles littering a foldout table under the awning. If she had her notebook with her, she'd flip to the page where she would already have sketched out a rough site map and make a note. *Alcoholics*, she might write. *Self-medicating retirees? Left high-stress jobs but hung on to bad habits?* On another pitch, the mother of a squawking toddler stands alone rubbing her eyes and taking deep breaths. *Postpartum depression. Hasn't slept in months, no family around to help, hides chronic anxiety from husband who believes family holidays are more important than childcare.* A middle-aged couple eat together without exchanging a single word or glance. *Infidelity? Communication issues? Unresolved grief?* People are so fascinating.

Katy is more difficult to read though. It might just be that Beth's brain is so busy building and tracking her cover story that she's missing things, but there's something distinctly opaque about her rescuer, like Katy is wearing some kind of mind shield.

Beth makes a list of known facts: Katy is from Sydney. She's a teacher who wears her uniform even when she isn't working. She's traveling alone. And she definitely has money. Her clothes and bad pixie haircut might suggest a low income, but so far Beth has clocked a laptop, smartphone, top-quality gas stove, and mini fridge. The HiAce is expensive, and the interior carefully styled.

As far as Beth can tell she's not cold or unfriendly, but not warm either; detached is probably the best word, and kind of vague. Generous for sure, a real Samaritan. She cares deeply about things, wants to do right by people, but doesn't trust easily: her eyes frequently dart around like flies in a hot room, searching for a way out. Physically she's bony and undernourished. Her skin is pallid and she's even missing a tooth, but her eyes are kind.

But the grief and stress probably account for a lot of that; she's probably going through some kind of emotional breakdown. It's understandable. Ambiguous loss is arguably the most painful and traumatic kind there is. It can be like living your life in a holding pattern. You can't get out, can't move on. Or so people think. But sometimes the questions themselves are the problem. Sometimes it's better to accept that to be human is to live without answers.

Still, control is a big thing for most people. When holes open up in life, people do whatever they can to fill them. And Phoebe clearly left a big hole, for Katy and probably for many others too. It's obvious from her Insta grid that she's sweet, fun, and a raging extrovert. Her smile is uninhibited, and she has a way of standing that oozes confidence and sensuality. She's the kind of girl whose existence in the world makes yours feel small, but which also gives you hope that there might be brighter things out there if only you could find them, the kind of girl everyone either wants to be or to have. The world really mourns the existence of people like that.

Katy on the other hand is a little awkward and nowhere near as attractive. She likely repels as many people as her sister attracted—which probably feels like shit but might not be such a bad thing; attention isn't always what it's cracked up to be.

Beth's heart twinges as she glimpses a little of Katy's pain—how brutal it would be to lose someone you loved so much—and her mind drifts, as it often does, to her own family. What are her parents doing right now? Having lunch? Entertaining? Is her mother shopping, her father playing golf? Whatever they're doing, they're not putting themselves on the line to look for her, that's for sure. But do they ever talk about her, think about her? She imagines calling them, turning up on the doorstep. *Hi, how are you, just thought I'd drop in.* How would they react? Unconsciously, she rubs at her wrist, the bones inside haunted by the ghost of a tight grip.

Her stomach settled, she sits back down at the table. What can she do to sway Katy's decision? What if she could help her find her sister? It might be true that no one knows what happened, but Beth can imagine. Because Phoebe's story sounds eerily close to her own.

She drums her fingers on the table. What is Katy doing out there? Who is she talking to? Pivoting in her seat, she nudges the nearest curtain aside, just a fraction, and—

A flash of silver, painfully bright. Her breath catches. *Shit.*

Letting the curtain fall, she jerks away from the window and slides down in her seat. A high-pitched whine starts up in her ears as all thoughts of Katy and her missing sister are bulldozed by a single instinct.

Hide.

CHAPTER EIGHT

Katy

The wind whips at my face as I step outside and slide the door shut behind me. "Yes?"

The man removes his sunglasses. He's maybe in his mid-to-late thirties with scruffy brown hair, olive skin, and dark eyes that crinkle at the sides. Average height, average build. Converse sneakers, khaki shorts, and a plain white T-shirt. A powerful scent dances in the air: a woodsy, spicy cologne.

His gaze slides past me and into the van. "So sorry to disturb, I wouldn't normally hammer on someone's door like that. I just saw your van and, well, what a coincidence!"

I blink. "Is it?"

"Well, I guess it's not that unusual, there are only so many campsites after all. But still, fancy seeing you here!"

I feel my cheeks redden. He must be mistaking me for someone else. But before I can say, *whoops, this is awkward,* the man plows on.

"I'm actually glad because I was a bit worried. After yesterday, I mean." *What?* "Yesterday?"

"At the beach camp? Around dinnertime? When you were, um . . ." He rotates one hand in the air in a gesture I don't understand. ". . . in a bit of a state?"

A state? My chest starts hammering. *Yesterday.* The night drive, the wine bottle. *There'd been a guy, I hadn't felt comfortable, Travel 101.* I examine the man's face but it's not familiar.

"Remember?" When I fail to respond, he shifts his weight and glances at his shoes. "Okay. Um. So, you were on the beach and—well, everyone was on the beach, someone had built a fire—and you came down and you were talking about . . . actually, I'm not sure, it was a bit of a muddle. You were quite upset?"

I frown. Shake my head.

"Some of the other campers and I, we were worried you might not make it back to your van, so I walked with you, made sure you got inside okay." He gives me an encouraging nod as if this should help.

None of this makes any sense to me. I don't know this man, and I don't remember being on a beach . . . but then I catch a brief sliver of memory: moonlight, looming faces, flickering flames. I think I remember dancing. And—*oh, god*—did I vomit? The pitying expression on the man's face seems like confirmation. And then I got in my van and *drove?* Why didn't anyone stop me? My face floods with heat.

The man says something that he probably thinks is comforting, along the lines of *don't worry, we've all been there,* but I can't look at him.

"I'm embarrassed to say I didn't catch your name," he says.

"Katy." I say it without thinking.

"Right." He smiles, nods, fiddles with his sunglasses. "Katy. It's good to meet you. Properly, I mean. And you're heading north?"

I stiffen. How does he know that?

"You mentioned something last night," he says, reading my reaction. "About going up the coast, not down. Said you were following some kind of trail? You showed me a photo, too. A woman. Phoebe?"

I feel like I'm falling. "How do you know her name?"

"Again, you mentioned it yesterday. I'm so sorry for your loss."

"My what?"

"Oh." He looks a little flustered. "Sorry, maybe I got it wrong? I thought you said that she . . . and you were very upset, so I assumed—"

"Yes. I mean, no. She's gone, but she's not dead. Just missing."

"Ah, that's right. I remember now."

"She hasn't been found yet, but that doesn't mean—"

"No, of course not."

"She could still be—"

"Absolutely. I understand."

Understand? Suddenly, I'm furious. I picture myself punching the man in the face, breaking his nose. *No, you don't. No one does, not even me. That's why I'm doing this. How could you possibly know how that feels?*

"I'm so sorry. This must be really hard for you."

He clearly expects me to say more, but I'm done. This is the strangest conversation I've ever had. "I have to go." I turn away.

"Wait," he says. "I don't suppose you've given any more thought to teaming up?"

"Huh?" My head is starting to hurt. The wind is stinging my eyes.

"It's just that I'm traveling alone, too. Maybe I could help."

Teaming up?

"I could pitch in," he continues. "See what I can find out. I'm pretty good at puzzles. And you look like you could do with some company." He stretches out an upturned palm. "Let me see that picture again."

I don't move. He looks harmless with his scruffy hair and unassuming clothes. But in the back of my mind alarm bells are ringing. "No."

"You sure?"

"I'm fine."

He shrugs. "No worries, just a thought. I'll leave you to it. But if you change your mind, I'll be right over there." He gestures vaguely over his shoulder, then he puts his glasses back on and smiles. "I'm glad you're okay."

I don't smile back. My fingers curl around the door handle.

"See you around." With a last lingering look, he turns and walks away.

CHAPTER NINE

Beth

Beth is still panicking when Katy steps back into the van and slides the door shut.

That silver flash. Curved roof and solar panels. Parked a short way along the opposite row of pitches is an Airstream, the same one for sure; how many other internationally imported polished aluminum trailers are there on the road these days? Palms sweating, muscles locked, she stays down, body curled to one side like a prawn.

Katy crosses to the sink, places her hands on the counter and stands there still and silent. Beth frowns. Unease slithers in her belly. Who had that been, outside? She clears her throat. "Everything okay?"

Katy turns. She looks puzzled. "Oh, sure, yeah. Everything's fine."

"Who was at the door?"

"Oh. No one. Just . . . campsite staff. Admin. Nothing important." She looks sharply at Beth as if seeing her for the first time. "What are you doing?"

Beth glances down at her contorted limbs. She should just sit up and act normal but it's not worth the risk of being seen. "I don't feel good. Just a headache. It's better if I lie like this."

Katy reaches out and touches Beth on the forehead. "Concussion?"

"Oh, no. I'm fine. Probably just a tension thing. Or dehydration."

"Well, you don't look very comfortable." Katy gestures to the bed. "Lie down properly, I'll get you some water."

Keeping her face turned away from the window, Beth climbs stiffly onto the bed and draws the curtains while Katy fetches a bottle of water from the fridge. Accepting it, she drinks then lies down with her head on the pillow. The previous night flashes through her head, the terror she felt while hiding under these same sheets.

"Just rest," Katy murmurs. "Everything will be okay."

Beth closes her eyes. *Last night.* Memories leap like fish from water. *The car, the footsteps, the screaming.* Her mind continues to wind back— *black night, cold air, keep going, don't stop*—and back—*bitch, look at me, never fucking ignore me*—and back—*I thought you understood the rules*— and back—*be confident, and quick*—all the way to what feels like the beginning of the end, just twenty-four hours ago.

"Found you," says a voice.

In a single swift move, Beth nudges the empty beer bottle under her chair and out of sight, simultaneously checking that the surfy guy in the pool is not paying her any attention.

"I left you a note," she says smoothly. "What about you, how long have you been up?"

He towers over her, hands on hips. "Awhile." He looks agitated, on edge, even more so than usual. His eyes are fixed on a point in the distance; something has clearly caught his interest but Beth can't tell what. "Time?"

Eyeroll. He knows as well as she does that she has neither a phone nor a watch. "Twelve-thirty maybe?"

He nods. "You ready?"

No. *The word tastes sweet on her tongue.* Not ready. Not now, not ever. *She sees herself not standing up and walking with him but running in the opposite direction, taking off like a bird and soaring through the air toward the glaring sun. Come back, he'd yell, but she wouldn't, not ever. Fly, Eliza, fly! The thought gives her goose bumps, like standing on the edge of a cliff and feeling an overpowering urge to jump. The call of the void.*

She won't, though. Jump or run. Not now, not ever. She knows exactly what would happen if she did.

Standing up, she takes his hand—but just as they're about to leave, there's a clatter to their right. The Airstream.

Beth stiffens. He squeezes her fingers. Game on.

Pretending to chat quietly, they watch in their peripheral vision as the door opens and the sleep-rumpled couple emerge stretching and yawning, stepping gracefully down onto the grass and tilting their heads to assess the weather. They chat softly, the man running his hands through the woman's hair, trailing his fingers across her back. She presses herself into his chest, and they both smile the kind of smile you only find on the faces of people who have everything.

Beth feels her jaw tighten. She hates them.

Which makes what she's about to do to them only marginally less appalling.

CHAPTER TEN

Katy

While Lily dozes off on the bed, I clean up around her, packing away the stove and washing out the mugs and generally making sure everything stays neat and tidy. I can't let things slide out of control again.

I leave her to sleep and step back outside. It's now calmer than it was. The wind seems to have dropped and the sun feels warm on my skin. I stand for a moment with my head tipped to the sky—*breathe*—before opening up the front passenger door.

Fusty air seeps from the cab. It smells like sleep. The quilt and pillow are still on the front seat, along with Lily's wet towel and her dirty clothes from the night before. I gather the towel and clothes, intending to add both to my laundry bag—but after a moment's thought, I change my mind. Squashing the clothes into a tight ball instead, I open the glove box and press them right to the back. Best not to wash them. Not yet anyway.

I shake out the towel, making a mental note to find a Kmart or something. Lily will need a whole new set of clothes; I didn't bring enough of my own for us to share for long. I pluck at the cheap material of my work shirt—*should probably treat myself, too*—and wrinkle my nose as an acrid smell wafts from beneath. *Gross.*

Slinging the towel over my shoulder, I grab the bodywash and head for the shower.

Under the falling water, I scrub and scrub and scrub and scrub.

The surreal conversation with Sunglasses Man plays over and over in my head like a bad movie. I'm not too shaken up about the gaps in my memory, blackouts are not new to me; it's more what he said. I hate that a stranger knows more about me than I do, for those few hours anyway. And there was something smug about his tone—like a pickup artist who thinks the deal's already done. Had he been the guy who'd made me uncomfortable? Maybe, but I honestly don't recall ever meeting him before.

I strain to recall for myself what might've happened the day before, all the things I might've said and done and all the ways I could've humiliated myself—but where the facts should be there's just a black hole. So what *do* I remember? I flew from Sydney to Perth. I got in a cab. I picked up the van, bought basic supplies, including wine, at a nearby supermarket. I set off, stopping in at all the same places Phoebe posted about until I reached the first campsite . . . and then I'm not sure. It was late. I picked a spot, paid for the night, and made a start on dinner. I remember opening a bottle of red but not how much I drank. Next thing I know I'm falling asleep behind the wheel and there's a car on my tail.

Scrub, scrub, scrub. My skin is bright pink. I drop my head and the water runs down my back in steaming rivulets. *This is absurd, I'm a mess, shouldn't be here, want to go home.* I picture my flat in Sydney with its clean lines, heavy doors and solid walls, everything tightly contained, perfectly controlled. On the road, there's nothing but wide open space, unpredictable and menacing. *I'm so sorry, Phoebe. I can't do this.*

'Course you can. Her imagined response pops immediately into my head. *Things are only as scary as you think they are.*

Classic Phoebe, afraid of nothing. If she were here right now, she wouldn't be hanging around the van. She'd be out there taking up space in the world, soaking up the sunshine as if shadows were things that happened to other people. *Come on Katy,* she'd say, her hand outstretched. *What are you afraid of?* She said that all the time, always lightly and with a smile as if the question was an answer in itself—and I never offered one of my own because I knew she wasn't really asking. But if she'd ever taken the time to listen, I could've given her a very long list.

I scrub myself all over one last time, then twist the faucet and dry off.

I walk back to my van with my head down, half expecting more random people to pop up and tell me I've behaved badly. I feel like the whole campsite is watching me, everyone projecting the same message: *you don't belong here.* But when I look up they're all just getting on with their own lives, minding their own business, looking after their own tiny corners of the world.

I scan the neat rows of tents, caravans, trailers, and motorhomes, looking for Sunglasses Man. *If you change your mind, I'm just in that van over there.* He'd pointed somewhere over his shoulder, toward the rear of the property. I wander around but can't find him.

Back on my pitch, I face what I think is the right direction and study all the vehicles in view. Sunlight spears my eyes and it hurts, like the light has shot right to the back of my skull. Why can't I *think*? Why did I ever think this was a good idea? What had convinced me that leaving my home and job to follow a social media account like a treasure map was a solid plan? I'd thought it would make everything clearer, but actually it's the opposite: everything is blurry and vague, the noises too loud, colors too sharp. Whatever I thought I would achieve, it doesn't feel so attainable now. Maybe I—

My thoughts grind to a sudden halt. There's something on the ground. A bright twinkle of color.

Edging forward, I crouch down. Lying in the dirt is a small object, bright and sparkly like a gemstone. Reaching down, my fingers close around something the size and shape of a matchstick. When I open my hand, my jaw falls open.

Oh my god.

Sitting in the center of my palm is a bobby pin, customized with glittery nail polish. Phoebe's favorite shade flashes in the sun: a brilliant coral pink.

When it was sunny they glittered in her hair like jewels.

I look up as if I might find her standing in front of me. I get to my feet and rotate on the spot, breathing hard, checking in every direction. This thing in my hand, this pin . . . it's *hers*. I know it is, I've seen it before, I'm certain. So why is it here? Maybe she dropped it back when she stayed here? But the chances of me stumbling across it on the exact same pitch a whole year later seem slim. Also, the pin doesn't look like it's spent twelve months submerged in soil. It doesn't appear to have recently resurfaced due to rain or wind or whatever else brings up the buried. Instead, the glossy pink lacquer looks fresh and clean, like the pin just fell from a hand or a pocket.

Tap, tap, tap.

I look back at the ground. The soil still bears the patterned imprint of Converse sneakers.

Phoebe, right?

Sunglasses Man.

So sorry for your loss.

I stare at his footprint.

If you change your mind, I'll be right over there.

I turn again to face the direction in which he'd pointed. In the distance, past the horses and the white stuccoed main building, a small cloud of dust is traveling north. A car is leaving the ranch and heading back to the main road. I watch it getting smaller and smaller until it disappears completely.

See you around.

I look back at the pin. My brain can't compute what I'm looking at. *What have I found? What am I holding? What is this?* But my body is not confused. For the first time in a long time, my body finally feels calm. Because deep in my bones I know exactly what this is.

My first clue.

CHAPTER ELEVEN

Wyatt

Another movie. A classic, one of Lucas's all-time favorites and now one of Wyatt's too. A story about vampires with a killer soundtrack, best experienced with the volume turned up to the max. Wyatt holds his breath as the villain steps forward, finally unmasked. *I'm sorry, Lucy. This is all my fault. David and my boys misbehaved.*

Beyond the living room, the rest of the house is quiet. Dad's on one of his out-of-area jobs again, which he hates but deems worth the effort because he can overcharge for the call-out, and his absence is louder even than the blaring TV. Shifting his position on the sofa, Wyatt knocks the volume up a little more. *I told you, boys need a mother*, says the villain. *It was all going to be so perfect. Just like one big happy family.*

Restless, he turns onto his back and stares not at the screen but at the wall opposite. His mind is curiously blank, hushed and peaceful as a snowy day. Must be the cold and flu medicine he's taking—not that it's done much good. The virus is still kicking around his body, enjoying its new home. The ache in his bones has subsided, but he can't shake the headaches and his guts are all over the place; for the last two days he hasn't been able to stray far from the bathroom.

Like the Noises, though, he's used to it. He gets sick like this a lot. Earlier in the year he'd caught a similar bug and had been laid up for a month. *You'll be all right,* the doctor had said. But Wyatt is worried that he won't. What if there's something seriously wrong with him, something that rest and fluids can't fix?

He actually heard Dad say it once. *There's something wrong with him.* Wyatt had been twelve and confined to his room for the evening because he'd hurled the TV remote at the wall during a tantrum. From where he'd lain curled up on the floor, he'd heard Dad outside on the driveway, his voice drifting in through the open window.

Honestly, I'm worried. I think there's something wrong with him.
You do?
Yeah, but I . . . ah look, it's probably nothing.
Oh, Rory, you just need time, you've both been through so much.
I know, but still.
Try to be patient, I'm sure it's just a phase.

The second voice had been their next-door neighbor, Mrs. Keating. Dad calls her Jill but to Wyatt she's Mrs. Creeping, because she's old and weird and pops up whenever Dad's out, knocking on the door with a jar of jam or some old piece of junk she no longer uses. *I thought you might like it,* she says. *You can have it if you want.* Actually, she doesn't do that so much anymore, she's started to back off now Wyatt is older, but she's still weird. Her shoulders are hunched and she walks funny. Also, her house stinks; Wyatt can smell it from the yard. And her eyes remind him of a lizard's.

Wyatt once tried to tell Dad about the smell and the weirdness, but Dad said not to be mean. He said Mrs. Creeping had been sad since her husband died, double sad since Mum left, and it was their job to make sure she had someone to talk to. *We have to look after each other, you know?* Wyatt did not know. He couldn't understand why the responsibility fell on them just because they happened to live next door, but Dad said it was what Mum would've wanted. *Your mother was a good person,* he said, *always asking Jill over for tea, checking to make sure she was okay. Now that she's gone, it's up to us to do the same.* That's why he weeds Mrs. Creeping's garden, mows her lawn, drops in when her Wi-Fi goes funny, and never charges her a cent. And in return Mrs. Creeping bakes the occasional cake and tells him he's doing a great job. *It's called community*, Dad said. *Fuck community*, Wyatt had replied under his breath. He'd rather be left alone.

In the living room, Wyatt's attention is brought back to the movie as the final confrontation plays out onscreen—*don't fight, Lucy, so much better if you don't fight*—but he can hardly hear for all the memories bouncing around inside his head. His eyes drift to the spot on the wall just beneath the light switch where three years ago the remote had gouged a divot in the plaster and spilled its batteries. Wyatt doesn't remember much else about that day, just the subsequent conversation outside his window—*something wrong, you've both been through so much*—but he knows it was bad. *He* is bad. Useless. Dangerous.

He checks his phone. Nothing. No calls or texts. No new notifications. His stomach gurgles. *Bad, bad, bad.*

Suddenly he can't be on the sofa anymore; he needs to move. Throwing his phone down, he gets up and leaves the house through the back door, emerging into the sun like one of the bloodsuckers from the film. The afternoon air is warm and thick but he gulps it down anyway, batting the flies from his face as he trudges over the patchy grass toward the Quiet Place behind the garage. In the shade of Mrs. Creeping's lopsided lemon tree, he sits on a stack of spare pavers and leans against the garage, letting his head fall against the fibro wall.

Bang, thump, shudder, shift.

He frowns, looks up at the sky.

Tumble, rustle, skid.

Turning, Wyatt examines the wall of the garage as if he might be able to see right through it. There's something inside, moving around. Or are the Noises just in his head, like everything else? *Something wrong, something wrong.* It seems increasingly likely that what he's been hearing for the last four years is not and never has been in the walls. Instead, they must be in *him*. If only he could punch a hole in his skull and rip them from his brain.

As the Noises continue, Wyatt reaches to his right and his fingers close around the cool bulk of a fat red brick. Sliding it aside, he plunges his hand into the roughly dug hole in the soil beneath, pulls out a Tupperware box and unclips the sides. The lid pops off and the contents glitter, teeming like a shoal of gold and silver fish. Wyatt regards his secret treasures, picks through them one by one before selecting a star-shaped pendant on a long silver chain, which he draws out with surgical precision and places in the palm of his hand.

Thud, thud. Shuffle-bump-hiss.

Reverently, Wyatt presses the treasure to his heart. He shuts his eyes tight and thinks of vampires, axe murderers, and demonic possession; seances and basements and monochromatic motel rooms. He summons the best scenes from his favorite movies, reciting the lines like prayers. *Come and play with us, Danny. God is in his holy temple. This is no dream; this is really happening. We all go a little mad sometimes.*

He holds the necklace so tight that the pendant cuts into his palm. And soon enough, the Noises stop.

Liked by **the_road_more_traveled** and **others**

pheebsinwonderland So here I am at Pink Lake / Hutt Lagoon and oh wow is this place magical! As you can see from the pics, the color of the water is unreal (comes from an algae called dunaliella salina) and the vibe is so peaceful. Don't get me wrong, I love meeting other people but there's nothing like a bit of "me" time to think and reflect!

Quick Tips: You can visit Pink Lake all year round but I recommend visiting on a clear day between 10 a.m. and 2 p.m. because that's when the colors will be brightest. The easiest way to get here is by car (5 hours from Perth via the Indian Ocean Drive coastal highway, all sealed roads)—pack a picnic so you can sit and soak it all up for a while, and bring a drone if you have one because the aerial views are absolutely stunning.
Tell me about your favorite thinking places! Where do you most feel at peace? Do you like the water, or the mountains? Maybe you light a candle or have some kind of grounding ritual Let me know!

(Image descriptions: 1. A woman in a yellow dress stands with her back to the camera, ankle-deep in strawberry pink water. 2. The same woman is now knee-deep with both arms raised to the sky, golden bangles glittering on her wrists. 3. The lake as seen from above: a strip of white salt-strewn shore and an expanse of pure pink. 4. Salt crystals pulled directly from the lake bed sparkle in the palm of a female hand.)

#pinklake #huttlagoon #wanderoutwest #westernaustralia #coralcoast #girlswhotravel #outandabout #peace

View all 55 comments

millielovescamping Thanks for the tips! So you can access with a 2WD? You don't need a 4WD?

wollongongwanderer73 Got my shot of inspo for the day! I like to meditate on the beach, so good for the soul.

goodnightpetergraham Beautiful hey? If you're still looking for free camps, I have some great recs 👇

lonewanderer66 Your content makes me want to travel. Where are you heading next?

authenticity_seeker I went in summer when the lake had less water in it and it wasn't as good. Less pink water, more crusty salt! I'd say April–October are the best months to visit.

20 May

CHAPTER TWELVE

Beth

Beth sits still and solemn in the passenger seat with her hands in her lap. Beside her, Katy is quiet, her eyes on the road, her hands at ten and two. The road disappears beneath them like murky liquid sucked through a straw.

Outside, the landscape is changing. Flat, arid earth and bleached colors are gradually giving way to rippling farmland and a more nuanced spectrum of color. Between stretches of lush green plains, burned orange driveways lead to squat stone buildings, and hills rise in the distance like trapped air bubbles. And even though Beth knows exactly where she is, has seen this view many times before, she keeps track of the GPS, mildly comforted by the familiarity of the route as displayed on the dashboard screen. The digital orientation—*you are here*—is a gentle antidote to the weirdness of sitting quietly in a small space with someone she doesn't know, which for some reason feels even weirder than it did in the dark the night before.

She glances at Katy. The silence is awkward, but she's glad for the opportunity to organize her thoughts. She runs through a mental list of obvious questions, trying to head them off before they're raised. *If you're traveling without a visa, how will you work? If all your ID documents are gone, how will you get new ones? Why exactly don't you want to go back to the States?* She concentrates on pulling "Lily" tight around her like an invisibility cloak, filling herself with false narratives until they feel real. She adjusts her physicality, playing on all the tropes she's learned from film and TV about what makes a good victim: damaged but sweet and compliant.

Trees slide by. Rusted gates and upcycled mailboxes. Handmade signs. ART STUDIO. WINDSURFING SCHOOL. FREE MANURE. HONEY SOLD HERE.

Katy hasn't yet mentioned anything about Beth's request-slash-proposition, but a favorable decision seems implied. She's still here, isn't she? They're moving, it's happening. Still, Beth mentally prepares for the alternative. She could try her luck elsewhere, hitch to Perth, show up at the bank and ask for new cards—not that it would do any good, she has no ID to prove who she is and there's nothing in her account anyway. What she really needs is her own car and a burner phone, but there's no chance she can make that happen any time soon. Even if she stole something she couldn't afford enough fuel to get out of the area, let alone the state.

Her fingers twitch, longing for a pen. She misses her notebook. It's so much easier to think when she can see her thoughts on paper, but even just the act of writing is soothing. She loves the simple sweep of ink over a blank page, the ephemeral made permanent, a relic of her university glory days. Textbooks, seminars, and tangible achievement. Modules and deadlines. *Neural pathways. Frontal lobe. Cognitive distortion. Negative reinforcement.* Magical words. Happier times.

She smiles . . . but then the memories curdle like milk.

"So," she says, breaking the silence. "When you get to these places, the ones on your sister's Instagram, what kind of things are you looking for?"

Katy purses her lips. "Clues. Signs. Anything unusual that might point to something we've missed."

"Hmm." Not much to work with there, but maybe Katy isn't ready to share details of her plan. How else can she be helpful? "It's wild that they couldn't find anything at all. What was the investigation like? Did it get national coverage?"

"Yep. TV, radio, everything."

Beth doesn't remember hearing about the case, but then she wouldn't. Her head was well and truly in the sand this time last year. "And they put a call out for information? Set up a campaign website, a Facebook page, that sort of thing?"

"Yeah, all of that. And we did everything possible on our end, too."

"We?"

"Me and my family. My parents are divorced, but they flew over here together, put pressure on the cops to widen the search. Plus we talked to friends and colleagues, searched through her apartment, did those press conference things."

"And no luck? You couldn't find anyone who could help?"

"Nope."

"Not even anyone who might've met her on the road?"

Katy shakes her head. "No. Which I don't get because there's no way she wouldn't have made friends along the way. She's very sociable."

And memorable. Beth thinks again of the photos, the long hair and stunning figure. Girls like that don't go unnoticed. "What about hashtags? Did you look through those?"

"What do you mean?"

"Insta, Twitter, YouTube, TikTok. It might take a while but if you search for particular hashtags and locations, you can check the background of photos and videos. You never know, someone might've captured her without realizing. I mean, the whole world is recording itself all the time, there's a good chance you'll find something."

"Huh." Katy says. "I haven't looked, but I'll check with the investigator."

A spasm of alarm. "You're in touch with the police?"

"No, just the lead detective, but he's hard to get hold of. And don't worry, if I do manage to speak with him I won't mention anything about you."

A pause.

Beth clears her throat. "I could have a look if you like? At the hashtags? I'm pretty good with social media."

"Mmm." Katy rubs her eyes. "Maybe."

Beth falls quiet, sensing she should stop. She can think of plenty more questions (What was Phoebe's state of mind at the time? Had she been in a relationship? Any recent breakups? Would you say she's a risk-taker? What are her interests?), and there would be even more angles that potentially even Katy herself hadn't yet considered.

But Beth knows better than to push, so she keeps quiet. Instead, she picks at her nails and looks out of the window.

A few minutes later, Katy heaves a deep sigh. "I honestly don't know how she lived like this."

"Who, Phoebe?"

"How did she not feel vulnerable all the time? I don't understand the appeal."

Beth thinks about it, takes a guess. "Freedom. Independence. Adventure."

"Okay, but what do those things actually mean? And do you really have to go so far from home to get them?"

It depends on what you mean by home, Beth thinks, but she's not the best judge. She mulls over what she's observed of others. She's never been fussy when it comes to people-watching, her interest extends to everyone, but solo female travelers are always captivating. The miracle of their autonomy, the audacity with which they claim it. *Who the hell are these women,* she would often think, *just wandering around doing life by themselves?*

"I think," she says at last, "that it's about lack of context. You leave everything behind—your background, your stories, your framework and routines—and it's just you in the moment. The past is forgotten, the future is unknown. You can be the truest version of yourself because there's nothing clouding it, and everyone else around you is the same. You have to meet people where they're at. It's the purest form of escape. That's why I started, anyway." That last part is true, at least.

"Escape," Katy repeats. She chews her lip. "So what were you running from?"

Beth sighs. Where to start? She's been running for so long. So many wrong turns and shitty decisions, too numerous to count. But her biggest mistake is never far from her thoughts. His name sits permanently in her throat, just waiting to be released.

"Lucas?"

"What?"

"I don't know about this."

"What the fuck are you talking about? You just said you were ready."

"I know, but . . ."

"But what?"

Inside Beth's stomach, butterflies are stirring. Conditions aren't quite right. The campground isn't as quiet as it ought to be. Most people have gone out exploring for the day but some of the more raucous groups have stayed behind. It's her job to keep track, but there are too many moving parts, though she doesn't know how to say it without sounding weak.

"Get it together," he hisses. "We're doing this."

She grounds herself by focusing on small details. A cloud in the sky that looks like a teapot. A leaf floating on the surface of the pool. A placard nailed to a nearby tree that reads, WELCOME TO WILLOWFIELD, HOME TO WESTERN AUSTRALIA'S MOST HAUNTED HOUSE! BOOK YOUR TOUR TODAY! *with an arrow pointing west to the crumbling remains of an old homestead. The whitewashed buildings stand pale and ominous in a sea of dry grass.*

"You paying attention?"

"Uh-huh."

She drags her gaze back to the couple. Their names are Tommy and Evie, and they're from the Gold Coast. Tommy runs a start-up currently making a splash with some new gym technology; Evie is a pharmaceutical rep. The Big Lap is their extended honeymoon. They chart their adventures in the Airstream with a freshly minted Instagram account—heavy on beauty, light on reality—from which they post daily stories and live videos from their real-time locations. They are loud and visible and love to connect with their rapidly increasing number of followers. Which is what made them so easy to find.

So far, everything has gone according to plan. Connecting with them has been a piece of cake. The campsite had enough space for walk-ins and check-in was swift. The perfect pitch—close enough but not too close—was readily available. A mechanical problem was fabricated with which Tommy was only too eager to help; solutions were found, stories were swapped, and soon they had themselves a party. By sunset they were all the best, loudest, and drunkest of friends. The whole campsite had seen and heard them. We are a group of four, *their raucous laughter proclaimed.* We are together.

"All right." *Lucas whispers, his voice hot in her ear.* "Let's go."

I don't want to do this anymore, *Beth thinks. Nevertheless, she forces her lips into a huge fake grin and waves an arm in the air.* "Morning, sleepyheads!"

The beautiful couple wave back.

Beth rubs at her temples as if she can squeeze the memory out like pips from a lemon.

"It's a long story," she says eventually.

"It's a long journey," Katy counters.

"Hmm. Can't argue with that." Beth thinks back to the beginning, before things got so fucked up. "I was a student, in my second year at un—" *shit, no, not university, they call it college in the States, and there's a special name for the second year,* "at college, a . . . sophomore, majoring in psychology. And I, uh, had a lot going on. Personal stuff. I fell behind and couldn't catch up, and the stress got too much."

"So you quit to go traveling?"

"Not exactly. I, uh, got kicked out."

"Kicked out? What happened?"

I have no idea, *she wants to say, but it's not entirely true.* What happened was a fish tank and a clock, the digital numbers emitting a lurid green glow. *I did something.* A dirty carpet and fat spots of red blood on pure white cotton. *Something really, really awful.* What happened was that Beth had made a terrible choice and it had changed everything.

But she can't talk about that either. Yet another in a long list of secrets.

"It's boring," she lies. "Main thing is, my parents went nuts. They're both very religious—and academics, top of their game, so they were always super strict about school as well as everything else. They wanted me to be just like them but told me constantly how hard I'd have to work, that my place in the world wouldn't come easily and if I wasn't careful I'd end up at the very bottom of the barrel. So, y'know, when I fucked everything up they did not take it well. Actually, that's an understatement; they lost their goddamn minds. We had a huge fight. And then some other stuff happened—" *starched sheets, latex gloves, more blood, how could you do this Bethany, you're a monster Bethany,* "and things got really bad, so I bought a plane ticket with my savings and left. We haven't spoken since."

She swallows, waiting for the judgment, but Katy's only reaction is to ask if that's the reason she can't return to the States.

"Kind of," Beth replies. "It's complicated." And that, thankfully, seems to be the end of it.

They drive quietly for what feels like forever but is actually just sixty or so kilometers of yet more trees, shrubs, and rolling gray road. They pass through a town with a servo and tavern, both of which are closed. A flock of black cockatoos rises up from a field and wheels away into the sky. At one point, Beth stiffens as a trayback ute materializes on the asphalt behind them—but then she blinks and it's gone, and the road is empty once again.

"Do you like podcasts?" Beth says, when the silence gets too much. "I know a few good ones if you're keen?"

Katy shrugs. "I prefer audiobooks."

"Yeah? What kind?"

"Anything really." She reaches for the media display on the dash, selects an audio app and hits "resume" on the first title that appears.

A syrupy voice wafts from the speakers. "You are not crazy," it says. "You are grieving. Your life has turned upside down, and your brain is working hard to process something that cannot and will not ever make sense."

Beth glances sidelong at Katy.

"When your brain is working overtime," the audiobook continues, "there's not much power left over for normal, day-to-day function, which is why you might put your keys in the fridge instead of in your handbag.

Why you walk into a room and forget the reason you're there. Why you might suddenly struggle to remember basic things like directions, words, ingredients, and names."

It's uncomfortable, like sitting in on someone else's therapy session, but Katy doesn't seem fazed; her eyes remain fixed dead ahead. Beth turns back to the window.

"You might feel confused or unable to focus. You may even lose whole chunks of time. This can feel like madness, but grief-related memory loss is often part of the process, as common as depression or insomnia. And it can last longer than you think."

They overtake a camper trailer, then a motorbike overtakes them. A convoy of Jeeps zip by in the opposite direction, panels flashing in the sun.

"But while brain fog can be bewildering, it's not always a bad thing. Think of it as your body's way of protecting you; your mind is trying to make your pain easier to bear. When someone we love dies, we—"

Abruptly, Katy reaches out and turns it off. "Choose something else if you want. I've heard that one already."

Thank fuck. Beth picks up the phone and scrolls quickly through Katy's library. She flips past other rubbish-sounding self-help titles—mindfulness, meditation, the power to heal, blah blah blah—and picks a novel, one that promises to be pacy and thrilling.

"Chapter one. The girl lay on her side with her knees bent and her hands drawn up to her chin. Her lips were parted, her eyes closed, and she looked peaceful, almost comfortable—so much so that if anyone were to pass the alleyway on their way to work, if they were to glance to the side and allow their gaze to fall upon the toes and hair and knees among the drainpipes and puddles and bins, they might think she was sleeping. That is, until they saw all the blood—"

This time it's Beth's hand that shoots out, hitting the power button so hard it hurts. "Sorry," she says. "Not keen on the narrator."

Katy doesn't respond.

The quiet returns. Outside, a dark mound whips by at the edge of the road. Stiff limbs, matted gray fur, lumpy innards soaking up the dust.

CHAPTER THIRTEEN

Katy

"Well, it is pink." I peer out the windscreen at water the color of a strawberry milkshake. "But magical? I don't know."

"Maybe we're too early," says Lily, rolling down her window. "The sun is still pretty low. And it's a little overcast. Doesn't Phoebe's post mention something about coming on a clear day?"

Leaning forward over the wheel, I stare up at the clouds. She has a point. Still, the tide line looks slimy, the shore thick with mud. The water looks like it smells. And I feel far from peaceful. There are too many other vehicles around, too many tourists doing the same thing, all taking the same picture. I watch two children scoop handfuls of natural salt from the shallows while their parents alternate between safety warnings and instructions to *look at the camera, Samuel, come on, give Mummy a smile*. Farther out, a thick-middled man tries unsuccessfully to find a spot deep enough to swim.

I urge the van onward to the main lookout, a rectangular viewing platform atop a small sandy rise, but all the parking spaces are already taken. Some people have set up chairs and blankets, others are flying drones and screaming at their kids that the candy-floss water is *not for drinking!* So much for the peace and quiet. Making a U-turn, I head back the way we came and find a less congested spot at water level. I cut the engine and lower my own window to let the breeze in.

Just ahead, a slender blond woman in a battered Akubra hat is walking slowly and wistfully toward the water, picking her way delicately over the salty residue and posing for her bearded, bare-chested partner who snaps photos of her with a proper long-lensed camera. Laughing at absolutely nothing, the woman takes off her hat and runs her hands through her hair, turning in a circle like she's in a music video.

"She looks ridiculous," says Lily.

"Agreed."

"I want her to fall over."

"Same."

"Want me to go push her?"

A laugh bubbles from my throat.

Lily opens her door. "I'm gonna go stretch my legs and find somewhere to pee. If Gigi Hadid over there is still throwing shapes when I get back, I will not be held responsible for my actions."

My mouth twitches into another smile. She's funny.

I watch in the mirror as she wanders away toward the lookout. Once she's a good distance away I reach into the glove box for the coral-pink bobby pin, now safely sealed inside a sandwich bag. I turn the bag over, examining the bobby pin through the plastic. It felt so significant yesterday but now it feels more like a coincidence, silly and meaningless.

I pick over my memory of Sunglasses Man. Does it mean anything that I found the bobby pin right where he'd been standing, or am I just making things up? I wish I'd thought to ask for his name. I'd inquired at the Ranch during checkout, but was told that giving out guest information is against campsite policy.

I dig out my phone, find Dust's number in my call log and hit redial.

"This is Dust, unfortunately I'm unable to get to the phone right now, but if you leave your name and number . . ."

Ugh. I leave another message after the tone. "Hi, sorry, Katy Sweeney here. Again. I just wanted to let you know that something happened yesterday and I think I might've found . . . well, I may have some new information."

I pause. Does the bobby pin actually constitute new information? Phoebe wouldn't be the only person in the world who customizes their hair accessories with nail polish. And even if I'm right and it *is* hers, what new light does it shed? Then again, the man, the footprint, the un-chipped lacquer . . . my gut says they're important.

"Look, please just call me back. You have my number. I'll wait to hear from you. Okay, bye." I hang up, then surprise myself by thrusting my middle finger at the screen. I throw my phone hard onto the passenger seat, where it bounces off the cushion and hits the floor with a clatter.

Falling back against the headrest, I close my eyes. The fog in my head is getting worse, like I'm permanently on the verge of a migraine, and thinking about Phoebe feels like chasing the end of a rainbow. Images swim around in my head like fish in a bowl: painting Easter eggs, hide-and-seek, making cubby houses, playing Bingo with our English grandmother. Kelly's eye, legs eleven, one fat lady, two little ducks . . . *That's us! Phoebe and Katy! Two little ducks, number twenty-two. Quack, quack, quack.* A tear slips from the corner of my eye.

I fish my phone from the footwell and open Instagram again. Phoebe's dress clings to her body like a second skin, the straps slipping over her shoulder to reveal a flash of yellow bikini, bright as the anger that flares in my chest. Perfect girl, the better one, everyone's first choice. So pretty, so happy. *Well, look where all that perfection got you, Pheebs. And look where it got me: still fixing your problems, still picking up all the pieces.*

I slam my palm onto the steering wheel.

Fuck you. I hate you for making me do this, for making me come here.

I bang my fist against the door.

If it wasn't for you, everything would be fine.

I breathe.

Sorry, Pheebs.

Inhale. Exhale.

I didn't mean it.

I think of the cupboard under the sink and all the wine stashed at the back, how good it would feel to let it numb me out, how much better off I'd be if just for a few hours I couldn't feel anything anymore.

No. No more of that. It doesn't help. It's never helped.

I drop my head. I am a terrible person. Not pretty, not happy, definitely not perfect. I pull the visor down and study my reflection in the mirror. My appearance and Phoebe's could not be more different. My face is haggard, thin, sallow, my hair short and unstylish after years of self-management. My eyes are sunken, and I smile with my mouth closed to hide the tooth I chipped and never got fixed. Instead of a bright sundress, I wear the same baggy shorts and T-shirt I'd pulled on that morning, the same T-shirt I wear to *work* for god's sake, and the thought of wearing a bikini makes me want to throw up.

I flip the visor shut with a bang and look out the window instead. Seconds later, a sudden gust of wind brings a smattering of sand and leaves, and I'm just about to roll the glass up when I notice another grasshopper. I let out a little *hah* of surprise as the insect hops from the window frame onto my thigh and rubs its back legs together. It looks just like the one from yesterday: my good omen, my tiny green friend.

"Hello," I whisper, leaning forward. "What are you doing here?"

The grasshopper waves its antennae at me. *It's okay. Everything will be fine.*

I hold my finger out, hoping it might hop onto my hand. "Are you following me? Did you hitch a ride?"

The grasshopper doesn't accept my invitation but it seems to nod, which I take as a yes. Reason tells me it can't possibly be the exact same insect, but its presence feels reassuring, a reminder of home: summer afternoons spent combing through the back garden, dirty knees and ice creams. One bright, sunny afternoon Phoebe and I had found crickets hopping around near the back fence. *Look at them jump! They go so high!*

Mummy, what are they? Mum had been cranky; she was on her way out to a "dinner thing," the neighbors were babysitting and she wanted us to get cleaned up. *Come on girls, pajamas please.* But we refused, continued to chase them, squealed loudly as Phoebe caught one. *Tell us, Mum, what is it?* We squinted into her cupped palms. *Does it have a name?* Mum's eyes were hard. *Put it down*, she said. *I mean it. Come on, inside, right now. I'm going to be late.* We persisted. *But this one is our friend! Can we keep it? Pleeeeaaase?* We wouldn't stop, and Mum got so mad that she—

But the scene starts to swirl and fade and soon I can't remember much about it at all.

Guilty and homesick, I quickly text Mum again: Still fine, don't worry, all going well. It's not true, but it's what she needs to hear.

I look back at my leg, but once again the grasshopper has gone.

CHAPTER FOURTEEN

Beth

Beth walks barefoot back along the road, heading directly for the large rock she knows is just around the corner past the lookout while simultaneously trying to appear as if this is her first time at Pink Lake. She's alert, conscious of every other person and vehicle around her, but there's also a small spring in her step, a barely discernible lift in her heart. She likes it here—the milkshake-pink water makes her think of *Charlie and the Chocolate Factory*—and it feels good to be back under such changed circumstances. The feeling, she realizes, is hope.

She's feeling a little more relaxed about Katy, too. The awkward drive had taken a turn for the better once they'd found a nice book to listen to, a sweet comedy about two unlikely friends sharing a flat, and they'd even swapped a smile or two. The atmosphere since has melted into something almost companionable and Beth has decided that despite a few quirks Katy is cool. She doesn't talk too much either, which is awesome, although Beth could do with knowing more about her. The information she's gleaned so far is a little conflicted.

For example, the van's stylish interior and decorative accents indicate an occupant with a zest for life and a passion for the outdoors, someone who reads lifestyle magazines, browses artisan markets, and makes curries from scratch, someone who has a very clear idea about who they are and how they want to present to the world. But Katy herself doesn't come across like that. She's not grubby or smelly, not like some of the other travelers Beth has encountered, and she mostly keeps the van clean—but image and personal grooming are clearly not priorities. And judging from all the canned soup and two-minute noodles in the cupboards she isn't bothered about cooking either. Socially she's a little awkward, definitely not what you'd call a people person, not like Lucas . . .

The thought shocks her and for several seconds she can't move. She stares at the ground, blindsided by a tidal swell of emotion: remorse, mixed with a strange variant of homesickness. All the things she'd initially found so attractive about Lucas come rushing at her: his charisma and charm, sense of humor and thirst for adventure, the infectious confidence with which he moves through the world as if it were designed just for him. She longs for him and hates herself for it.

Becoming aware that a nearby couple are side-eyeing her, she pulls herself together and strides away with her head down, heading around the corner to where a thin track leads into the scrub. She nudges her way through overgrown bushes to the big rock and tucks herself into its shade. Then, checking first for snakes, she hitches up her dress and squats in the dirt.

The optimism she'd felt just moments earlier has now soured into something close to substance withdrawal: an oily, irresistible need, and a growing certainty that survival is not possible or even desirable without instant satisfaction. She hasn't even considered how Lucas might be feeling after everything that happened. She can almost hear him: *I'm sorry, I didn't mean to, it's not my fault, I don't want to be like this, I don't want to hurt you or anyone else, I hate myself, I want to be different.* Same old story—but is it possible she overreacted? Just because someone is a bad person it doesn't mean they aren't also good, and vice versa. Both could be true at the same time. And she knows better than anyone what it feels like to lose control, to carry a darkness within. She was in fact lucky to have Lucas, because who else would have her? He loved to remind her of that. *You're dreaming if you think anyone's gonna love you after what you've done.*

Bladder empty, Beth makes her way back to the road. Perhaps if she'd stayed, she could've helped him. They could've saved each other. They were, after all, a team.

After breakfast, Tommy unhooks the trailer from their Pajero while Evie packs a beach bag. Their interactions are smooth and comfortable, demonstrating the ease and success of the partnership.

Beth stays on task by anchoring her thoughts to the moment, packing away, washing up, making a shopping list, all the while remaining highly attuned to both Tommy and Evie's movements and those of the surrounding campers. Which are likely to be off-site for the day? Which are staying, which are checking out? How empty is the campsite likely to be within the hour, and how long might it stay that way?

Both couples are ready to leave at the same time. They climb into their respective cars: Tommy waves from behind the wheel, Lucas pips his horn. Then they all drive together along the winding track that leads from the ranch to the main road. At the crossroads they split off—Troopy to the left, Pajero to the right—and a few more horn honks later, Lucas and Beth are alone.

Beth catches her reflection in the wing mirror as the pretense falls from her face, her features dripping and melting like candle wax.

Lucas drives for fifteen minutes before doubling back and returning to the campsite. As they approach the gate again, Beth's heart begins to hammer. What if someone sees them? Fortunately, her predictions prove largely correct. Except for one or two late starters, most of the campers have cleared out for the day.

Lucas brings the Troopy to a slow stop in front of the Airstream, engine still running. "Don't think," he says. "Just do. The quicker the better."

Beth nods and scans the pitch. The Airstream is nicely boxed in by the neighboring trailer and the tent behind, both entrances facing conveniently away, and the occupants of the tent have even hung a side panel from their gazebo for extra privacy. How helpful. With the Troopy now parked in front, anyone would have to come right up close to get a clear view of the Airstream's front door.

Lucas hands Beth his phone along with a small silver key. "Be confident,"
he murmurs. "And quick."

The key, recently purchased online, shines bright in Beth's palm. It's a mi-
nor miracle that most RVs and campervans (also tool cribs, side boxes, pickup
shells and lockers) are made with universal locks and the keys are readily
available online; it makes things so much easier—unless the owners are savvy
enough to have changed the locks, which generally they're not. Please work,
she begs it. They usually do, but occasionally you get one that sticks or catches.

She raises the phone to her ear, glances at Lucas, waits for the green light.
He nods once. Go.

She gets out of the car. "Hey, Evie," *she's saying into the mouthpiece be-*
fore her foot even hits the ground. "Yeah, we're back. Where is it again? . . .
Behind the door, next to the couch, got it . . . Yep, Tommy gave us the key."
She pauses, listening to the dead silence. "Oh, no worries at all, we had to
come back anyway . . . Yeah, we'll see you down there. Save us a spot!"

It's unlikely that she'll be noticed. Besides the fact that there's hardly
anyone around, it's a general rule of life that no one really cares what other
people are doing as long as they themselves are not directly affected. But the
fake phone call covers their backs, just in case.

Hanging up, she tucks the phone into her pocket and forces herself to the
door, key at the ready. Lucas's voice bounces around inside her skull. Rule
number one. Never hesitate. Commit and keep going. *She slides the key*
into the lock. Holds her breath. Turns it.

The door opens.

Inside, the Airstream is messy but beautiful. The kitchenette has a mar-
ble counter, white cabinets, and brass tapware, and there's an actual bath-
room with a toilet, shower, and walls lined with tiny hexagonal tiles. Beth is
tempted to linger—there's so much to admire—but there's no time. Drone,
she thinks, spotting it on the table. Laptop. iPad. Powered cooler. Bluetooth speaker. *There's also a portable espresso maker the size and shape of a*
Nalgene bottle, a brand-new leather weekender bag, and what looks like a
designer goose-down jacket. Jackpot.

Ignoring the iPad (too risky) and the bag (too bulky), she puts the speaker, laptop, espresso maker, drone, and jacket inside the cooler. She replaces the lid, then carries it outside, across the pitch and into the waiting Troopy, only remembering at the last minute to run back and lock the door of the Airstream behind her.

Lucas drives them to a field in the middle of nowhere. The journey takes about thirty-five minutes, the last ten on dusty side roads. Beth sits silently in the passenger seat, chewing her nails. Neither of them says a word the whole way.

In one corner of the field is an abandoned barn. Parking as close to the fence as possible, Lucas turns off the engine and pockets the keys. He gets out, opens up the Troopy's back doors, unlocks the storage bench, and pulls Tommy and Evie's cooler from inside. Then he puts the cooler into an industrial-grade bin liner, climbs over the fence, and carries it through the long grass to the barn.

Beth watches as he chooses the best spot and stashes the bag. He takes a photo of the hiding place on his phone, taps out a message, adds the photo, and hits send. Then he picks his way back to the Troopy, fires up the engine, and turns it around in three neat points. Without speaking, they head back toward the main road.

As they pull out onto the bitumen, a black trayback ute approaches from the opposite direction and signals for the same turn. As Lucas speeds away, the ute turns onto the track and trundles over the rutted track to the old barn.

As Beth returns to the HiAce she sees Katy at the lookout, cornering tourists and showing them Phoebe's photo, but doesn't join her. Instead, she trudges miserably down to the lake's edge and paddles in the fairy floss water. Salt crystals crunch under her feet.

"Any luck?" Beth asks when Katy finally runs out of people to talk to.

"No." Katy's eyes rake the ground, searching for god knows what. "Waste of time."

Back in the cab, Katy enters her next destination into the GPS (Kalbarri, Beth notes: an impressive stretch of coastal cliffs and national park, another sixty kilometers of wide-open space, another forty minutes' drive) and as she does, Beth experiences the distinct scratchy sense that someone, somewhere, is watching her.

It's only in her head, of course; she knows that the "gaze feeling" stems largely from the belief that one is being watched, not the act of watching itself. But she also knows that the brain does a lot of work beneath the surface.

She checks the mirrors, turns in her seat, scans the lookout and the lake. No one is looking her way, as far as she can tell. Still, the tingly feeling persists and she keeps one eye on the road all the way to the next stop.

CHAPTER FIFTEEN
Wyatt

It's late. Wyatt is at the back door, watching the darkened yard through the flyscreen. Outside, something is moving: a shadow near the garage, quick and smooth like the ripple of a flag or the flick of a coattail. He can feel it, too—and not for the first time. This shiver on his skin, the sense that the air out there is charged with a presence other than his own, is not unfamiliar to him. For some time now he has carried the sense that something is coming for him, closing in fast, but he can't tell when or how it will strike.

"What are you doing, mate?" Dad lumbers into the kitchen, all leathery skin and gardening scars, the handiwork of spades, shears, and secateurs.

"Nothing," says Wyatt, closing the door. "Just thought I saw something."

"Like what?" Dad opens the fridge, cracks a beer, and sinks half of it in one go. His eyes are glassy, his skin puffy. He's working too hard, sleeping too little.

"Just a shadow." Wyatt knows not to bother him with the truth.

Dad grunts. "Gotta stop watching those movies, mate. They're messing with your head."

Wyatt frowns. Dad never pays attention, never takes him seriously.

This is exactly why he started going to Lucas with his problems instead. Sure, his brother gives him shit, but he always listens in the end.

He remembers the time he'd admitted to seeing Things, and Lucas had told him about Mum. He was thirteen: thin as a sapling and so weak from regular head colds and chronic coughs that Lucas had taken to calling him Sick Boy. As usual, they'd been watching a movie.

"Hey," he'd hissed from the window.

"Huh?" Lucas barely glanced up from his phone. The TV was blaring. *Don't you swear at me, you little shit*, a woman yelled, her face twisted. *All I do is worry and slave and defend you, and all I get back is that fucking face on your face.*

"Come here."

"Why?"

"I think there's someone in the yard."

"Don't be a sook."

"Serious."

"Nah."

"But I *saw* something."

Lucas turned to look at him with a sneer on his lips, an expression only made more intimidating by the fat bruise around his left eye, the result of a fight down at the pub. "Bro, maybe it's the ghost. She probably got tired of waiting at the beach, going straight into people's homes now. Best lock all the doors and get your crucifix out." He did his best evil laugh.

Wyatt knew he was supposed to join in, but besides the joke being factually incorrect—crucifixes were for demons and vampires, not ghosts—it wasn't funny. The town *was* haunted and everyone knew it. The malignant spirit of a murderess stalked the bay at night, pulling people into the ocean and eating their souls.

Turning back to the window, he peered again through the glass, suddenly reminded of a different story, a book or a film he saw years ago, something about a demon from another dimension who hid in a girl's bedroom but never truly revealed itself. Every time the girl glimpsed the demon, she'd turn around and it'd be gone. He couldn't remember the details but whatever it was had given him nightmares so bad he'd called Mum into bed with him every night for a week. She'd shuffle through the dark, slip her arms around him and hold him tight. *We're under a force field,* she'd say, pulling the sheets over their heads. *Snuggle zone, activate! Nothing can hurt us now.*

If he still couldn't get to sleep, she'd tell him stories about her life before she met Dad, tales of life on the road. Bali, Vietnam, France, Nicaragua. Bunny chow, pupusas, halo halo, and dahi puri. She taught him how to say *nǐ hǎo,* and *grazie,* and *quisiera los huevos revueltos por favor.* For a long time she lived in her van, Lola—which, until she left, had sat in their driveway like a loyal dog waiting for its owner to come home. Lola popped up in most stories, mentioned with a smile as if Mum was recalling experiences shared with a real person, a much-loved old friend. Sometimes she let Wyatt play inside, sit behind the wheel, pretend he too was off on a journey. She played "Hotel California" on the record player and danced with him around the kitchen. *The world is astonishing, my little man. And Ningaloo is the most magical corner, the last wild place on earth. You're the luckiest kid in the world to live here. There's nowhere else I could ever settle.*

Finally he would drift off with his head on her shoulder, her voice weaving dreams made from reef and gulf and cape, the three systems that make a whole. He'd fall asleep to lessons about whales (they can split their brains in half!) and turtles (they're as old as the dinosaurs!) and manta rays (they have to have to swim constantly to stay alive!). She'd leave the curtains wide open so he could always see the stars. For a while, he'd genuinely believed she might be a star herself, fallen to earth like in that movie with Claire Danes. With her long hair and shimmering salt-kissed skin, she was just as beautiful. Even her name is celestial. Nova: "the creation of a star."

"What if it's Mum?" he said, his palm pressed against the glass.

"Hmm?"

"The things I keep seeing. What if it's not a ghost or just shadows? What if it's Mum? What if she wants to come back?"

Lucas stared at him then paused the movie. "Dude, what? You think Mum's in the yard?"

Wyatt's face flushed but he was already committed, figured he might as well keep going. "I just feel like maybe she's going to come back one day. I keep expecting her to show up."

"Oh, mate." Lucas shook his head and his tone changed. "She left. You know that. She didn't want us. She wanted to travel. She wrote that letter."

Wyatt did know, he'd read the letter and heard the story many times over, but he still couldn't quite bring himself to believe it. And whenever he and Lucas talked about it there was always something in his brother's tone, like Lucas knew something Wyatt didn't. "She might change her mind one day though, right? It's possible."

Lucas was quiet. Then he patted the seat beside him. "Alright, come here, sit down, let me tell you something. I, uh—well, *we* should've been honest from the start but Dad said you were too young. And it is a hard thing to understand, but maybe you're old enough now."

Wyatt perched on the arm of the sofa. "Old enough for what?"

Lucas cleared his throat. "So, Mum did leave. But about a month later, she disappeared."

Wyatt absorbs this information, folds it into his body like eggs into flour. "What do you mean?"

"They tracked her to Broome. She was there for a while, and then it looked like she'd turned around and was heading back this way. They thought she might've been on her way home. But then she just vanished. Her van and everything. There was a big search, but she was never found."

Wyatt stared, transfixed. How had he never heard this before? Surely it had made the news? But then he'd been sick a lot that year and stayed mostly at home, so maybe he missed it. He could feel the questions building behind his eyeballs, bulging from his temples, but his tongue wouldn't give them shape. "I don't get it," he said.

"I'm sorry we never told you," Lucas said. "You were just a kid—and

I guess we hoped we wouldn't have to. But it's been years now and as much as we want to believe she's still out there, maybe we all need to accept the possibility that she's, y'know . . . not." His voice cracked a little on the last word.

Afterward, Wyatt locked himself in the bathroom and searched for his mother's name on the iPad. *NOVA*, he typed, *CLEARY.* Too young? Fuck off. He was thirteen, and old enough for plenty of things.

When her picture appeared on the screen, her beautiful features excruciatingly clear, something surged inside him: a pulsing nebula of fury. For so long he'd thought his Mum had abandoned him, but what if she hadn't? What if someone had taken her away? He had no idea who would do a thing like that, but if it was true he would find them. And he would kill them.

Sure, it was all a bit Liam Neeson but he'd meant every word. Two years later though, and he still hasn't managed either.

Still lingering at the kitchen window, he watches as Dad opens the fridge, grabs a piece of leftover pizza, and ambles back to the living room to watch the footy, leaving Wyatt alone again and wishing hard that his brother was still around. At least then he had someone to talk to.

Liked by **the_road_more_traveled** and **others**

pheebsinwonderland Day 6! Made it to Kalbarri, the traditional lands of the Nanda people—and if you like your adventure served with jaw-dropping vistas and an adrenaline rush then this place is your jam. You've got epic surfing, majestic cliffs, vertiginous views, and of course the beautiful Murchison River that winds through the town. I loved spending time here, and my personal recommendations would include the many hidden tracks from the coastal cliffs to the beaches below as well as the stunning hiking trails through the river gorges. The Skywalk is well worth a visit, and the views from Z Bend Lookout are outstanding.

Sleeping-wise, it can get busy here but if you're not a big planner or everything's booked out, don't worry, there are a couple of decent rest stops back out on the highway (notable features include firepits, red river gums, and actual toilets—gasp!). If you're not used to them, free camps can be unsettling at first, but as long as you're smart they're perfectly safe. Contrary to the advice dished out by certain travel guides and websites, I do not believe you need gimmicks like self-defense rings ("stylish and convenient!") or anti-rape underwear (what?). Besides food, water, some form of communication, and a good working knowledge of your van, all you really need is common sense. Remember: always trust your gut. And if something's off, just leave.

Hit me with your best safety tips! In the meantime, happy traveling.

(Image descriptions: 1. A picture-perfect view of a river winding across a valley floor as seen through a naturally formed hole in sandstone rock. 2. A massive metal platform juts out 100m above a spread of green-speckled hills. 3. A woman with long hair stands in a lush gorge, gazing out between two boulders toward the Murchison River. 4. Surfers check out the sunrise while waiting for a set at Jakes Point. 5. Striated orange cliffs tumble into vivid blue water. 6. A frosty bottle of beer stands on a red rock, backlit by the setting sun.)

#kalbarri #westernaustralia #solofemaletravel #safetytips #safetravel #womenwhowander

View all 82 comments

lenslens_180 Hard agree, common sense is all you need! Most people are pretty cool, you have to be unlucky to run into real trouble.

starfish.and.coffee Always share your itinerary with friends / family and check in often so they know where you are. Also, nothing is too much when it comes to safety, we have to take care of ourselves.

lonewanderer66 You've inspired me—I'm booking a trip around WA. Maybe we could meet?

goodnightpetergraham So glad you loved the free camp!

notlost_justwandering A ring? Nail polish? Anti-rape underwear? WTF??? And why is it always *our* job to keep ourselves safe?

21 May

CHAPTER SIXTEEN

Katy

We're hurtling along State Route 139 when my phone starts buzzing, the screen lighting up with a call from Mum. I'm not comfortable updating her with Lily in here with me—I'm not yet ready to explain the situation—so I let the call ring out.

Fortunately Lily only glances at the screen once, then without comment goes back to staring out of the window.

"Is it weird that you don't talk to your family anymore?" I ask once the buzzing has subsided. "Do you miss them?"

She shrugs. "Yes and no. I feel sad sometimes, but it is what it is. I can't change it, and I can't change them. But I can change how I respond. I mean, they're gonna see the world the same way no matter what I do."

"What way do they see it?"

"Just very black and white. Like, there's good and there's bad. You either toe the line or you don't. And if you're good then life is easy, but if you're bad you're a write-off, and there's just no in-between. Which basically means you can't make any mistakes. And they don't ever talk. Not to each other anyway, and not about anything that actually matters."

That strikes a chord. "My parents are the same," I say. "When something bad happens they gloss over it, pretend it's not happening. Or they say things like, *Oh well, can't be helped, like there's nothing to be done about anything, ever, you just have to accept it.* And it got so much worse after Phoebe. They both just shut down." I glare at the phone. "I'm glad to be away from them."

"Me too." Lily shoots me a wry smile. "For the most part."

"The most part," I repeat, returning it.

Halfway to Kalbarri, Lily asks if she can put on some music. I haven't listened to music in the van yet, most songs remind me too much of Phoebe, but I tell her to go ahead and she searches the app for something she says is perfect for the moment. Moments later, guitar chords strum from the speakers and an earthy, soulful voice comes in over the top. It's good. I like it.

"Who is this?" I ask.

"Xavier Rudd." Lily grins, her head bobbing in time with the beat. "Don't tell me you've never heard this one?" She slaps her palms on her knees and sings along with the refrain. *"Road trippin'."* She lowers her window and stretches out her arm to high-five the breeze. *"Road trippin'."*

A harmonica chimes in. The lyrics are beautiful; they seem to flow directly from the landscape around us, from every plant, flower, and animal, and straight to my heart. I find my head moving too, and in that brief moment I catch a glimmer of what Phoebe saw in all of this.

Road trippin'.

I'm glad to be away.

When I reach the cliffs I follow Phoebe's itinerary to the letter. At Jakes Point, I watch neat lines of turquoise waves peeling into little tubes. I try to guess which rust-red rocks Phoebe might've stood on and approach local surfers to ask if they know anything about a vanlifer called Phoebe traveling in the area this time last year. I pose the same questions to families walking the sealed trails at Pot Alley and Natural Bridge, and by the time we reach the town of Kalbarri itself I'm marching into coffee shops and tourist offices, showing Phoebe's photo to baristas and asking tour operators to check their systems for any bookings made under Phoebe's name. Everywhere I go, I collect more flyers and business cards in an attempt to build a directory of people she might've met or talked to, places she might've been that might not have made it into her posts.

Frustratingly, though, I find nothing of value. No one knows, saw, or remembers anything at all. Worse, no one seems to care.

Phoebe's posts don't specify where exactly she stayed that night so I can't know for sure I'm in the right spot, but I make my best guess based on what little information I have.

Lily and I pull up at the rest stop just before sundown and get out to look around. It's not much, just a clearing with a few sub-basic amenities, but there's enough dappled sunshine for the place to appear reasonably unthreatening. Fine for one night, anyway.

We make hurried use of the remaining daylight, whipping up an unremarkable store-cupboard dinner then taking turns to scurry to and from the poorly maintained toilet before it gets too dark. While Lily takes the collapsible tub outside to wash the dishes, I wipe the counters, sweep the floor and shake out the rug—so much dust and dirt everywhere, so hard to keep on top of it—then I close all the curtains, place a towel on the floor and wash as best I can with cold water and hand soap, an experience so unpleasant I'm straight back to wondering how anyone could possibly enjoy living this way.

Swapping places so Lily can do the same, I wipe the dishes dry and stack them neatly back in the tub, then we both brush our teeth and go to bed. In the back of the van, I check the doors, windows, and extractor hatch, tugging on each handle until I'm certain it's firmly closed. Gripping the keys, I press the button on the fob and the locking system engages, then press it three more times just to be sure.

I run through Phoebe's safety list and mentally tick off all the things I have in place: personal alarm, flares, flashlight, mobile power bank, first aid kit, jump leads, jerry cans, paper maps, travel apps. I run a drill in my head of where each item is kept and how to use it. Only then do I lay down on the bed and pull the sheets across my body.

Outside, darkness gathers.

CHAPTER SEVENTEEN

Beth

The sky blazes orange as Beth follows Katy around the van, trying hard to listen to a detailed rundown of what seems to be the van's entire instruction manual. She's exhausted, the hypervigilance draining her of any energy that being "Lily" has not already zapped, but she doesn't want to be rude. So she pays as much attention as she possibly can to Katy's safety mandates. Always check and recheck the locks, make sure the windows are secure, keep a constant eye on the fuel tank . . .

"Never let it dip below half," she says. "That goes for the water tank too. Too full and it burns extra fuel, too empty and there's not enough spare in the case of an emergency."

Beth supposes she should be grateful. The fact that Katy is showing her this stuff has to be a good sign, right? If she was planning on dropping her off in the nearest town, what would be the point of a demonstration? Then again, it's all a bit much. Half of what Katy's telling her saying isn't strictly necessary. She and Lucas weren't nearly so fastidious with the Troopy.

A pang of nostalgia. *Isn't that the kind of thing they use in the army,* Beth had asked the first time she laid eyes on Lucas's pride and joy, *to drive soldiers around in?* And Lucas said that, yes, traditionally it was exactly that: a troop carrier, but with a full camper fit-out. Pull-out kitchen, fridge/freezer, water tanks, and solar panels. A dining area that converts to a bedroom, and a canvas pop-top with mechanical risers that increase the height of the roof when parked. *Everything you could ever need on wheels.* It sounded surreal to her at the time—how could a single person possibly live in a car, let alone two people? But what's really surreal is how such a thing had so quickly become her home.

"Latch the cupboards and drawers when you're not using them," Katy is saying. "It's just good practice so then we don't forget and risk everything falling out when the van's in motion."

Beth nods. They move on through point after point—and then just when it seems to be all over, Katy issues instructions on using the fire extinguisher and first aid kit with such urgency that Beth can't help but check their surroundings for signs of imminent disaster.

"So you go through all of this every day?"

"Twice. First thing in the morning, last thing at night."

"Wow. That's commitment."

Katy shrugs. "Yeah, well. Gotta stay safe."

Beth climbs into her makeshift bed feeling hollow. All that time and money and effort spent trying to stop the sky from falling when people like her can bring it crashing down in a mere heartbeat.

Back at the campsite, Beth and Lucas take the Haunted House tour with half a dozen others. Lucas asks lots of questions, engages with the guide, and makes everyone laugh with a bad impression of a ghost. Beth knows she's supposed to do the same—be loud, be big, be memorable—but she can't muster the energy. As the other tourists follow the guide from room to room, gasping at the story of the old man who'd shot himself and the little boy who got stuck in the well, she hangs back, pressing herself against the walls, paying attention again only when the guide gets to the part about screams that can still be heard over the paddocks, and the cries of the boy's grieving mother that seem to echo through the halls.

After the tour, Tommy and Evie still haven't returned. Lucas makes a sandwich and plays on his phone while Beth sits on the grass and bites her nails. The sun beats down on her shoulders like a punishment.

Soon enough though, Lucas's energy shifts. "All right," he says, nose in the air like a dog catching a scent. "Game on."

Beth raises her head to see the Pajero gliding smoothly through the rows of tents and caravans. She swallows. Here we go.

Lucas gives her a loaded look. Keep your shit together. Then he opens the Troopy's back doors and starts rummaging through their belongings. "Have you seen our camera, babe?" he says loudly.

"Second drawer down," Beth replies.

"Nope, not there."

"Really? Are you sure?"

The Pajero rolls to a stop and Evie waves from the passenger window.

"Hey, guys!" Tommy calls, brandishing a bottle of Jose Cuervo. "Hope you're ready for round two because we got tequilaaaaah."

Lucas gives them a half-hearted thumbs up. "I can't find the power bank either," he says turning back to Beth.

"What are you talking about? It's right there, inside the door."

"It's not. See for yourself."

Mr. and Mrs. Airstream make their way over, their smiles turning to frowns of concern. "What's going on?" says Tommy.

"My phone," moans Beth. "My credit card."

Lucas kicks a tire.

"You guys okay?" Evie asks.

"Not even close." Lucas rakes his fingers through his hair. "I hate to say it, but I think we've been robbed."

The campground manager meets the catastrophe with a flat expression. "You sure?" he says, his jaws working a piece of gum. "You didn't just misplace them?"

"No, we didn't misplace them," says Tommy, furiously. "We went for a surf, these guys did your lame-arse ghost tour thing, and when we got back there was all this stuff missing. They noticed first"—he jerks his thumb at

Lucas—"and then we checked our place and realized we'd been hit too. Our cooler's gone, our drone, new speaker, my fucking laptop."

Beth blinks. He hadn't even noticed the espresso maker.

"I've got a business to run," Tommy rants. "How am I supposed to work now?" He slams his fist on the desk.

The manager doesn't flinch. He looks Tommy up and down.

Behind him, Evie is crying, her face in her hands.

"You have insurance, right?" Beth whispers.

Evie nods. "But that drone was a gift from my brother. It was special." She bursts into fresh tears.

"Our camera." Lucas paces back and forth, hamming it up. "I hadn't backed up our pictures yet. And they took our solar panels! How are we gonna go off-grid? Our trip is totally fucked."

Beth stays quiet, her insides roiling.

Tommy eyeballs the manager. "You have cameras, right? Let me see the footage."

"Sorry."

"No cameras?"

The manager takes the gum from his mouth and drops it into a bin. "What were your names again?"

"Tommy and Evie Wicks," says Tommy.

"Eddie and Eliza Wiseman," says Lucas.

"Right." The manager speaks slowly, as if validating the feelings of a child. "Well, we'll refund your stay, but there's not much I can do about the rest. You signed the waiver on check-in. The safety of your vehicle and personal belongings is your own responsibility. I suggest you report it to the police and get onto your insurers. Worst-case scenario, you get a payout."

"Fuckers," mutters Tommy, already googling the number for police assistance. "I can't believe this shit."

"Who even does something like that?" wails Evie.

"Sick sons of bitches," says Lucas. "Hope they get hit by a truck."

Beth heads outside, her bloodstream tar-thick with guilt. She thinks about the guy in the pool just hours earlier; the pretty woman with the shampoo-ad *hair, her freedom so tangible she could almost taste it. She thinks of all the many Tommys and Evies and Airstreams she's encountered, all the mistakes she's made, and all the ways she's trapped, and decides that she too hopes they get hit by a truck. At least then it would all be over.*

And she's shocked to realize that she means it. In that moment, she hates her life so much she'd do anything to disappear from it. Anything at all.

CHAPTER EIGHTEEN

Katy

When I wake, it's gradual, like rising gently from seabed to surface.

Everything is dark but not entirely quiet. I can hear something: tires on gravel, and the faint *crunch, crunch* of footsteps.

I open my eyes. I'm in bed, lying under the sheets in exactly the same position I'd fallen asleep. I sit up and listen, but whatever was making the noise has stopped. Probably an animal. Or maybe just a dream. Pulling back the sheets, I shuffle to the end of the bed, reach for my water bottle and take a sip.

Crunch.

I twist my head toward the door of the van so fast I hear my neck crack.

Crunch, crunch.

It sounds like someone treading very lightly and carefully over gravelly ground. Someone trying not to be heard.

I check the windows and doors: all shut, still locked. Then I tug the nearest curtain aside, just a fraction, but as far as I can see there's no one out there, and everything is exactly as it had been the night before. No new arrivals, no sleepy travelers ambling to the toilet with a flashlight.

I shine the torch through the glass anyway, flashing it toward the trees. Then I angle the beam down so it points at the ground, and the light catches the edge of something. A pile of something, right outside the van.

Warily, I slide open the door, just enough to see through. In the dirt are stones, several mounds of them, stacked one on top of the other like little cairns. And nestled among them is a piece of paper weighed down by a rock.

I step down and reach for it. It's an A4 sheet, folded once. Printed on the page are several paragraphs of black type and two color photos. The first shows a long dusty road winding through an expanse of red dirt. In the second, a woman stands in shadow, looking back over her shoulder as if preparing to run, mouth stretched wide in a silent scream. Across the top is a headline in bold capitals.

BLOOD ON THE HIGHWAY, it reads. *IS THERE A SERIAL KILLER ON WA'S ROADS?*

CHAPTER NINETEEN
Wyatt

"Go for a walk," Dad says, barely looking up from a spread of invoices. "Get some fresh air."

Wyatt thinks it's a shit suggestion, but he's finally feeling a little better—enough to feel bored hanging around the house anyway—and he can tell Dad's getting pissed off with him being there all the time, so he pulls on a T-shirt and slouches toward the door.

"And stay away from the old lake," Dad adds.

What a pointless thing to say. Besides the fact that everyone knows to stay away from the old lake—the way they bang on at school about that stupid sinkhole, anyone would think it's the world's first and only sign of climate change–related soil erosion—no one *wants* to go. *It's just a fucking hole in the ground,* he feels like screaming. *It's not even interesting.*

He goes to visit Gracie instead, bypassing the streets and the houses, looping around the back way toward the highway. He's out of breath by the time he reaches her, his eyesight clouded with spots of bright light. Climbing the last of the hills, he reaches automatically for her silver bands and gives them a friendly pat, expecting them to be ice cold but finding instead that they're hot as the sun itself. Chastened, he snatches his hand away. He'd forgotten that about Gracie. In summer, she could burn you.

Turning his back on her twisty, glistening beauty, Wyatt sits on the sandstone plinth and gazes out at the view. From her position at the top of the hill, Gracie can see the whole town. He wonders if she ever gets bored of it: the spread of ocean, the wide open sky, the speckle of houses and caravans that used to feel so big to him but now seems so small. Now he understands just how insignificant his home is, how removed from the rest of the world. Outside of Western Australia, there are probably only a handful of people who have ever heard of Gracious Bay.

Hadn't stopped Mum from loving it, though. *Ningaloo. The last wild place on earth. There's nowhere else I could ever settle.*

Lucas feels differently. *Fucking shithole town. Arse-end of nowhere.* It's always been a thing with him, how much he hates the place. He couldn't get away fast enough, and now hardly ever comes back.

Wyatt remembers the exact day he realized that his brother would not stick around forever. At twenty-three, Lucas had been working for Dad for years, mowing lawns and cutting trees and laying pavers, and Wyatt assumed life would continue like that forever. *Cleary and Son.* At some point the "*Son*" part would become plural, and that would be that. But then suddenly Lucas developed an obsession with cars. He saved up and bought some massive army-looking thing from a used dealership in Exmouth—little more than a wreck, but with heaps of "potential"—and for months, that's all he did: bang and drill and polish, fix up spare parts and install them as if by magic.

At the time Wyatt had thought it was a cool hobby, something that Lucas did with his spare time. But then one day he'd wandered outside and found his brother no longer tinkering but sitting in the driver's seat, bare feet propped against the open door, thumbs tapping rapidly on his phone, and for some reason Lucas had looked different. Adult. Other-worldly. He'd been a man ever since his sudden and curious metamorphosis around age seventeen, but at what point had he got so tall and broad, so composed, so ridiculously good-looking? His sandy hair was stiff with salt and his green eyes shone emerald-bright against leathery sun-lashed skin. He looked like a model or an actor. And for the first time it occurred to Wyatt that Lucas might have outgrown the Bay, and possibly never belonged there at all.

"What are you doing?" Wyatt asked, glaring enviously at Lucas's smartphone. At thirteen he still hadn't been deemed old enough for his own.

"Making friends," Lucas replied without lifting his eyes from the screen. "Come here, I'll show you."

Wyatt sat in the passenger seat and Lucas showed him pictures of all the girls he'd met online, beautiful creatures with long hair and slender limbs who wrote him long missives about far-flung places and sprinkled Lucas's own posts with little red love hearts. "What do you think of this one?" Lucas pointed to a girl with silky black curls. "Might meet up with her. Cute, hey?"

Wyatt shrugged. What was he supposed to say? The decade between them sometimes felt like centuries. "I like what you've done with the car," he said, changing the subject.

"Troopy."

"Huh?"

"It's not a car. It's a Troopy. Troop carrier. Come on. I'll give you the tour."

Retrospectively, Wyatt understands that the overly long demonstration that followed had been his brother's way of apologizing in advance for what he was about to do. He was also trying to win Wyatt over, justify the dream, sell it like a showroom salesman. With great pride, Lucas had explained how he'd gutted the back, installed thermo-acoustic insulation and knocked up a pinewood frame. He'd maximized storage by installing handcrafted drawers, hatches, consoles, pockets, and shelves, and he'd made two couches that transformed into a queen-size bed. "The roof pops up too," he said, "for extra sleeping space. Then the fridge will go there, the stove fits in here . . . there'll be an awning, water tank, side ladder, the works. Pretty sweet, hey?"

"Yeah, so sweet." But Wyatt's belly was a nest of snakes. "Why would you want all that? You have everything you need here at home."

Lucas's smile faltered and he dropped his gaze. "Listen, mate," he said after what felt like a very long pause. "You and me, we'll always be close. But things are changing. *We're* changing. We each have our own path. And I want you to know that when the time comes for you to find yours, you don't have to stay here. Understand? You can leave. Go as far away as you like."

Wyatt was caught off guard. *Leave?* Was he joking? "Okay," he said, waiting for the punch line.

But Lucas's expression remained serious. He dropped his voice and spoke so quietly that Wyatt had to strain to hear. "This town is fucked. And you will be too if you stay."

A chill spread through Wyatt's body like a cold wind. "Okay," he said again. "Sure."

Lucas glanced up through the windscreen at the afternoon sky and the light dimmed as bulbous clouds swallowed the sun. Then he clapped Wyatt on the shoulder. "Wanna go for a spin? We can head up the highway to the old fire trail road and you can have a crack."

Wyatt brightened. "You'll let me drive? Really?"

"Come on, dickhead, get in." And just like that, Lucas was back to normal.

But Wyatt had never forgotten that day. In a way, it was when everything had changed.

He stared down at the town again, trying this time to see it through his brother's eyes. But his head feels thick and his eyes are starting to burn, so he takes his leave of Gracie, gently brushing her shining steel curves with his fingertips before pushing himself off the plinth and setting off back through the scrub toward home.

Liked by **sunshine_and_poses** and **others**

pheebsinwonderland: Let's talk about roadhouses. The other day I listened to a podcast interview with a lady who's been traveling around Australia pretty much all her life, and she said that 20 years ago they were terrifying. You'd rock up and there'd be no one around, just a few dudes, truckies, miners, and you'd have to fuel up and get the hell out. But now they're like travel community hubs, often full of music and good food, perfect if you want to break up your journey with coffee and a chat with other vanlifers. I wasn't sure at first—anyone seen Texas Chainsaw Massacre? 🙁—but I can confirm they're delightful. I think my number one rec so far has to be @redgumroadhouse: great coffee, comfortable motel rooms, and super friendly staff (don't miss their tattoo photo wall, especially if you yourself have ink!).

Tip of the Day: It's a good idea to plan your stops ahead of time because fuel stations can be few and far between and you don't want to get caught out. Also, for all fellow astrology fans, Jupiter and Mercury are working their mojo magic tomorrow which means plenty of collaboration, tolerance, and community spirit all round. A good time to travel!

Hit me with your best tips, fave pit stops etc. Where should I go next? As always, suggestions are welcome!

(Image descriptions: 1. A flashing neon sign that says Welcome to Red Gum, Finest Pit Stop In The West! 2. A campervan parked on a fuel station forecourt under a bright blue sky. 3. Bright pink bougainvillea spills over a wooden sign that says Overnight Parking This Way. 4. A takeaway coffee cup sits on a table with a red and white cloth in front of a large window with a view of the forecourt. 5. Three acoustic guitars hanging on a plain white wall. 6. Another wall, this one covered with a huge colorful display of photographs, each showing a tattooed body part.)

#redgumroadhouse   #australianroadhouses   #travelpitstops #solofemaletravel #needcoffee #fuelup #vanlife

View all 45 comments

saltyhair_sandytoess Awesome working sheep station just up past there! Great accommodation and hot showers! And the coffee cart on the Carnarvon foreshore is UNREAL, you have to go.

redgumroadhouse Thanks for the shout-out, so glad you stopped by!

lonewanderer66 WA is even more amazing than I expected, but I have questions, check your DMs.

goodnightpetergraham "If I have any more fun today I don't think I can take it!" 🙈😆

lolathelovebus Can we talk more about safety? Do you have any more tips?

23 May

CHAPTER TWENTY

Beth

The van speeds north over impossibly straight tarmac toward Shark Bay, the paved bitumen stretching out before them like a runway. Sitting stiffly in the passenger seat, Beth stares down at the crumpled piece of paper in her lap, the four short paragraphs streaked with dirt.

"What is it?" Katy keeps saying, her fingers wrapped tight around the wheel, her knuckles bone white. "What does it mean? Why was it outside? Who put it there?" The HiAce is gathering so much momentum Beth keeps half expecting it to take off into the air.

"I don't know," she says. "Let me read it properly."

BLOOD ON THE HIGHWAY—IS THERE A SERIAL KILLER ON WA'S ROADS?

We've all seen the movie. A sunburned psychopath who isolates three young backpackers in an abandoned mine. A blood-soaked young woman running through the outback. A title card claiming that around 30,000 people go missing in Australia each year, many of whom are never found. And we've all wondered about that statistic, haven't we? Because surely it's an exaggeration? Surely the filmmakers are wrong? Unfortunately, they are. Believe it or not, the updated figures are even more staggering. In 2021, police received over 53,000 missing persons reports nationwide, and while the vast majority were located there are still roughly 2500 people who remain missing to this day. So where are they? And what happened to them?

As the hunt continues on the Coral Coast for 41-year-old vanlifer Vivi Green, reported missing earlier this year and last seen in the Ningaloo area, and as WA alone sees a significant surge in reports specifically concerning missing backpackers and tourists, locals and visitors alike are asking the same questions. So what are the answers? Perhaps travelers in the area are getting lost while hiking or falling into gorges. Wild animals or riptides could be to blame. Or maybe there's another reason, something more sinister. It's not hard to imagine, is it? The road-trip horror stories are endless: haunted crossroads and beaches, hitchhikers who suddenly materialize in the back seat of your car, supernatural entities who melt your tires and stuff up your gearbox.

And it's not all ghosts around the campfire, either. Hands up if you've heard the one about the fruit picker stabbed in her dormitory by a fellow farm worker? The Canadian held captive in a pig shed after applying for a housekeeping job on Gumtree? The British backpacker killed by her Tinder date? There have been more travel-related murders, abductions, and assaults in the last five years than ever before. And now a recent spate of van thefts, auto break-ins, and suspected intrusions have visitors to our beautiful state second-guessing their security. One family claimed an anesthetic gas had been pumped into their camper to ensure they stayed unconscious during the robbery. Sounds wild, doesn't it? Sure. But not as wild as those statistics. So what's going on?

Yes, we've heard the tall tales, we've all seen the movies, we know they're all just stories. Or are they? Think about it. All those missing people . . . they've got to be somewhere.

Beth reads over the words again then goes back to the beginning. "Where did you find it again?"

"Right outside the door," says Katy. "On the ground."

"Maybe someone dropped it?"

"No, there was a rock weighing it down. And *who*? We were the only people there!"

The HiAce bounces over a pothole and Beth's hand flies instinctively to the door handle. They're going too fast, twenty over the limit, and she hasn't had a chance to catch her breath since she woke up to find the engine revving and Katy in the driver's seat, babbling about something she'd found. They motored out of the rest stop in such a hurry that Beth hasn't yet peed or eaten or properly figured out what the fuck is going on. "Sorry," she says, her pulse matching the speed of the van. "Could you . . . I mean, would it be okay if you slowed down a little?"

"What?" Katy checks the gauge. "Oh, sorry, sorry, I'm just . . ." She brakes and the needle drops. "I'm freaking out."

"I get it, but let's just take it easy. Think rationally for a minute."

"Okay, yes, you're right, I know you're right."

Beth smooths out the page over her knees. "Firstly, what even *is* this? A news article? A letter? A school report?"

She runs over the detail, taking notes in her head. Overall, the piece is not sophisticated. The movie reference, even without the picture of the lead actress mid-scream, is clear but unoriginal. Whenever backpacking and Australia are mentioned in the same breath, someone is bound to say something like *don't get chopped up by a farmer now, will you?* The synonymity is such that anyone would think that the outback is full of more psychos than red dirt.

Then there are the unverified stats: *2500 people remain missing to this day.* No attributed source, no footnotes. It could easily be some kid's homework, fallen from a Big Lapper's trailer, left behind, and forgotten. Or it could be a page printed from a scaremongering news website, but there's no date or name attached, no URL or any indication of which outlet the article might've appeared in.

The coincidence of the subject matter is definitely weird though—as is the specific mention of the search for a solo vanlifer up near Ningaloo, the exact same area in which Phoebe disappeared. *Vivi Green.* The name rings a very faint bell, but she can't think why. *Vivi, Vivi.* The bell tolls once more, then stops completely.

Beth scans the last line and shudders. *They're all just stories . . . or are they?*

"Okay, let's say someone did leave it—"

"They *did*," Katy says. "There were stones everywhere, piles of them, which were *not* there when we went to sleep."

"Right. Okay, well, let's say that someone did all of that. What would be the purpose?"

Katy's answer is quick-draw fast. "To scare me."

"You think someone's deliberately trying to scare you?"

"Or tell me something. Maybe someone knows where Phoebe is or what happened to her, and they want me to know they know. Maybe they're playing with me. But I think it's a message."

"But to what end?"

"I don't know!" The needle on the speedometer creeps up again. "All I *do* know is that note is for me. Someone left it there for me to find."

Beth doesn't push it, but she isn't so sure. What if the note *is* a message, but it wound up in the wrong hands? What if it was intended to be read not by Katy but by her? The thought takes root. And the more she reads over the words, the more convinced she becomes.

Someone knows.

CHAPTER TWENTY-ONE

Katy

Red Gum roadhouse first appears on the horizon as distant flashes of light, a heat-induced mirage, a disco-themed oasis. But the closer we get, the more distinct the lights become until finally they take the shape of caravans, cars, trailers, and trucks, all gathered under a large canopy. A little closer, and I can make out fuel pumps and flashing signs. COFFEE! SOUVENIRS! FRESH SNACKS! FREE CAMPING!

I pull off the road and into the melee. People mill around, shuffling back and forth across the forecourt with takeaway coffee cups and pies. Ragtime piano music filters through hidden speakers and floats through my open window on a cloud of fumes.

Choosing a free pump, I get out and fill my tank with trembling hands. *That note* . . . who would leave something like that for me? Who would write it in the first place? Someone who knows about Phoebe, I'm certain of that. But what do they know, and why would they choose to tease me with the information like this? And what did the piles of stones mean? They reminded me of memorial sites, burial grounds.

I return my attention to the roadhouse. Phoebe's photos—the spill of bougainvillea, the texture of the light, a shot of the motel cleverly angled and filtered to create a trendy Palm Springs vibe—make the place look much nicer than it actually is, but then I guess that was the point. In reality, the motel's rooms promise little more than a roof and four walls. Through the windows of the main building, I glimpse the red-and-white check of the restaurant's tablecloths and what I guess must be the tattoo photo wall.

When the tank is full I park the van in the bays that sit a little way off the forecourt. "Are you coming in?"

Lily shakes her head. She looks tired.

"Okay. I'll get us some food and coffee."

I walk back across the forecourt, dialing Dust as I go. His voicemail clicks in again. He must be screening my calls. I briefly consider scrapping the plan and driving the eight or nine hours to Exmouth right now, show up in person and force him to speak to me. Instead, I leave another message telling him we need to talk then call twice more just so he knows it's urgent. He needs to hurry up if he's going to run tests on the things I've found.

Inside, I find a takeaway counter with a chalkboard menu, a neat line of glass-fronted fridges, and a row of heat lamps warming a selection of sausage rolls and pies. The restaurant is to my left, checkout counter to my right. The rest of the space is crammed with various road-trip-related products and rotating gift stands.

I pay for the fuel, then head immediately for the restaurant and its feature wall of snaps. Some are fresher than others but each one shows a close-up of a tattoo. I spot a dragon on a thigh, a windmill on a biceps, and what looks like a bottle of sauce or relish on a bony ankle. Weaving around a couple of gray nomads having the matching whale sharks on their shoulders photographed by a bearded staff member, I step right up close, scrutinizing every image. Two turtles peek out from behind an ear, petals cascade down a rib cage, a calavera skull observes me from the base of someone's spine . . .

My heart stops. *There!* About halfway down on the left-hand side is a compass. Without thinking, I reach out and pluck the image from the wall. *It's her! Oh my god, it's Phoebe!*

"Lily, look!" I cry, before remembering she'd stayed in the van. Whirling around, I approach the staff member. "Hey. Sorry to interrupt, but did you take this picture?"

Both he and the gray nomad couple turn to look at me. "Uh, you're not really supposed to touch those."

"I know, sorry, but I really need to know." I shove the photo in his face. "Do you remember anything about the person in it?"

The bearded man gives me an odd look, then squints at the compass. "Don't think so. Might not have been on shift that day."

"Oh." The disappointment burns. "Well, can you tell me who was?"

"Um, well, do you know when it was taken?"

"This time last year. May twenty-third, or twenty-fourth." I flip the photo around to check for a time stamp but there isn't one.

"A year ago?" The guys laughs. "Whaddya think I am, a bloody elephant?"

The two nomads smile politely. One of them seems to be watching me with interest.

"Would you happen to have CCTV footage?"

"Sorry mate, we don't keep anything older than a month." He turns back to the nomads with a slight eyeroll. "Ladies, thanks for your time, we'll get you up on the wall pronto."

He returns to work, leaving me staring at the photo. It's Phoebe, there's no doubt whatsoever. The trough of her spine, the swell of her hips, the twin depressions just above her butt that she referred to as "back dimples" . . . I'd know them anywhere. I close my eyes, press the image to my heart. *Where are you, Pheebs? Where did you go? What happened to you?* The photo might be a dead end, but I know I'm getting closer to finding answers. I can feel it.

I think about Dust and the bobby pin and that horrible note, the shadow under the tree and the whisper in the dark. Sunglasses Man and the maniac driver that almost ran me off the road. And then someone touches my shoulder, the briefest of taps.

"Hello again," says a voice at my side.

CHAPTER TWENTY-TWO
Beth

Beth waits in the HiAce as Katy heads inside to pay. Her bladder is once again bursting but she's too afraid to go to the bathroom just in case Lucas is here or happens to pass by. This was one of their most frequent stops, owing mainly to the fact that it's one of just two fuel stops on this 180-kilometer stretch, so if she's going to bump into him anywhere it'll be here or somewhere like it.

She shuts her eyes, blocking out all the tourists, miners, and farmers bustling around in their own little bubbles, the truckies and tradies shuttling from one job to the next. The air around her smells of eucalyptus, diesel, and pies. *How is this my life? This is not my world. How did I get here?* Her mind answers with a slideshow of pictures: a river, a row of shops on a dark city street, a tank full of fish. She sees herself as if in a movie, standing in a bathroom with vomit on her dress. Her family seated at a long table like a board of trustees, her mother's phone bearing a single text message on the table between them. And Lucas, sitting beside her in a different car on a different stretch of road.

"That was fucking brilliant," he says as they drive away. "Absolutely bang on, could not have gone more smoothly. I wish that dump did have cameras, then I could've watched that shit back on loop."

In the passenger seat, Beth stares out of the window.

"I mean, we got lucky with that pitch. It was perfect. And the key worked a treat. It didn't stick, did it?"

"No," Beth says. Then, realizing he expects her to say more, adds: "I thought it might, but it didn't."

"That's right it fucking didn't. You know why? Because I know what works." Lucas jabs a finger into his sternum. "Right? Don't I know? Someone needs to give me a goddamn medal."

She gives him the admiring smile she knows he wants, and he grins back.

"God, I'm good. I am the king."

He turns to her, one eyebrow raised, expecting confirmation. And she grants it, because while he definitely is not the king his smile is preferable to the alternative and some income is better than none. Also, he's right. He is good at what he does.

After almost a year of playing the Bonnie to his Clyde, Beth is still cautious and conflicted—but Lucas is cool, confident, efficient, and unwavering in his self-justification. He's also creative, which means they now have a variety of schemes for different scenarios. Sometimes he chooses remotes spots and they observe vehicles from a distance, learning the owners' routines and predicting their movements until they know what to expect. Other times he'll see an opportunity and they'll just go for it: in and out, smash and grab.

His preferred method though, is what he calls the Victim Technique. Step one, identify mark remotely using social media. Step two, engineer a "chance" meeting. Step three, befriend mark. Step four, steal goods. Step five, return to scene of crime and play the victim. Step six, celebrate.

He's taught her that social media makes it easy to get to know the marks without giving yourself away. You see their life in close-up, but you're nowhere near them and never run the risk of being seen. The best targets are the ones who post live rather than waiting until after they leave a location; it's easy to communicate with them, comment on their posts, slide into their DMs, strike up a rapport. And if the account holder likes to show off their build, you can even get a detailed overview of the vehicle's layout, commit the floorplan to memory, spot security weaknesses, and identify hidden storage.

It doesn't always work out, of course. Sometimes they virtually follow travelers who unexpectedly change course. Sometimes a targeted campsite is full. Sometimes they identify a mark only to lose them when they unexpectedly stop posting. Sometimes the stars just don't align. You can't control everything, Beth said to him once. "Like hell I can't" was his reply.

For a while he was convinced that a GPS tracker would be the best solution to most of these problems, and he nearly ordered one before realizing how expensive, impractical, and risky multiple usage would be, at which point even he had to admit that there would be some targets he just could not hit. But four times out of five the social media method works a treat—and when it doesn't, Lucas just uses his intuition. He says that the Big Lap route up and down the Coral Coast has so many obvious stops, so many "unmissable" tourist attractions and perfectly 'grammable photo opportunities that you almost don't need social media. Everyone ends up following one another whether they intend to or not.

"Trust me," he told Beth at the beginning. "I grew up around here. You pass the same travelers again and again, pull up next to them in car parks, watch them all take the same photos. They all think they're going their own way, but it's like one mass convoy."

He explained that because so many follow the itineraries prescribed by guidebooks and travel websites, their vehicles are like bulletin boards on wheels. Do they have a surfboard? Fishing equipment? Hiking gear? A snorkel on their 4WD, red dirt all over their wheels? All of these things, plus a well-placed conversation or two, could tell you almost precisely where they'd just been and where you were likely to see them next.

Lucas also explained there was a uniform look, a way of speaking and dressing and moving through the world that marked you as One of Them. And if you were One of Them, people would fall over themselves to share space, barbecue, fish, dive, drink, maybe even watch their stuff while they went for a swim. "Tribe mentality," he'd say, "is our secret weapon."

Furthermore, as long as they stick to smaller items—electronic devices, computers, specialist camping, and fishing gear—the cops will never attend the scene. Most people who report property theft are given an incident number that they can then pass on to their insurers, and that's about it. "Statistically," he says, "most travel-related crime is committed by local repeat offenders already known to the police, so that's their first port of call. No one's looking for two middle-class vanlifers in an expensive Troopy." Beth tries to remind herself of that during a job—no one's looking, One of Them—but it doesn't always help.

Fortunately some jobs are slightly less stressful than others. Storage hatches or emergency windows can usually be popped with a screwdriver, which makes for a clean enough hit. Car windows are broken quickly with a little force exerted on the glass at one point location with a small sharp object. And, as it turns out, the movies are right and plenty of locks can be picked with a bobby pin bent into the right shape. Her personal preference is always to simply unlock the door with a key and walk right in, as she did with Tommy and Evie's Airstream.

But however they do it, it's always horrible. Once they broke into a five-berth Maui at night while the owners were asleep, which was so traumatic she almost passed out. Afterward she made Lucas promise they would never do it again.

One thing never changes though. The goods, once stolen, are transported to a prearranged drop-off point where a shadowy "contact" collects and moves them on as quickly as possible. The contact then stores the goods in a "cache," the location of which Lucas keeps to himself, from where they're "processed" and sold on. About a week later, payment for the goods is transferred into Lucas's bank account. A well-oiled machine, as he likes to say.

Beth doesn't worry too much about those details; she figures the less she knows about that side of things the better. She does worry though—all the time—that they will get caught. She's convinced that one day someone will see them and the police will be called, or a mark will spring them mid-operation and become violent. She worries that all the marks will end up in the same place or connect on the socials and all the stories will come out, the similarities too close for coincidence. But of course Lucas has an answer for that, too. He says that if they're smart, keep moving, change course often, spread out the hits, take breaks, rotate their own fabricated socials, vary their *names, clothes, stories—if she follows his rules, they'll never get caught. Because he's great at this shit. He's the king.*

He always forgets one important factor though. You have to read the room. You can't just target anyone. And that's Beth's special skill. Susceptibilities, proclivities, the chinks in people's armor; she can spot them a mile off. He might be good with a plan, great in the field. But when it comes to understanding people, the crown is hers.

She opens her eyes. There's that tingle again. *Gaze feeling.*

Sitting up, she studies the forecourt, the bowsers, and the shop. There are fewer vehicles than before. And it's getting dark. How long has she been sitting here? Did she doze off? And where's Katy? Still in the roadhouse? What's taking her so long?

She's about to get out and check when she spots something ahead. A boxy four-wheel drive parked beneath a tree just short of where the highway resumes, lights off and nose toward the road as if it can't decide whether to stay or go. The light thrown by the roadhouse doesn't quite reach it so Beth can't see exactly what kind it is or even the color, but something about it chills her blood.

Just beside it is a tall patch of deep shadow. She stares, trying to make it out. Is it a person? The shadow moves. Yes. A man, one hand raised to his ear as if talking on the phone. He's looking her way.

Shit. Biting her nails, she glances at the shop, the restaurant, the motel. *Where are you Katy? What's taking so long?*

When she looks back the shadow man is still there, still watching.

CHAPTER TWENTY-THREE

Katy

I look up to see the nomads standing in front of me. Both are in their early-to-mid-sixties: one is tall and wears a patchwork dress, the other is short and round with red-rimmed glasses. Her black T-shirt says GLASTON-BURY '95, and she's holding out a napkin as if it's something I might need. It was her who'd touched my arm.

I frown at the napkin and a split second later become aware that my face is wet. "Sorry," I say, wiping my eyes. "Have we met?"

"We were at the beach camp near Jurien Bay," says Glastonbury. "Sandy Cape. Big ol' silver caravan? You were on the pitch just across from us."

"Right." Her face is vaguely familiar but I don't remember meeting her recently, if ever.

"What's going on, darl?" says Patchwork. "Are you in some kind of trouble?"

"No, I'm just . . . looking for someone." Automatically, I dig out my phone to find a photo.

The nomads lean in. On the screen, Phoebe is kneeling on a beach made entirely of tiny white shells, a half-drunk bottle of Corona on the ground beside her. She's smiling with her whole face, her eyes creased with joy.

"Who's that then?" says Glastonbury, peering through her gaudy spectacles. "Your sister?"

Sister. The word rises inside me like a bubble. I love that our shared DNA is so apparent. "Her name's Phoebe. She went missing while traveling in this area a year ago."

The nomads gasp in unison. "Missing?"

"Any chance you recognize her?"

Glastonbury takes a closer look. "No, I don't think so honey, but gosh"—she presses her hand to her heart—"I'm so sorry, that's just *terrible*. What happened?"

I explain, and both their faces contort with pity.

"Oh, sweetheart, I can't even imagine what you've been through."

"And no answers at all. Oh, your poor parents."

"I suppose she might've been attacked, poor love. We've heard stories from up that way."

"There are some rough spots for sure."

"The things you read in the news now, you've got to be so careful. And she's not wearing much, is she, bless her."

Not wearing much? The comment is jarring. I look again at the picture. Phoebe is on a beach. She's clearly just been swimming. But the woman's tone seems to imply some direct correlation between the yellow bikini she's wearing and the Bad Thing that happened to her, almost as if the swimsuit itself could be to blame.

Discomfort spreads through me and, feeling as exposed as if I'd just shown my own body to a couple of total strangers, I quickly choose a different picture, a shot where Phoebe is fully dressed. It's a selfie from her final post, taken on a nondescript road with her van positioned in the background. Once again, she's smiling and peeking coyly over the top of her mirrored sunglasses. I've seen it countless times before, but all of a sudden my attention catches. There's a reflection in Phoebe's sunglasses, one I've never noticed before. I bring the screen closer to my face. It's some kind of sweeping silver thing, small but distinct. I pinch my fingers, preparing to zoom in—

"Where's your boyfriend anyway?"

All my muscles contract at once. I look up. "My what?"

"Boyfriend," Glastonbury says. "The guy you were with when we chatted at the beach camp. Is he waiting in the car?"

There's a roaring in my ears. *Boyfriend? Chatted?* "Wait, hold on. We talked? Had a conversation?"

"Sure, on the beach. Not for long—and actually, come to think of it, your man did most of the talking. You were pretty quiet, but he told us you were tired, you'd both had a big day and needed to go to bed." She frowns. "You don't remember?"

"I . . ." My cheeks grow hot. "I'd had a bit too much to drink that night."

Patchwork makes a face. "Really? You didn't seem drunk to me. Sleepy, yes; maybe a little zoned out. But not intoxicated, or not in the extreme."

I'm reeling. The floor tips under my feet. I suddenly recall a box of fusilli and a jar of sauce. I'd made pasta; I can see the pan of water bubbling on the stove. Next to it, the wine bottle stands open, along with two glasses.

"Sweetie?" Glastonbury's expression is serious. "That *was* your partner, right?"

I'm frozen by their sudden scrutiny. *Boyfriend?* Beneath my shirt, sweat beads on my chest and drips into my bra.

"What's going on, honey? It's okay, you can tell us."

They're both regarding me closely. I feel like there should be a tape recorder between us, a two-way mirror on the wall. I don't know what to say. I'm so confused.

Trust your gut. And if something's off, just leave.

"I have to go."

"No, wait—"

"Sorry, I just remembered that I, um, I'm late for something."

"Please, just wait a second, let's figure this out—"

But I'm already out the door. They don't understand. No one does.

Outside, the sun is sinking, the sky purpling like a bruise. I'd only planned to stop for a few minutes, how is it so late already?

Boyfriend.

Hurrying back across the forecourt, I think again of Sunglasses Man, snippets of what he said running through my head. *A bit of a state. We were worried. I walked with you. So sorry for your loss.* It has to have been him at the beach camp, but why don't I remember him? And why would he pretend to be my boyfriend?

You look like you could do with some company.

Had he drugged me? Is that what happened? Had he put something in my drink and knocked me out? Had he then followed me through the night, chased me to Plains Ranch? Had he come to talk to me the next morning, perhaps even followed me as far as here? Suddenly the bobby pin and the note feel less random then they had before, but I can't figure out what holds them together. And what does any of it have to do with Phoebe?

Remembering the reflection I'd noticed in her final post, I stop just shy of the van and dig out my phone again. I find the photo and zoom in on her mirrored sunnies. *What is that?* Something sweeping and silver . . . a spaceship? A water feature? No—it looks more like a sculpture or a statue, a twisting, shining shape made of steel and mounted on some kind of box. I feel like I've seen it before, but where?

I look up at the sky, my stomach sinking. Yet again it's getting potentially too late to drive. I wonder if maybe it might be smart to park up around the back and stay here at the roadhouse until morning. Maybe with a bit of rest my brain will start to work again. I turn to face the driveway that leads around the main building to the overnight parking area. All except for a small caravan in one corner, it's empty. Also dark and creepy. I contemplate a night spent lying awake listening to trucks pulling in and out. All those tires, all those footsteps.

Deciding firmly against it, I hurry to the van and open the driver's side door. "Lily," I say, "we have to go."

But the cab is as empty as the parking area. Lily isn't there.

I pivot on the spot, scanning my surroundings. "Lily?" I say, trying not to sound alarmed. I can't see her. She's gone, disappeared, just like Phoebe. I start to panic. What do I do? If something has happened to her, if she's been taken from me too, if she's hurt, I won't ever forgive myself, not ever, *oh god, Lily, I'm sorry, I let you down, I shouldn't have left you, please be okay—*

"Katy."

I spin around. It's her, she's okay, she's hurrying toward me wiping her hands on her dress, face a little flushed but clearly unharmed. I exhale. It's fine, she's fine, she just went to the bathroom. I'm so relieved I can't speak.

"Let's get out of here, hey?" Lily says, hopping into the passenger seat. "This place has a bad vibe."

In silent but firm agreement, I get behind the wheel and we drive quickly away.

CHAPTER TWENTY-FOUR

Wyatt

The walk has taken it out of him. Too much, too soon, Dad says.

Wyatt is back in bed, eyes stinging, throat sore, belly tender. And now a rash has broken out over his ribs, though Dad called the doctor and apparently it's just part of the virus. As long as his temperature stays stable, there's nothing to worry about. *Tell that to my sweat glands,* he thinks, kicking off his damp sheets.

Thud, bump, tumble, bang.

Noises, noises, so many noises. They float through the air like dust motes, settling on nothing, belonging nowhere.

Rustle, scuffle, hiss.

They won't let up; not even his treasures can ward them off. He's sure it's the demon, the one from that old film—or had it been a dream?—roaming around at night, tapping little messages on the walls and the doors, trying to access the bedrooms. Sometimes it hides in the garage and drags itself around in the gloom.

But there's nothing he can do. He's spent the last year trying and failing to identify the source and no one else, it seems, can hear it. Dad's had the pest guy in, he's been up in the roof himself several times, but other than the usual possums there's no evidence of anything.

As a last resort, Wyatt had even tried filming the house, an idea that had come to him on the day that Lucas finally left home. It was another hot morning—blinds closed, TV on, fan blasting—and Wyatt was in his usual spot on the sofa, trying to study (*Macbeth believes he can see the ghost of Banquo. Starting with this extract, explain to what extent you think Shakespeare presents Macbeth as a man who is in control*). But he was having trouble concentrating; ever since Lucas had told him the truth about Mum, Wyatt couldn't stop mining the internet for information. Unfortunately, he'd barely found anything, just confirmation that Mum had indeed disappeared and there had been a big fruitless search. He *had* unearthed a few rumors of a serial killer, whispers of an emerging "pattern," but exactly what that pattern was no one could say, and not even Google would explain why. So in the end he was left with only one option: to sit around at home and do his schoolwork.

He forced his eyes back to the iPad, back to *avaunt and quit my sight* and *blood will have blood*, back to the shut blinds and a movie for company and the stale stink of his own inadequacy.

And then Lucas appeared in the room, the green of his eyes bright as gemstones. "Man, I love that film," he said, pointing to the TV. "A classic. I've taught you well."

Flushed with his brother's approval, Wyatt pushed his iPad aside and they watched the scene together. Onscreen, two women were deep in conversation. *It's not the house,* one said to the other. *It's me. Wherever I go, it goes.*

"Listen," Lucas said all of a sudden. "I need to tell you something. I'm going away for a bit. In the Troopy. A work thing. Dad's expanding the business, wants me to scope out some new opportunities."

Wyatt picked at a hole in the sofa, poked his finger deep into the stuffing. "For how long?"

"Not really sure. Two or three months maybe? I'm leaving tonight."

The movie played on. The world continued to turn. But in that moment something inside Wyatt had stopped like a clock.

Lucas barreled on into the silence. "So, anyway, this is for you." He thrust his iPhone under Wyatt's nose. "Thought you could do with one. You're nearly fourteen now."

Wyatt blinked at the offering. "But . . . don't you need it?"

"Got myself an upgrade." Lucas sat bird-like on the edge of the sofa and produced a second phone from his pocket, brand new, the latest model. "But my old one's only a few years behind. I've wiped it clean of all my stuff so it's ready for you to set up, and it's got heaps of storage so you can download games or whatever. Even better, you can call me whenever you want. Got that? Whenever."

The look on Lucas's face was meaningful, but Wyatt couldn't manage a response. A chasm had opened inside him, a great yawning crevasse. Somehow he knew Lucas wasn't ever coming back. He doesn't remember much about what happened next, only that he'd gripped the phone tight, as if it might anchor him to something safe, and focused on the sound of the movie until gradually Lucas's voice faded away, replaced by overlapping unscripted dialogue.

We've heard banging on the walls. Scratching sounds, like, you know, like dragging down the wall kind of scratches.

I'm taking care of this. This is my house. I'm gonna solve the fucking problem.

We can record all night. Got the tripod, wide-angle lens, get the whole room, EVP recorder, just to catch any sounds.

Now I'm in control. I'm making progress.

When Wyatt finally opened his eyes, the room was empty.

And that's when the idea hit. *Control. Progress.* That's what he needed. Otherwise everyone would keep leaving, and his life would stay the same forever.

Opening his palm, he studied Lucas's phone. *His* phone now. He began setting it up, signing in, syncing it with his iPad. He ran a little search, watched a few tutorials, downloaded a couple of new apps. Then he walked around the room, trying out different angles.

Eventually he stopped in front of the bookcase and carefully positioned the iPhone with the lens facing out. "This is my house," he murmured. "I'm gonna solve the fucking problem." Then he returned to the movie and skipped forward to when things got really interesting.

Thing is, though, while the fictional experiment had worked a treat, Wyatt's had not. The setup had gone well: Lucas's phone, positioned discreetly on the bookshelf, acted as a security camera and live footage was sent via a surveillance app to the "viewer" device, aka Wyatt's iPad. The recordings came through in little bursts and remained there for seven days, after which they were automatically stored in the cloud. But apparently whatever was in the house didn't show up on camera. It was very disappointing.

Still, he kept the phone there as much as he could because you never knew. And what use was it otherwise? It's not like anyone ever called him or texted.

Thud, thud, bang, rattle.

Wyatt covers his ears with his hands. Sitting up, he stares out of his bedroom window at the garage. *Stop,* he begs silently. *Please, whatever you are, just stop.* He strikes his fist against his skull. *Get out, get out, get out.*

And then the garage door swings open.

Wyatt holds his breath. Is this the moment? Is the demon about to reveal itself?

But it's just Dad, putting his tools away, swapping them out for a lawn mower and whipper-snipper, wiping his shiny forehead with mud-caked gloves.

Wyatt collapses back onto his mattress. *It's me. It's all me. None of this is real. There is no demon. The problem is me.*

Liked by **lonewanderer66** and others

pheebsinwonderland Following a LOT of requests for safety tips, I'm reposting my Safety Gospel list. But please bear in mind that besides locking your door and using your common sense there's not much you really need to *do* to stay safe on the road. In any given situation our biggest problem is usually our own fear—and that's what so great about solo travel! It teaches you to cope in situations where you might otherwise panic and give up. Remember, oftentimes things are only as scary as we think they are.

Do you agree? Let me know!

(Image descriptions: 1. A handwritten list of safety travel tips written on an A4 piece of lined notebook paper entitled The Solo Travel Safety Gospel According to Phoebe. 2. A white van stands alone on a red dirt road. The surrounding landscape is flat and dry, the sky wide and cornflower blue. 3. The same van is shown from the rear, traveling along a gray strip of bitumen toward a bright orange sunset. 4. The van is now parked on a clifftop overlooking the ocean. A woman in a white t-shirt and bikini bottoms sits in the open doorway hugging her knees to her chest. She's gazing out over the water and smiling.)

#safetygospel #solofemaletravel #safetytips #vanlife #staysafe #useyourhead #costalhighway #westernaustralia

View all 77 comments

later_allygator Thanks so much for these amazing tips Pheebs! You're an inspiration.

ellerymackieliveshere Hard disagree, with the caption at least. Our fear is not the problem. *We* are not the problem. Women are not making shit up, the threat is real. Less victim blaming and more responsibility please.

goodnightpetergraham Tell the story about the car at the lookout, that's a good example.

aroundtheworldwithmacymay Best tip I can think of is USE YOUR VOICE. If a guy gives unwanted attention, just calmly and firmly say no. No placation or modification, and def no apologies. Just NO.

lonewanderer66 Great tips. But you know that safety is an illusion, don't you? If someone really wants to get to you, they will.

25 May

CHAPTER TWENTY-FIVE

Beth

They drift through the twilight without speaking, both deep in thought. Katy had found a picture of Phoebe at the roadhouse, which was exciting but also frustrating because no one had been able to tell her a thing about it, and Beth was still unsettled after the thing with the man in the shadows.

Leaving the van had been stupid; she should've just stayed inside with the doors locked, but she couldn't help it. He was just standing there staring at her, and while that wasn't exactly a crime she knew it was only a matter of time before he did something. The shadow man had known that too and he was enjoying it, biding his time, waiting to see if she would break first—which of course she had, bursting suddenly from her seat and racing across the forecourt toward the women's bathrooms where she'd barricaded herself in a stall and vowed never to leave. But obviously she couldn't actually stay in a roadhouse toilet for the rest of her life, so eventually she'd snuck a peek outside and spotted Katy flapping around the HiAce, clearly looking for her. The shadow man appeared to have gone along with his van, so she'd jogged back and pretended everything was fine. And in a way it was, because what had actually happened? Nothing. At least, nothing specific anyway. It had just been a feeling, an overreaction.

Then again, for reasons she can't quite explain, she's sure that had been the figure's intention: to make her uncomfortable without doing anything explicitly threatening. *I'm just standing here,* he could've said if asked, *what's the problem?* That kind of gaslighting had been Lucas's specialty. That's not to say he hadn't also fucked with her in more overt ways, because he had, and with great success.

She thinks immediately of the time he left her alone overnight, just four or five weeks ago. They'd been on their way to make another drop at some random field in the middle of nowhere, another abandoned barn, and they'd both been on edge; it was dark, neither had eaten, and their adrenaline was pumping following a close call with the owner of a brand-new oversized off-road caravan. Lucas was in a foul mood and Beth had hit a rare wall, so when he lost his shit she lost hers right back. "I'm out," she screamed, getting out of the car and storming off toward the barn. "I'm done. I hate you, I hate this life, I don't want to do it anymore. I'm leaving." It wasn't smart—and it wasn't realistic either because where was she going to go? But it was true.

She'd braced herself for the usual escalation, after which she would inevitably be overpowered and forced back to the car. But instead, Lucas had stayed in the Troopy, sitting motionless behind the wheel, just watching her. She'd waited by the barn, half sulking, half preparing for a fight. Then the Troopy had begun to move, sliding away into the night like a fish into dark waters, and Beth had watched in stunned silence as the taillights got smaller and smaller until they disappeared completely and she was alone in the middle of nowhere with no keys, no phone, no money, and no food or water. *Asshole,* she thought. *He'll be back.*

It was a full hour before she considered the possibility that she might be wrong. *No,* she thought. *He wouldn't do that. He's just teaching me a lesson, he wouldn't leave me, he'll be back.* And thirteen long and terrifying hours later, he was. "How could you do that," she'd bawled as Lucas drove back into the field. "I tried to find my way back to the road but I couldn't, there's nothing around here, I don't know where I am, I could've died." Lucas had cried, too. He took her in his arms and wept and promised he'd never, ever do anything like that ever again. Beth wanted to believe it so badly that she forgave him, and for a whole week, he treated her like a baby bird. But things changed after that. *You need me.* That had been the lesson. *You are helpless without me. And you'd better pay attention because anything could happen at any time.*

Beth stares through the window at the darkness outside. Is he out there right now? Has he been following her the whole time? The darkness stares right back, forbidding and inscrutable.

CHAPTER TWENTY-SIX

Katy

"Her tattoo is cool," says Lily, pointing to where the picture I took from the roadhouse is propped up behind the gearstick. "What does it mean?"

"It's a compass," I say, making a mental note to find a more permanent place for the photo, somewhere I can see it all the time. "Phoebe got it on her twenty-first birthday. It symbolizes adventure and always knowing the right way to go. Something like that anyway."

"Do you have any ink?"

"No. We were supposed to get the same one in the same place but I chickened out last minute." I smile, remembering the tiny shop and the artist who'd had his own face tattooed on his neck. *Don't*, I'd urged, squeamish at the sight of the needle. *Don't do it.* But of course she did, all by herself.

"What's she like?" Lily says.

"Phoebe?"

"Yeah. What kind of person is she?"

I hesitate. *Apples in the car, brown cores in the cupholder. The last few centimeters of any drink. Lacquered bobby pins, glittering like jewels.* An image of her old bedroom passes behind my eyes. "She liked plants but couldn't keep them alive. She lined them up on her windowsill but always forgot to water them."

Lily seems puzzled, and alarm swells beneath my breastbone. *Wrong answer.*

I dig deep for something else. What were her politics, her dreams? What did she talk about over dinner with friends, what songs did she play in the car? How do I not know these things? "She was perfect," I say at last. "Beautiful, funny, creative, joyful. People loved her."

"Perfect, huh? Wow, there are so few of us out there."

I smile. "Okay, maybe not perfect. She could be annoying sometimes, a bit ditzy. As a kid I was always having to bail her out of trouble, rescue her from stupid situations."

"Like what?"

"Oh, she played with fire, got herself stuck in trees, crossed the road without looking. One time she ran away from home and no one could find her but me. I was always telling her off, which she hated, so she would always blame me whenever she got caught doing the wrong thing, told everyone I'd made her do it." I chuckle. *Little turd.*

"Were you close?"

"When we were little, yes. Inseparable actually, even though we were total opposites." I feel my smile growing wider. "Phoebe was like this delightful baby elephant, just blundering around and making everyone laugh, and I was her weird anxious shadow. But I think that's why we made such a good team. We were like two halves of the same whole."

"Like yin and yang."

"Exactly." She was the light to my dark, the sweet to my salt. The lit match to my bucket of water.

"That's so lovely," Lily says. "I wish I'd been close like that with my brother, but we never really got each other. And then as adults we grew even further apart."

"That's what happened with Phoebe and me. We grew apart, lost touch. We were fine, and then suddenly it was like I was this bossy big sister, always ruining her fun, and she outgrew me. She never understood how much we needed each other. But it's like that song, isn't it? If you love someone, set them free."

Lily nods emphatically as if I've said something wise but my words sound hollow, even to me. If I'd really loved her, if I'd kept her close, maybe she'd still be here.

"What do you think happened to her?" Lily whispers.

The question catches me off guard and the answer pops immediately into my head. *The same thing that happened to you.* And it takes me a second to realize that I believe it. I can't say it though, not yet. The thought is still just half formed.

"I don't know." I press my fingers to my cheeks and they come away wet. "Sorry. It's just hard. I miss her."

"Oh my god, no," says Lily, "*I'm* sorry. What a thoughtless question, of course it's hard. I didn't mean to upset you, we can totally talk about something else."

"It's okay, I like talking about her. Sometimes it feels like I'm forgetting, like my brain is deliberately trying to block her out." The admission feels shameful.

Lily sighs sympathetically. "If it helps at all, that's normal. With grief, I mean. It's like your audiobook said: it's just the brain's way of minimizing the effects of trauma. It removes anything it deems a threat—memories, experiences, associations—and temporarily confines them until it feels strong enough to let them out. So, as far as your mind is concerned remembering Phoebe is an unsafe act. You're rattling the locks, banging on the doors, attempting a heist. So the brain issues a lockdown, reinforces security. It's quite clever, really. But it doesn't tend to last, the memories will come back eventually."

I nod. Everything she's saying makes sense to me on a very deep level. "Did you learn all that at uni?"

"Yeah. I wanted to be a therapist. But I didn't finish, so." She shrugs.

"You would've been great at it. You still could be."

"No," she says firmly. "I'm too much of a mess myself."

"I don't think so."

"Oh, you have no idea. And I'm not even counting my current predicament."

"So, tell me." I look at her. "What happened? Why did you get kicked out?"

Lily groans. "I can't use the long story excuse again, can I?"

I give her a small smile. "Didn't work the first time, won't work now."

She sighs. "Fine. But you won't like it. And you won't think much of me after."

CHAPTER TWENTY-SEVEN

Beth

I did something awful.

She tries to front it out, make it seem like what she's about to share is no big deal, but inside Beth is terrified.

You're a monster, Bethany. A monster.

She considers making something up—*I stole something, I got in a fight*—but Katy has just been so vulnerable with her that she feels compelled to tell the truth, or a fraction of it at least. What's more, she wants to. There has to be some honesty among all the lies, and the need for someone to see her after hiding for so long feels akin to a desperate thirst after days of no water. But where to begin? She turns to the window, searching the night as if for help but it's like there's nothing beyond the glass. If it weren't for the headlights illuminating the road in front, the HiAce could be floating through space.

"There was a lot of pressure on me growing up," she says at last. "That's not an excuse, by the way, it's just a fact. My parents wanted my brother and me to be successful in ways that mattered to them, so it was a constant battle to meet their standards. I tried, but I just couldn't be what they wanted and the only way I could deal with their disappointment was to lean into it. I acted out a lot, did the wrong things, hung out with the wrong people, yadda yadda. Somehow, though, I scraped through with good enough grades for college, so off I went."

Beth remembers the excitement of her first day, not at an American college obviously but Melbourne University. It had felt like an opportunity to become exactly who she was supposed to be, cast off her old skin and grow a new one.

"But finding my place was harder than I'd expected, so I fell back on old habits. I drank a lot, dabbled with drugs, became the party girl who always knew where the good times were. It was all a bit predictable. What did come as a surprise though was how much I loved classes. I'd only chosen psychology because it was the one thing I didn't think I'd hate, but as it turned out, Psych 101 and me were soul mates. I stopped partying so hard and studied instead; I started acing all my tests, exams, and assignments. I became obsessed with true stories, real-life cases. You know, the man who took his wife for a hat, the woman who hallucinated dragons. But then I fucked it all up by falling in love with one of my tutors."

His face flares in her mind like a struck match. *Whatever our souls are made of, yours and mine are the same.*

"Looking back it was all such a cliché, but at the time he was so charismatic and charming, and he made me feel smart and valued, so of course I loved him. We'd make each other laugh in tutorials, we'd talk for hours after seminars. He told me I was mature beyond my years and that we had a unique connection. And I couldn't untangle him from my love of learning, the adrenaline rush of achievement, so the two felt like the same thing. Emotionally, it got pretty intense. And then . . ."

A surge of nausea. She sees the river, twinkling lights reflected on its inky surface; a fancy lobby and a mirror-lined lift. The fish tank, *Romeo and Juliet*. Green numbers on a clock and a dark wood bookshelf.

"I went to his apartment and we slept together. I don't really remember it, which at the time I'd blamed on being drunk even though I'd only had two vodkas, but I do know I was sick because he made me clean it up afterward. I was mortified. I didn't tell anyone because he'd asked me not to, and I was fine with it because we were in love. But then just days later, he ghosted me."

Beside her, Katy listens, quiet and still. No comments, no judgment. Yet.

"It hurt so much," she continues. "I was so ashamed, I couldn't eat or sleep, so obsessed with winning him back, I couldn't study. It got worse and worse, and then one day I told a friend who suggested I might've been raped—which really shocked me. I mean, I hadn't said yes; in fact, I distinctly recall not really wanting to sleep with him that night, I'd just wanted to talk, but I couldn't remember much else about what had happened so I couldn't say for sure that I'd said no. And it wasn't like he'd dragged me kicking and screaming into an alleyway, which was how I'd always defined sexual violence. But then I thought about it, especially those two vodkas, and I wondered if maybe I'd been drugged."

Katy inhales softly and makes a small sound on the out breath, like *mmmm*.

"So then I tried to report it but it was way too late for testing, and because I'd been known for my partying no one believed me anyway. Everyone, including my parents, bought his side of the story, which was that nothing even happened in the first place and I'd made the whole thing up because he'd rejected me."

Beth pauses to take a deep breath. "When I found out I was pregnant, I went by myself to the clinic. It was horrible. My parents had always been stridently pro-life and I thought about Satan and hell the whole time, but I knew having his baby at nineteen was not what I wanted. I could not, would not, sacrifice my entire life in the name of his short-lived appetite. I swore I would never, ever tell them what I'd done, but then a woman from my mother's book group saw me in the car park and that was that. Two days later, Mum and Dad told me I was no longer welcome in their house."

Katy sighs again. "That's when you saved up to go traveling?"

"Nope. I broke into my mother's banking app and stole from them. I used that money to buy a flight to Sydney—all the solo travel sites said Australia was one of the safest places for a woman alone—and picked up a shit secondhand van once I touched down. Then I got on the road, moved from one cash-in-hand job to another, and found myself here in WA. And that, as they say, is the end."

But of course it wasn't. It was just the beginning. Because just weeks after leaving Melbourne and arriving in a small coastal town just north of Perth, Beth had met Lucas.

They drive. Beyond the window, the world slides by. Blue-gray clouds gather on the horizon. There'll be rain later.

Something bulky flies through the air and lands in Beth's lap with a thud. She looks down to see Lucas's wallet nestled between her knees.

"Sort that out, will you?" he says.

"Right, yeah, sorry."

Opening the wallet, she pushes a slim wad of cash aside and eases the cards from their plastic pockets: driver's licenses, Medicare cards, bank cards, all fake. She lifts the rubber mat at her feet and selects new IDs from the brown envelope hidden beneath—Lily, American, traveling with her brother on a holiday visa—then tosses the old ones inside before tucking the envelope back under the mat. As she's sliding each new card into the wallet, she's careful not to disturb the only thing that ever stays between the fake-leather folds: a faded photograph of a copper-haired kid, maybe eight years old, standing on a parched lawn in front of a house with a blue door. Just within shot are the corner of a window, the edge of a veranda and a slice of guttering. The summation of what she knows of Lucas's origins.

The boy in the picture is clearly Lucas's sibling, though she only knows for sure because despite their different coloring they basically have the same face. That, and Lucas has mentioned a brother once or twice when drunk, along with a mother who walked out one day for some unknown reason and never came back—but otherwise he barely mentions his family and never, ever talks about home unless drunk. She doesn't even know where home is for him, except that it's somewhere north of here, up the coast, a "piece of shit" holiday town, nothing to it but a "dumb shipwreck and a statue of a whale." "I'm never going back," he said once through a vodka fug. And that's fine by her. She has no desire to meet his family anyway, not anymore.

The ginger kid looks cute though. She likes his dimpled smile and the way his gangly body looks poised to run the second the picture is taken. In Beth's head he's warm, kind, funny, all the things that Lucas can be in his better moments. And sometimes she catches Lucas taking the photo out when he thinks she's not looking and staring at it with fondness, which suggests that the two are, or used to be, close. But his reticence also implies some kind of bad blood or ill feeling. She never presses him for answers, though. She understands what it's like to have a past you can't talk about.

Before she realizes what she's doing, she slides the photo from the wallet and brings it close to her face. She studies the boy's smile, wonders where he is now. He could be any age, doing anything, anywhere at all, but in that moment he looks happy. The house behind him looks warm and welcoming, the blue door like a piece of the sky.

"What are you doing?"

"Sorry," Beth says, automatically. She tucks the photo back behind the plastic. "There was some dirt on it, and I—"

Lucas's hand shoots out so fast she has no time to block it. He shoves her upper arm hard, the blow thudding through the meat of her muscle right down to her bone. The impact sends her flying into the door and her skull connects with the window frame.

"Don't touch that." He snatches the wallet back. "Did I say you could touch that?"

"No."

"Then why did you?"

"I'm sorry."

With one hand still on the wheel, Lucas riffles through his wallet with the other, checking the cards, counting the cash.

"It's all there," Beth mutters, her head throbbing.

"Better be."

They lapse into silence. Lucas's eyes dart from mirror to mirror, from passing car to passing car. Beth sits beside him, resisting the urge to rub her aching arm. If she draws attention to herself in any way it'll just make things worse.

She turns back to the window and watches the clouds. Fly, Lily, fly.

"Lily," Katy says when she's finished, "I am so, so, sorry that even a small part of that happened to you." And she says it with such compassion and gravity that Beth has a weird urge to laugh, because Katy doesn't even know the half of it and also because fuck, her life is bleak. But she doesn't because it's the first time anyone has said anything like that and she doesn't quite know what to do with it.

A short while later, Katy yawns and rubs her eyes. "Sorry," she says. "I'm so tired. I don't think I can drive anymore."

"You want to stop and rest?"

"Yeah. Is that okay?"

"Of course."

At the next available rest stop, Katy pulls in and the van trundles off the road.

CHAPTER TWENTY-EIGHT

Katy

The rest stop isn't ideal; it's a little farther off the highway than I'd like and quite exposed, but I can't keep my eyes open any longer. The GPS says my next campsite is two hundred kilometers away, roughly two hours of driving, some of which is on what looks like a smaller winding road through a World Heritage–listed area. Phoebe's corresponding post says that I'll find pristine coastline, rugged national park, turquoise lagoons, an astonishing array of marine wildlife, and even the world's oldest known fossils, but none of that will be of any benefit now that the sun has gone down. I won't be able to see a thing. There'll be kangaroos on the road, and who knows what else. If I attempt it, I'll have to go slow; two hours will become three, and I can't risk falling asleep at the wheel again.

I bring the van to a stop next to a large shrub and start my safety checks while Lily makes us something to eat. I can't stop thinking about her story. It's so sad, but it also chimes with me in ways I can't quite pinpoint. It makes me think about how much we go through all by ourselves, under the surface. How little we actually know about other people's pain. It makes me wonder how much I knew about Phoebe's and what she might've been experiencing around the time of her disappearance. I've always assumed that whoever took her from the world was already here, waiting to claim her—but what if the threat had followed her from home? What if she'd been running from something that eventually caught up? Or . . .

I stop still. What if she's *still* running? What if I'm right and she *is* alive, but not in danger? What if she doesn't want to be found?

No. I shake the thought off. *No way.* If Phoebe was able to let us know she's alive and well, then she would've done just that.

I check the tires, the oil, the buildup of dust and dirt on the bumpers and grille. Inside, I can hear Lily humming. *What do you think happened to her?* My knee-jerk response comes back to me—*the same thing that happened to you*—and again I feel an odd sense of certainty.

I look out into the night, at the vast shadow-shrouded plains. What if I'm right? What if there's a connection? If I could somehow unlock Lily's memory of that night, if together we could figure out what happened to her, we could take it to Dust. I think about Lily's unwashed clothes and imagine handing them over to the police along with Phoebe's bobby pin and the note I found. Solid facts, DNA samples . . . he wouldn't be able to ignore me then.

I'll call again tomorrow, decide what to do from there. He can't hide from me forever.

After a dinner of canned soup and cheese sandwiches, Lily and I turn in.

She climbs into the front and makes her bed while I lock all the doors and run through my inside checks three times before curling up on the mattress. I stare up at the fairy lights, reluctant to plunge myself into darkness just yet. Thank god for solar power.

It takes me a while to fall asleep. I can feel collapse creeping in like a tide but I'm still wired, on high alert. Through a gap in the curtain I stare at the stars, somehow knowing that somewhere out there Phoebe is watching them too. I think of sliding doors, overlapping worlds, layers of alternate dimensions and the membranes between them. I imagine that by penetrating them I could reach through time and pull her close.

"I miss you, Pheebs," I murmur. "Talk to me. Tell me what to do."

In the dream, Phoebe and I are standing together under a starless sky, on the shore of a vast body of water. The surface is black and glassy as a mirror.

I'm so glad you're here, I say to her, my fingers wrapped tight around hers. *I've missed you so much.*

I missed you too, says Phoebe.

I wish you would come back.

Phoebe shakes her head. *I can't.*

Why?

You know why.

A breeze blows in over the water, rippling the surface, and Phoebe's long hair flies out behind her like a cape.

I lay my head on her shoulder. *I'll never stop looking, Pheebs. I promise I'll find you.*

Phoebe's grip on my hand tightens. *No. Don't. You need to stop.*

What?

I mean it. Give up. Go home. Leave me here.

I don't understand. I'm close to tears. *Why would you want me to leave?*

Phoebe's eyes are on the water, her face resolute. *Because I love you. Because I want you to be safe. Because I'm scared.*

Why? I grasp her shoulders. *Pheebs, what are you scared of?*

Just when I think she isn't going to answer, she lifts her gaze and finally her eyes meet mine—but then she stiffens.

What is it?

Shhh. Her skin is ashen.

What's wrong?

Listen.

I tune into our surroundings. At first all I can hear is the hushed lap of the black water. But then I become aware of tinkling notes, a song riding the breeze like butterflies. Somewhere, the gentle wail of a child in distress. And footsteps, slow and steady.

What's happening?

A beam of light, shockingly bright, sweeps across the water.

Phoebe, what's going on?

Beside me, Phoebe is rigid with fear. She grips my hand so tight it hurts. Then she looks right at me and utters a single word.

Run.

CHAPTER TWENTY-NINE

Beth

Beth dreams of a wolf circling the van, sniffing at the doors, trying to get in. She hears it scuffling in the dirt, drawing shapes on the ground with its claws. She can smell it, too; the wolf is wearing cologne, something expensive and woodsy. It howls, and the sound is human.

She wakes. The air inside the cab is cold and fresh and smells of soil, and she's wrapped tight inside the quilt, must've burrowed deep inside while she slept. The window is open, the night rolling in through the top third: she'd kept it open last night promising Katy on pain of death that she would close it before she went to sleep, but she must've forgotten, she was so tired . . .

She snuggles down even further, goes to turn over, then stills. There's an unfamiliar scent in the air. Fragments of the dream return: the wolf, the cologne. She inhales and the same spicy aroma hits the back of her throat. And then someone outside coughs. It's faint, barely perceptible, but real. Beth's eyes fly to the open window. *Katy?* No, the tone was too deep for a woman. But it didn't sound like Lucas either; she knows his cough and that was not it. Maybe it's the police or a national park ranger, come to inform them that what they thought was a rest stop is in fact private property . . .

A light flickers on in the back.

"Lily?" Katy's voice is tense.

"Mmm?"

Silence. A scuffle of blankets.

Beth holds her breath and doesn't move.

The noises stop. The scent dissipates. The light in the back flickers and swings.

There's a long pause.

"Lily," Katy whispers again from the back.

"Yeah?"

"There's something out there."

Adrenaline surges through Beth's body. Her limbs fizz with the impetus to run.

"What is it?"

The locking system clunks and the back door slides open.

"Oh my god, Lily, they're *everywhere*."

"What is?"

No answer.

"Katy?"

Shit. Grabbing the spare flashlight from the glove box, Beth gets out too. The night is cool but not chilly. To the east, the horizon glows red; dawn is coming. She steps forward and her foot knocks against something hard. She swings her beam wider and the light catches pointy shapes in the dirt, pale things emerging from the earth like . . . leeches? Fingers? Hands? A growing forest of tiny ghost trees? No. Stones. Countless piles of them, arranged neatly and left at the door like gifts.

"Fuck me," she breathes. There are too many piles to count but there could be as many as fifty or sixty. "What are they?"

"I don't know," Katy replies, appearing at Beth's side, "but it's the same thing I found at Kalbarri. The night with the note."

They both sweep their flashlights around but can't see another piece of paper. Wide-eyed, Katy juts her chin toward the front of the van and together they circle it in silence, picking their way through the piles of stones, moving slowly around the front to the side and all the way to the back. Katy is right: the piles are everywhere. And there are lines, too. In places, the stones have been organized into some kind of pattern. No, letters. A very clear *W*, then what could be an *I* and two *L*s.

"What the hell . . ." Beth shines her lights outward, into the bushes and the plains beyond, bracing herself for someone to jump out and rush at them. Her mouth is so dry she can barely swallow.

"Hey." Katy's voice is coming from the other side of the van, back where they started. "Come and look at this."

Beth follows the sound, tiptoeing over more stones, more piles, to where Katy stands in front of the open side door, pointing her torch inside. "Look," she says again.

Joining her, Beth adds her own beam. "Oh, holy fucking fuck."

The floor of the HiAce is covered in dirt. Despite Katy having swept and cleaned the night before, the laminate is now speckled with dry grass and tree bark, the rug smeared with rust-orange marks in the unmistakable shape of—

"Are they . . . ?" Katy murmurs.

"Footprints," Beth confirms.

They edge closer, torches outstretched. The light shines over the counter, the drawers, the sheets, the mattress—

"There's something on the bed," Katy says.

Beth can see it too, a small object, soft and golden brown, sitting in the middle of the mattress. An animal, surely? Pulse thudding, Beth steps into the van.

Behind her, Katy gasps.

It's hair. Human hair. A long, glossy lock. Caramel blond.

CHAPTER THIRTY

Wyatt

It's funny how you can spend your whole life surrounded by things and never really notice them. Take, for example, the family photos on Wyatt's living room wall; they've been hanging there ever since he can remember, he passes them every single day, but it's only now, when he's too sick to leave the house and has endless time on his hands, that he's really *seeing* them.

There's him and Lucas at five, six, eight years old. There's Dad holding a fish. There's Mum looking angelic in a park. And here's Mum *and* Dad, with Nan and Pop and four other people he's never really seen before.

He steps closer to the frame and places his fingertips lightly on the glass. Two couples, one older, one younger. The older couple have graying hair and both wear glasses; they seem to be Nan and Pop's age. The younger couple are more similar to Mum and Dad: youthful, wholesome, and ever so slightly dorky. One of them, the girl, looks weirdly familiar. Something about the eyes and the shape of her jaw.

Taking the frame off the wall, he opens the back and removes the photo. On the back of it someone has written January 1999 in spidery scrawl. *The Clearys: Bruce, Maree, Rory and Nova (plus Rory Junior, due next year). The Greenaways: Lionel, Raelene, and the new Mr. and Mrs. Keating, Jill and Keith.*

The two older couples have their arms around each other. The men are big, broad, and sun-roasted; their smiles are hearty but their eyes are mean. The women lean in coyly as if roped into a dare. Rory Junior obviously refers to Lucas, who was born in April of '99 and is clearly visible as a swollen bump under Mum's shirt. They're all standing in a dated, much less landscaped version of Wyatt's backyard.

Mr. and Mrs. Keating. Jill.

Wyatt looks again at the dorky young woman. Bloody hell, it's Mrs. Creeping. Or the girl she once was.

Just then, something passes by the kitchen window and Wyatt looks up to see a figure disappearing out of sight. His breath catches. There's someone in the garden.

Abandoning the photo, he walks slowly and quietly to the kitchen and stops by the back door. What will he find when he goes out there? An actual person? Or is this just another mind trick? A hallucination?

What he finds, of course, is Mrs. bloody Creeping. She's standing in the middle of the lawn, staring at the garage. *Shit's sake.* He rolls his eyes. *Should've known.*

Crossing the grass, he taps her on the shoulder. "Hi, Mrs. Creep—I mean, Mrs. Keating. Can I help you?"

She jumps, apparently startled. "Me? Oh no, I'm fine. But maybe *I* can help *you*?"

"Me?" Wyatt tries to keep his face still. "Um . . . Nah, I'm good."

There's an uncomfortable pause. Then Mrs. Creeping says: "I'm so sorry your mum isn't around anymore. I do miss her, you know."

Wyatt is confused. It's been six years. A little late for condolences. But he doesn't want to be rude. "Right, yeah. Thanks." Then he adds, "I'm sorry your husband isn't around either. You must miss him, too."

Mrs. Creeping smiles. Her teeth are gross. But up close he realizes that she's not as old as he'd thought. *The Greenaways* . . . Lionel and Raelene, and Jill must be their daughter, who'd become Mrs. Keating when she married Keith. The Greenaways had lived next door. Dad and

Mrs. Creeping must've grown up together. Which means they are in fact the same age. Wyatt's mind is blown.

"Would like to come over to my house?" she said. "I have milk and cookies."

Eww. "Not really. Thanks, though." He wonders if it would be mean to just come right out and tell her to go home.

"I'm very fond of you, Wyatt," she says at last. "I've known your family a long time."

He swallows. "Uh-huh."

"I know you. I see you. I understand exactly who you are. I know everything."

Lady, Wyatt thinks, *you are cracked.* Then: *If you know everything, tell me where my mum is.*

The yard is dead quiet. Mrs. Creeping smiles again as though she can read his mind. And then she pulls something from her pocket and offers it out. It's a stone, perfectly smooth and round. Taking hold of Wyatt's wrist, she presses it into his palm.

He blinks. "What is it?"

"For remembrance," she says. And then without another word she ambles away in the direction of her own house.

Liked by **goodnightpetergraham** and others

pheebsinwonderland Greetings from Shark Bay—or Gutharraguda as it is known to its traditional owners, the Malgana, Nhanda, and Yingkarta people. This stretch of almost 1500km of coastline is now a UNESCO-listed World Heritage Area and contains so many natural attractions lined up one after the other that it feels like a wilderness theme park but without the crowds: a new wonder around every corner! It's a real mix of desert and ocean, like yin and yang. There are about 130 registered Aboriginal heritage sites including quarries, rock shelters, and burial sites. And it has this incredible vibe—I've been trying to put it into words, but I guess sometimes there just aren't any. As someone said to me recently "you don't see nature, you feel it."

Highlights: the pristine beaches and rugged national park; the turquoise lagoons and hidden bays. All the many dugongs, turtles, dolphins, and sting rays swimming around, plus the world's oldest known fossils! Shell Beach is extraordinary (no sand, just shells) and Little Lagoon is perfect for a sunset swim. You can base your-self at laid-back Denham, Australia's westernmost town, or up at the idyllic Monkey Mia resort (the bar does killer cocktails, just sayin'), and from there join lots of other visitors on a multi-stop beauty spot hop. So funny bumping into all the same travelers along the way!

(Image descriptions: 1. A woman with long hair and a yellow bikini sits on a shore made entirely of tiny white shells. She's holding out a handful toward the camera and smiling. 2. A spectacular view of the ocean as seen from the Eagle Bluff lookout. 3. The red-earth mouth of a cave at a sacred Indigenous excavation site near Monkey Mia. 4. The same long-haired woman from image 1 sits on a

different beach with her feet in the water watching three
beautiful dolphins who have come to feed in the shallows.
5. A frosty margarita is positioned in front of an incredible
sunset. 6. Selfie of the long-haired woman, who is smiling
so hard it's a wonder she can still feel her face. The sunset
is reflected in her sunglasses.)

#sharkbay #denham #monkeymia #dolphinfeeding #shellbeach
#solofemaletravel #vanlife #neverwantittoend

View all 63 comments

lonewanderer66: Anyone ever tell you it's rude to ignore people??
I'm not sure you're as nice as you make yourself out to be.

risinggeministories: Hey Pheebs, great shots, are you planning on
passing through Adelaide at any point?

goodnightpetergraham: Idyllic if you don't mind a tussle with an
emu, right? Haha.

adsandjaxgooffgrid: Pheebs, Francois Peron is off the hook,
need 4WD though. And don't miss the cold drip at @morning-
peopledenham.

emmeline_jojo: Hi Pheebs, are you planning on hitting Karijini?
We're heading down that way from Broome, two girls on our own,
would be cool to meet up!

27 May

CHAPTER THIRTY-ONE

Katy

The lock of hair sits on the table between us like a feather.

"You're absolutely sure it's Phoebe's?" Lily says, chewing her nails.

"Positive." In this light the color is less caramel and more peanut butter and honey, but there's no doubt it's hers. It makes me think of our first haircuts and the baby curls Mum saved, preserved forever in brown envelopes and kept in her bedside drawer.

Lily nods slowly and purses her lips. "Shit just got real, huh?"

Exhaling hard, I lean back in my box seat and let my head fall against the window. Through the open door of the van, another new view spreads itself wide. Rows of identical cabins with pitched roofs and balconies, huge caravans and trailers, palm trees and neat lawns. Gleaming amenities, flawless facilities, and a never-ending stream of sunshine.

Phoebe was right: the Monkey Mia resort *is* idyllic, almost like a film set. In fact, this time her photos are so accurate I feel like I've stepped into them. It occurs to me that maybe I'm dreaming again—a speculation compounded by the sudden appearance of four gigantic emus that dart out from behind a nearby bush and make a beeline for a trailer whose absent occupants have neglected to clear away their lunch. I watch as the emus attack the leftovers like a pack of teenagers then casually saunter away as if denying all responsibility. I can't help but smile. It's oddly satisfying that despite all the manufactured perfection nature still has the run of the place.

Lily and I sit in silence. There doesn't seem to be much to say—or not yet anyway. Shit has indeed got very real, but neither of us know what to do about it. All those stones. So many little piles, and the lines that looked like letters as if someone had been trying to spell out a message. Whoever is responsible, they must've been at it all night.

My phone buzzes. Startled, I tear it from my pocket as if drawing a gun, hoping hard that it's Dust . . . but no, it's just Mum again, checking up on me for the third time this morning.

I mute the call—I can't tell her about the hair, not yet, I don't know how to explain, I need to speak to Dust first and figure out what it means—then send a quick text. Sorry, driving, bad signal, call you later.

Lily gives me a questioning look, but says nothing. We both return to our thoughts.

"I'm so hot," says Lily at last. "Do you think I could . . . do you have a swimsuit I can borrow?"

I don't, but suggest we walk over to the main building to see if they have one in the gift shop. We both need to get out of the van anyway.

While Lily browses a rack of locally made clothes and merch T-shirts, I wait outside and call Dust, preparing the inevitable voicemail message in my head. But to my shock, he answers.

"Yes?" His voice is low and wary. "Detective Dust?"

I'm so shocked that for a moment my mind goes completely blank. "Oh," I stammer. "Hi, hello. Sorry, I didn't expect—"

"Who is this?"

"Katy Sweeney. I've been trying to reach you. About Phoebe? I need to speak to you—"

A groan rumbles from the speaker. "You need to stop. I told you, we're doing all we can."

"I'm sorry, I sure you're busy, but—"

"I am. Very busy indeed."

"I know, but—"

"No, Miss Sweeney, you don't know, or you wouldn't be harassing me."

I stop short. "Harassing? How am I *harassing* you?"

"You know exactly what I'm talking about."

What? He's a detective. This is his case. Doesn't he want to hear what I have to say? "Please, you have to listen. I just found—"

"No, *you* listen." Dust's voice is cold. "And actually *hear* me this time, all right? Let me do my job. I am doing everything possible. I will be in touch if and when I have news. Okay? Now, please, for your sake and mine, stop calling me. Just *stop*."

He hangs up.

I stare at the screen, clench my jaw. What's wrong with him? Why won't he talk to me? It takes all my self-control not to hurl the phone at the shop's wall and smash it to pieces.

Lily emerges from the shop to show me a patterned one-piece she thinks might do. "It's the cheapest I could find," she says, "but if it's too much we can just leave it."

I smile—"It's fine!"—and follow her inside to pay, but all I can think is *I can't do this anymore. I want to go home.*

Again, Phoebe's voice pops into my head. *Then why are you still here?*

It's a good question. Why *am* I here? I could just leave. I don't have to be here in this faraway land. No one forced me to come, the choice was mine—so why did I make it? What am I truly looking for? What do I really want?

The questions make me shiver, like when you brush up against something unseen while swimming in murky waters.

CHAPTER THIRTY-TWO

Beth

It's still early, but the resort bar is already busy. Groups of people fill the spacious deck, chatting around long trestle tables and on cushioned lounges. Strings of little bulbs twinkle above their heads as a dreadlocked man on a small stage plays folksy songs on a guitar.

Beth follows Katy to a long timber counter at the front with a clear view over the beach, clocking the entrances and exits and taking note of the clientele. As far as campsites go the resort is pretty fancy—and a thief's paradise, so many high-end vehicles and expensive equipment. But Lucas would never have targeted somewhere like this: the security is too tight, too many cameras, the check-in process too thorough. That doesn't mean he won't show up though.

They pull out a couple of barstools and a waiter brings them menus. Beth glances at hers then puts it down again. She and Katy haven't yet eaten out together and she's not sure what's expected of her.

It's a beautiful evening: the setting sun is putting on a fine show, and the ocean is a shimmering mirror in which the shifting sky admires itself. Suddenly tiny black triangles appear on the surface. "Oh, look," she cries, unable to help herself. "Dolphins!" A pod of about six or eight are making their way across the bay, their slick fins shining in the sun.

"You've never seen dolphins before?" Katy asks.

"Of course. Just not for a while." How to explain that she'd been living among this beauty for almost a year without really seeing it? How can she articulate the reasons why? She grins as one dolphin leaps from the water then disappears again with barely a splash, feeling like her eyes are open for the first time in ages.

Katy announces she's having the calamari and a margarita. "What will you have?"

"Nothing for me, thanks. I'm not hungry." She's ravenous but can't bear to ask for anything more, not even a basket of fries.

Katy goes inside to order. While she's gone, Beth takes inventory of the patrons. A middle-aged couple play cards in the corner, while a group of four fresh-faced backpackers on the neighboring table clink their frozen margaritas. Three kids eat pizza while their parents drink beer. There are no other women on their own. There is, however, a cute guy sitting alone at the back, nursing a Corona. Tallish, maybe just over six foot, and slender with messy hair and sunglasses pushed up on his head.

Beth looks away then back again. Why is she drawn to him? Maybe she just likes his artsy, bookish vibe. He's the kind of dude you'd find three espressos deep in a Melbourne laneway, the kind she once thought she'd end up with. Again, she finds herself marveling at how far she's traveled from herself, how unrecognizable her life is now.

Suddenly the man looks up, right at her. Their eyes meet, and he smiles. She feels her cheeks redden. He raises his beer as if toasting her, an adorably awkward gesture, then he drains the bottle, gets to his feet and, with a final backward glance, leaves via the bar area.

Beth watches him go. The moment was brief but it has stirred something in her: a tiny spark of hope that one day she might reclaim that lost life. That she might still end up with someone nice.

Lucas seems rejuvenated. He says their next job will be a big earner, he's got some ideas. He's so jovial that he insists on picking up some whiskey and a takeout, a special "treat" after a hard day's "work."

With boxes of Thai food cooling in her lap, Beth watches the sun sink toward the horizon as they speed out to a free camp just off the highway. They set up the pop-top, make the bed, and pull out the camp chairs, then Lucas builds a fire as the clouds turn pink. After dinner, they pass the whiskey bottle back and forth between them until the last drop is gone.

The shadows deepen. Lucas scrolls on his phone, his face bathed in the screen's eerie light. Beth watches the flames, her hands limp and useless in her lap. We can't afford two phones, *Lucas had said early on.* We only need one between us, anyway. *And she'd agreed because it was true, they couldn't afford to pay two bills, they were already sharing everything else, and actually she'd be quite happy to give hers up. Less temptation to check in on her former life, more incentive to forge ahead with the new one.*

What she hadn't agreed to (or didn't think she'd agreed, it was hard to be sure) was that Lucas be sole custodian of their "shared" phone on the basis that she is "flaky" and "careless." Again, he has a point; she is both of those things and many others besides. But still it seems unfair. As does the decision—his, of course—that her phone be placed "in storage" with all the rest of her stuff: real driver's license and bank cards, as well as make-up, books, and a whole bunch of her clothes he wasn't "keen on."

"If this is going to work," he said shortly after he'd invented the Victim Technique, "we can't have any of our personal stuff lying around. If the shit hits the fan, we don't want anyone knowing who we really are." He'd bundled the whole lot up in a plastic bag and left it at a drop-off point to be collected by his contact and kept safe in the cache. "Don't worry," he told her, "we can get it all back whenever we want. It's just safer this way." And it had made sense at the time because she didn't have any money so the bank cards were useless, and she was terrified of getting caught. Also, she was in love, and when you were in love all kinds of stupid shit made sense.

Now, though, the logic doesn't seem to hold. And it's becoming increasingly clear that "get it all back whenever we want" means that Lucas can do what he wants when he wants, but she has no say.

She tips her head back and counts the stars, itching to scroll through something mindless herself. "Aren't you going to talk to me?" It comes out more petulant than she intended.

He looks up. *"What about?"*

"Anything. The weather, the roads. Tell me a bedtime story."

He smirks. *"A bedtime story?"*

"I don't know. I just can't take this silence anymore."

"All right, let me think. Umm . . . Okay, I've got one. You ready?"

"Are you serious?"

"You asked."

"Okay, then."

"All right. Once upon a time, back in the old days, there was this guy up in Darwin. A shipping merchant."

"A shipping merchant? What is this, the Brothers Grimm?"

"Shush, let me finish. So this dude was rich and successful and had everything he could ever want, including a beautiful young wife, who he loved more than anything in the whole world."

He's slurring, his words bleeding into one another, but he's also relaxed. There's no crackle of volatility, no immediate sense that things could go south. Beth feels her muscles loosen.

"So, this wife was smoking hot but insane. She needed round-the-clock medical care, which the merchant provided as best he could while also working like a dog to build his business. He hired the best doctors, paid for the best available treatments. He never let her out of his sight, even going so far as to bring her with him on his sea voyages."

Beth's eyelids grow heavy. She tucks her feet beneath her and rests her head against the back of the chair.

"In 1869 he sailed from Darwin to Fremantle with a shipment of wool and pearl shell, and of course the wife went with him. But only a few weeks into the trip, she just fucking loses it. She starts thrashing around and screaming that she's going to kill everyone."

Beth looks up. *"What?"*

"Yeah. So the merchant restrains her in his quarters, but somehow she gets loose. She goes down to the hull with a candle, sets fire to a barrel of booze, and the whole ship goes up in flames. It sinks to the bottom and everyone on board dies."

"No, really?"

"Well, a few crew members survived but yeah, basically everyone. Anyway, the ship sinks and the bodies of the drowned wash up on a nearby beach, all burned up and charred, including the merchant and his batshit arsonist wife. Bits of their skin float in on the tide for months."

Beth makes a face. "Gross."

"And here's the best part." He turns to her with a sloppy grin. "One hundred and fifty years later or whatever it is, you can still see her ghost wandering around by the water, looking for more people to kill."

"Don't be silly."

"I'm serious. If you went there, you'd see her for yourself. And all that charred skin."

"Ugh. Not quite the bedtime story I had in mind."

"Great for a campfire though, right? And I'm claiming bonus points because it's true."

"Liar."

He shrugs. "Okay, fine, maybe not the bit about the skin. But anyone in my town will tell you about the ghost. We've all seen her at some point. If you haven't, you aren't a real local."

Beth nods slowly. Aha. A story from home. He really is drunk. "Sounds like a great place to grow up."

Lucas falls quiet. The flames crackle. "It really wasn't," he says at last, his face suddenly serious. "I hated it."

He looks so sad that Beth reaches for his hand.

"There was something in the air," he says, lacing his fingers with hers. "In the walls. Did I ever tell you that?"

"No. What kind of thing?"

"It was everywhere."

"What do you mean?" A breeze dances over Beth's skin, tugging at the hairs on her arms.

Lucas stares at the fire. "I used to go into town sometimes, at night while everyone was asleep." His voice is so quiet Beth has to lean closer to hear him. "I'd go to the beach, the boat ramp, all the way out to the statue.

I'd walk a loop around the pub. In the dark, in the quiet, I could hear it, feel it."

"Feel what? What was it?"

He squints into the shadows, his brow furrowed as if trying to solve a tricky math problem. "I don't know, exactly. I never did figure out if . . ." He trails off, then presses the heels of his hands to his eyes.

"Hey." Beth squeezes his hand. "You okay?"

Lucas is still for a short while longer, then he blinks and shakes his head. "Yeah. Sorry. Too much grog. Going to bed." He gets unsteadily to his feet, staggers to the Troopy, opens the back doors and climbs in.

A few minutes later Beth follows, packing away the chairs then clambering up into the pop-top and sliding onto the mattress beside him. She tucks herself in next to his sleepy body; he takes her hand and brings it to his cheek.

"Love you."

"Love you, too."

And in that moment, in the dark beneath the canvas, she means it.

She falls asleep and dreams of a giant maze. All night long she runs around corners and into dead ends, breathlessly calling his name and trying in vain to find him.

"What are you thinking about?" says Katy, returning from the bar.

Beth shrugs. "Just, y'know, last night," she lies. "And all the things that are happening."

"Right." Katy's energy has shifted. She pulls out her stool and sits down like she's about to chair a meeting. "About that. I've decided we need to stop thinking and start doing."

Beth sits up a little straighter. "What do you mean?"

The dreadlocked man finishes his song and thanks his audience. While everyone else in the bar claps, Katy leans forward and says, "I mean that it's time to make a plan."

CHAPTER THIRTY-THREE

Katy

The waiter brings my order—*two* serves of calamari and *two* margaritas, plus a side salad and a bowl of sweet potato fries just in case—and batting away Lily's protests, I hand her a set of cutlery. "Eat," I say. "You've barely had a proper meal in days."

She relents, and after a few eager mouthfuls we get straight into it. I say that the hair planted in the van is proof that whoever hurt Phoebe is following me—following *us*—and that he might be the same person who attacked her.

Lily is hesitant but doesn't disagree.

I then tell her that we need to identify that person and, leaving out the fact that I've already spoken to and been outright dismissed by Dust, explain that if she still doesn't want to involve the police we need to investigate by ourselves. Thing is, I'm not sure where to start.

We bat a few useless ideas around and then Lily brings up something I said about Phoebe having a reckless nature. "No offense," she says, "I'm just spitballing here, but it seems to me that she wasn't being especially careful. Like, she was a bit of an obvious target."

"What?"

"Just . . . okay, look at her Insta." Lily points at my phone. "Let's say someone saw her pictures and became jealous or fixated. It would be pretty easy to track her movements."

"It would?"

"Sure. I mean, I'm no expert but on a route like this I'd imagine you could guess roughly where someone might go from where they've just been, even if they don't share their itinerary online."

"Which Phoebe did," I say, thinking of her very first post.

"Well, there you go then. Also, if somebody posted live from their location you'd see where they were in real time—and from there it's very easy to make contact, you just send a DM."

My skin crawls. "You think Phoebe was communicating with someone?"

"Oh, for sure, probably lots of people. Here, let me show you."

I bring up Insta and pass her the phone.

"All right, let's see . . ." Lily scrolls and clicks. *"Awesome working sheep station . . . great coffee . . . let's talk more about safety . . .* aha." She passes the phone back to me. "See there? *There are some great beaches, I'll DM you the details.* And she's replied, look. She says, *thank you so much.* So she's communicated privately with at least one of these people but almost certainly many, and any could've struck up a private friendship. You've read through them all, right? Checked the usernames, had a look at their profiles?"

I hesitate. I don't like to read the comments, they make me feel sad and angry, but clearly that's a mistake. "Of course," I lie.

"And? Have you noticed anyone who comments more regularly than others, perhaps seems more friendly?"

I don't reply. I've got nothing.

"Well, the police would've looked for sure," Lily says. "These interactions might even have been among the last she had before she disappeared. They didn't mention anything?"

"No." That at least is true.

"You use Insta, right? Like, for yourself?"

"Not really. It's mostly just to follow Phoebe." The thought of putting myself out there for everyone to see makes me feel ill.

"What about Facebook? TikTok?"

"No. I don't understand the appeal."

"Oh. Well, it's a good way to make friends."

I shrug. "I don't need to make friends. They just show up in the back of my van."

Lily grins. "Very funny. Point is, it's not hard. You can even call people if you want, arrange to meet. Sometimes it's the only way to socialize on the road. You should get onto it."

I think about that until my head starts to spin. Just how many friends had Phoebe made?

"You okay?" Lily asks.

"Yeah, I'm just . . ." *Overwhelmed. Incompetent. Confused.* "This all just feels like a lot."

"That's because it is." Lily says gently. "Especially for one person. But I can help."

"You really think someone might've been tracking her?"

She shrugs. "It's possible."

"How?"

"Oh, easy. A person's socials presence says heaps about who they are, right? Their tastes, personality, history, sense of humor, world view, it's all right there. And then you've got facial recognition, social mapping apps that correlate profiles across different platforms . . . like, it's super simple to find out where someone's been and predict where they're likely to go next, but you don't even have to do that if you just make friends. You just get their attention, fabricate some common ground, strike up a conversation, and away you . . ." Lily trails off, her brow furrowed.

"What?" I prompt.

Lily hesitates, then shakes her head. "I don't know. It's just a theory."

CHAPTER THIRTY-FOUR
Beth

After dinner they head back through the resort to the HiAce. Katy walks a few steps ahead, appearing and disappearing like a ghost as she passes through pools of lamplight. Beth hangs back, deep in thought.

It might be the same person who attacked you.

At first, Beth had dismissed the idea. *Not possible,* she wanted to say. *You have no idea what happened to me. How could you? I've been lying from the start.* But now . . .

She pushes the thought away. She couldn't even discuss the possibility without confessing the whole truth, and if Katy knew even half the extent of her deception that would be it, she'd be back out on her arse. The only option is to do exactly what Katy asks, play along, try to find Phoebe some other way. Then again, if there *is* a connection she needs to find out as soon as possible.

At least there are two of them on the job—although, thinking about it, Katy's likely to make things harder not easier. She's put a lot of effort into this mission to find her sister but her plan isn't exactly logical. Maybe she's on drugs. Beth hasn't seen any medication, but if Katy's taking something it might would explain why her thinking sometimes seems a little muddled, and why she's obsessed with poring over Instagram rather than gathering factual information.

For example, if Beth were in Katy's shoes, she'd start with police records; the case file might not be easily accessible but she could at least make an FOI request. She'd comb through the news reports, find the names of any witnesses or persons of interest. Then she'd cobble together a more comprehensive timeline and try to retrace Phoebe's steps from there—but instead of wasting time talking to random travelers who almost certainly weren't in the area last year, she'd go straight to hairdressers, bartenders, and pharmacists, the people in any local community who have their fingers on the pulse, the kind of people she and Lucas tended to avoid. She might approach local women's shelters and domestic violence support groups, because what if Phoebe is deliberately hiding because it's not safe for her to be found?

Another option would be to pay a hacker to get into Phoebe's private accounts: bank, phone, Medicare, Service NSW. She could target the true crime forums, see if the amateur sleuths had any interesting theories . . . and that's just the obvious stuff. There's so much on the internet, so much you can do with it as a tool to find people.

As Lucas knows all too well.

When they arrive back at the van, Beth sets up her bed then gathers her towel and toothbrush ready for a quick shower.

"I'd like you to stay," Katy says at her back.

Beth turns, caught off guard. "Huh?"

"For as long as you like. Free of charge. I'll pay for food, fuel, campsites, new clothes, whatever you need to get back on your feet."

Even though it's exactly what she wanted, Beth is overcome with a swell of guilt. "Oh, Katy . . . you don't have to. You've already done more than enough to help me."

Katy shakes her head. "We'd be helping each other. And if we find Phoebe, or proof of what happened to her, then I'll give you the van."

"You'll *what*?"

"Well, I won't need it anymore, will I? I'll have done what I came to do."

"Yeah, but . . . shit, Katy, are you for real?"

"Papers and everything."

Beth laughs. You don't just give away a campervan. The HiAce is worth thousands. Is Katy out of her mind? "You're joking, aren't you? This is a joke?"

"No." Katy looks mildly insulted. "I'm serious."

Slowly, Beth allows herself to consider the possibility. Owning the van would be like winning the lottery. More than that, it would be a get-out-of-jail-free card. She wouldn't have to steal again; she could travel freely and legitimately. Or she could sell it, put a deposit on a rental, get a real job. She could begin again. It's almost too much to contemplate.

"But what if we can't find her? What do we do then?"

Katy gives a small shrug. All her movements are small. "What have we got to lose?"

It's a fair point. Except for Katy herself, Beth has nothing to lose at all.

CHAPTER THIRTY-FIVE
Wyatt

The stone is off-white, oval-shaped, and about the size of an AirPod case. Wyatt turns it over and over in his palm, passing it from one hand to the other like a bar of soap.

For remembrance.

Taking his iPad from his desk, he opens the browser and types *stone for remembrance* into the search bar. The top results include a standardized design for war memorials, a quest item in a Japanese video game, and an array of engraved "memory ornaments" available to purchase from a Perth-based crematorium for the bargain price of $140. Wyatt's stone is similar but nowhere near as polished; it looks more like it's been plucked straight from the ground.

He also finds a local news article reporting the rise in popularity of rock cairns or rock towers across the state, saying that hikers are stopping along trails to build little stacks of stones traditionally used as navigational aids. "It's vandalism," one ranger is quoted to have said. "The disruption to the natural environment is potentially very damaging." Another website claims the stacks have nothing to do with navigation and are instead part of a local tradition. "It's how we remember our dead," says a Ningaloo resident. "Stones are placed at sacred locations to honor those we have lost."

He tries again, including words like *death, ritual,* and *witch,* but finds nothing more sinister than hippies promoting the use of crystals as grief support tools. Maybe it really was just a kindhearted gesture.

Outside, an engine growls in the driveway. Dad's home.

Peeking through the window, Wyatt watches as Dad parks up and gets out, red-faced and sweaty and covered in earth. The post-work routine is always the same: stretch and yawn, unload tools, take tools to the garage, grab beer from the fridge, take green waste to the tip—then it's home, dinner, bed, up again at sunrise. The bed of his ute is filled with trimmings, tree branches, and green sacks bursting with freshly cut grass. He looks exhausted. He's been on the job all day and Wyatt feels bad for him.

But then a different feeling seeps into his system like a gas leak. As Dad carries his tools across the grass, releases the padlock on the garage door, opens it up, and slips inside, it occurs to Wyatt that although Dad is in and out of that shed all day long (he never realized just how often until he was stuck at home for weeks with nothing to do), he always keeps that door locked, even bolts it when he's inside, and never asks Wyatt to help. In fact, Wyatt is amazed to find that he can't recall ever having been in there, not even as a child. It's always been Dad's space, his private sanctum, a place full of dangerous machinery and not in any way suitable for the eyes or the clumsy little bodies of children. That's always been the way, and he's never thought to question it.

Now though, he considers the garage, thinking about the Noises and the intensity with which Mrs. Creeping was staring at it when he found her in the yard the other day.

He waits for a minute or two, then gets to his feet, drops the stone into his pocket and makes his way through the kitchen to the back door. With its two murky windows, the garage seems to glare at him from across the lawn, and as he approaches he realizes that, as with the family photos, he's never really *seen* it; it's just one of those things that's always just been there.

He pauses, examining the stained walls, the ragged roof, the rickety drainpipe. It's just a shack, really. Needs a real fix-up. Stepping forward, he reaches for the door handle and—

He hears them. The Noises. Clear as anything.

Bumble tumble shuffle thud.

And just underneath, a soft whispering.

He edges closer. Voices. Two of them. Dad . . . and a woman.

Wyatt listens closely. It's Mrs. Creeping. She and Dad are inside the garage together, having a conversation: hushed and discreet. The words aren't clear but they seem to be—

The door flies open, and Wyatt jumps back.

"What the hell are you doing?" says Dad, bursting out and almost tripping over his son.

"Nothing. I—I was just . . . um . . . hungry."

Dad gives him a hard look. "So go get a snack."

"Right. Will do. Do you want one?"

That look again. "Nah, mate. Gotta go dump those cuttings before dark."

They stare at each other.

Without another word, Wyatt heads back toward the house but pauses at the screen door, one foot on the step, on hand on the frame. Behind him, Dad shuts the garage door and secures the padlock, then, with a final backward glance, he climbs into the ute and disappears back down the driveway.

Wyatt watches him go. Beyond the fence, Mrs. Creeping's house looms. The windows are dark, the doors all closed. There's no sign of her, or anyone else.

And though the light begins to fade and the afternoon air grows cold, Wyatt stays there for a long time, just standing in the doorway with his hand in his pocket, turning the white stone over and over between his fingers.

Liked by **daisyellajones006** and **others**

pheebsinwonderland Welcome to Yinggarda country! Subtropical and super friendly farming town Carnarvon is best known for its fruit and veg (the area provides 80% of WA's total crops) and has a lovely central waterway, several delightful cafes, an Aboriginal Heritage and Cultural Center and a very pretty cactus farm. The perfect place to stop, rest, and replenish supplies.

And rest, incidentally, is exactly what I need. I think I might be going through what I've heard other SFTs call a "dip"? Which is fine, that's life, and actually sometimes the down days are a good excuse to lay low and appreciate small wonders instead of big ones. Example: I took a spontaneous dip in the river yesterday. I was walking through town and there were all these kids splashing around having a ball, so I thought, why not? I had my swimmers on under my clothes so I stripped off and left my stuff on the grass. I was only gone for ten minutes but when I got back to shore someone had TAKEN MY CLOTHES. For real!! Not my bag, thank god, but still, who does that? Kids, I reckon. Anyway, there I was, dripping wet and half-naked in the middle of town, and this family came over and gave me a t-shirt so I could at least walk back through town to my van safely. How kind is that?? If you're reading this, lovely family, thank you and let me know your address so I can mail it back!

So, onward and upward. And don't worry, I'll be back to my usual cheery self once I've taken some time out.

(Image descriptions: 1. A pristine blue waterway shimmers beneath towering palm trees. 2. A woman in a straw hat wanders through an abundance of spiky cacti. 3. An enormous and slightly careworn satellite dish watches the sky like a giant eyeball. 4. A selfie of a happy woman about to go for a swim. 5. The outraged face of a dripping wet woman whose clothes have just been stolen. 6. The offending patch of grass that did not safeguard said clothes and has very little to say for itself.)

#vanlife #randomactsofkindness #mysaviors #clothesthief #notcool #givememydressback #solofemaletravel

View all 167 comments

dan_thevanman Love Carnarvon—did you check out the Space and Technology Museum? So good!

mavisgetsaroundabit That's messed up!! But what a delightful family—so sweet! And so #vanlife.

lonewanderer66 Oh dear, not the yellow dress I hope? You must've been terrified. What will they come for next?

goodnightpetergraham Totally okay to have a down day, happens all the time. Here if you need.

free_spirit1994 Sorry to hear, some people like to ruin everyone's fun. Love your photos, you're so inspiring.

30 May

CHAPTER THIRTY-SIX

Katy

The café's wicker chairs are not deep or comfortable but my body seems to think it's in a king-size bed; my spine has turned to jelly and I'm struggling to keep my eyes open.

I watch through the window as the small town of Carnarvon goes about its business. Across the road and to the right is a playground and public toilets. To the left, a terraced sandstone promenade. People amble along the palm-lined waterway, eating ice cream and snapping pictures of the war memorial. I imagine Phoebe among them, peeling off her dress, stepping over the grass and into the water. I see her emerging, dripping wet, to find her clothes gone. I picture Sunglasses Man slipping away from the scene, a ball of yellow material in his hands. The image is so real, I almost stand up and give chase.

A waitress sets a flat white on the table, my second since I arrived, and looks pointedly at the empty chair opposite. "Can I get you anything else?"

"No, thank you." I stifle a yawn. "My friend has gone shopping. She'll be back soon. I'm sure she'll order something then."

Unlike me, Lily left Shark Bay feeling refreshed. I insisted on taking a turn in the front seat last night (another reason why I didn't sleep) so she could try the bed, and this morning she has a whole new energy: very perky and motivated. She played music all the way here, singing along to artists I've never heard of, bands with names like Dulcie, Vallis Alps, Youmi Zuma, and the Japanese House. When we arrived, I gave her some cash to buy some new clothes and she skipped away like she was off to grandma's cottage. She said she wouldn't be long, but it's been half an hour already and she's still not back.

I sip my coffee. The café is quiet but not completely empty. Besides me, there's an elderly couple at the back and a man in a high-vis vest waiting for a takeaway. At one of the tables outside, a pregnant woman tries unsuccessfully to feed a sandwich to a little girl in a yellow T-shirt. The little girl is climbing on her chair and banging the tabletop with a spoon.

It's an odd place: part coffee shop, and apparently part tourist information office. The walls are covered with hand-painted signposts pointing in different directions—PERTH, 893KM. BROOME, 1460KM. ALICE SPRINGS, 2873KM. SYDNEY, 4690KM—and posters advertising whale watching cruises and the weekly growers market. Any spare space is taken up by display racks packed with flyers, a selection of which I've fanned out on the table in front of me, along with the note-slash-news-article I found in Kalbarri. I've reread it three times now but still can't make sense of it.

Minutes slide by. Lily is still not back.

At the table outside, the little girl in the yellow T-shirt has finished banging her spoon on the table and is now crawling around under the table. The pregnant lady, presumably her mother, is making a case that it's time to leave. I can hear them arguing through the open door.

"No," the girl whines. "I don't want to go. I made a friend."

I watch the tussle with mild interest. I wonder if I'll ever have kids. My clock is ticking; isn't that what they say? Having babies is what women are supposed to do. *Stuff that,* Phoebe used to say, *I'm never having kids, looks like a death sentence to me.* But I'm on the fence. What else am I going to do with my life?

"But Mum, it's lonely," the little girl is saying. She has now emerged from under the table and is holding something in her hands. "It wants to come home with us. Please?"

The mother peers into her daughter's palms. "Sweetie, no. Grasshoppers don't live in houses."

My skin prickles.

"Come on. Put it back, time to go home."

"Won't. It's my friend."

I'm catapulted into the past. Summer days. Dirty knees and ice creams.

Honey, no, they're meant to live outside.

Please? She can live in my room. I'll look after her. She wants to eat cake.

They don't eat cake, silly billy. They eat leaves and seeds. See how it even looks like a leaf? That's called camouflage.

But—

"Hey." Lily flops into the empty chair opposite and places two bulging paper bags on the floor. "I'm sorry I took so long. I went to Coles for underwear and toiletries, and then the place on the corner actually had some really nice stuff."

"That's okay."

When I look back outside, the mother has won the standoff. The little girl is carefully placing the insect back where she found it.

"Did you get what you need?"

"Yes, thanks. Shorts, two shirts, and a pair of thongs." She hands me the change.

"That's it?" I flick through the notes. She's only used half of what I gave her. "You didn't want anything else?"

"Well, I didn't want to spend it *all*. It wouldn't have felt right."

I reach across the table and place the money in front of her. "Keep it. You need it more than I do."

She hesitates, a bunch of expressions passing over her face. Then pockets the notes. "Thank you."

The waitress returns and she orders a juice. "Found anything useful?" she asks, pointing at the flyers.

I sigh. "Not really. I googled the headline but all I got were mentions of some movie from 2008 and an album by someone I've never heard of. The by-line brought up a few pieces about suspected serial murderers in Perth, one in Claremont in the mid-'90s and another in Willagee in 1986. There was something up in the Northern Territory near the WA border around 1987, but nothing near Ningaloo or the Coral Coast."

"What about the woman mentioned by name. Vivan someone?"

"Vivi Green. Last seen in the Ningaloo area. It's weird, the name feels familiar but I don't know why." I search her up on my phone again and show Lily what I discovered. "She was a massage therapist, yoga teacher, and permanent vanlifer who was on her way to Ningaloo in February of this year. Says here that she vanished just days after texting a friend that she was looking for a job. The text was sent from a short way north of Carnarvon, and then her phone pinged off a tower somewhere northeast of Lake McLeod."

"That's south of Exmouth, right?"

"About two hundred kilometers. No one has heard from or seen her since. Or her van for that matter."

Lily looks at me but says nothing. She doesn't have to; I know what she's thinking. *No van. No suspects. No trace.* Just like her. Just like Phoebe.

"The estimated date of her disappearance," I continue, still reading from the screen, "is February fourteenth."

"Four months ago."

"Vivi's family are still looking for her . . . there's a GoFundMe campaign, a Facebook page." I scroll through the posts and comments. "Listen to this. *She's been known to drop off the grid occasionally, but it's not like her to just disappear . . . She loved her independence, but she always checked in.*" Without my own Facebook account I can't post anything or privately message the admin, but I bookmark the page anyway. Maybe Lily's right and it's time to get over my fear of social media.

Lily and I read the article again. *Fruit picker stabbed. Single mother held captive. Backpacker killed.* All true stories, Google tells us, but none of them took place here in WA.

Putting the phone down, I pick up my coffee and a flyer comes with it, stuck to the bottom of the cup. I pluck it off and am about to drop it back on the table when my heart stills.

"What?" says Lily, immediately alert.

I turn the pamphlet over. "Marine Paradise Awaits," the front cover announces in curly yellow font. The main picture—shimmering turquoise water lapping at a white sandy beach—is overlaid by two smaller photos. The first is a scuba diver swimming with a whale shark. The second is a sweeping metal sculpture.

"Oh my god."

Lily gets up from her seat and comes around to look over my shoulder.

I point at the sculpture. It's rendered in ribbons of shining steel and mounted on a sandstone plinth. Quickly, I grab my phone and find the image of Phoebe, the one from her final post. I turn the screen around so Lily can see the mirrored lenses of her sunglasses. "See the reflection?" I zoom in, then point again at the flyer. "It's the same thing, isn't it?"

She leans closer. "It's hard to say. I think so. What is it?"

I'm not sure. It looks like it could be some kind of large fish, body curved in a c-shape, head up, tail down. I think I see fins, and a wide boxy head. I open out the flyer and scan the text boxes. *Commissioned by the Australian Marine Conservation Society and inspired by grassroots initiatives to protect Ningaloo from industrialization, this stunning 18-foot stainless-steel sculpture known to locals as "Gracie" is said to be one of the most beautiful pieces of public art in the world.*

"Where is this?" I say.

"Gracious Bay," Lily reads. "Or just outside. It's a small fishing town on the Ningaloo reef just north of Lake McLeod."

I let go of the flyer and it flutters to the table. The shape reflected in Phoebe's glasses and the sculpture on the flyer are the same. Which very likely means that Phoebe was not on her way out to Karijini the day she disappeared but was in fact on the road in or out of Gracious Bay.

"Holy shit," whispers Lily, almost to herself.

I nod. Once again, I don't need to ask what she's thinking. Vivi Green's last known location. *Ningaloo. Lake McLeod. Gracious Bay.*

But for me though, it also means something else. It means I've had it all wrong from the start. When Phoebe vanished, she was not where anyone thought she was. The police, Dust, even me . . . we've all been looking in the wrong place.

CHAPTER THIRTY-SEVEN

Beth

Beth excuses herself and goes to the bathroom, following the waitress's directions out of the café and around the corner to the facilities shared by all the businesses in the precinct. Bolting herself into one of the stalls, she flips the toilet seat down, dumps her shopping bags on top, and unfolds the flyer she just swiped from the table.

Gracious Bay.

Her skin tingles. She scans the other pictures and text boxes, skimming through information about local hiking trails, lookouts, the backpackers hostel, and the franchised holiday park. On a simple map of the town center she finds the words "beach," "pub," and "boat ramp." Common enough words for a coastal town. But then on the back page, she reads about a 116-tonne schooner wrecked off the reef in 1869. According to a sepia photograph and the caption below, the ship was named the "Eleanor" after the owner's wife, whose spirit is said to haunt the area.

A chill slides down her spine.

A piece-of-shit holiday town . . . A dumb shipwreck and a statue of a whale . . . One hundred and fifty years later you can still see her ghost wandering around by the water, looking for more people to kill.

The realization hits her like a migraine.

Gracious Bay is Lucas's hometown.

That's where he's from, where he grew up, where his family lives.

And unless Katy changes her mind completely, that's where she and Beth will now be heading.

Closing her eyes against a barrage of memories, she sags backward against the door.

Lucas stands at the bowser, filling the tank and scanning the forecourt.

Beth watches him in the wing mirror. In his singlet and boardies, he looks just like every other Aussie road-tripper, but behind his high-end sunnies (stolen, obviously) his eyes are everywhere. They both know the roadhouse well but, as Lucas is constantly reminding her, it's important to stay alert. Also inconspicuous. Get in and out, quickly and quietly.

He taps on his phone as he waits for the car to fill. He's so busy, so distracted, always thinking ahead, forging plans, searching for their next mark, scrolling, scrolling, scrolling, working out where to go next, always moving, never slowing, never even coming close to putting down roots. That hadn't always been the plan. When they first met, she'd been waitressing at a seafood joint just outside of Perth; he walked in and ordered a lobster roll and that had been it: thunder, lightning, the works. She'd handed in her notice just a few days later on the proviso that they would apply together for "proper" jobs. But then Lucas changed his mind. He didn't want to work for The Man. He wanted to be master of his own destiny. Hers too, apparently.

"Fuck." Lucas's voice is muffled through the glass.

She cracks the window.

"Just checked the account," he hisses through the gap, "and there's shit all in it. We should've got heaps more for that last drop." He bangs a fist against the door.

Beth flinches. "Can you talk to them?" Not that she has any real idea who "they" are.

He answers by shoving cash in her face. "Go pay for the fuel." The bank notes sail into her lap like paper planes.

Inside, the shop area is busy. She waits in line at the checkout, hands over the money, then wanders around, browsing the souvenirs and picking up snacks, stalling for time. She can't face going back outside, not yet. The sound of Lucas's fist on the Troopy's door is still ringing in her ears. She's used to these bursts of aggression now, but they still shake her up. Not quite in the same way as they had the first few times, but still.

After the very first blow, a mighty crack to her right cheekbone that sent her flying into a table, she'd reeled for weeks, swinging back and forth between rage and self-pity, fear and disbelief, until finally landing on compassion. He'd sobbed afterward—what's wrong with me, why did I do that, I'm so fucked up—so hard that she'd ended up comforting him. "It's not that bad," she cooed, "it was an accident, look, the bruise is fading already." He promised he'd never do it again, convinced her it was a one-off. But then it happened again. And again.

Of course she'd tried to leave, walked away from a campground while he was taking a shower, all the way to the main road and beyond. She'd even got as far as the highway, but then the truckie who offered her a ride jammed his hand up her skirt, so she'd had to run away again, at which point she realized she had absolutely nowhere to go, no money, and no means, and if she ran any farther she'd probably end up dead. So she'd turned around and started walking back. A short while later, the Troopy had pulled up beside her and that had been that. She hadn't tried it again.

She stays in the roadhouse as long as she can before heading back outside.

"Are you going to pay for those?" says a harsh voice behind her.

She turns around to see a man in a red polo shirt, the roadhouse logo embroidered on the pocket. "I'm sorry?"

"Those." He nods at her hands. "I didn't see you pay."

She looks down. In her arms were the snacks she'd picked up while "browsing." She hadn't meant to take them; she hadn't even meant to buy them. "Oh," she says, "I'm so sorry, I was miles away. I hadn't even realized."

"Heard that before," says the man flatly. "I'm gonna need you to come on back inside so we can—"

Beth panics. "No, you don't understand. I really didn't mean to take these."

"Just step back into the shop—"

"I just forgot. Really, I would never steal anything . . ." The lie stings more than any other she's ever told. *Fuck, Lucas will be so mad.*

"Look love, I really don't have time for this." The man takes her elbow.

Beth pulls away. *"No, you don't get it—"* Please don't hate me, *she thinks, trying to telepathically push the words into the man's head. This isn't who I am.*

"If you don't come back inside, I'll have to call the police."

"Please, I—"

"Sorry, is there a problem here?" Suddenly Lucas is at her side, his hand on her back.

"The problem," the man says crossly, *"is that this woman is trying to steal from me."*

"No," Beth moans. *"No, I would never."*

"I'm so sorry." Lucas is calm and smooth. *"It's my fault. My wife isn't well and I shouldn't have let her come in on her own. Of course we'll pay for the items."* He takes Beth's elbow in what to anyone else would seem like a gesture of support. *"Come on, Samantha, let's go back inside and get this all sorted out."*

The manager softens. *"It's fine. Just give them back and we'll call it quits."*

"No, no, I insist."

Returning to the Troopy with the cookies and Lucas's hand clamped around her arm, Beth's legs feel like jelly. *That had been close. Too close. She'd been so stupid.*

Lucas opens the passenger door and she climbs in. Silently, he walks around to the driver's side and gets behind the wheel. There's a pause while he revs the engine.

"What the fuck is wrong with you?" Lucas spits. *"You could've fucked everything up."*

Beth sinks further into her seat. *It's true, she could have. But she didn't. And now she'll have to pay the price.*

Outside the stall, there's a squeak followed by a loud bang.

Startled, Beth clutches the flyer to her chest. The bathroom door. Someone has just walked in. She presses herself to the very back of the stall and holds her breath.

Shoes slide over floor tiles. The footsteps are heavy and slow. They seem to be approaching Beth's stall. They get closer and closer. Then they stop.

She looks down. Under the door, she can see the shadow of the person's shoes. She can hear them breathing. She eyes the lock on the door, assesses its strength.

Seconds turn into minutes.

The shoe-shadows move. The footsteps start up again. One of the taps is turned on. It runs for a long time, then stops. *Shuffle, shuffle, shuffle.* The main door squeaks again, then shuts with another bang.

Silence.

Pulse rattling like a high-speed train over unstable tracks, Beth sits down hard on the toilet. *I can't do this anymore.* No one can live this way forever, always on edge, never feeling safe, always waiting for the other shoe to drop. She needs to get out of the state, go to Queensland or back to New South Wales, get as far as possible. *I need that van.* The sooner she can give Katy some answers, the quicker this will all be over.

Breathe, she tells herself. *You know what to do. You'll survive. You always do.*

Folding the flyer into a small square, she drops it into her pink shopping bag, flushes the toilet, and—cautiously, vigilantly—leaves the bathroom.

CHAPTER THIRTY-EIGHT

Wyatt

Bursts of laughter fly from the kitchen and bounce from room to room, mixing with a soft pulse of music and the smell of Dad's "famous" chilli crab spaghetti. It doesn't happen often, Dad hardly ever brings women back to the house, but he must really like this one because she's been here twice this week and he's been much less cranky as a result.

Wyatt sits in his bedroom with a pounding headache, trying not to listen. She seems okay, this woman, but she won't stick around no matter how hard Dad tries to persuade her. They never do. The town is always full of blow-ins; some stay just for a day, others for weeks or months, but the carousel is always turning. But the only other option as Wyatt understands it is to date someone else who grew up here and that, as Dad says, would be like going out with your cousin.

It doesn't matter anyway; Wyatt's not interested in Dad's love life. What he really wants to know is what's in the garage.

When the laughter fades a little and Fleetwood Mac is replaced by the sound of the TV, Wyatt cracks his door and peeks out into the hall. Dad and his date have moved into the living room; the coast is clear. He pops another couple of acetaminophen and washes them down with water, then slips from the bedroom and tiptoes through the chilli crab stink of the kitchen, out the back door, and into the darkened yard.

It's sticky out tonight. The moon is newly waxing and the cicadas are raucous. Wishing he had his phone (it's still on the bookshelf in the living room, he remembers with a flush of shame, currently recording a whole bunch of stuff he really doesn't want to see, and which would get him into a whole heap of shit if Dad found out), Wyatt approaches the garage as stealthily as he can manage, squinting into the gloom to find the door. He feels for the handle, then the bolt and the padlock, but no matter how hard he tugs and yanks, the lock holds fast and the door remains shut.

With lock-picking (no idea) and ramming (how, and with what?) firmly out of the question, he circles around the back, searching for another way in. But because the garage shares a wall with Mrs. Creeping's own shed and sits astride both their properties, there's only so far he can go before the fence cuts him off. Checking quickly that Dad is still otherwise occupied, he tries the cobwebbed windows—but predictably they too are locked. He could smash one, he supposes, but Dad's wrath wouldn't be worth it. Instead, he wipes the dirt away with his sleeve and presses his face to the glass.

He can't see much, just darkness and shelves, tools and gardening equipment, but it's enough to confirm that despite his vague theories of monsters and vampires and captive axe murderers, the garage is in fact empty. There is something though, sticking up from the ground. It's way too dark to say for sure, but Wyatt thinks it looks like a stick or a stake, or one of those tennis pole things with the ball on a string.

Unable to glean anything more illuminating though, he gives up and heads back to the house.

As he's returning to his room he bumps into Dad on his way back from the bathroom.

"Hey, mate," Dad says, grinning widely. "You right in there? Got everything you need?" His skin is flushed, his eyes glassy, and there's a smudge of sauce on his chin.

Suddenly disgusted, Wyatt gives him the stink eye. "Oh, yeah, fine thanks. Having a bloody ball, aren't I?"

He whirls around and is about to slam his door when Dad stops it with his foot. "Mate," he says, cajolingly. "Don't be like that. She's all right you know."

Wyatt looks up at him, some fierce but unidentifiable emotion burning inside him. "Tell me something about Mum," he blurts. "Right now. Please?"

"Oh." Dad's face falls. "Oh, mate. Where's this coming from?"

"I don't want to forget her," Wyatt says, then immediately regrets it. Why does he have to say shit like this out loud?

Dad leans against the doorway and sighs. "Okay, let's see . . . well, I guess one of the main things was that your mother loved nature. Remember? It was one of my favorite things about her. My idea of a good day was a couple of beers in front of the footy, but she was always wanting to go hiking and swimming and whatnot. She loved that lighthouse—what's it called, the one just north of Exmouth?"

"Vlamingh."

"That's it. She saw the beauty of life and wanted you and Lucas to experience everything it has to offer. To her, the world was a great big dessert and she wanted to eat it all."

To Wyatt's surprise, Dad's eyes fill with tears. It's the most bizarre, electrifying thing. Never, not once, has he seen his father cry.

"You once told me she was crazy," he says.

"Did I?"

"Yeah. Psycho, you said."

Dad shifts his weight. "Well, I mean, she had her issues for sure. But that wasn't the only thing about her, you know? She was also smart and funny and she loved you kids like mad. Lots of things can be true about a person at once. Okay?"

Wyatt nods. "Okay."

"All right."

Dad lumbers away, and Wyatt returns to his room. But instead of feeling better, or at least reassured, he feels worse. Angrier, and full of dark thoughts.

Shaking with tension, he listens through the wall as Dad and his date bring their plates back to the kitchen. *She's all right you know.* He hears the clink of cutlery on crockery and imagines running back out there and stabbing the bitch in the eye with a fork. He sees the prongs entering her eyeball, the blood hitting the splashback, the holes that would be left in her head. It's strange, but the images seem so real.

Liked by **lonewanderer66** and **others**

pheebsinwonderland Day 16 and I am in love with the Quobba
Coast. A lot of people bypass this detour just north of Carnarvon
but they shouldn't because this magical place is definitely worth
the effort. About 30 mins drive from the main highway you'll find
an incredible stretch of rust-colored cliffs and an area called the
"blowholes" where jets of white spray shoot into the air as powerful swells are forced through sea caves (best seen as the tide
is coming in). And don't miss the Aquarium, a protected area
of shallow water perfect for snorkeling, or the beautiful campground—a travel community favorite.

On a separate note, I just want to say thanks to the mostly wonderful Insta travel community for all your support. I get some
pretty wild messages on here, some of which I REALLY don't appreciate, and it's nice to know I'm not alone. However I think we
need to be more aware of the language we use around solo female
travel, e.g., comments like "you must be so scared," or "you're so
strong to travel alone" or even "be careful." The intention is sweet
but it's like a self-fulfilling prophecy: the more we tell ourselves
we're unsafe, the more we'll believe it.

Thank you again to y'all offering support and encouragement, you
really keep my spirits up! Love and peace.

> (Image descriptions: 1. A woman stands with her arms
> raised on a road under an enormous sign that says KING
> WAVES KILL. Behind her is bone white sand, dry seagrass
> and a strip of sparkling ocean. 2. A 15m (ish?) jet of wa-
> ter erupts from within a slab of limestone and bursts into
> the sky. 3. A majestic stretch of rough limestone cliffs
> are pounded by relentless waves. 4. A view of a crystal

clear and perfectly calm lagoon as seen through the open back of a campervan. 5. A woman floats on her back in said lagoon with her arms outstretched. Beneath her, coral, shells, and fish are clearly visible. She is in heaven.)

#quobbablowholes #pointquobba #theaquarium #coralcoast #solofemaletravel #vanlife #doesntgetmuchbetter

View all 121 comments

eloiseisalive85 YES! The predator/prey narrative is so ingrained that violence against women feels natural, almost expected. But change only happens when we refuse to accept the unacceptable.

lonewanderer66 Think I saw you on the beach today, was it you? Check your DMs.

r8chelm8rix First world problems mate. Check your privilege.

dollymollymandy I'm confused. It's good to be careful, right? Especially when it comes to men, they're just so much bigger and stronger. We have to protect ourselves as best we can.

goodnightpetergraham 👏 You're amazing. Enjoy those blowholes.

1 June

CHAPTER THIRTY-NINE

Katy

At the end of a long tarmac road edged with orange sand and sparse vegetation we are met by a T junction and the *KING WAVES KILL* sign. Turning left, I follow the signs to the campground.

Lily winds down her window. There are the limestone cliffs, just as Phoebe described. And there are the jets of water, forced upward through the caves. The Aquarium is just as clear and pretty as in her photos, but I can't muster any interest. It's hard enough just keep my eyes open. The last two nights have been uneventful—no footsteps, no stones, no new gifts left anywhere nearby—but still I can't sleep. A part of me wonders if we might finally have shaken the stalker (perhaps Lily was right and whoever it is wouldn't dare follow us into somewhere as secure as the resort) but I'm too preoccupied with Phoebe to give it much thought. The sculpture plays constantly on my mind. I've called Dust another three times but no joy. I can't wait to tell him he's had it wrong this whole time.

We reach the campground. Wide, flat, and perched right on the edge of the ocean, it's pretty desolate. No power, water, or facilities—just sand, cliffs, and turquoise water. And ancient-looking fishing shacks, dotted among the sites, their corrugated walls decorated with sun-bleached animal skulls.

I choose what I assume is an empty pitch—a swept patch of ground with a view of the Aquarium—and get out of the van. I count the hand-ful of other vehicles: gigantic shining trailers, boxy motorhomes, four-wheel drives, and vintage campers. I clock their positions. I check out the trailer on the neighboring pitch, a long complicated-looking thing with all sorts of extensions popping off the sides like tumors. The owners, a family of five, are getting ready to go snorkeling. I eye them with suspi-cion, waiting for them to eye me back, but they're too busy to notice us.

Looking out at the infinite expanse of blue, the gently curving hori-zon meeting nothing but limestone at each end of the headland, I feel simultaneously safe and extremely unsafe. We are right at the edge of the world. No one could find us here, not even if we wanted them to.

Around lunchtime, a fat plate of cloud rolls across the sky and provides some relief from the heat. I open up the back of the van and lie on the bed, listening to the distant thump and crash of the waves while cursing and checking my phone for signal. One bar of 4G is not going to cut it.

I make sure to keep an eye on Lily, too, as she explores the site. Oc-casionally she slips out of view behind a van or a small tree and I grow anxious until she reappears.

"Here's a conundrum," she says when she returns. "No toilets." She stands chewing her lip for a minute or two, then turns on her heel and heads for the trailer next door. Lying low, I watch with alternate stabs of anxiety and envy as she approaches the snorkel family—both adults leggy and bronzed, their three children like little golden-haired fairies—and strikes up a conversation, endearing herself immediately with laugh-ter and goofy gestures.

Twenty minutes later, she's back, triumphantly waving a strip of pa-per. "Next door have a 4G power pack with a signal-boosting antenna. They gave me the code so we can use their Wi-Fi."

I sit up. "Seriously?"

"Even better," she adds with a wry smile. "They have a portable toilet with a privacy shelter, and we can use that too."

CHAPTER FORTY

Beth

Beth snoozes outside in one of the camp chairs. It's warm but not hot, breezy but not windy. The lull of the ocean and the occasional *whooomph* of the blowholes is sending her to sleep. Three nights now with no major events, and her body seems to have interpreted that as a sign she can take a breather. All she wants to do is nap and swim, nap and swim.

"What am I looking for again?" Katy calls from inside the van. She's been lying on the bed for an hour now—clearly her body also got the memo—but now she's back to scrolling through Phoebe's Instagram.

"Anyone who pops up a lot," Beth replies sleepily, "whose tone might be more intimate or who's gunning hard for camaraderie. Basically someone who might be trying to win Phoebe's trust."

There's a pause. "How about this guy? @lonewanderer66."

Yawning, Beth pushes herself out of the camp chair and heads into the van. "Scoot over." She slumps down on the bed next to Katy, who points at the screen.

"See? He comments on almost every single post."

"Uh-huh." The user's display image is a sunrise. They scroll through, checking each comment. *"Your photos are beautiful, do you sell prints?"* *"Your content makes me want to travel. Where are you heading next?"* *"I'm*

booking a trip around WA. Maybe we could meet?" "Sounds like they connected, maybe made some plans."

But as they continue to read, the comments get a little strange. "*WA
is even more amazing than I expected, but I have questions, check your
DMs . . .*" "*you know that safety is an illusion, don't you? If someone really
wants to get to you, they will . . .*" "*Anyone ever tell you it's rude to ignore
people?? I'm not sure you're as nice as you make yourself out to be.*"

"Wow," Beth says. "Bingo." Inside, her mind races. *lonewanderer66.*
It doesn't sound like a handle that Lucas would use; he'd be more likely
to choose something benign and approachable. Then again, she's never
been party to all his online interactions. He could have all sorts of account names she doesn't know about.

"Okay," she says, "I'd definitely start there. Check his profile, his bio.
How many followers does he have, how active is he, do they have any
mutual friends, what was his latest post? And then, depending on what
you find, maybe flick him a message, ask some questions."

Katy nods wearily and rubs her eyes.

"It's so weird that they never found her van," Beth says, standing up
to get a drink. "Access to her belongings would make things so much
easier." She grabs a fresh bottle of water from the fridge, screws off the
cap, and takes a gulp. "DNA, obviously. Receipts can tell you a lot. There
are always secrets stuffed inside toiletry bags. And her phone. That would
obviously have been ideal." She drinks again. The water is deliciously
cold. "Do you have anything on yours?"

Katy looks up. "Like what?"

"Well, like anything from Phoebe, either before she left or during the
trip. Emails, texts, updates from the road."

Katy looks away again. "Phoebe was a caller. She didn't do texts."

"Right." Unlikely, Beth thinks, but not impossible. Some people are
like that; they travel to avoid contact with the wider world. Any messages
they do send are brief and perfunctory, they post missives and write blogs
so they don't have to answer questions or repeat themselves a hundred

times, and if Phoebe had indeed ghosted Katy as an adult then it makes sense that she wouldn't have heard from her.

"She would've reached out if she was in trouble though, right? You mentioned that she was always making mistakes and you had to bail her out. That doesn't sound like someone who solves her own problems."

Katy exhales slowly. "I guess not."

"So, have you spoken to her friends?"

Katy nods.

"And they couldn't help?"

Head shake.

"Did the cops look through her emails?

"I don't *know*," Katy suddenly yells, "they won't *speak* to me."

Beth's eyes widen. *O-kaaay.*

There's an awkward pause, then: "Sorry." Katy leans forward over the table and massages her temples. "I shouldn't take it out on you. It's just that I've been calling and calling, trying to get the answers to some of these questions, but the lead detective refuses to answer. He actually told me to stop *harassing* him. So I don't know what they did or didn't do."

Beth nods. It doesn't strike her as normal for investigators to freeze out family members after a case is closed, but what does she know? "Just a thought, but have *you* tried breaking in?"

Katy looks stunned. "Into what?"

"Phoebe's emails. Her socials accounts. If you can guess her Insta password you'll have access to all her private messages. You could see exactly who she was talking to."

"Maybe." Looking like she needs a couple of matchsticks to prop her eyes open, Katy picks her phone up again. The flat light from the screen makes her face look even more pale and drawn than it already is.

Beth leaves her to it. For someone who claims to be desperate, Katy doesn't seem to be trying very hard. Then again, sometimes all it takes is a fresh pair of eyes. It's a fact of life that the longer you live with something, the harder it is to see.

CHAPTER FORTY-ONE
Katy

"I have an idea," I say as Lily and I wade through the shallows of the lagoon on our way back to the van.

We've been for a walk to the blowholes, sat on sun-warmed rocks overlooking the vast spread of ocean and watched as waves pummeled the cliffs, and the experience has done something to me. I can't explain exactly, but as the surf crashed and salt water burst from the ground like roman candles, spraying us with cool droplets, I had a brief moment of *something;* comfort, or a sense of return, almost as if I'd lain back down in my childhood bed after spending decades away from home. I felt small too, dwarfed by the size of the sky and the rock and the water. I placed my hand on the ground beneath me and felt . . . I'm not sure. Magic, or the next best thing. For the first time, I could glimpse a little of what Phoebe loved about this life, and it filled me with energy and hope.

"Tell me," says Lily.

"Well, I listened to this book a while back. About hypnotherapy? And I've been thinking, I don't know, maybe we could try it?"

She shoots me a look. "You want to try hypnosis."

"Kind of." I feel embarrassed now, but I keep going. "I just think it's worth a go. You know, to help you remember what happened."

She's quiet. I brace myself for laughter, or flat-out rejection—and fair enough. I'm not an expert; I'm not even trained. But then she shrugs. "Why not?" she says. "Can't hurt."

I shouldn't have been surprised. We're on the same page, Lily and me. We're in this together.

"Just relax." I say, making my voice as soft as possible. "Clear your mind and allow it to wander."

We're in the van. Lily is lying on the bed with a pillow under her knees and her eyes closed.

"Take a few deep breaths. I'm going to count back from ten, and when I reach one you're going to be back in your old van, trying to find that sundial. Okay?"

Lily nods, her face peaceful.

"Ten . . . nine . . . eight . . ."

I glance outside. It's cloudy again. A few drops of rain spatter against the glass, the first of the trip.

". . . seven . . . six . . . five . . ."

Lily takes another breath.

". . . four . . . three . . . two . . . one. Okay. You're in your van, looking for the sundial. Tell me what you see."

"The steering wheel." Lily's voice is dreamy, her face completely blank. "The windscreen."

"What's outside?"

"Black sky. Dark night. Dirt track."

Another surge of energy. She's in it. She's back in the past. *This is going to work.* "Do you know where you are?"

"No. I'm lost. I need to pull over."

"Okay, go ahead." I pause. "Are you stopped now?"

"Yes."

"What can you see now?"

She swallows. "Not much. A track. Bushland."

"Nothing else?"

"No."

"Can you hear anything?"

"Yes."

"What is it?"

She pauses. "Stones."

My heartbeats faster. "Is someone coming?"

"Yes."

"Are they close?"

"Yes, but . . ."

"But what?"

Lily's expression shifts. She frowns as if concentrating. "Sorry, I—"

"Stay with it."

She stills and falls quiet. I hold my breath, worried she's breaking her trance. *Please,* I want to say, *we're nearly there, we're so close.* I watch her face. *Come on, you can do it.* She's quiet for a long time. But then her breathing changes. Her chest bounces with rapid inhalations, and a tear slides from one eye.

I lean forward, my own breath catching. Something is happening.

CHAPTER FORTY-TWO

Beth

When Katy first suggests some "therapy" in an attempt to unearth the "hidden memory" of her attack, Beth very nearly giggles. *What do you think this is*, she wants to say, *a slumber party?* Was she about to pull out a Ouija board too, play "light as a feather, stiff as a board"?

And Katy's a schoolteacher anyway, what does she know about therapy? All that woo-woo stuff—hypnosis, past-life regression, guided imagery—it's mostly a crock of shit. Researchers had once believed that the brain worked a bit like a filing cabinet: all a person had to do to recall a forgotten event was find the right file. But recent studies have proved that the process is actually more creative, more reconstructive—and therapeutic hypnosis is problematic in that remembered information can be distorted and even "falsified." But Katy is keen as a bean, and convinced that the technique will work, so Beth has no choice but to play along.

When they arrive back at the van, she does as she's told and lies down. She sinks into the mattress as Katy begins her countdown. At first it's not so bad. She acts a little scared, authenticates her performance with what she knows of trauma and PTSD. She raises the pitch of her voice and inserts a little tremor. A part of her even enjoys it. But because Katy has no idea what she's doing it's like playing Let's Pretend with a five-year-old: no real plan or technique, just the same basic questions over and over.

"Your mind has blocked out the trauma," Katy keeps saying. "But it's still there. We just have to find the place where it's hidden." *That's literally what I told you yesterday*, Beth wants to reply. *Stop parroting me.* But she doesn't. She just relaxes and waits for it to be over.

But then something happens. As Katy's words swirl around her, she finds herself sinking. It feels like she's falling. The ground opens up . . . and suddenly, horrifyingly, she's back there, in the Troopy, trapped beneath a crushing weight of fake IDs, fuel pumps, cash, and cookies, choking on the horror of what happened next.

"You stupid, stupid bitch. What were you thinking?"

Lucas is yelling. Has been for a while now. Beth had hoped he might run out of steam by now, but the more he yells the angrier he seems to get.

"Were you trying to get caught on purpose? Or did you actually think, after everything I've taught you, that it was a smart fucking thing to do?"

She stares blankly out the window. The land rolls like an endless black sea, the sky above a charcoal chasm. Stars wink in the gaps between smoky clouds. Fly, Beth, fly.

"I told you to pay for the fuel, not go shopping for snacks." His eyes are all over the place; he's wired, like he's high, and who knows, maybe he is. "And cookies? What are you, eight?"

"I was hungry," Beth heard herself say.

"Hungry?" Lucas barked out a single mirthless laugh. "We're both hungry, Beth, that's why we work. To get money so we can eat more than just fucking cookies."

What we do isn't work, *she very nearly says but doesn't. Better to stay quiet, wait for the storm to pass. He'll calm down eventually, apologize, give her the usual story about how it's not his fault, his mother left and it messed him up, blah blah, poor broken boy, just needs someone to love him, understand him, take care of him. They'll make up and everything will be all right for another couple of days until it isn't again. And then they'll go round and round like a record on loop, playing the same sad song over and over until the end of time.*

"How can I trust you after this?" His voice is getting louder. He's driving too fast. "How can I be sure you won't do it again?"

Beth tries to tune out, focus on other things. There's a faint repetitive buzzing coming from Lucas's pocket: someone is calling over and over. On the road ahead, two gleaming red eyes: the taillights of a campervan, cruising below the speed limit.

Lucas speeds up even more. "I thought you understood the rules. I thought we wanted the same things. I thought we were good together." He shoots her a look, expecting a response. When she doesn't give it, he yanks the wheel sharply and they swerve over the white line into the oncoming lane.

Beth gasps and her hand flies to the door.

"Look at me."

She doesn't. Can't. They're getting closer to the camper. "Lucas," she murmurs. "Slow down."

He swerves again and again, enjoying himself. And is it just her imagination or is Lucas leaning forward in his seat now, eyes fixed on the camper. Is he chasing it?

"Lucas," she says again. They're right behind now, dangerously near. If the camper stops suddenly, they'll collide for sure—and as if to prove the point the camper brakes, just a little. "They're letting you pass. Just go around."

Ignoring her, he urges the Troopy on until its bumper is within kissing distance of the camper's. His mouth is a grim tight line, his jaw set. It's as if he has some issue with the van, like the driver is the source of all his problems—but Beth knows it's her, she's the problem, and if Lucas hurts this person because of her she'll never forgive herself.

"Lucas, stop. We're going to crash."

But that's what he wants, clearly. He's trying to kill them both.

She grips the sides of her seat and braces her legs against the floor, waiting for the moment of impact . . . then, right at the last minute, the HiAce veers abruptly off the road, clearing the way for Lucas to plow on victorious, and Beth turns in her seat as they pass, trying and failing to meet the eyes of the driver and communicate an apology.

Muttering under his breath, Lucas turns back to the road, his phone still buzzing in his pocket. They keep going, speeding through the void. Beth closes her eyes. He speaks; she detaches. I'm rubber, you're glue. Sticks and stones may break my bones.

"Are you even listening to me?"

There's a pause.

And then Lucas brakes, so hard that the tires screech. Thrown forward, Beth cries out and her seat belt locks and cuts into her neck. The Troopy stops and Lucas cuts the engine. He turns to face her, his body so close she can feel the heat of his breath.

Beth shrinks back against the door. There are a few seconds of absolute quiet, and then Lucas lunges forward and all her air is cut off.

"Don't. Fucking. Ignore. Me." His hands are around her throat. "Never ignore me."

Beth fights for breath. The pain is intense. The crush of his fingers, the grind of her bones . . . Her lungs spasm, her eyes water, her skull bulges with trapped air, trapped blood. She tears at his hands, kicks out with her feet. Her lips move soundlessly: stop, stop, stop.

Lucas's teeth are bared like an animal, his eyes bulge white in the dark. His body is stone, his arms like steel. She twists in her seat, legs thrashing in the footwell as her entire body fights for air but still he holds her down. Her ears pop and her spine buckles.

I'm going to die.

The thought crystallizes as her vision blurs.

He's murdering me.

And then, as the pressure builds to an excruciating climax, he lets go. Her lungs open and she gulps down air, but he isn't done. He hits her twice, hard, in the back of the head. He grabs the stolen cookies, tears open the packet and grinds a handful into her mouth until her lips bleed. Then he pushes her against the window, grabs the key from the ignition, grips it like a knife and hangs over her, poised as if to plunge it straight into her artery.

That's when he stops. Pulls away. Throws down the keys.

Beth crumples, throat stinging, head exploding, lungs pumping.

Lucas is wheezing too, banging his fist against the steering wheel and moaning. "Fuck, look what you fucking did, you fucking . . . why would you . . . goddamn it, fuck . . ."

Go. Now.

Without even thinking, Beth finds the handle and pulls, topples back into the night, hits the dirt like a bag of meat, and then somehow she's up and running, soaring into the night like an eagle, fly, fly, fly!

"Where ya gonna go, ya dumb cunt?" *Lucas screams behind her.* "We're in the middle of fucking nowhere."

She runs, precious air burning like fire in her crushed windpipe, the sound of her labored breathing only barely covering the sound of his laughter.

"Fuck." Panting hard, Beth scrambles across the mattress. "No, get off me, get away."

"Lily—"

"Don't call me that."

"What's wrong, what did you—"

"Get away from me, don't touch me."

"*Lily!*"

She doesn't even realize she's screaming until there's no breath left to use.

CHAPTER FORTY-THREE
Katy

I sit in the van with my phone in my hand, watching Lily through the window. She's swimming in the lagoon, paddling around like a child. She dives under the water, bobs back up, then repeats the process all over again. She's so vulnerable. I can't tear my eyes away.

Following the hypnosis, and Lily's reaction to it, something has happened to the two of us. A kind of softening or melting. The therapy worked; she remembered her attack. She hasn't yet shared with me the finer details of what she saw but I know she knows what happened. Which means we're closing in on the truth. But suddenly there's less of a rush because we've reached some kind of unspoken agreement.

It's been a whole week since that night on the road between Kalbarri and Shark Bay. Seven days without night noises or things found in the morning. Both Lily and I are starting to think that we might've lost our stalker. And Quobba feels safe, somehow—relatively speaking, anyway. The community is warm. Twice now we've eaten dinner with the family next door, some delicious concoction Lily made using spices on the rack that I've never touched. She plays with the kids and enchants the parents with interesting, thoughtful conversation. For a shy person, she's surprisingly good with people. We're growing closer too, building a real friendship. We swim (well, she does, I wade) and read books borrowed from other campers and talk. It feels like a spell that neither of us wants to break. So it looks like, for now at least, we're staying put.

Which suits me because I'm helplessly tired. I don't even have the energy to ask about Phoebe, show her photo around, and pose my usual questions. I've lost my appetite, my brain feels foggy, and fatigue sits viscous in my chest like the flu. But as long as Lily's around, I'm okay.

Out in the lagoon, I smile as she dives under again and wait for her to resurface before forcing my attention back to Instagram.

Have you tried breaking in? You could guess her password.

I log out of my ghost account and stare at the Sign In screen. I type in Phoebe's username, but the password field remains empty.

Talk to me, Pheebs. What is it?

The cursor blinks.

But you already know.

Do I? I close my eyes and think of her as an adult, glowing and vivacious and adorable. A teenager, bouncy and impulsive and changeable as the weather. A child, curious and playful, a pile of sheets and cushions in her arms. *Let's make a fort. This can be our clubhouse. No one else allowed in but us. Knock three times and say the password.*

But what is it?

Phoebe's voice comes back to me. *No, Mum, I'm not telling! Only we know the password. Katy chose it because she's the best at deciding things, and she said we could only ever have one for the rest of our lives because otherwise we'd keep forgetting and get locked out of the clubhouse, and we can't tell anyone else, ever!*

I open my eyes. Stare at the screen, the blinking cursor. Surely not.

I start typing, my fingers moving fast in a well-practiced pattern. *whatkatydidnext.* I press enter, but nothing happens. I think again. *Two little ducks. Quack, quack, quack.* I type the password, this time adding the number 22, and tap submit.

I'm in. *Holy fucking fuck*, as Lily would say.

I navigate straight to the message inbox. A long queue of unopened, unread messages swims in front of my eyes. I open the first few.

Hi Pheebs, I just want to say privately how much I love your account, it's so inspiring.

Pheebs! Thanks for all you do. I've been in a dark place in my life lately and your posts have really kept me going.

Hi Phoebe, I'm a solo traveler currently in Southeast Asia. Can you offer me any advice on how to start my own blog?

I can't see anything from lonewanderer66. Not yet anyway.

I do, however, find my mother's name. Apparently every other day she sends a few hopeful lines—hi, it's me, are you out there, please call or text, we just want to know you're safe—but gets no response. I keep scrolling, scanning the heading for anything that might suggest that Phoebe is still alive and using the account but she hasn't replied to anything since before June 3, the day she disappeared.

And then I spot lonewanderer's display image, the sunrise. It's next to the name Chris Craig. I click into the message and find a very long chat thread—though "chat" is wrong because it's all one-sided. Fifty-seven messages over a period of three weeks and not one reply from Phoebe. I scroll right back to the beginning.

Hey Pheebs, you'll know me from the comments as lonewanderer66 but my name's Chris and I'd love to get to know you better.

Hey, great post today. I'm interested in buying your photos for my wall, do you sell prints? I think you're so beautiful.

Phoebe. You drive me crazy. Your body, your hair. I can't tear my eyes away, can't stop thinking about you. I feel like you see me too, that every post is meant for me. You want me to find you, don't you? You want me to know where you are. I'm right aren't I?

My stomach tightens; I can feel my pulse in every part of my body. I scroll further, noticing the gradual change in tone.

You think you can play games? What, you're too good for me? I will not be ignored. I'm here, and closer than you think.

I'm going to hunt you down and make you see me. I'm going to make you do all kinds of things.

Safety measures? Haha. I will blow your house down, cunt. I will crawl through your window in the middle of the night and then you will know me. You won't be able to get enough. You cannot imagine how close we're going to be.

About halfway through there's another shift but no less disturbing.

So sad to hear that people have been unkind. I can't believe anyone would be so cruel. I hope you know that I would never do anything like that. And I will bury anyone who hurts or upsets you.

I'm here to take care of you, Pheebs. I hate to think of you all alone out there.

How are you doing? You all right? Just checking in. Let me know you're safe, okay?

The final three messages are so dark I can't even take in the words.

Bitch, I'm going to choke you till you beg. I gave up my job for you. I gave up my life, and you won't even speak to me?

I'm coming for you. I will find you. Then I will find your family. Go ahead and hide if you want, it just makes it more fun.

Watch out for me, I'm on my way. See you soon, Pheebs.

I drop the phone and sit in silence.
lonewanderer66. Chris Craig.
He's the one. He knows where she is. I found him.

CHAPTER FORTY-FOUR

Beth

Peeling off her dress and dropping it onto the sand, Beth adjusts the straps of her new swimming costume and lowers herself into the lagoon, stretching out her arms and pushing off in a gentle breaststroke. The water is deliciously cool, and so clear she can see all kinds of fish: tiny blues ones, yellow ones with black stripes. She spots a turtle and several starfish. She glides over anemones and shells. Out here, she feels different. The events of the last eleven days—the last month, the last year—fall away and she's left feeling light, like she weighs nothing.

Holding her breath, she dives down and lets the ocean hold her for a moment. The gentle currents cradle her like a baby. *It's okay,* she tells herself. *You're okay.*

Resurfacing, she looks back toward the van. No sign of Katy. She's starting to feel horrible about lying. She had an opportunity to confess when they did that stupid hypnotherapy thing and she gave herself a panic attack, but it just wouldn't come out. And now it feels like they're not just mutual means to mutual ends anymore; they're becoming friends, which really complicates things.

She's pretty sure Katy's hiding things too though; she's so spacey and inconsistent, and her behaviors don't fit any psychological mold Beth can think of. But then, grief is complex and trauma is powerful. And it's none of Beth's business anyway. On the whole, sharing the HiAce hasn't been too bad, not nearly as cramped and awkward as she'd expected, and without the relentless eggshell-treading and hypervigilance she's been free to experience vanlife in a whole new way.

She swims in languid circles until her fingertips start to wrinkle. Floating over a particularly bright patch of coral, she finds a clear patch of seabed to stand on. Her toes touch sand and she straightens up. Running her hands through her hair, she thinks about home, her old living room, her parents' dining room table. She imagines what kind of home she might one day make for herself, on her own terms. What kind of job she might do, what kind of person she might be. The thoughts are soothing.

She turns back toward the beach. The tide is rising, creeping back over the wet sand toward the dry, returning to the rocky crevices and sea caves it has left exposed. She's about to strike out for the shore when she catches sight of a man on the beach. He's lying on a striped towel, propped up on one elbow with his legs stretched out on front of him. Messy hair. Shorts and T-shirt. Artsy vibe. He's reading a book. As she's idly wondering which one it might be, the man looks up and her heart flaps. She's seen him before. It's the cute guy from Monkey Mia, the one who smiled at her at the resort bar. Her cheeks burn and she dives under the water.

When she comes up again, the guy is still looking her way. Is it him? She thinks so. He's swapped his thick-rimmed glasses for Wayfarer sunnies but she's pretty sure. He smiles and lifts his hand in a goofy little wave. Definitely him. Butterflies stir in her belly.

She starts to swim toward the beach, thinking again of that imaginary home, her imaginary job. She pictures kicking off her shoes at the end of a long day, pouring a wine, putting her feet up, throwing on some music. Tentatively, she adds a second glass to the scene, a second pair of shoes. Because maybe there's someone else at home with her. A kind, artsy guy who reads. Messy hair and Wayfarer glasses.

Then again, maybe not. As she cuts through the water, Beth realizes that she hasn't ever been on her own, not really. From the earliest age possible she's had a boyfriend. Even during her party years, there was always someone to whom she was at least casually attached. But out there in the water, she glimpses the person she might be underneath. The woman just waiting to break free.

Beth, Beth, Beth.

Me, me, me.

I, I, I.

When she gets back to the van, Katy is yelling.

"I don't understand why you won't listen to me," Katy spits, pacing in front of the sliding door and furiously jabbing the air with the index finger of her free hand. "You're supposed to be the detective, why aren't you interested? I have all this information that . . . No, *you* don't get it, and I'm sick of trying to explain . . ."

Beth hovers uncertainly, unsure if maybe she ought to head back to the beach.

"I *know* that, but if you'd just give me five minutes of your time then you'd . . . What? *Why?*" Katy pauses to listen, her expression darkening. "But why would you *not* want to hear it? Don't you . . . No, that's not at all what I . . . No, you listen. I cannot believe that you would—"

Pulling a towel from the back of one of the camp chairs, Beth dries herself off.

Katy ignores her. "No, don't you dare hang up," she says into the phone. "All I need is five minutes and you . . . no, please, don't, please, please—" She stops, then goes completely still. Slowly and with a visibly trembling hand, she takes the phone from her ear.

"What's going on?" Beth asks.

Katy's doesn't respond right away. "That was the investigator," she says after a beat. "Dust, the one who worked on Phoebe's case. He still won't talk to me, even though I . . ." She stops again, and her eyes fly around the campsite. "You haven't seen anyone hanging around, have you? Anyone strange?"

"What?"

"Anyone who keeps popping up, who might possibly be following us?"

Beth wraps the towel tightly around her shoulders. "What do you mean?"

"Don't talk to anyone. No one at all, okay? Not even the people next door."

"Why?"

"Just don't. Not anyone. It's not safe." She pulls Beth inside the van, slides the door shut and closes the curtains. "Look at this." She taps on her phone and passes it over.

Beth peers at the screen. It's an Instagram inbox, but it takes her a beat to grasp what it means. "This is Phoebe's? You guessed her password?"

Katy nods. "I was looking for lonewanderer66, but the messages don't come up under the handle, they come up under the user's actual name. Look for Chris Craig."

Beth looks—but only a few messages down the list, her heart stops dead.

"You were right about the private communication," Katy continues, "but it wasn't mutual. Phoebe doesn't even reply to him. His messages . . . they're so horrible. He *stalked* her, and he must've found her and hurt her, and now he's coming after me—and maybe he came after you! We have to find him and stop him, he . . ."

Katy is babbling, her tone frantic, but Beth barely registers anything she's saying; she can't even see the name Chris Craig, because nestled among all the other messages is a name she *does* recognize. Two words, eleven letters, rising from the screen and filling her vision until the rest of the world drops away. It dances on her lips, begging to be spoken out loud.

Lucas Cleary.

And even though she was half expecting it, she's still floored. *Fuck,* she was right. Numb with shock, she puts down the phone. *Lucas, you shit, what did you fucking do?* And behind it, another thought, small and pathetic: *you gave her your real name?*

Behind her, Katy is still rambling about stalkers and Chris Craig, and Beth has to turn away because she can't *look* at her, everything Katy believes is wrong, and in so many ways it's Beth's fault but she can't—

She stops. Stiffens. Stares at the floor. In the corner, folded twice and tucked just behind the van's open door, as if someone has quickly returned a borrowed item, is a piece of paper. And Beth doesn't have to pick it up to know what it is. She doesn't even have to guess.

Another fucking note.

Reaching down, she opens it up and starts to read.

DEAD END—A DEEP DIVE
INTO MURDER ON THE ROAD

Picture it. You're a girl traveling alone. The wind is in your hair, the sun is shining, and the world is your oyster. But something isn't right. A strange feeling begins to niggle at you, a sense that you're being watched. Everywhere you go, you feel eyes tracking your every move, footsteps pounding the ground behind you. The feeling grows and grows until you know it in your bones: someone or something is coming for you, and you will not survive.

But what is it, this mysterious threat? As discussed in the first installment of this investigation, the dangers of the road can, and often do, take a number of different shapes. If the campfire tales are to be believed, the danger lies in the supernatural. For example, the abandoned homestead at Willowfield near Leeman is said to be haunted by a farmer who shot himself after his young son fell into a well and died. Visitors to the homestead have heard screams and moans coming from the old buildings and suspect the farmer cannot rest until he finds who is to blame.

Several deaths and unexplained incidents along the long stretch of road between Kalbarri and Shark Bay are rumored to have been caused by the "Minilya Hitchhiker," a woman in a red dress who appears at the side of the road with her arms outstretched, and who disappears from the back seat of your car once picked up. And at

Gracious Bay on the Ningaloo coast, it's said that the spirit of Eleanor Flannery, who in 1869 drowned the entire crew of a merchant
ship when she set fire to the hull, still roams the local beach at night
calling for new victims to follow her into the sea.

Or could the explanation be a little more pedestrian? As pre-
viously reported, a rash of recent van robberies up and down the
Coral Coast has police wondering if local thieves are taking notes
from Europe. One family traveling through the Lesueur National
Park claimed they'd been gassed while they were sleeping, an as-
sertion that chimes with a series of high-profile crimes committed
in France between 2006 and 2018 during which burglars allegedly
pumped gas into their victims' villas before ransacking their rooms.
At least three families in campervans also reported waking up feeling dry-mouthed and nauseous after thieves used air vents to do the
same. Medical experts have repeatedly asserted that there is no gas
in the world that is sufficiently safe, potent, undetectable, or cheap
to be used in this way—but in an age when the medical industry
is unable to keep pace with an ever-innovative black market, how
can we know for sure?

Let's face it, the most obvious explanation for the recent surge in
traveler disappearances has to be a serial killer. The name most of us in
this country associate with traveler deaths is Ivan Milat, who between
1989 and 1992 brutally murdered at least seven backpackers on and
around the Hume Highway in New South Wales. Milat's methods
were varied but three of his victims suffered knife wounds that sev-
ered their spinal cords and rendered them helpless, and all were alone
and vulnerable. But how common is a monster like that? Despite the
publicity afforded to serial murder, the reality is that it accounts for
only a very small proportion of all known homicides.

So what if it's not the killer that's prolific but the place? Since
1970, at least twelve people have either vanished or perished along
the isolated eight-hundred-kilometer Flinders Highway between
Townsville and Mount Isa in North Queensland, earning it the

nickname "Highway of Death." These incidents have commonly been attributed to the work of a single "thrill killer"—but criminologists now increasingly believe that multiple perpetrators are to blame: a host of psychopaths all gravitating, for some as yet unknown reason, to the same remote location.

To make it worse, it's hard to separate fact from fiction. Take the infamous "Cuckoo Killings" stories that dominated the subReddits in 2020 and 2021. These terrifying rumors of traveler disappearances, vehicle theft, and identity fraud had the whole vanlife community up in arms until they were finally and conclusively debunked.

So what is the truth? As friends and family of missing vanlifer Vivi Green continue to hunt for answers months after her disappearance, tourists all over WA are asking themselves exactly that. What is out there? What is coming for me? And how can I protect myself?

Whatever the answers, there are plenty of reasons to be afraid.

CHAPTER FORTY-FIVE

Wyatt

Fever dreams. Fork prongs, tennis poles, and a famous chilli crab. A strobing swirl of star-shaped pendants and egg-shaped stones spins through the air while the crab plays "Hotel California" on repeat.

Wyatt, Mum calls through a haze of smoke and fire. *I'm here, I'm hiding, come find me.* A different mother, the lead actor in his favorite scary movie, takes her place. *I never wanted to be your mother. I was scared, it wasn't my fault, I tried to stop it.*

Wyatt tosses and turns in bed, his sheets once again sweaty and damp. He's lonely and scared and sick, why is he so *sick*? His head thumps all the time, with or without the paracetamol that for some reason makes him feel drowsy, and though he's chronically lethargic he can't sleep—like, *ever*. It's been going on for so long that he can't remember the last time he felt well, can't recall a time when he didn't feel sore and breathless and nauseous and tense . . .

No, wait, he *can* remember: a month or two ago, he'd felt healthy then—yes, he can see himself, smiling and happy, sitting on the porch, walking to the beach, chatting online with a friend—yes, a *friend*, he'd had one . . . but then he'd lost her, because he'd done something so fucking bad that he'll hate himself for the rest of his life, something so awful and cruel that he shouldn't even be alive anymore—and, in fact, the thing he did is probably what made him sick. Yes, that's it, that's why. Because this is what happens to people who hurt other people: the Bad Things just rebound onto them, burrowing like worms deep down inside their bodies and poisoning them until they can no longer breathe.

Choking, he throws off the sheets and sits up in bed, wishing so hard he could just call out again and Mum would come running. But Mum isn't here anymore. Wyatt was supposed to find her, but he failed.

The broken promise weighs heavy in his bones. But he's started to wonder if, in the end, he might not have to find whoever or whatever took Mum away. Lately he's begun to feel that *they,* or *it,* will come to *him.*

Liked by **lonewanderer66** and **others**

pheebsinwonderland Milestone post! Almost 3 weeks ago I set off on a trip of a lifetime: a solo drive around the entire circumference of Australia. 1200km and a whole lot of adventure later, I've completed my first leg. Hello, Ningaloo. Cue the celebrations!

Also cue some introspection. These last 18 days have taught me so much. Vanlife is beyond incredible—but while it might look easy from the outside, in reality it can be tough. Sometimes solo travel is lonely, uncomfortable, and grubby. The long stretches on the road can get boring, and nights alone can be scary. Some aspects of publicly sharing the journey have come as a surprise, too. I'm grateful to have connected with so many fellow travelers, and the comments have mostly been encouraging. But some people have, I'm sorry to say, been hostile and hurtful. I've also realized that sharing my experience doesn't always serve me. I'm constantly hunting for the best pictures, the best way to articulate what I'm seeing and/or dress it up for show, with the result that I'm actually missing it all. So I'm taking a break, just for a few days.

With Jupiter in Gemini and Pluto in Aquarius right now it's a great time to trust my intuition and mental strength, so I've decided to change up my plan and head inland to Karijini to hike the gorges and swim in the pools (any last-minute tips greatly appreciated—kindness and love only please!). After that, who knows? Wish me luck! I promise to report back afterward.

(Image description: A selfie of a happy, adventure-smitten woman in sunglasses taken on a long empty stretch of road. Her beloved van is in the background, just in shot. And she's got a huge goofy smile because tomorrow marks the start of a new mission: to be more present and alive in the moment.)

#vanlife #solofemaletravel #onsomenewshit #mindfultravel #takingabreak #karijini #ifyouneedmeillbeinthedesert

View all 202 comments

hillary_j_weddings Great idea—but make sure you head back to Ninglaoo and swim with the whale sharks! It was the highlight of our whole trip!

taratamarama23 Seconded! Karijini is breathtaking but don't miss Ningaloo, it's the best part of WA.

goodnightpetergraham ☺

cathandmartyontheroad Dales Gorge Campground has toilets, barbecues, and picnic tables, but they don't take bookings. Also, there's flooding between Karijini and Port Hedland so if you're heading to Broome find an alternative route.

rubyy_every_dayy Good call Pheebs, get back to nature. It'll transform the way you travel.

lonewanderer66 What a coincidence, I'm also heading to Karijini. Check your messages. See you soon.

3 June

CHAPTER FORTY-SIX
Beth

Beth packs up their pitch while Katy paces up and down, calling Detective Dust over and over again.

"We should go," says Beth, putting away the last of their food and securing the cupboard doors. "Let's talk on the road."

"We should just call triple zero," Katy says, with the cracked expression of someone unlikely to listen. "Report Phoebe's disappearance all over again. They would have to contact Dust, or assign a new investigator. Either way—"

"You know," Beth interrupts, fighting a wave of panic, "I'm not sure that's the best idea. Let's just cool our jets, take some time to think."

It takes a little more persuasion but eventually Katy relents. They both climb into the van and the HiAce rolls slowly out of Quobba campground. They pass the blowholes and the *KING WAVES KILL* sign, heading back toward the highway.

In the passenger seat, Beth's thoughts tear around like toddlers. *A rash of recent van robberies.* The gas thing was ridiculous (she and Lucas never used gas, that was an urban legend, where would you get it, with what would you pump it, and through where?) but the meaning is clear. Someone knows. And they want her to know that they know.

But who? Chris Craig? Katy is convinced of his guilt, but his messages strike Beth more as someone making frustrated, empty threats. She bets that if she could track the guy down he'd be some broke-arse thirty-year-old red-pill dickhead still living in his parents' basement somewhere in Midwest America. And there's nothing specific enough in his messages that would necessarily tie him directly to Phoebe's disappearance. Unlike the evidence building up against Lucas. And if Lucas is behind the notes too, they take on a whole new and even more complex meaning.

Interestingly, there's a name on the note this time: "WILLIAM," scrawled in pencil on the back of the page in the top left corner, which initially seemed pretty definitive but which on reflection seems like less of a signature and more a hurried reminder; like, *call the vet's, don't forget to buy milk.* Maybe it's just a coincidence, someone's recycled scrap paper. But then Katy reminds her of all those stones left outside the van, and the lines arranged to resemble letters. *W. I. L. L.* So what does that mean?

Whatever—priority one has to be stopping Katy from reporting anything to the police. If that happens, they will both be required to give statements. Beth will have to explain why she doesn't have ID or money or belongings. Her parents will be contacted, and she already knows what happens when *they* get involved. The cops will bring Lucas in too, and they'll both be arrested because there's no way he'd go down without dragging her with him. And then she really would know what it is to be trapped.

Beside her, Katy is still banging on about Dust and triple zero.

"Maybe it's better to be careful," Beth says as they turn back onto the highway. "We don't yet know who or what we're dealing with. Let's keep going, see what we can find at Gracious Bay, and if you still want to call the cops, we can do it from there. What do you think?"

In the driver's seat, her bloodless fingers wrapped tight around the wheel, Katy doesn't respond.

CHAPTER FORTY-SEVEN

Katy

"What do you think?" says Lily.

It's a good question. I think that I'm in hell. I think that if I had any doubt that I'm being followed then this dispels it. Leeman, Kalbarri, Shark Bay, Gracious Bay . . . that's my journey, stop for stop. Knife wounds. Spinal cords. My stomach heaves.

Outside, the landscape is flat, barren, and hostile. Nothing but dry grass, dead-looking shrubs, and scratchy black branches stretching endlessly under a taut, cloudless sky. I glance at my phone. Along this stretch of road, there's no signal at all, no bars of 4G, just three little letters in the top right corner of the screen: *SOS*.

Know what else I think? That this second article feels like a set of instructions. Whoever is following me, writing to me, leaving hair in my van, and dropping bobby pins like breadcrumbs, they don't just want me scared, they want me terrified. They want me to run, to imagine all the things they could do when they catch me, all the things they might've done to Phoebe. They are steering me too obviously toward a scenario in which Phoebe is dead. They want me to stop looking for her.

And that name. *William*. There were the stones outside the van, of course, laid out to spell the first four letters. But more than that, it feels oddly familiar—besides the fact that it's common. Is it a message? A threat? Some kind of calling card?

Lily is frightened, I can tell. And she has every right to be. But nothing bad will happen to her. I won't allow it. I want to tell her that. *It's okay,* I want to say, *I'll protect you.* I want her to know that I will keep her safe if it kills me. *Everything will be fine, I promise.*

But the truth is that I don't know how to stop things from hurting us, that I can't figure it out or keep either of us safe. So I say nothing, and we drive the rest of the way without exchanging another word.

CHAPTER FORTY-EIGHT

Beth

They drive and drive and drive some more. The road between Quobba and Gracious Bay is mostly flat and dominated by scrappy black bushes. Huge termite mounds rise periodically from the grass like the heads of terra-cotta soldiers, and in the distance the land bunches up like a rucked rug until it reaches the ocean.

Beth sits quietly, thinking. "Would you mind if I take a look through those messages again?" she asks. "I didn't get time to read them properly back there."

"Sure," Katy says after a beat. "Go ahead."

Picking up the phone, Beth opens the app, accesses the inbox and, with a sharp pang of anxiety, taps on Lucas's name.

The chat thread is so long it takes her a while to scroll back to the start. Lucas, it seems, had initiated contact well before Phoebe had set off on her trip, kicking off with a banal question about campervan conversion. Phoebe had shot back a cheery reply and offered some advice on how to find the right vehicle. Lucas thanked her and introduced himself. A few more travel questions later, the messages became more friendly.

"Wait, your username is goodnightpetergraham, right?" Phoebe wrote at one point. "So do I call you Peter or Lucas?"

"Lucas," he replied. "That's my real name. Peter Graham is the main character from my favorite film."

"Which film is that?"

"Ah, if you have to ask it's clearly not one of yours."

Beth frowns at this. Lucas's favorite movie is Tarantino's *True Romance*. There are no characters named Peter Graham in that. She feels oddly shut out, left in the dark.

She keeps reading. Lucas checked in regularly before Phoebe left Sydney, and then they chatted several times a day from the moment she left Perth. After Kalbarri he asked what she'd really thought of the free camp, and she replied that it felt perfectly safe and asked for his thoughts on WA highlights: tours, hikes, beauty spots, cafes, etc. He told her about the Ningaloo reef and his hometown, describing it as the most beautiful place on the planet, the last wild place on earth, in possession of a magic he could never truly articulate because "you don't see nature, you feel it."

He rattled off facts and anecdotes, demonstrating a level of interest in the natural world Beth had no idea he possessed. "Did you know," he said, "that whales can split their brains in two? When a mother whale sleeps, one whole half of their brain stays awake to keep an eye on their calf while the other half just shuts down. Amazing, huh?"

They shared stories and made each other laugh (according to the emojis, anyway). Their travel chat dissolved into an easy banter that led to an exchange of pictures: a sunset-over-water shot from Phoebe, a selfie on the beach from Lucas. A picture of Phoebe chilling in her van was met with one of Lucas sipping a beer on his porch at home—and with a sickening lurch, Beth recognizes the piece-of-sky blue of his door, the one she saw every time she opened his wallet. The sight of his face sends Beth's heart into spasms: he looks younger, happier, more alive.

And it only gets more uncomfortable from there. In a single day Lucas divulged more about his family than he'd told Beth in a year, especially about his adored kid brother. "Pheebs, you'd love him," he said. "He's so funny and clever and sweet and wouldn't hurt a soul. You know those rare people in life who you'd trust with just about anything? That's Wyatt for me." In return, Phoebe tells him about her strained relationship with her parents: her mother's depression, her father's alcoholism, and her belief that she inherited both. (*Like sister, like sister,* Beth thinks, her train of thought diverting briefly to all the wine she's spied under the sink in the van.)

Lucas's responses are considerate and nonjudgmental—which is perhaps the hardest pill for Beth to swallow. There he is in black-and-white, the boy Beth fell in love with, who made thoughtful observations about the world and sang loudly in the car and could talk to anyone. A man who did not lash out or spit when he yelled or drive his fist into people's faces, who would never dream of behaving like that. Where did that boy go?

A terrible thought: was it possible he'd never left at all? Reading his words, Beth wonders if perhaps she's made all that bad stuff up. What if his rage and abuse were all just in her head? Worse, what if the problem had never been him but *her*? The thought makes her want to vomit.

She sits up when she finds a mention of Chris Craig.

I have a stalker, Phoebe wrote.

I hope you don't mean me, lol, replied Lucas.

Obvs! No, it's this random dude called Chris. Username lonewanderer66. I've never met or replied to him but for some reason he thinks we're destined to be together. It's super creepy.

Oh yeah, I see him in the comments. You need me to take him out?

Haha. Settle down, John Wick.

Beth could easily spend all day reading the whole thread but she doesn't have time so she skips forward to their final correspondence. So I was thinking, Lucas wrote on June first, that if this stalker guy is really freaking you out then maybe you should go dark for a while. Write a false entry saying you're going somewhere you're not, then do what you want for a few days. Go somewhere peaceful and beautiful and enjoy travel for its own sake. If you stop posting about where you are then the asshole won't be able to find you, and then maybe he'll get bored and leave you alone.

Good idea, Phoebe replied. Where on earth might I go? 😉

I know a nice place by the beach, if that sounds like your thing?

That wouldn't happen to be the last wild place on earth, would it?

Might be. Your call though.

Hmm. I do enjoy a wilderness. Address?

141 South Beach Street, Gracious Bay.

I'll think about it. 😳😊

Beth stops reading and puts the phone back where she found it.

"What do you think?" Katy asks softly.

Beth hesitates, her head still full of the day they first met. *Of all the cheap seafood joints in all the world.* How charming he was . . . but what did she know then about Lucas's past? What does she know about it now? Not much. But she's (probably) more acquainted with his present than anyone else. She knows his moves, methods, triggers; she's very well attuned to his temper. She even knows his (their) phone number. So if he *does* have anything to do with Phoebe's disappearance, she's best placed to find out.

She imagines simply calling. *Hey, it's me, so sorry about running off, I just have a quick question* . . . It blows her mind that after everything, Lucas might hold the very piece of information Beth needs to end all of this for good. How ironic that in this new and bewildering moment, he is both her prison and her key.

Obviously she can't ask, though. So she'll have to find out some other way—preferably before the police get involved or Lucas makes a new move.

"Scary," she says at last. "I think it's all very, very scary."

The turnoff to Gracious Bay is marked by a single signpost, after which the road becomes narrower: dunes to the right, scrub to the left. It dips down into a gentle valley, curves around a grassy bowl that looks like it might once have been a lake, then starts to climb up again to the top of the next rise. "Gracie" rises from the crest, her winding steel bands glinting in the light.

Katy pulls over and both she and Beth get out to take a closer look. The sculpture really is pretty, and looks even more like a whale shark up close. Beth circles it several times, trailing her fingers over the plinth, its edges worn smooth by the hands of countless others, and wonders how many times Lucas has sat here. Probably too many to count. It looks like the kind of place kids would sneak out to, cheap cider concealed in their schoolbags, the promise of a hookup tingling beneath their skin.

Beth watches Katy as she takes pictures, re-creating Phoebe's shots, and for the first time it strikes Beth as really quite creepy. Is this an investigation, she thinks, or some kind of vanity project?

They set off again, coasting around bends until the town spreads out before them: a crescent-shaped cluster of residences and businesses built around a glistening cyan bay. They pass placards advertising dive schools, tours and cafes, and a large sign that says, WELCOME TO GRACIOUS BAY—NOT JUST A PRETTY PLACE! in cheerful vintage lettering. A smaller one follows, warning against dingoes.

On the main street, Beth opens her window. Gracious Bay appears to be a typical rural-coast community: picturesque and peaceful but with a slight undertone of precarity. Sun-leathered backpackers walk barefoot into coffee shops; retirees push trolleys into a tiny IGA. There are bakeries and bait shops and at least a dozen tour operators. Beth spots signs for a school, a medical center, and a library. They pass a backpackers hostel and two large holiday parks full of caravans before they hit the bright sparkle of the beach.

Katy pulls into the car park, kills the engine, and slumps back into her seat with a heavy sigh.

"Are you all right?" Beth asks.

Katy doesn't reply. Her face, already pale and drawn, looks especially hollow today. Her cheeks are sunken, her jawline extra sharp, and her limbs seem even more twig-like than they had when they'd first met.

"Why don't you stay here in the air con," Beth says. "I'll go take a look."

She steps outside onto the hot bitumen. Even though she's never seen Gracious Bay before, it feels strangely familiar—or meaningful at least. Everything makes her think of Lucas. He grew up here, he knows the town inside out. The whole place hums with his presence.

The ocean is separated from the car park by a strip of stabilized dunes and a public service area with picnic benches, shade sails, toilets, and a fish-cleaning station. To her left, a paper poster has been taped to a utility pole. MISSING, it says. HAVE YOU SEEN VIVI GREEN? Beth heads straight for it. Up close, an attractive curly-haired woman in her early forties smiles out from a photograph, a small gold hoop dangling from her septum. *Last seen February 14th on the Minilya-Exmouth road driving a blue TRAKKA Akuna A2M-E, registration plate 1HF 1VG. If you have any information, please call . . .*

February 14. Valentine's Day. She and Lucas had spent the afternoon at Jurien Bay, curled up in the shade of a tree, their sand-speckled limbs so intertwined it was hard to tell whose was whose. Briefly, her chest feels like it's about to cave in.

Behind her, she hears the door of the HiAce and Katy pads across the car park to join her. They contemplate the poster in silence before wordlessly agreeing to follow the fence line toward the boat ramp. Beyond is a lookout fitted with a narrow bench and an information placard. They climb the steps and scan the bay. The ocean is mirror-still, protected by the reef and two long spits at either end. Children play in the shallows while farther out snorkel pipes pop out of the water like little submarines.

Beth reads the placard, running her fingers over the illustration of a ship with many sails. *In 1869 the merchant ship* Eleanor, *a 116-tonne two-masted wooden-hulled schooner, was destroyed just off the reef at Gracious Bay when a fire was deliberately lit in the hull. The culprit was said to be the ship's namesake, the young and mentally unstable wife of the shipowner who unexpectedly flew into what survivors described as a "violent fit of uncontrolled rage" just a few days into the trip.*

At the age of eighteen Mrs. Flannery had been placed under medical supervision in Darwin at the request of her husband but, "unable to be parted from her for even a moment" (as he wrote to his brother in 1868), he decided that a sea change would do her good and installed her in his quarters aboard the vessel he'd named for her. The Eleanor *was to sail for 100 days, stopping at Port Walcott then on to Fremantle with various cargo including wool and pearl shell. However, it caught fire as it passed unexpectedly close to the Ningaloo Reef and sank to the bottom, taking with it all twenty souls on board, including the merchant and poor mad Eleanor herself. The bodies and most of the ship's debris eventually washed ashore on Gracious Bay beach.*

Some say Eleanor's spirit haunts the shores to this day, her appetite for human life as yet unsated, and many have seen her on the rocks and on the sand. Look for her when the moon is full and the tide is low; listen out for her call. But don't stay too long, or you might not live to tell the tale.

Beth shivers. *Tell me a bedtime story.* Firelight dances before her eyes, whiskey burns on her tongue.

Katy nudges her and juts her chin at a white weatherboard building at one end of the beach, the words GRACIOUS BAY HOTEL written in large letters along one side. "Come on," she murmurs.

Reluctantly, Beth follows.

"Hi ladies," says the bartender. "What can I get you?"

From the outside, the pub is very pretty: freshly renovated in a modern-coastal style, sophisticated with a laid-back holiday vibe. Inside, however, the Hamptons-inspired elegance brushes up against other styles with confusing results. There's a coffee counter decked out like a Hawaiian beach bar, a "fine dining" restaurant area, and a TAB/Sportsbet and pokies room with a neon sign above the entryway that says LITTLE VEGAS. Dominating the back half of the building is a tiki-style bar area with a dance floor and DJ booth, the walls of which are plastered with posters advertising themed nights—Two-Shot Tuesday, Free Drink Friday, Ladies Night, and something mysterious called a Shrek Rave. The many disjointed parts are unified by a combined smell of dry ice and fried food.

"Just water, please," Katy says. "Two glasses."

The bartender makes an "I don't think so" face and pours two highballs of coral-pink cocktail, each garnished with fresh orange and cherry. "On the house," she says with a wink. "Because if you're ordering water, it's clearly your first time at the Gracie."

"Oh," says Katy, eyeing her cocktail as if it might be poisoned. "Okay."

Beth swipes hers from the bar without a second thought and takes a long glug. Alcohol is one hundred percent required, poisoned or not.

Katy pulls out her phone. "Do you know this person?"

The brunette peers at the screen. "It's hard to tell with those sunnies, but I don't think so."

"Her name's Phoebe. She was here this time last year?"

"Oh, then definitely no. I'm new, just started a month ago."

Katy sags, then perks up again. "Do you know the name Chris Craig?"

"Um . . . no?"

"You sure?"

"Pretty sure."

"What about Vivi Green?"

"The chick on the posters? The one who went missing?" The bartender narrows her eyes. "What are you, journos?"

"No, we're—"

"We're looking for some friends," Beth says quickly, cutting Katy off. "They were supposed to meet us here. And we're just curious about the posters. It's scary when things like that happen. We just want to make sure this is a safe place for us to be."

"Safe?" The bartender snorts. "What do you want, a guarantee? Some kind of stamp?"

Beth tries to catch Katy's eye: they're not getting anywhere here, and the longer they keep trying the more memorable they'll be.

"This town is just like any other," the bartender continues. "As long as you know how to look after yourself, you'll be fine. But if you're looking for reasons to be afraid, you're gonna find them. And if you're scared of traveling, maybe you should just stay home."

Wow. Beth feels like she's just been slapped.

"As for your friends? You might want to check the wall. Most back-packers who pass through here end up on there. Especially the pretty blond ones."

Both Beth and Katy followed the bartender's gaze to a wall to the right of the bar filled with photos. When they take a closer look they find that the pictures are mostly of young women, either on their own or in groups, all doing shots, chugging beer bongs, dancing on the bar and holding cocktails high above their heads with their eyes half closed. Some appear to be having the time of their lives; others look like they're about to spew. Many photos miss the women's faces entirely and show just boobs or a butt. In neon letters above the display is a sign that says: GRACIE'S HALL OF FAME. Someone has crossed out the "F" and replaced it with "SH."

Beth looks for long caramel hair, a bright toothy smile, and a yellow sundress, but Phoebe is nowhere to be seen. In the bottom-left corner, though, she finds a much younger Lucas, flushed and shaggy-haired, one arm slung over the shoulder of a girl with bangs and a spectacular cleav-age. She looks swollen and sweaty and off her face, but he looks great: clear-eyed and happy. *There he is,* Beth thinks. *My lost boy.* Except he doesn't look lost. On the contrary, he looks very much found.

She looks around again at the pub. Mismatched decor and spiky bar-tender notwithstanding, it's an okay place. The sun will set over the water later, and the whole place will glow with golden light. The town, too, seems small but sweet: a close community with an exotic landscape and a sometime party vibe.

Sounds like a great place to grow up.

It really wasn't. I hated it.

Why? What had been so terrible? Why had living in a van and stealing for money been a preferable way to live? She walks toward the window and the picture perfect view beyond.

There was something in the air. It was everywhere.

What do you mean?

I'd go to the beach, the boat ramp, all the way out to the statue. I'd walk a loop around the pub. In the dark, in the quiet, I could hear it, feel it.

Beth reaches out with her senses but all she can hear is the distant ping of the pokies, the low hum of human bustle, and an occasional bark of laughter.

"Come on, let's go."

Katy appears at her shoulder, and they make their way back outside.

CHAPTER FORTY-NINE

Katy

Something has shifted. Since the emails, since *I will find you*, since *I will find your family*, since *See you soon, Pheebs*, I haven't been myself. Chris Craig's messages buzz in my head like blowflies; I can feel his words in my mouth, almost as if they're my own. Except they can't be because I would never, ever say anything like that. But I also feel like I don't know anything for sure anymore. My stomach keeps heaving as if something is trying to fight its way out; my eyes aren't working, everything is blurry, and I can't tell what things are just by touching them either, like my brain has forgotten half of what the world contains. Names run rampant through my mind—*Chris Craig, William, Phoebe, Dust*—repeating like a song until they no longer make any sense.

Chris Craig. I checked his profile but there were just thirteen pictures of sunrises-slash-sunsets, similar to his display image. I googled his real name plus username but couldn't find any other public profiles. Also, the date the account was created is recent and matches up with when Phoebe started her trip—all of which suggests a troll account, according to Lily. I thought about sending a message of my own but she says we need to be careful, we don't want to make things worse.

Lily also says I shouldn't call triple zero, not yet. She thinks that if the guy *is* somewhere nearby, it might give us an advantage. We could get to him before he gets to us. Which makes a certain kind of sense—but suddenly all I want is for this to be over now, for someone else to take responsibility. I don't want to read through any more messages or search any more campsites. I have proof of sorts now, but I can't bear to contact Dust even one more time. I really need to call Mum and tell her what I've discovered—she deserves to know, we all do, that's why I'm here in the first place—but I don't dare dial her number. All I want to do is disappear. I feel . . . changed. Nauseous and achy, but also hyperaware like I have superpowers. My immediate surroundings are less clearly defined, but the things inside my head have become brighter and more distinct, and my memories of Phoebe are no longer elusive but precise and frequent. I can hear her voice, see her face, smell her perfume. I'm even catching glimpses of her—a flash of yellow in the corner of my eye, a lick of caramel hair disappearing around a corner. It's like she's here with me, leading me somewhere. And maybe she *is*. I have this strange feeling that whatever I'm supposed to find is here in this town, just waiting for me to show up.

I'm close, I just know it.

I'm just no longer sure that's such a good thing.

CHAPTER FIFTY

Beth

The lecture hall is empty. Beth sits at the front, notebook open and pen poised, slightly unsettled because class is about to start and where are the other students? A man appears, charismatic and charming. Smiling warmly, he approaches her desk and she understands that today's lesson is just for her.

If a man has lost a leg or an eye, he says, *he knows he has lost a leg or an eye; but if he has lost a self—himself—he cannot know it, because he is no longer there to know it.*

She writes that down. They're learning about a case where a formerly nonviolent man killed his wife during a psychotic break. The act of murder compounded the psychosis and the man became convinced he was not himself but a member of his own defense team. He even tried to question witnesses in court, claiming he was a lawyer called Barry.

Beth and the man are discussing the complexities of this when the door opens and her father walks in. *How could you do this,* he yells. *You're a monster, Bethany. A monster, a monster, a monster . . .*

She wakes up in the van, in the bed, alone. Her father's voice drifts in and out of the hush like a distant foghorn. Hauling herself upright, she rubs her eyes and waits for the dream to leave her. *If a man has lost a leg or an eye.* One day, once this is all over, she'll go back to uni and finish that damn degree.

She gets out of bed and goes to the fridge for some water, and as she does cool fresh air tickles her skin. A draft. She turns, looking for the source. The door is closed, the windows, the roof vent. Goose bumps rise on her arms. Hoisting herself up on the kitchen counter, she peeps through the hole in the partition wall. The front cab is empty. Katy's quilt and pillow are bunched up in a ball under the steering wheel. And the passenger door is wide open.

Tugging some clothes on, Beth opens the door and steps out into the night. Gracious Bay Holiday Park is whisper quiet. A breeze pushes gently through ancient eucalypts and a full moon shines floodlight bright in the sky.

"Katy? Are you here?"

She treads a circle around the van but Katy is nowhere to be seen. Bathroom dash? Probably. But it's not like her to leave the door wide open.

Beth is contemplating the amenities block when she spots another piece of paper, on the windscreen this time, folded twice and tucked under the wiper. *Oh, shit.* Alarm shoots outward from her chest to her fingertips. She looks around, studying the other vans, the tents, waiting for movement. Nothing.

Cautiously, she picks the piece of paper from the wiper, takes it into the van, and flicks on the light. She expects more chunky paragraphs, more horror stories. But instead she finds a phone number written neatly in black biro and just three small words.

Are you safe?

Beth hunts through the front cab but turns up nothing but sand and snack wrappers. She reaches under the seats and pulls out pieces of orange peel, several withered apple cores, and an empty wine bottle. In the glove box she finds paperwork for the HiAce, the first aid kit, Katy's "evidence" bag—and absolutely nothing else.

Shoving the new note into her pocket, she turns the light off and goes back outside. *Where the fuck am I going to find a fucking phone?* "Katy," she hisses again. "Where the hell are you?" No reply. *Bloody hell.*

Closing the doors, she sets off into the night, dodging guy ropes and camp chairs, looping around the amenities block and back toward the main entrance. She can't see Katy anywhere.

When she reaches the office, she peers through the windows in the hope that there might be someone at reception—but the building is dark and the doors are all locked. Drawing in lungfuls of salty air, she leaves the park and heads down the deserted main road into town. Nothing is open, there are no public pay phones and no one around to ask, so she makes for the beach instead. At least she'll have a better view of the place from the lookout.

Climbing the steps, she stands on the platform and scans the sand, the water, the car park—

"Hello."

Startled, she turns to find a man sitting on the bench in the corner. Shorts and a T-shirt. Messy hair and thick-rimmed glasses. *Artsy guy.* Her heart flutters—but then Katy's voice come back to her. *You haven't seen anyone hanging around, have you? Anyone strange?* Instinctively, she takes a step back.

Artsy Guy raises his hand in an awkward little wave. "Sorry, didn't mean to startle you. I was just . . ." He gestures vaguely at the ocean and the sky. The moonlight bounces off his lenses.

Beth stands frozen, unsure what to say.

"Wait, don't I know you?" He tilts his head, then snaps his fingers. "Yeah, I've seen you before. At the, uh, resort place. Shark Bay?"

"Monkey Mia." Beth's pulse is doing laps. No book this time; instead, he's sipping from a can of something. Two more sit on the bench beside him, still sealed, and an empty rolls on its side at his feet. The air smells faintly sweet.

"You were at Quobba this morning, too," he continues. "I saw you swimming. Wow, isn't it funny how you run into the same people again and again?"

She doesn't return his smile.

He clears his throat. "Sorry, I'm, uh, taking up space here. I'll leave you to it."

"No," Beth says. "I'll go. You were already here."

"No, please, I insist." Getting to his feet, he gathers his cans, dropping one in the process. "Whoops. Sorry, I'm aware this is not a good look. I only got into town a few hours ago and felt too wired for bed. Want one? I'm not usually a bourbon man but turns out it pairs beautifully with a moonrise."

Beth says nothing. She knows she should leave, that it's a bad idea to be alone in the dark with a strange man. But for some reason she can't. Her feet seem glued to the floor.

"I'm Jesse," he says.

"Beth." She regrets it immediately. All those fake names at the ready and she gives her real one?

"Beth," he repeats. "Good to meet you. Traveling alone?"

"No. With a friend. She's, uh, showing me the vanlife ropes."

"Cool. And what do you do when you're not traveling?"

"Um. I work in, uh . . . sales. Distribution. Gadgets and stuff. You?"

"I'm a writer. Working on a travel book. Hence the travel. Here, are you sure you don't want one of these?" He holds out one of the cans. "There's no way I'll drink them all."

Don't you dare, she tells herself. *Go back to the van and go to bed.* But then she thinks of the HiAce, all its cavities and crevices and unfamiliar smells, the constant layer of dirt, and the fact that nothing is hers. She thinks of all the campgrounds she's been through, the Troopy with its fug of stale breath and seldom washed sheets, the beat-up VW T4 she'd fled Sydney in, and suddenly she's desperate for something uncomplicated, just a normal conversation with a normal guy, someone who doesn't know her or want anything from her, someone with whom she could stop pretending, even just for five minutes, because why can't she have that? Why shouldn't two people just hang out under the stars, have a drink and get to know each other? Is it so bad to take a chance once in a while? Does it have to be all *safety first* and *read the room* all the damn time? Can't a woman just let go and enjoy the ride?

Before she can stop herself she's accepting the can from Jesse's out-stretched hand. Her fingers brush his. Electricity crackles in the air between them—

But then she stops. Something is wrong. There's oddly familiar scent in her nose, spicy and woodsy. It reminds her of . . .

All the hairs on her arms stand on end. Another breath in, and she's back on that dark dusty track in the middle of nowhere, the clink of stone on stone and a potent smell of cologne floating in through the par-tially open window. She drops the can.

Jesse frowns. "What's wrong?"

"You. You were there. That night."

Jesse's brow crinkles. "Sorry?"

"On the track, off the highway. *You* put those stones outside the van. You've been following us the whole time." She pulls the crumpled note from her pocket and holds it out. *Are you safe?* "Was this you? Did you put this on our van? Is this your number?"

Jesse's expression wavers, just for a split second, but it's enough.

"It is." Beth presses herself into the corner of the balustrade. "It *was* you. Those articles too. Your name isn't Jesse, is it? It's William. Or Chris. Shit, are you Chris Craig?"

"What are you talking about? Who's Chris?"

"Oh my god, fuck this." Beth makes for the stairs but Jesse, or who-ever the hell he is, extends an arm like a barrier and blocks her path. "Okay, wait. Let me explain?"

"Nope." Backing away, she glances over her shoulder and down to the dunes below. Could she jump the balustrade, run to the beach?

"Please, Beth."

"Why the fuck would you do that?" She looks back at him. "Why would you leave notes outside someone's van? What were you trying to do?"

"Notes, plural?" He looks genuinely confused. "I left my number, in case you needed me, but that's it."

"*Needed* you?"

He steps toward her. "Well, maybe not me specifically but—"

"Get the fuck away from me."

"All right, okay." He puts his hands up as if *she's* the threat. "Just please, give me two minutes. I promise, I'm not going to hurt you."

Heard that one before. She looks at the dunes again. Would the balustrade hold her weight?

"My name *is* Jesse," he says, quickly. "Jesse Anderson, and I'm a writer. Mostly freelance, and just filler stuff so far but trying to break into investigative journalism. I'm working on a podcast, an *Unsolved Mysteries* kind of thing, but I needed firsthand accounts, people's lived experiences, something original as opposed to the usual spooky crap, and I couldn't find anyone willing to talk to me. Until Katy."

Beth wonders, if she rushed at him suddenly, could she get past and make a bolt for the HiAce?

"It was at this campsite, a beach camp near Jurien Bay. A bunch of us had a fire going and she was wandering around looking pretty upset, so I asked if she was okay and she told me about Phoebe. It got my attention. I'd been following the search for Vivi Green and wondered immediately if there might be a connection, possibly also with other missing backpackers. I knew that if I could tie it all together I'd have a real story on my hands. So I asked Katy if I could interview her."

Beth eyes the cans. How much has he had? Enough to slow him down? Is there anything around she can throw at him or use as a weapon?

"Honestly, it was unethical," Jesse continues. "She seemed kind of out of it. A couple of other campers noticed and expressed concern, but I was desperate to keep her talking so I told them we were a couple so I could walk her back to her van. Which I did, and it seemed like I might be getting somewhere, but then she got upset. Like, *really* upset. I tried to calm her down and, well, that's when I noticed it."

Beth looks up. "Noticed what?"

Jesse frowns. "It's hard to explain. At the time I thought she was drunk but . . ." He scratches his chin. "It's like, have you seen her blank out? You know when just stops talking and her eyes go all vacant? The way she changes when she gets upset? And at night . . . she sleepwalks, doesn't she? I wasn't sure exactly what was up, but I have a sixth sense for these things and I just knew I was onto something bigger than just a missing sister, something I could *really* write about. But I couldn't persuade her to talk to me so I—"

"Stop." Beth holds up a hand. "*Sleepwalks?* I mean, no, she doesn't, but how the hell would you know a thing like that?"

"She does. And I know because I saw her. At the beach camp. When I couldn't get Katy to open up, I cut my losses, went back to my own van and pulled together a few samples of my work, short pieces I'd written as part of my pitch. I thought if I could get her to read my work then she might understand how serious I am, that I want to help her get answers. I even suggested we travel together in convoy. I thought we could help each other."

He sighs. "So then I took the pieces over to her van, intending to tuck them under the wiper or whatever, but the side door was open. I knocked and called out, but she wasn't there. So I put the articles on the edge of the counter and I had a look around to see if I could see her. I was worried, y'know? Campers don't often leave their vehicles open like that in the middle of the night, and like I said she was a bit of a mess. Anyway, I eventually spotted her on the beach. She was standing at the shoreline with her feet in the water, just staring into space and swaying slightly. She stayed there for like twenty minutes. And then she turned and kind of lumbered like a zombie back to her van, got in, closed the door, and that was that. Until . . ." Jesse looks sheepish. "I saw it again. Later."

"What do you mean, later? When?"

"At a rest stop near Kalbarri. And then again on that side road. The one with all the rocks. Which, by the way, I definitely did not put there."

"Wait, what? How did you know we would be in those places?"

He grimaces. "Christ, this is going to sound totally insane. I, uh . . . put a tracker on the van."

All the air rushes from Beth's lungs. "You did *what*?"

"At the beach camp. That's how I knew she'd be at the horse ranch, the rest stop, the roadhouse, and so on."

"You were at Plains Ranch?"

"Yeah, I knocked on the door, tried again to talk to her."

Beth thinks back. *Everything okay? Who was that at the door?* She'd been too busy hiding from Mr. and Mrs. Airstream to look for herself.

Jesse wags a finger at her. "I was pretty surprised when I saw you, by the way. Where did you come from?"

"You can't track someone without their knowledge," Beth splutters, ignoring him. "That's so fucking illegal." Not impossible, though. Or difficult. Any idiot could order one online, she knows that firsthand.

Jesse groans. "Look, I know, it wasn't cool, but just listen. So then I followed you guys around Kalbarri, watched Katy do her thing with her sister's photos and all the questions. I tailed you to the rest stop, saw her sleepwalk there as well, then all the way up the highway to a roadhouse. I parked up and watched her through the window, talking to someone in the restaurant. She sat down, I assumed she'd be there a while so I went to find a bathroom. But when I got back, you guys had gone and one of my tires was flat."

Beth scans her memory of that night, too. *The shadow man.* Had that been Jesse? Or someone else?

"That cost me some time," Jesse continues. "By the time I set off again it was pretty late. I thought I'd really have to motor to catch you guys up, but when I checked the app you were just sitting on the road about thirty clicks away. I thought maybe you'd broken down. I wanted to help, but I didn't want to scare you so I parked some distance away with my headlights off, then got out and walked. The van's door was open and the lights were on, so I went closer to check it out but she wasn't there."

"Yes, she was." Beth remembers the noises, Jesse's cologne, and Katy's voice in the back of the van. "We both were."

"Well, I didn't get close enough to see you, but I did see her. I was checking out the weird rocks around your van—again, not me, I thought maybe you guys had built them as some sort of protective trap—and then she just comes lumbering out of the dark in exactly the same way as before, like a zombie. I hid—even though she couldn't see me, she was blatantly fast asleep—and then she got in the van, and I thought that was it until a few minutes later when she starts shining her torch around. So I got out of there."

"So, you didn't leave those articles outside? At that place, or at Kalbarri?"

"No. Like I said, I gave them to Katy at the beach camp, put them on the counter in her van."

Beth stares at him. How is he saying all this so casually, like it's something people do every day?

"Anyway, so then I followed the tracker to Monkey Mia, by which time I'd decided it wasn't Katy I needed to talk to but you."

"But *why?*" Beth explodes. "*Why* would you follow two women in a van for almost nine hundred kilometers? What the hell did you want to talk to either of us about that could possibly justify that?"

Jesse inches forward, his expression earnest. "Again, it's really hard to explain but I knew from the start that there was something going on with Katy. And I was right, but I never would've guessed that—"

"Don't come near me." Beth squeezes herself even farther into the corner of the lookout. "Stay away."

"Sorry," he says, even as he continues his approach. "I get that I'm totally stuffing this up and I never should've followed you but I really need to talk to you, I need tell you something."

"No." Beth tenses her muscles, prepares to run. "I don't want to hear it."

He keeps coming. "I googled Phoebe Sweeney."

"Stop talking."

"You know what I found?"

"Come closer and I'll scream." She scrabbles at the balustrade, testing for wobbly planks, loose nails. She looks down again at the sand and bushes below. Could she outrun him on the beach?

"Beth, stop. Katy is dangerous. She's not who she says she is."

Be confident. And quick. In one swift move, she lashes out with her foot and catches Jesse in the chest. Winded, he staggers back, and she takes the opportunity to hoist herself up and over. Pushing off the balustrade, she swan dives into the night.

"Beth, don't!"

She lands hard on her side, the scrubby bushes barely breaking her fall, and her shoulder pops with pain, but somehow she finds her feet and keeps going, stumbling breathlessly down the slope and toward the water.

The slope flattens out and the soft sand becomes hard as she picks up pace, sprinting as fast as she can away from Jesse. This fucking town. *Sounds like a great place to grow up.* She should never have come here. *Don't stay too long, or you might not live to tell the tale.*

She splashes through rippling shallows with no real idea of where she's going or what she'll do next—and then a figure rears up before her.

She trips, her chest seizing with pain. Pins and needles run up and down her hands and arms, stars cloud her vision, and her knees give way beneath her. The last thing she sees before she drops to the ground is a woman gliding fast over the sand toward her, arms outstretched as if eager to claim her.

CHAPTER FIFTY-ONE

Katy

I open my eyes. I'm not in the van. I'm outside, on the beach with my feet in the water, still dressed in the clothes I went to bed in. Baby waves ripple over my bare toes.

I look up—dark sky, moon, and stars—then turn in a slow circle. *Phoebe?* I had the same dream again, the lake and the sweep of light, her hand in mine. The feeling returns: that sickening drop in my belly like going upside down on a roller coaster. I can still hear her voice, as clear as if she's standing right behind me—*William, William, William*—but when I reach for her she's gone.

How did I get here? I used to sleepwalk as a kid but I haven't for years . . . or not as far as I know, anyway. I look back toward the car park, shuddering at the thought of my body walking all that way without me. If I hadn't woken up, how far in might I have gone? All the way? The shuddering turns into a shake. I turn back to the sea, feeling its pull.

And then I see her. Lily. She's running fast, flying over the sand, splashing into the shallows, eyes wide, mouth stretched, and she's heading straight for me. I move toward her, *what's happening, are you all right?* And then she's falling, crumbling onto the sand, landing in a heap, and rolling onto her back, face tipped toward the moon.

I rush to her side. "Lily!"

She shoves me away.

"Lily, it's me, it's Katy."

She stares at me, her chest heaving. "A man," she says. "Up there . . . the lookout . . . following us . . ."

"What? Where?"

"Over there." She points vaguely at the dunes. "Please . . . get away . . . run . . ."

I smooth her hair back from her face. "Hey, it's okay, it's just me. I'm here, I've got you."

"No, need to leave . . . he followed us . . . tracker . . . on your . . ."

I can barely hear her; the words are just sounds. "Come on, we can talk back at the van." Hauling her upright, I guide her up the beach, away from the water, and back to the car park.

Again, she mutters something about the lookout, but as far as I can see the platform is empty.

"What were you doing at the beach?" I wrap a blanket around Lily's shivering body and press a glass of water into her hands.

"Could ask you the same," she says, through chattering teeth. "Woke up and you were gone. I found a . . . a new note." She fishes in her pocket and pulls out a damp piece of paper.

Unfolding it, I find a phone number. There's something written above it, but I can't see what. The paper is too wet and the ink has run.

"I tried to find you. Got as far as the lookout. And that's . . . that's where he was."

"Where who was?"

Lily takes a sip of water and lets out a slow breath. "He says his name's Jesse Anderson. He's a writer, a journalist . . . wants to speak to you about the story."

"A writer?" I shake my head. There's something weird about what she just said, something I can't pinpoint. "What story?"

"Phoebe. He said he met you at some beach camp and has been following you ever since."

"Following me?" Something unlatches in my chest. *Jesse. Beach camp.* I put the note on the counter and search for "Jesse Anderson writer journalist" on my phone. A crop of images come up: mid-to-late thirties, scruffy brown hair, olive skin, and dark eyes. It's him. The man at the horse ranch who tapped on my door and knew Phoebe's name—*Sorry for your loss. I'm pretty good at puzzles*—who'd apparently taken care of me back at some beach camp of which I had very little memory, who informed me I'd been in a "state," and near whose shoe print I'd found Phoebe's bobby pin. *Your boyfriend.*

"Did he hurt you?" I manage.

"No. I thought he might, but . . . no."

"Chris Craig. It has to be. That must be his real name. Or the name he uses online?"

Lily shakes her head. "I don't think so."

"But the notes he left . . . And all the clues. He *wanted* me to know that he knew about her, knew that I was trying to find her. And he *was* stalking us, you just said so. It *has* to be him."

Lily's face twists. "I know it looks that way, and I could be wrong, but he seemed to be genuine. Really fucking bad at his job, obviously, and quite probably a sociopath. But I don't think he was lying."

I press my fingers to my eyes. I've got that feeling again. Something about what she's telling me feels wrong, but I don't know what. My head feels like it's about to explode. Tiny spots swim like fish behind my eyeballs. "But," I manage, "if this Jesse person *isn't* Chris Craig then why would he follow me?"

"He thinks there's a link between Phoebe and the woman on the posters. What's her name? Vivi Green. He wants to write your story and sell it to some paper or magazine or whatever. Y'know, missing vanlifer, grief-stricken sister trying to find answers, an unexpected connection to an unsolved mystery. He said he approached you at the beach camp and asked if you'd do an interview."

A hazy recollection darts out of the depths—*I don't suppose you've given any more thought to teaming up?*—then sinks back down again.

"He told me you said no, so he gave you some examples of his work, articles he'd written about missing people. He thought they might convince you to speak with him, take him seriously."

"Wait," I say. "Those notes . . . he said he *gave* them to me?"

"At the beach camp. He sort of posted them through the door. Which, if it's true, means the first two weren't left for you to find after all, they were already in the van. They just sort of turned up, probably after a cleanup or something, and you assumed they'd been planted."

I gape at her. Already in the van? But how would I not have seen or known about them? And I don't have *any* memory of Jesse asking for an interview, or even telling me he was a journo. "What about the clues?" I say. "The bobby pin, the hair, the piles of rocks, and the William thing."

"I don't think that was him."

"Why? How?" There can't be a *second* person trailing us.

"Because I think he would've mentioned it. He admitted doing worse things."

"Worse?"

Lily winces. "He put a tracker on the van. He knew where you were the whole time. Watched us both like a creep."

My mind screeches another sharp corner. "He put *what* on the van?"

"A tracker. Actually, it's probably still there." Shrugging off the blanket, Lily puts her glass down, opens the door, and steps outside.

When I follow, I find her on her knees by the back left tire. "It might be difficult to see," she says, feeling around inside the wheel well, "but it should be around here somewhere." Rising again, she pushes past me and crouches by the front left wheel where she repeats the sweep before moving on to the front bumper and the front right wheel. "He would've put it somewhere easy to . . . aha, got it." Lily reaches into the arch and tugs at something. There's a faint metallic click. "See?" She holds up a very small black cube the size of a nine-volt battery with two metal circles on the top.

But suddenly I'm not looking at the tracker. A horrible realization has sunk deep into my flesh, sharp and cold like the point of a knife pressed to my throat. I stare into Lily's eyes, nauseous with disbelief.

"Katy?" she says. "What's wrong?"

I open my mouth but the words get stuck. Because the jarring feeling, the thing I couldn't pinpoint, the weirdness that's been bugging me throughout this whole conversation . . . I see it. I know what it is.

CHAPTER FIFTY-TWO

Beth

"What's wrong with your voice?"

Beth feels like she's plunging off a cliff. Panicking, she plays back what she's just said—or rather, *how* she's said it—and the ground shifts beneath her.

Fuck.

Her accent.

Lily.

In her distress, Beth has forgotten the pretense and dropped her American alias. Everything she's said since Katy dragged her off the beach has been spoken with a cadence and inflection as Australian as Katy's own.

For a moment, she thinks she might vomit. But amid the fear is a shard of relief. She can stop now, give up the ghost. It was, after all, inevitable; she couldn't pretend forever. It's possible she even self-sabotaged just so she could drop the burden of deception. *Enough now, time to rest.*

"I lied," Beth says simply, the words coming out like a sigh. "The visa, the sundial, everything. I wasn't traveling alone. And I wasn't attacked—at least, not in the way you think. My name isn't even Lily.

It's Beth. Beth Randall. And I'm not from the US, I'm from Melbourne."

One she starts, it's impossible to stop. The truth gushes from her like clean, fresh spring water. She tells Katy everything. And as she does, a little of herself returns.

CHAPTER FIFTY-THREE

Katy

As Lily—no, *Beth*—peels back layer after layer of lies I'm left feeling un-skinned, like she's taken my actual flesh and bones along with everything I thought I knew about her. Also small, because if she hadn't slipped up by accident when might she have told me? I think back over all our conversations, all the things she's shared, all the ways we've bonded over travel and loss and our families, and wonder if any of it was real. Why wasn't I worth the truth?

"I'm so sorry," Beth says when she's done. "I should never have lied. I know I don't deserve forgiveness. I've been so stupid. But I'm telling you the truth now. About everything."

I don't know what to say. I can't process what's happening.

"I really was hurt that night," she continues. "I genuinely did need your help, and I'm so incredibly grateful that you gave it." Her face crinkles up and tears dribble down the sides of her nose. She wipes them with the hem of her T-shirt. "I'm a shitty, shitty person. I don't deserve even one good thing."

I know I should say something nice but I can't. I don't know how.

"You have no reason to let me stay," Beth says, wiping away fresh tears, "but please don't kick me out. I'll do everything I can to be useful. I can still help you find out what happened to Phoebe; I *want* to help.

I'll cook and clean and sleep up in the cab. I'll figure out a way to pay you back every dollar you've spent on me. And I promise on my life, I'll never, ever lie to you again."

She stops speaking. I'm overwhelmed—and physically unstable, as if my body is now just a network of tunnels about to collapse. I'm angry; furious, in fact. But after hearing her story I can also understand her reasons. And now we, my van and me, are all she has left. Without us, she has nothing.

"Beth," I say, trying it out. "Beth. Okay. I think maybe . . . we can start over."

Her face lights up. "You mean it?"

I hesitate, thinking back to the first time she asked to stay. I have an opportunity to make a different choice this time, disentangle myself, forget I ever met her. But I can't. I just can't.

I nod. "Of course."

"Oh my god, thank you. I know I don't deserve it. Honestly, I don't understand how you can be so kind to me but I'm so grateful that you are."

Of course she doesn't understand. How could she after all she's endured? But I do. I get it.

"It's not about kindness," I say. "It's about being a team. Because that's what we are now. And who else in the whole world does either of us have?"

CHAPTER FIFTY-FOUR

Beth

The next morning, Beth wakes in the bed to find Katy fast asleep beside her. The previous night rushes back—the note, Jesse, the beach, the tracker, how she confessed everything to Katy and cried her eyes out, and how Katy forgave her. Fingers entwined, they both lay down afterward, silently agreeing that neither should be on their own overnight, and almost instantly Beth fell into one of the deepest sleeps of her life. Looks like the same was true for Katy too. She's dead to the world, her breathing deep and even. A little pale and clammy, too. Maybe she's coming down with something.

Beth checks the time and finds that it's almost midday. Sliding quietly off the mattress she grabs her wash bag and a towel and leaves the van through the side door. Outside, the air is warm but the sky is heavy with cloud. She walks to the bathroom, feeling bad that even after all last night's honesty she still hasn't mentioned Lucas's messages. Half of her just doesn't want to believe it's true.

And after all, maybe this is a big fuss over nothing. In the shower, she wonders: what if Phoebe just got sick of being stalked and went dark for a while? Maybe she was already unhappy or running from something at home. Maybe she enjoyed her new off-grid lifestyle so much, she stayed that way. It's possible that she visited Lucas, said hi, and moved on. She could now be living her best life in Patagonia or Cuba or Greece. Beth knows better than anyone how easy it is to disappear.

Imagine, Beth thinks as she brushes her teeth, *if Phoebe were to be found safe and well and happy.* How relieved Katy would be, how grateful. All the red in Beth's ledger would surely be wiped clean away.

With an idea churning away in her mind, she dries her hands, fixes her hair, and heads back to the HiAce knowing exactly what she needs to do next.

Leaving Katy sleeping, she sets off into town, striding out along the main tourist drag, eating an apple as she goes. She passes dive shops, bus stops, a community bulletin board. Café after café after café. The sky is even darker now, bulging with the threat of rain.

She walks the three blocks to the pub, then right again into what appears to be a more residential area. Garages and gardens, swing sets and trampolines. The modest homes of locals. *141 South Beach Street.* She repeats it like a mantra for over an hour until finally she finds it right at the edge of town.

The street itself stretches almost all the way from the ocean to the scrub. Like most others in Gracious Bay, it's wide and exposed, the bitumen rough and potholed. Cars sit on browning lawns as if they're not sure of their place. In one or two yards, the Australian flag flaps languidly from poles, the material sun-bleached and ragged.

Number 141 is at the end farthest from the ocean, the second last on the street. Beth stands in the shade of a tree, staring across the road at the powder blue door. It looks almost the same as in the photo, just a little timeworn and missing a redheaded kid in the foreground. It's a detached single-story cottage, old but well maintained, with a magnolia tree sprouting from a neatly mown front lawn. The garden is simple but nicely kept: a few succulents, fresh woodchip, and a wide driveway to one side.

Beth looks up and down the street. The neighborhood is oddly quiet. No one outside gardening or mowing the lawn or washing the car, no twitching curtains or wafting food smells. There aren't even any barking dogs. She's about to cross the road when she stops and ducks back behind the tree. Something is moving on the driveway. A car, backing slowly out into the road. Her breath catches when she sees the model: a black ute with a tradesman's canopy.

You.

It feels like years since she last saw it, but also no time at all. All those drop locations, the various fields and barns and silos and bridges. She remembers each one as if it were yesterday.

She waits until the ute passes, not daring to breathe let alone risk a look at the driver. And when it's gone, trundling down the road and disappearing around the corner, she waits some more. She watches the house, yard, and driveway. And when she's as sure as she can possibly be that no other cars are about to emerge, she hurries across the road and up the porch steps to the front door.

The wooden boards creak under the soles of her sandals. She peers through a couple of windows, considers knocking on the door. What would she do if someone answers? *Hey, what's up, my name's Beth, is Lucas home? I'm his ex, I just left him. Do you happen to know if he killed a woman called Phoebe? Oh, and if there's anything in there that belongs to me—bank cards, driver's license, a couple of cute dresses—I'll have it back now if that's okay?* She eyes the house next door, calculating what she might say if a neighbor gets suspicious. *Hello, I'm Jane, I'm collecting a package for my friend while she's away on holiday; this is number fourteen, right?*

She taps lightly on the blue paint, but there's no answer. Heading back down the steps, she goes around the side of the house to the driveway, which seems to be shared with number 143. At the end is a double fibro garage with a pitched roof, divided at the apex and painted two slightly different shades of cream. The doors are different too: the left-hand side is a metal roller, the right a three-part bifold with mottled glass windows.

The backyard is just as neat and bland as the front: a square of lawn with an old rotary clothesline at its center, several strings of which are missing, and a frangipani tree in one corner. At the rear of the house, Beth counts four windows, three large, one small, and a screen door atop three concrete steps. At the far end, a paved patio area is protected by a translucent lean-to covering.

Beth weighs up her options. The small window is promising; beyond the mesh of the flyscreen, she can see clearly that the sash is open. But a door is always preferable and this one looks pretty flimsy. It shouldn't be too hard.

Don't think, just do. The quicker the better.

In the sky above, a faint rumble of thunder.

CHAPTER FIFTY-FIVE

Wyatt

"I have to run out," says Dad, striding through the kitchen on his way to the front door. "Just gotta get rid of today's cuttings and chase up a few invoices. You'll be all right?"

Wyatt looks up from the sink, a wet dishcloth in his hand. "Sure." Through the living room window he can see Dad's ute parked in the driveway, its tray bursting with branches and leaves.

"If Lucas gets here before I do, just tell him to go ahead and dump his stuff in the usual place."

This strikes Wyatt as a mildly odd thing to say—what stuff, what usual place?—but Dad's already halfway out before he can ask.

"And you don't have to do all that," he calls, waving a finger at the cluster of cleaning products on the counter. "Don't get me wrong, it's great, but don't go nuts."

"It's fine. I want to do it."

Dad throws him a baffled glance before continuing on his way. "Just like your mother," he says over his shoulder. Then the front door swings shut and he's gone.

Wyatt washes the last of the dishes and places it carefully on the drainer. He's already vacuumed, dusted, tidied away the piles of dirty laundry and all the stray shoes; there's only the bathroom still to go—

and he wasn't lying, he really is happy to do it all. Lucas is coming home again, maybe for good this time, or so he said on the phone, so it's important that both he and Dad think it's a nice place to be, even though it isn't, not really, and it's getting worse.

Wyatt doesn't just hear and see things now, he feels them too, like all the strange sights and sounds are animals sniffing around his feet, brushing up against his legs and pawing at his skin. The dream is back, the one he used to have night after night as a kid, the one about the demon from that old movie, and it's bleeding into reality. He sees the demon stalking through the house at night, trailing its fingers along the walls, slipping out into the yard and disappearing into the garage. In the moments between asleep and awake, Wyatt thinks that's where it must live, this demon, out in the garage. He avoids it now, never goes out to the pavers anymore, has abandoned his trinkets, left them in the hole like offerings. And right on cue, as if his thoughts have summoned them like a spell, there they are: the Noises, muffling shuffling, crunching, creeping. He stops to listen. The sounds are coming from the yard.

Automatically, Wyatt ducks away from the window, presses himself to the wall, then sneaks a look, half expecting the dream-demon, half expecting Mrs. Creeping again—but what he sees is neither. The woman—girl?—in the yard is young. And pretty. Wyatt doesn't recognize her. For a heart-freezing moment he's convinced it's the ghost, Eleanor Flannery, come to drag him into the sea. But—he takes another peek—no, the girl is real. And apparently casing the house.

He watches, still and silent, as she examines the windows, peers up at the roof, approaches the back door. Wyatt edges away toward the hallway and his bedroom, his nervous system tingling. If Dad were here, he'd go straight out there and demand to know what's going on. If this were a movie, the hero would go toward the scary noise, not away. But Wyatt knows better, cannot even count the number of violent screen deaths that could've been avoided if only the hapless characters had found the right place to hide.

The back door rattles. The handle turns. She's coming in.

Like a shadow, Wyatt slips down the hallway and into the linen closet. And as the door swings open and the stranger in the yard enters his house, he crouches down, covers himself with a towel and makes himself small.

CHAPTER FIFTY-SIX

Beth

Beth pokes her head around the door, which was surprisingly unlocked. Lino floor, acrylic benchtops, cheap electric stove. A circular six-seater dining table, worn and scarred from years of use. Hallway to the left. She stands on the threshold for as long as she can, breathing slowly, attuning herself to the building, listening for any sign that there might be still someone home. After several minutes of absolute silence, she steps forward into a fug of store cupboard spices and multi-purpose cleaner, underlaid with human musk. There's a bleach smell too. The house has been cleaned recently.

If she had any lingering doubt that this is Lucas's family home, it disappears when she sees the photos. His face is all over the walls: as a toddler, schoolboy, teenager, and beyond. Birthday cakes and bouncy castles, fishing trips, and Christmas trees. She sees the brother too, the kid from Lucas's wallet, aging slowly in a series of five school photos. Moving to study a selection above the dining table, she notices that Lucas had much lighter hair as a child. His eyes were brighter too, almost amber instead of the mocha brown she knows.

Her stomach turns and she averts her eyes, forcing them elsewhere. She moves farther into the kitchen. The house is old but someone has tried hard to make it a nice place to live; there are as many decorative accents—jugs and vases, refrigerator magnets, house plants—as there are cracks and watermarks. She opens a few cupboards and finds neatly stacked crockery and carefully placed mugs.

Beyond the kitchen is a living room with a threadbare carpet and an equally worn rug. An L-shaped sofa, a coffee table, and two mismatched armchairs draped with patterned throws. One wall is dominated by an enormous flat-screen TV positioned above a cheap-looking entertainment unit. Another holds oversize shelving, the boxy type sold in Ikea and Kmart, each square holding a messy array of knickknacks and sun-faded schoolroom drawings. One picture frame, fancier than the others and prominently placed, contains a slightly misty enlargement of a willowy woman with long golden hair sitting outside on a picnic blanket—and Beth double-takes as she passes it, her skin prickling with what she thinks at first is recognition. *Phoebe?* But no, on closer inspection the woman in the photo is older and slimmer, her earthy Joni Mitchell vibe slightly at odds with the prissy daisy-patterned cardigan she's wearing. She's leaning toward the camera with a half smile as if about to tell a secret, a sweet silver necklace gleaming at her throat. Lucas's runaway mother, Beth assumes. But the resemblance to Phoebe is unnerving.

She stares at the photo for several minutes before a sudden rumble from outside diverts her attention. A car? A truck? A neighbor wheeling their bin out to the street? No. Thunder again, still faint but getting closer.

She waits for it to pass, then tiptoes around the room, running her hands over dusty surfaces, opening drawers and inspecting the shelves. She doesn't find any of her belongings but she does find a battered iPhone on the bookcase, a power cord trailing from its port to an unseen plug socket somewhere behind the unit. Beth taps the screen with her knuckle and it lights up with a standard lock screen. She swipes up. Passcode. *Damn.* She takes it anyway, pulling out the charger before sliding it into her pocket.

She creeps back out of the living room and to the hallway off the kitchen. Daylight spills through two open doors on the left-hand side.

Another door stands ajar at the very end. Two more on the right are closed. How weird it is to be here. She'd spent so much time picturing Lucas's house, imagining what it would be like to meet his family, to spend weekends and holidays with them. She runs her fingertips over the faded wallpaper, marveling at how many times he must've done the same—

She stiffens as a sudden noise pierces her awareness, a faint click or a creek, so quiet she can't be sure she hasn't imagined it. She listens, waits. A bird caws from somewhere in the yard, rough and grating like the squeak of bedsprings. A distant car horn beeps three times, a cheerful greeting rather than a warning. Nothing from within the house.

Cautiously, Beth moves on. The first door in the hallway leads to a cramped laundry and toilet, the second to a bedroom that smells strongly of boy. She lingers in the doorway of the bedroom, taking note of the single mattress on the floor, the balled-up quilt, the sheet tacked up over the window in place of a curtain. Snack wrappers litter the floor, clothes and shoes have been flung into corners. Movie posters line the walls, mostly horrors. *The Lost Boys, A Nightmare on Elm Street, Wolf Creek, Hereditary.* A chunky laptop sits on a desk littered with notebooks and pens. She checks through the drawers and wardrobe but again comes away empty-handed.

She backs out, ensuring the door stands ajar at exactly the angle she found it, then nudges open the two doors on the right: a linen closet packed with towels and a tidy if damp-smelling bathroom.

The last door at the very end of the hall leads to another bedroom with a small window that looks out onto the backyard. She studies the unmade double bed with its squashed pillow and thin patterned quilt, the built-in wardrobe with its wide-open doors. There doesn't appear to be much inside, just some sweaters, shirts, jeans, and shoes, all more obviously masculine than feminine. The room looks exactly like it was styled by a woman whose presence has long been missing.

She checks the shelves, the drawers, but finds nothing more interesting than loose paperwork and a jumble of electrical cords. In one of the bedside tables, though, she discovers a significant amount of prescription meds: benzodiazepines, according to the labels. Antidepressants. The name on all of them is Rory Cleary, which she presumes must be Lucas's father? There are some unmarked bags too, full of random tablets, as well as a few disposable syringes. Beth presses her finger into the corners of the drawer and it comes away coated with grains of white powder.

Leaving everything as she'd found it, she goes back to the kitchen and steeples her fingers against her lips. If there's no one to talk to and nothing of interest to be found, what's her next move? What is she even looking for, besides her stuff? She's not exactly sure, but her gut is telling her something is here.

She scans the ceilings for a loft space, checks unsuccessfully for a basement. And then her gaze falls on the kitchen window—or rather, what lies beyond.

Interesting.

Pushing open the back door, she returns to the yard.

CHAPTER FIFTY-SEVEN

Wyatt

Curled up tight in the linen closet, Wyatt listens to the intruder moving around the house. Who is she? Why is she here? What does she want? He pats his pocket, thinking that now would be a great time to text Dad and tell him to come home, but it's empty. His phone is in its usual place on the bookshelf.

He can hear her padding quietly from room to room. Her footsteps are soft and quiet and slow. It doesn't sound like she's taking or breaking anything; it sounds more like she's looking for something. But what could she possibly want in here? There's nothing valuable, besides the TV. What would he do if she *does* go for the TV? He immediately thinks of a movie where three kids break into a blind man's house only to find out that he's a psycho. Could Wyatt embody that man's vengeance to do what he did? It's a pointless thought.

Then his heart knocks violently against his ribs as the door of the linen closet opens and light spills inside, through the fabric of the towel over his head. He holds his breath. One . . . two . . . three . . . The door closes again, and thank fuck, because what would he have done?

He listens. The girl is in Dad's room now, rummaging through his stuff. Not for long through—now she's back in the hallway, passing the closet, padding through the kitchen. Silence. Then the back door creaks and the house is quiet again.

He lets time do its thing. *Not yet, too soon, just wait.* After an indeterminate pause, he crawls from his hole and stands up. Creeps cautiously from room to room. The girl has gone. Nothing appears to be missing.

He's about to fetch his phone from the living room and call Dad when he stops. Stares. Outside in the yard, the door to the garage is standing wide open.

CHAPTER FIFTY-EIGHT

Katy

I wake up alone. Lily is gone and the world is shaking. The van is shuddering, the mattress vibrating, the curtains sway over my head—but no, it isn't the van. It's me. I'm convulsing, cold, so cold, teeth chattering, limbs numb, skin damp with sweat. My pulse beats mud-slow in my ears, a heavy Doppler throb, and my chest is a balloon about to burst.

"Lily?" Then I remember: that's not her name. "*Beth*." The name feels odd on my tongue. "Beth, are you here? Hello?"

I curl up onto my side. I need help. There's something wrong with me. I roll back again and stare blankly at the ceiling. My eyesight is filled with strange spidery patterns, words that wriggle like sea snakes in the air. I squeeze my eyes shut and they go away. I open them again, and they're back. I blink. The words are on the walls, they cover the ceiling—and the more I stare, the more I realize it's just the same seven letters over and over, and not in my head but real, written in black pen all over the inside of my camper: the walls, the floor, the cabinets, the countertop.

William, William, William, William, William . . .

I lurch off the bed and to my feet. Someone has been in here while I was sleeping. Someone has scribbled all over my home. Beth? No, not her, she wouldn't do this, not after everything we've been through, not given her recent honesty. So who then?

Chris Craig.

It has to be. Rage blazes inside me, spreading outward from my center until I am consumed. I have to find him. All of this, it has to stop. I grab my phone from the counter and bring up Phoebe's Instagram. I go straight to the messages and scroll for his name—then stop. My vision flickers, then narrows as another name leaps from the screen and burrows into my brain.

Lucas Cleary.

Bells start to ring, unbearably loud. *Lucas.* Temples throbbing, I think back to last night, to Beth's confession. She told me she hadn't been attacked by a stranger after all; she hadn't even been traveling alone. She told me she'd been trapped, controlled, and abused by her boyfriend. She said his name was Lucas.

I click into the message, scroll through the thread. It's long. There are pictures, too. Little red hearts everywhere. My guts slide around as though filled with eels. *Lucas.* Shaggy hair, tanned skin, stubbled cheeks. *You don't see nature, you feel it.* Broad shoulders, long legs. *You know those rare people in life who you'd trust with just about anything?* Bright green eyes, sweet smile. *Go dark. The last wild place on earth.*

I was wrong. Chris Craig is no one. He means nothing. This is who I've been looking for. *Lucas.* Beth's goddamn boyfriend.

Lies. All of it.

She knew. All along, she *knew.*

I race through the messages again.

I know a nice place by the beach.

Address?

141 South Beach Street.

I straighten up. My blood is burning. South Beach Street. That's where Beth's gone, that's where she is right now, I know it in my bones. She's left me and gone back to him. She's known the truth about Phoebe this whole time. What do I do, what do I do . . .

Look. Phoebe's voice in my head, another imagined answer. *Look, look, look.*

Not now, Pheebs. I don't have time to decipher her codes, but she won't shut up.

Look, Katy. Look, look, look.

I whirl around. Look at what? Everything's just as it was: closed curtains, balled-up shirts, ugly spindly writing on every damn surface—but then I see something: a bright triangle of turquoise poking out from underneath the rug.

Yes. Look.

Reaching out, I nudge the rug with my finger and it folds back to reveal curly yellow font. "Marine Paradise Awaits." It's the flyer, the one I picked up in Carnarvon: diver on the left, sculpture on the right. I must've dropped it. But why would Phoebe want me to see it?

I open it out. Pictures and text boxes. Backpackers hostel, holiday park, a map of the town, something about a shipwreck . . . and then, as I turn to the very back page I feel all the blood drain from my face.

William.

Abruptly, the shivering stops and I am filled instead with a strange calm.

William.

Well, how about that. Yet again, I've got it wrong.

William isn't a person.

It's a place.

CHAPTER FIFTY-NINE

Beth

Like the house, the garage is old and almost certainly riddled with asbestos. The corrugated roof is speckled with lichen, and black dirt crawls the once-white fibro walls. There's a small window in the side wall, and a jade-green hinged door, the paint bubbling and peeling like sunburned skin. A padlock hangs from a rusty bolt. Beth gives it a tug. Locked. *Damn.* But it's only small—thirty millimeters, probably only three or four pins, a cinch compared with an entire caravan.

She slides a bobby pin from her hair and bends it into the shape Lucas had taught her. Less than a minute later, the shackle swings away from the body. Throwing a quick look over her shoulder, she frees the padlock from the bolt, draws back the latch and the door creaks open onto a dank, yawning darkness.

Thunder rolls, louder this time, each rumble separate and distinct.

Inside, the garage smells of earth, dust, and chemicals. She can't see much at first, but as her eyes adjust to the gloom, she can make out bags of soil, a lawn mower, whipper-snipper, and wheelbarrow, all neatly lined up against the walls. A rusty barbecue, an old electric heater, a broken floor lamp . . . no room for a car, the ute is clearly kept outside. As she moves farther inside, she finds coils of hose, fishing poles, a couple of deck chairs, and an old washing machine. Tools displayed on a pegboard, fertilizer spray, and plant pots on heavy-duty shelving. Nothing out of the ordinary—except for a metal pole about a meter high, bolted to the center point of the floor. The surface of the pole is discolored and mottled with rust. A long chain trails from a loop at the top, like something a really terrible pet owner might use to tether a dog. Both the pole and the chain look years old, but some marks appear to be new. There are dark smears of what might be oil at the top, even darker drops on the floor at the base.

Unable to imagine what its use might be, Beth backs away and inspects the contents of the shelves: mostly cardboard boxes, some empty, some full of household odds and ends. Glancing down, she notices that the floor in front of one unit toward the back is free of dust, as if just one neat square has been swept clean and the rest ignored. There are drag marks, too. The shelf, she realizes, has been repeatedly pulled away from the wall.

Without thinking twice, she hooks her fingers around the side and pulls. Despite its size, the shelf slides easily over the floor. Behind it is a large sheet of plywood about the size of a fridge, which wobbles when nudged. *Unsecured.* Beth tugs at it and the whole thing topples forward, falling against the shelf with a soft thud. Peering behind, she sees a gap in the wall where a section has been crudely removed and sealed from the other side with yet another sheet of plywood. *Curiouser and curiouser.*

Like the first, the second sheet of plywood isn't secured either. She manages to inch it aside a little, creating enough of a gap to peek through into the neighboring garage, and finds yet another shadowy space, similar to the Clearys' but with even more shelves and no window. There's barely any light at all.

She takes the stolen phone from her pocket, activates the torch, and shines it around. More shelves line the walls, lots of them, sturdy and metallic like you might find in a warehouse, all packed with lumpy shapes. She squeezes herself all the way through the gap and stands up. The items, whatever they are, have all been wrapped carefully in plastic. She picks one up and can tell through the wrapping that it isn't a gardening tool or a plant pot. It's an appliance: black, smooth, and about two hand widths in length. She peels back a little of the plastic and sees a familiar silver logo.

Oh my god.

Ripping the rest of the wrapping away, she weighs the gadget in her hand, registers the familiarity of its size. The espresso maker. She runs her hands along the next shelf and finds a drone. A Bluetooth speaker. Laptop. Portable cooler.

Holy shit. Tommy and Evie. The Airstream.

She keeps going, recognizing camp chairs, stoves, fridges, freezers, hunting knives, barbecues, scuba fins, dive computers, wet suits, cameras, fishing rods, reels, spears, scooters, duffel bags, iPads, audio systems, smartwatches . . . she knows them all, has touched them all.

The cache.

Lucas's contact.

It's his father. The whole operation is a family business. But this is the neighbor's garage. Does that mean there are more people involved than she thought?

Frowning, she works her way around the edges of the room, sliding her fingers between each object, quietly and carefully searching among and behind and between, because if the stolen goods are here then might her stuff be with them? Once she's completed a full rotation, she starts again from the beginning and about halfway around she accidentally nudges a bulky item on a bottom shelf. The item topples onto the floor with a soft thud, and as Beth bends to replace it she spots an aluminum storage box shoved to the back. For something so tucked away, it's neither dusty nor dirty. Instead, it looks well-used.

She drags the box off the shelf, pops both button locks and lifts the lid. Inside is a black canvas bag, a duffel with circular ends and a long thick strap. She tugs at the zip and the bag opens up like the slit belly of an animal. When she sees the contents, Beth feels her jaw drop.

Money. A shit ton of it. Fat bricks of cash like in a movie.

Pulling the bag right out of the box, she rummages through it. The wads are bundles of twenty-, fifty-, and one-hundred-dollar bills. She can't even guess at what the total might be. Is this what the Clearys made from what she and Lucas stole? When they were paid barely enough to live on?

Her eyes drift back to the box. There's something else in there: another bag, also black but smaller and made of plastic. She shines the torch. It's a bin-liner wrapped tight around a package. Her heart lifts. The shape is tantalizingly familiar.

Please, oh please let it be what I think it is . . .

She rips a hole in the plastic and a phone falls out. Sweet baby Jesus, its *hers*. Dead, but still intact. And then *bloody hell* she's holding her credit cards, driver's license, Medicare card, her favorite shorts and crop tops and mini dress, she's cradling them like long-lost children, tears rolling down her face, whispering her thanks to god, the universe, and whatever else answers the prayers of people like her. Everything she needs to be free is right there in her arms.

Well, almost everything.

She eyes the duffel bag. In a weird, twisted, totally criminal way, the money within belongs to her . . . doesn't it? It, like the phone and the cards and the clothes, is hers.

Be confident and quick.

Moving swiftly, she wraps her cards and phone up in the clothes and shoves the lot inside the bag with the cash. She takes the stolen phone from her pocket and switches it off—unless she trips over a charger for hers on the way out she might still need it, and she can't risk it being tracked—then hoists the strap over her shoulder, gets to her feet and ducks back through the hole in the wall, replacing both sheets of plywood as she goes. Back in the first garage, she drags the shelf into place, hurries past the strange metal pole and barrels through the door, thinking of nothing but the road and Katy and the HiAce, getting in and driving away from Gracious Bay as fast as possible. Her face meets the sunlight and—

There's a boy in the yard.

He stands on the grass, arms hanging loosely at his sides, lips parted in surprise. Fair skin, green eyes, and copper-colored hair. *The kid in the photo.* Lucas's brother. He's grown, has to be fourteen at least, maybe fifteen or even sixteen.

He stares at Beth. Beth stares back. Time abandons its post.

The kid speaks first. "Who are you?" His voice is unsteady. "What are you doing here?"

Beth's mind is completely blank. She can't think of a single valid excuse for why she's on this person's property, why she's emerging from his garage with a bag on her back. She grips the strap. Her mouth opens and closes. And then she does the first thing that comes to mind. She lunges forward and shoves the boy hard in the chest, barely waiting for him to hit the ground before running full pelt toward the side of the house.

Dimly, she registers the sound of the back door. "Hey!" someone calls.

She turns and, *fuck,* it's Lucas, stepping from the house, his jaw dropping fast, *fuck, fuck, fuck!*

Adrenaline surging like rocket fuel, Beth achieves a hitherto unknown level of speed and focus, sprinting around the side of the house and down the driveway, duffel bag banging against her hip, eyes fixed only on the road on the road on the road, but shit, here they come, two sets of footsteps pounding the gravel behind her, and she knows she won't be able to outrun them, they're too fast, too big, too strong, and she's weak and small, but she has to try, she can't let him catch her, not again, she'd rather die, and she got away once so she just might again, if she's lucky, if she's fast, so she keeps going to the end of the driveway, over the lawn and across the street, and she really isn't doing too badly until she runs smack into the bonnet of an oncoming van.

CHAPTER SIXTY

Katy

William.

I drive, pushing my foot down as hard as I dare.

South Beach Street.

The ocean rushes by, the boat ramp, the pub.

Lucas.

I pull hard on the steering wheel and the van screeches around a corner. Another corner and I'm there, an ordinary road with ordinary houses and cars and mailboxes. I slow to a crawl, searching for numbers, searching for *her,* but somehow she finds me first, comes flying out from behind a house to the left, a blurry breathless shape moving comet-fast over dry grass and gravel and into the road, head whipping back over her shoulder—and then a second person appears, also running, a man with the same shaggy hair and broad shoulders from Phoebe's messages, *Lucas, Lucas,* his eyes flashing with fury and fixed on Lily, on Beth, *Get the fuck back here,* he yells but she doesn't even slow, she runs straight toward me and—

I slam on my brakes and yank the wheel. The van swerves, the bumper missing Beth by only a few inches, and she crashes shoulder first into the side panel. She looks up, her eyes white with fear—then she grabs the nearest handle and pulls. The sliding door opens and she throws herself inside just as the man called Lucas reaches her and I watch in the wing mirror as he grabs her ankle. She kicks hard, once, twice, but he's not letting go, so I throw the van into reverse, slam my foot to the floor, and the van screeches backward, fast enough to shake his grip. He goes down on all fours and, seeing my chance, I force the stick back into drive and accelerate again, aiming the HiAce right at his head. He's almost under my wheels, but at the very last minute he rolls away and the van crushes the garden fence instead of his skull. I reverse again, farther this time, then stop, engine snarling. *Lucas, Lucas,* still on the ground, an open target. I press the pedal, get ready to drive . . .

He looks up, right into my eyes, and a single thought slices me in two.

William.

Something changes. My focus shifts, and a deep knowing rises up inside me.

This is wrong. It's all wrong.

I breathe in, and out. Then I stamp down on the pedal and pull the steering wheel as hard as I can in the opposite direction. The wheels spin and we're moving, screeching away in a mess of fumes and black tire marks like jet contrails, out of town and back toward the highway, leaving Lucas and South Beach Street far behind us.

The side door slides shut. In the back of the van, just under the sound of the engine, I can hear Beth breathing.

CHAPTER SIXTY-ONE
Wyatt

"What the fuck happened, Wyatt?" Lucas is panting hard, his face red and furious.

"I don't know! She was in the house, and then—"

"In *here*?"

"Yeah, but I didn't know who she was or why she—"

"What did you do?"

"I—I hid."

"You hid?"

"In the linen closet?"

Lucas stares at Wyatt. "A little girl breaks into your house and you *hide* in the *linen closet*? What the fuck, man?"

"Well, she wasn't *that* little—"

"What the hell are you both talking about?" Dad is standing in the doorway, his face aghast. "Did someone break in?"

Lucas nods. "A girl."

"Shit." Dad moves further into the room. "She take anything?"

"She was a pro for sure," Wyatt says, trying to get in first before Lucas throws him under the bus. "She came into the house while I was here, I thought she looked dangerous so I hid in the closet, and when I came out she'd gone into the garage."

Dad's eyes go so wide Wyatt can see the whites above his irises. "The garage?"

"I don't know what she was doing in there, but she came out with a black bag."

Dad curses under his breath and drops his head. When he looks up again, he and Lucas exchange a look. "You know her?"

Lucas nods. "And the van."

"What van?"

"She got picked up by someone in a white HiAce camper. I've seen it before, here, outside the house."

"Seriously? Did you get a look at the driver?"

Their voices are low and urgent, their words like balls passed between members of a tight, effective team—and slowly it dawns on Wyatt that Dad and Lucas have been doing something without him. *The garage. The bag. The van.* They are part of something that he knows nothing about. Hurt and betrayal rise like acid from his belly to his throat.

"Fuck, Lucas," says Dad. "You know how much is in that bag? We have to get it back, *now*." He turns to Wyatt. "What did she do right before the garage? Which rooms did she go in?"

Wyatt is about to say he doesn't know, then realizes that in fact he might. His phone. He hasn't checked the surveillance footage in a long time but the app is still running, the camera still recording every time he puts the phone on the shelf to charge. He should've deleted it ages ago, he never finds anything but, you know, just in case. He runs to get it . . . but the bookshelf is empty.

"Oh," he says. The charger cord trails limply from the power socket. "She took my phone."

"What?" Lucas follows him. "What are you on about?"

"My phone. Well, yours. The one you gave me. It was here, on the shelf. I'd been using it to—"

Immediately, Lucas pulls out his own phone and dials. "Turned off." A tense pause. Then, "Wyatt, go get your iPad."

"No, wait," Wyatt says, "I had this app that I—"

"I said, get your fucking iPad."

Wyatt does as he's told. He unlocks the screen and Lucas takes over, bringing up the Find My app and locating the device. It shows up as a little green dot on a map of Gracious Bay.

They all watch as the dot travels out of town and turns north on the main road.

Lucas grabs his keys and heads for the door. Dad follows, but Lucas tells him to stay. "You stay on the phone and tell me where they go. They could be driving awhile."

"What are you going to do?"

"I'm going to find her," Lucas says. "And then I'm going to fucking kill her."

CHAPTER SIXTY-TWO

Beth

Beth lies on the floor of the van, trying to catch her breath. She hadn't imagined it: he was there, she saw him. And he saw her take a bag full of cash from his actual fucking house. If he hadn't gone full psycho on her before he sure as shit would now.

Twisting around, she gets to her feet, trying to see through the back window. So far the road is clear, but that doesn't mean he won't appear at some point. Thank god for Katy; her timing was unbelievable. *How did you know where I was,* she wants to ask, but it doesn't feel relevant. She's alive and leaving Gracious Bay, and that's all that matters.

"How far?" Katy calls from the front cab.

"What?"

"The turnoff."

"What turnoff? Where are we going?"

"The *flyer.*"

"Huh?" Beth turns back to see that Katy is poking a folded piece of paper through the partition wall.

"Look for William Wilson."

William? Beth struggles to her feet, takes the flyer and folds it out. It's the Gracious Bay pamphlet. The sculpture, the shipwreck, the pub . . . She skim reads the text boxes. "I don't know what you mean. What am I looking for?"

"Back page," Katy shouts.

Steadying herself against the kitchen counter, Beth flips the flyer over to where a walking tours map shows the different routes into the national park: trails, access points, and rest stops. She tries to read the writing but can't quite hold the paper steady. "Can't see it," she says, giving up. "Listen, let's keep going, up to Exmouth or something, find somewhere safe to stop. We can figure things out in the morning." She scans the back window. Still no sign of the Troopy.

"William Wilson," Katy insists. "Look for the trail. There's a map. Directions."

Reluctantly, Beth looks back at the map. It seems strange that Katy hasn't yet asked her what happened in Lucas's house, why she was running from it at top speed or who was chasing her. Katy hasn't asked about the duffel bag either. As far as she can tell, Katy's attention is entirely elsewhere.

Studying the flyer again, she finds a hike called the Wreck Beach Firetrail. *This route is currently closed*, the flyer says, *due to ongoing maintenance following the opening of a sinkhole in 2016*. She identifies the trail on the map. It starts at a place called William Wilson Rest Stop.

"Got it," Beth calls. "It's about six kilometers from town. You go out to the main road, loop around the old lake site, then back toward the ocean again via an unsealed road. You sure you want to go there though? It looks pretty remote."

"I'm sure." Katy answers. "Phoebe is telling me to go there."

Beth frowns. Phoebe is *telling* her?

"Which way?" Katy asks, when they reach the main road.

"Um . . ." Beth looks back at the map. "Take a left."

Katy turns. The van speeds up

Outside, the harsh landscape rushes by.

William Wilson Rest Stop turns out to be a flat, dusty clearing set back from the road with a rickety sun shelter and a faded information placard, and if it weren't for the ragged strips of caution tape and a sign instructing visitors to KEEP OUT due to unspecified DANGER, it might feel like a long-forgotten hideout, the kind of place adults would return to after many years away and reminisce about rope swings and first sips of beer.

Katy pulls up in a corner and kills the engine. Beth tugs one of the curtains aside and peers out. There's not much to look at, and no one else around. The setting sun is shining through a gap in the clouds, painting everything gold and casting long shadows over the dust.

"What are we doing here?" she calls.

No answer. The driver's side door opens and closes, and then the van is quiet.

"Katy?" Beth reaches for the sliding door, but as she does she hears the clunk of the locking system. She pulls the handle but the door doesn't budge. Shielding her eyes from the last of the sun's rays, she peers outside again. Katy is nowhere to be seen. She bangs on the glass. What the fuck is happening?

To the east there's a slow roll of thunder, followed by a flash of lightning. Storm clouds are gathering. Beth waits and waits, but Katy doesn't come back. She tugs at the door again, tries the windows but they won't open either. How is that possible? Surely you could get out from the inside even if the van was locked? There must be a button, like a child-lock or something. She hunts in vain, then attempts to get into the cab through the partition wall, but the little window is too small to crawl through and the plywood is fixed too firmly in place.

She tries the drawers and cupboards, hunting for a spare key or a service manual, anything that will tell her how to unlock the car from the inside. She doesn't find one, but she does come across Katy's phone nestled in the blankets on the bed, which is something. Only two bars of 4G and just nine percent battery but enough for a call if she needs it. She places it on the counter, then kneels on the floor and peers under the sink and into storage hatches. A section of paneling below the bed turns out to be another drawer—she hadn't noticed before because there's no handle—and she tugs at it until it slides all the way out. Inside the drawer is a box file containing, Beth realizes with a dull plunge of disappointment, Katy's chaotic collection of cards, flyers, and receipts. No instruction manual though.

She's about to put both the file and the drawer back where she found them when something among the detritus catches her eye. It's a business card, white and glossy with a green logo. She picks it up and stares at it. The emblem is a picture of a sweeping brush trapped inside the circle of a magnifying glass. *Dust,* it says. *Detective.* But it's the words beneath that really hold her attention.

Confused, she turns the card over to find a website and a phone number. Reaching for Katy's phone, she taps the screen and swipes up. *Enter your passcode.* She thinks for a moment, then presses and holds the side button. "Siri," she says. "Make a phone call." A line of text appears: *Who would you like to call?* Beth recites the phone number on the card. Siri pulses, then dials.

The call connects, and a male voice answers. "Yep?"

Stunned, Beth flounders for words. "Um . . . hi. Is this, uh . . . is this—"

"Hello? Anyone there?"

"Dust?" she says finally. "Is this Detective Dust?"

The line seems to clear. "Close enough." The voice on the other end is sandpapery with a strong rural accent. "What can I do for ya?"

"Sorry," Beth stammers. "You're a police detective, right? An investigator?"

The line crackles with a heavy sigh. "Christ alive, we gotta change that name." Then in a fake cheerful voice, the man says: "No, love, we're a cleaning service. Would you like to make a booking?"

Beth stares again at the card. *The Dust Detective: Residential, Automotive, Commercial.*

"Are ya there, love?" says the man.

"Yes, sorry, I'm here, I just . . ." She swallows. "Look, this might sound strange but I'm looking for a police detective called Dust who investigated the death of a woman called—"

"Ah shit," the man interrupts. "Listen, lady, I've had a real gutful of this. I've told you a hundred times, I'm not a fucking police detective. Never have been, never will be. But I will get the real police involved if you don't stop hounding me."

Beth reels, her brain suddenly required to make sense of a reality where Katy had not been calling a detective all this time, she'd been calling a *cleaner*. "I'm not . . . I haven't been calling, it wasn't me," she says eventually. "I'm just a concerned friend of the woman who has. She's been . . . unwell."

The man softens enough to confirm that over the last few weeks Katy has indeed been in frequent contact. "Whoever she is, she's gotta stop. I mean, I've tried to be kind because, y'know, she's clearly not all there. But I'm out of patience now, right? I've got a bloody job to do."

At first he assumed the calls to be the prank work of kids. Then when they continued, he pegged it as a wrong number. "I told her, you've made a mistake, but she just kept calling, sometimes upward of four times a day. It was like she couldn't hear me, like she was having this whole other conversation in her head and nothing else was getting through. It pissed me off to begin with, and then I just felt sorry for her."

The man told Beth that both his mother and wife had suffered from dementia and he knew a lost mind when he encountered one. "I figured it'd be easier just to play along; poor thing seemed upset enough already. So next time it happened I pretended to be the police guy, told her I was doing everything I could and I'd be in touch with any news. That seemed to calm her right down. She got off the line, and I thought that would be the end of it. But then it started up again and honestly it's starting to wear me out. And this isn't even my business, it's my daughter's, I just help her out with the bookings."

"Why didn't you report the calls?" Beth asks. "Or block the number?"

Another big sigh. "Ah look, I thought about it, but what good would it do? And even if I knew how to block her, I wouldn't. Like I said, it's not my business, and I didn't want to bother Alisha with any of it, she's got enough on her plate. I figured if I have to answer a few calls, tell some crazy lady I'm with the police then, so be it. But then it got a bit much, y'know?"

"I'm so sorry," says Beth. "I'll make sure it doesn't happen again. How long did you say you've been getting the calls?"

"Not too long. About a month?"

Beth apologizes again and thanks the man for his time.

"I really hope this Katy person gets the help she needs," he says before hanging up.

Beth stares at the phone in her hand, the screen blank. Then she brings up the lock screen and stares at the word *Emergency* beneath the keypad. Her thumb hovers, ready to call. Then her eyes slide to the computer bag stuffed full of money, her own dead phone, and bank cards. She imagines the police arriving, having to explain.

Shit.

She throws the phone back on the bed. Why hadn't she tried harder to verify Katy's story in the first place? Why hadn't she asked to see her ID? What kind of idiot gets into a van with a woman she barely knows and just accepts everything she's told without any kind of substantiation?

A scared idiot. A desperate idiot. An idiot hoping to catch a break.

It doesn't matter. She made her own bed and she's stuck in it now. She rubs her eyes, Jesse's voice rolling around in her head, pleading with her just the night before—*Katy is dangerous, she's not who she says she is.* Lines from his articles fly around her head like birds in a cartoon. *Cuckoo Killings. Vehicle theft. Identity fraud.* Where is his third note, the one he did actually leave for them? She last saw it after she and Katy had returned from the beach; she'd shown it to Katy, it had been wet, Katy had read it . . . then she'd put it on the counter. It isn't there now though, so where is it?

Searching again, she eventually finds it down the back of the kitchen unit, stuck in the gap between the counter and the window. Picking up Katy's phone again—only five percent battery now—she reads Siri the phone number.

Jesse picks up on the third ring. "Hello?"

"Jesse, it's Beth."

"Beth? Oh my god, I've been trying to find you but the tracker—"

"We found it, threw it away."

"Right. Shit, listen, I'm so sorry about that, and about what happened at the lookout last night, I never meant—"

"I'm not calling about that," Beth snaps, peering out of the window again. "Last night you told me Katy was dangerous and I want to know why."

"I, er . . . where are you right now?"

"Doesn't matter."

"Is this your number or Katy's?"

"Just tell me. What do you know about her—and what did you find out about Phoebe?"

"Maybe it's better if we meet?"

"*Now*. Quick, the phone's about to die."

"Okay, fine, sorry." He pauses. "So, I searched online and there's literally nothing about Phoebe's disappearance. No police reports, no news pieces or op-eds, not even a mention in the local rags. I couldn't find anything to do with the investigation at all. But I did find a LinkedIn profile. She's also on a staff page on a New South Wales college website, and both seem to suggest that not only was Phoebe very much *not* missing this time last year, but she was in a totally different state."

The words blow through Beth like a cold wind. "I don't understand."

"Phoebe worked as a student support officer. When I looked into the college, I found a staff bio. She was actively employed there all last year, including June third. I also found a bunch of photos. One was taken at a Sydney fundraising event. In February."

Beth frowns. "Of last year?"

"No, *this* year. Like, four months ago."

She shakes her head. "No."

"Google it, you'll see for yourself."

"But her Insta posts, all the captions and locations—"

"They're from this year, not last," Jesse said. "It's an easy mistake to make. On Insta, the year is only included in the time stamp if the post was published the previous year, not the current. If the post is from this current year, it's just the day and month. You probably didn't clock it because Katy's story had already been cemented in your mind and you didn't have any reason to question it."

Beth shakes her head but can't deny that he's right. She hadn't really engaged with Katy's story—at least not to begin with, she'd been too focused on her own agenda. And when she had engaged, Katy had granted only very limited access: a quick peek before she'd whip it away again.

"Phoebe Sweeney didn't go missing last year," Jesse continued. "But she may have disappeared more recently. The last time she posted online was just over four and a half weeks ago."

"What?"

"I checked her socials and it looks from various comments and replies like going off-grid isn't unusual for her, but a whole month with no contact is pushing it. Her family and friends are starting to worry."

Beth whirls in a tight circle, counting the days. Four and a half weeks ago, Lucas had left Beth's side for the first and only time in a year. He abandoned her overnight in that fucking barn. Whereabouts had they been at the time? Not near Gracious Bay, but close enough.

And the messages. She'd been so shocked at seeing Lucas's name in Phoebe's inbox that once again she'd failed to take note of the date. If she looked again would the time stamp confirm Jesse's story?

It hits her like a train. If it's true, it means that Lucas was communicating with Phoebe *recently*. While he and Beth were together. While she was robbing vans for him and sleeping in his bed. "I don't believe you," she whispers, the phone pressed to her ear.

"You have no reason to," says Jesse. "But I promise you, it's true. And another thing. I couldn't find anything about Katy either. Like, nothing at all. So I looked a bit deeper. There are a few family snaps on Phoebe's socials—not many, just a handful of her parents, an aunt here, a grandparent there, but no siblings. I checked Mum and Dad out. Phoebe's parents are both very successful art dealers who co-own several galleries in Sydney. Their bios mention just one child, not two."

"Huh?"

"I found something Mrs. Sweeney wrote for the *Guardian* a few years ago, a think piece about motherhood and creativity. In it she talks about her daughter, Phoebe. Her *only* daughter."

The bottom drops right out of Beth's world. "What does that mean?"

"It means that there is no sister. Never has been. Katy has been lying to you."

Beth feels like she's falling. Everything is spinning. Katy *lied*.

Or did she? Words and pictures flash through Beth's mind. Had Katy ever actually said that Phoebe was her sister? Or had Beth just assumed?

"I don't know exactly what's going on," Jesse is saying. "But you need to get away from her. I think she—"

Outside, there's a noise. Beth pulls the phone from her ear. She turns toward the window. The sun is down, the afternoon light fading fast. The sky is like a giant bruise.

"Beth?" Jesse's tinny voice buzzes through the speaker. "Are you still there? Where are you? I can pick you up."

"A rest stop," Beth whispers, resuming the call. "William Wilson. But—" The phone cuts out. "Jesse? Jesse, you there?" *Shit*. The battery is dead. And the charger's up in the front cab. She tosses the phone onto the counter, then stills. There's that noise again. Footsteps?

Dropping to her knees, Beth tries to shove the box file back in the drawer but it won't go. Pulling it out again, she sweeps her hand around the cavity, frantically feeling for the obstruction, and her fingers touch something squashy and soft. It feels like a plastic bag. She grabs hold of it and pulls but can't get it out. *Shit*, she *cannot* be caught rifling through Katy's private stuff . . . Panicking, she pulls harder and the plastic rips. Things tumble from within the drawer cavity and—

Hair. Human hair, lots of it, all over the floor like a spill of snakes. Long wavy tendrils the color of caramel.

A ball of wrinkled material, lemon-yellow, and stiff with dark, dried bloodstains.

And a crumpled piece of A4 lined notebook paper, across the top of which is written *The Solo Travel Safety Gospel According to Phoebe*.

CHAPTER SIXTY-THREE

Wyatt

Wyatt and Dad are in the kitchen, glued to the iPad screen. They watch the green dot travel all the way along the main road north then left again back toward the ocean. It slows down, then pulls off the road and stops altogether.

"What the fuck?" says Dad softly.

"Why have they stopped?" adds Wyatt.

Dad speaks into his phone, relaying the location of the green dot to Lucas on the other end. "William Wilson," he says. "The old rest stop just past the crossroads . . . yeah, that's the one. Make sure you handle it right." The edge in his voice is sharper than Wyatt has ever heard it.

Lucas's tinny voice confirms that he's not far behind. "I'm hanging up. Call me back if they move."

Very slowly, Dad puts the phone down and places both palms on the dining table. "Who is this girl?" he whispers. "What was she doing in my house?"

"I don't know. But we have her on camera, so we can just show the cops and they can deal with it. Lucas doesn't need to do anything."

Dad's eyes narrow. "What?"

Feeling like a hero, Wyatt explains about his surveillance app.

"Everything she did, in here at least, is recorded. All we have to do is go back to the—"

"You've been filming the house? For how long?"

"Just a few months. Since Christmas, I think? I wanted to see if—"

"A few months?" Dad's face has gone white.

"Yeah." Wyatt is suddenly much less sure of himself. "Was that . . . did I do something wrong?"

Dad stares at him. Then he slams his fists onto the tabletop so hard that Wyatt scoots backward against the wall. "Fuck," Dad howls. "*Fuuuuck.*"

CHAPTER SIXTY-FOUR

Beth

Transfixed, Beth's eyes travel down the list. *Don't go exploring in remote areas. Avoid driving at night. Trust your gut. Dress appropriately, don't stand out. Keep a weapon on board, something you can use in an emergency, e.g., cricket bat, scissors, corkscrew. Have fun!* ☺

Pressing her face to the window, she scrutinizes the dusk beyond the glass. All is still. She tries the other side. No sign of Katy, not yet. Up in the sky, thunder growls.

Barely breathing, Beth reaches inside the drawer cavity and scoops more items from the back. Mirrored sunglasses. Necklaces, earrings, bangles. Short shorts. A yellow bikini top. And a flat, plastic card. Beth turns it over. It's a NSW driver's license. The face in the photograph is the same as on Instagram. And the name printed below is Phoebe Eloise Sweeney.

Beth retches. *Oh, Katy, what did you do?* The whole time they'd been traveling together, she'd never once doubted the authenticity of Katy's grief; her behavior may have been baffling at times but the underlying pain was so real. The intense affection with which Katy spoke about Phoebe, the way she cried when she thought she was alone . . . had it all been pretense? Surely not. A person can't fake it one hundred percent of the time.

Says the girl who faked it one hundred percent of the time.

Wasn't Beth herself guilty of the exact same thing? Hadn't she maintained her own lies so diligently there'd been times when she felt she might be disappearing? Yes, but something doesn't quite track. She thinks back over the last two weeks, all the oddities and what she'd assumed to be grief or stress-related behaviors. She hadn't been able to read Katy as well as she usually read others; she hadn't been able to find a psychological mold that fit. But then she remembers her dream. The empty lecture hall, the lesson that was meant just for her.

But if he has lost a self—himself—he cannot know it, because he is no longer there to know it.

The murder case. The man who'd killed his wife then lost his identity, believing himself instead to be a defense lawyer. She remembered it clearly; it had been one of her favorite case studies. The guy had been convicted but his sentence had been commuted following a diagnosis of post-traumatic dissociative disorder. *When the mind experiences severe trauma,* his medical team had said at the time, *it shuts down and erases everything like a failed hard drive.* Poor "Barry" had no idea what he'd done.

Is it possible? Beth considers the holes in Katy's story, her woolly thinking, and obsession with Instagram. *Let's say someone saw her pictures and became jealous or fixated. It would be pretty easy to track her movements.* Had she handed Katy her own playbook without realizing? Worse—had Katy even given herself away without Beth even noticing? *I don't need to make friends. They just show up in the back of my van.*

Another noise outside sends her back to the window. Something is moving in the dark. Seconds later, a flicker of lightning catches Katy in its strobe, her scrawny silhouette moving slowly back over the dirt toward the van—and Beth is struck by a horrifying thought. Chris Craig. The stalker. She'd assumed it was a man behind those messages, but it could just as easily have been a woman.

A surge of panic sends Beth to the door, grabbing the handle and pulling as hard as she can, but the locking system holds tight. She almost laughs. How ironic she knows so much about breaking into vans but nothing about breaking out . . .

And then there's a flicker of light, coming from the direction of the road. Beth cups her hands to the window. Twin beams are cutting through the shadows, gliding between trees. A car. Tourists, pulling into the rest area.

Oh, thank Christ. She gets ready to wave and shout—*help me, I'm locked in*—but as the car gets closer, her heart recoils. Behind the glare of headlights, she recognizes the white paintwork, snorkel, and bull bar of the Troopy.

Her blood freezes.

Found you.

It's Lucas. Somehow, he's here.

CHAPTER SIXTY-FIVE

Beth

"Where's the money, Beth?"

Lucas's voice rings out in the dark, muffled by the glass. His silhouette, backlit by the Troopy's headlights, comes closer, gets larger.

"I see you," he yells. "Get out of the van."

Beth doesn't move.

A beat. Then Lucas strides out of the night, right up to the van, and smashes his fist against the window. Beth lurches back and stumbles over the black duffel bag, still sitting on the floor where she'd thrown it earlier.

He bangs on the door and yanks the handle. When it doesn't open he drives a foot into the paneling. Then he stops. Beth sees him turn slowly away from the van. He glares into the shadows. "Who the fuck are *you*?" he says.

She follows his gaze. Something is moving. Another shadowy shape.

Beth watches as Lucas draws a phone from his pocket, activates the torch, and points it into the dark. Illuminated in the weak beam, Katy looks like a ghost. She edges forward, her expression blank.

"That your van?" Lucas shouts, gesturing at the HiAce. "Answer me: is that your fucking van?" Another pause.

The torchlight disappears as Lucas puts the phone away. He walks right up to Katy and grabs her T-shirt. She twists away and the material rips. Adjusting his grip, he drags her toward the HiAce.

"Friend of yours, babe? This an ambush? One of you pretends to be stuck in the van while the other hides in the dark? You gonna take my car as well as my money?"

Lightning flashes, and briefly it's as if someone has turned all the overheads on. Beth stares at the scene: Lucas bending Katy's arm behind her back, Katy trying to push him away. She cries out, struggles to free herself. He pulls her close, wraps one arm around her neck and the other around her waist. Beth watches them grapple in the dust, bewildered. Who is the bigger threat? Is she safer inside the van or out? What would she do if one of them gets in? How would she defend herself?

Keep a weapon on board, something you can use in an emergency.

She opens the cutlery drawer and selects a knife. But could she actually use it?

Outside, Lucas has managed to turn Katy around and is now screaming in her face, demanding she open the van. Katy isn't responding; her eyes are open, her face pale. She's completely frozen.

Beth's sense memories kick in.

Don't ignore me.

"Stop!" She bangs on the glass. "Lucas, no!"

Never ignore me.

Lucas punches Katy hard in the mouth, and Beth gasps as Katy's head snaps back. There's a bright flash of blood, then Lucas releases her tattered shirt and she falls to the ground. Once she's down, he winds back his foot and kicks her hard in the ribs.

"No!" Beth yells, pounding on the glass. "Please, please, stop!"

Lucas keeps going, repeatedly driving his foot into Katy's body as if she's just a sack of grain. Beth looks at the knife in her hand.

Q: How do you break a car window?

A: By exerting force on the glass at one point location with a small sharp object.

Gripping the handle tight, she drives the tip as hard as she can into one corner of the glass. Cracks spread from the point of impact, and a small chunk falls from the frame with an almost musical clatter. Through the hole, she sees Lucas look up. Pivoting, she reaches under the sink, grabs a full bottle of wine and throws it hard, shattering the rest of the pane. The wine hurtles out as fresh air rushes in; there's a smash, and burgundy liquid splashes across the dirt. Without stopping to think, Beth drags the quilt from the bed, tosses it over the window frame to cover the jagged shards, and throws herself out.

She lands on her back and the air is knocked from her lungs. Her shoulder pops again, and pain floods her body as she rolls over, grasping for the knife. Where is it, she's not holding it anymore, where the fuck did it go? She scrabbles in the dust, but the knife is gone.

From the corner of her vision, she sees Lucas turn to face her. Instinctively, she grabs the next best thing, a shard of broken glass, and pushes herself to standing.

"You're getting pretty good at that," Lucas says, sounding mildly impressed. "Throwing yourself out of cars, I mean. Though I'm not sure it's an especially marketable skill."

Beth brandishes the shard like a dagger. "Stay away from me."

"Or what?" Lucas laughs. "You'll stab me? That's funny." He steps toward her.

Beth backs away. He's right, she can't stab him. The sharp edges of the glass are already cutting into her palm; she won't be able to apply enough pressure. "How are you even *here*?" The intention is fury, strength, backbone, but the effect is more like a childish whine.

Lucas laughs. "You know, for a semi-educated person you're really fucking dumb. Like, I get why you went for the money, but why, Beth, *why* would you take a *phone*?"

Beth stiffens. She'd forgotten about the phone she'd swiped from the house. She pats her back pocket, feeling its bulk. "But I switched it off," she murmurs.

Lucas tuts. "Come on, babe. Even when a phone's off it'll still show up on the app. A little dot, gliding along a lonely road. Hanging out in a random rest area in the middle of the goddamn night. It's almost as if you *wanted* me to find you."

Her stomach drops so sharply she winces. She *is* dumb. Just a dumb bitch who can't do anything right and has never been good enough. A stupid little girl with nothing going for her.

And nothing left to lose.

From the deep of the night, a dingo howls. Lucas's attention wavers, just for a split second, but it's all she needs. She throws herself forward, swiping at him with the shard of glass and knocking him off balance—but it isn't enough. Lucas blocks her with a raised arm, then shoves her backward into the side of the HiAce. She hits the ground tailbone first and the back of her head smacks against the door.

Thunder. Three beats. Lightning. Dark.

"You're dead," Lucas says, towering over her. "You know that, don't you? You and whoever this cunt is." He flings a hand in Katy's direction. Then he kicks Beth hard in the solar plexus.

She hears a crack. Her diaphragm spasms, contracts. She writhes on the ground, breath caught, lungs stunned. The world blurs and fades.

When light and sound come back, Lucas has returned to Katy who is still face down in dirt, her bare limbs pearly against the black earth. He stands over her with his fists balled and his feet firmly planted: a fighter's stance. "Who are you, bitch?" he growls. "What game are you playing?" He grabs the back of her tattered T-shirt *and lifts her upper body several inches from the ground then lets her drop. Katy doesn't even try to break her fall. She is inert, unresponsive.*

Beth gets to her knees, reaches out, and her fingers close around a rock. "Hey," she croaks.

Lucas ignores her. "Tell me," he yells at Katy's lifeless form. "*Who. The fuck. Are you?*"

He waits a beat, then punches her in the back of her head. She is inert, unresponsive. Her T-shirt has ridden up, exposing her back, and as Beth creeps forward her attention is caught by something rising from the top of Katy's shorts, a black shadow extending over her sacrum . . .

Oh, shit.

Her eyes widen, and for a moment the world stops turning.

Oh, no.

Lucas grabs Katy's hair. "Answer me."

That's impossible.

But Beth knows she's wrong. It's not just possible, it makes perfect sense. Her mind snaps into razor-sharp focus. She knows what she has to do.

"Hey," she says, louder this time.

Pretending he hasn't heard, Lucas winds his leg back again, readying his foot.

She strides toward him: three steps, two steps, one. "I said hey, motherfucker."

He hears her that time. He turns, a coiled spring.

But she is waiting. "Don't *ever* ignore me."

She raises the rock and brings it down hard onto his skull.

CHAPTER SIXTY-SIX

Katy

Get up.

It's dark. I'm lying face down on a cold, gravelly surface. Dirt in my mouth, mud on my tongue, the coppery taste of blood.

Now.

My left eye socket is throbbing, the skin around it tight and fat as a cushion. Broken glass glitters in my narrow line of sight.

Move.

Muscles screaming, I haul myself up onto all fours, hands and knees grinding against grit.

Push.

Tiny stones drip like rain from my bare stomach and thighs, leaving my flesh pocked with their imprint, and I keep going, *push,* I get a foot down, dig my toes in, another foot, *push,* and I'm up and swaying.

Run.

A noise, somewhere behind me: a dull crack. A gasp, a groan. The sound of something falling from a great height, hitting the ground with a thump. And then a voice calls my name.

Pure fear surges through every part of me.

Hide.

CHAPTER SIXTY-SEVEN

Beth

Lucas goes down in stages. He stoops, like he's ducking under a particularly low beam. Clutching his head, he staggers forward. He falls to his knees, makes a sleepy yawn-like sound, then topples over, twisting on the way down as if suspended in water. He lands on his back and stays there.

Dropping the rock, Beth edges forward. She nudges him with her foot.

"Lucas?"

He is still.

Thunder rolls.

She bends down, ready to spring back if he moves. He's still breathing; she can see the rise and fall of his chest. But for how long? How hard did she hit him? She has no way of knowing, she's never cracked anyone on the head with a rock before. *Fuck.* Should she call an ambulance?

Lightning flashes, and a scratchy sound at her back sends her spinning around just in time to see Katy scrambling to her feet and lurching off into the dark. "No!" she shouts. "Come back!"

Katy doesn't stop. She disappears through the fence and into a tangle of trees and bushes and shadow.

"Katy!" Beth calls again. "Where are you going?"

Shit. She looks back at Lucas. No matter what he's done, she can't leave him here to bleed out or have a seizure or whatever it is that happens with head injuries. What if he has brain damage? But . . . She looks back at the darkness into which Katy has just disappeared and knows she can't let her go either.

Seconds pass. Her eyes bounce from Lucas to the bushes to the van.

Tick, tick, tick.

Goddamn it.

Making a decision, she pulls the stolen phone from her pocket, switches it on and waits for the lock screen. *Come on, come on.* Two bars of 4G. When the keypad comes up, she taps *Emergency.* "Ambulance," she says when the operator answers. "And police." She gives the bare minimum of detail before hanging up.

Hurrying to the van, she hauls the quilt off the ground, throws it back over the window, hoists herself up and climbs inside. She grabs only what she needs and crawls out again. Then she activates the torch and takes off after Katy.

CHAPTER SIXTY-EIGHT
Wyatt

Wyatt is scared. Dad is acting weird. His face is completely drained of color and he won't stop pacing. He calls Lucas over and over again but Lucas isn't picking up. He asks question after question about the stolen phone and the surveillance app: exactly how long has it been operational, why did Wyatt put it up, what position was it in, show me, was it pointing over there or over there, where are the recordings kept?

"Have you watched the footage, mate?" Dad says, placing both hands on Wyatt's shoulders. "Is there anything you want to tell me?"

"No."

"Anything at all?"

"No!"

"You sure?"

Thunder rolls outside. The air feels electric.

Wyatt isn't sure what Dad wants him to say. Is he mad because Wyatt violated his privacy by filming his date? Or is Wyatt guilty of something much more serious?

"I had a girl over," he says, flushing hot with mortification. That's what it must be—it's the only thing he can think of. "And I fucked it up."

Pinned down by Dad's dark glare, Wyatt confesses how he took his brother's advice and made a friend online. It was surprisingly easy, just one quick message and they were away. She was a vanlifer just like Mum—she even *looked* like Mum—and she was clever and funny and even though she was a few years older she'd seemed to really like him. The only thing was that he lied to her—which was wrong, but he *had* to! There was no way anyone would've wanted to connect with the real him, so he'd made up a cover account using photos and videos from Lucas's phone pretending to be him. And that had worked out just great, until his new friend hinted that she was in trouble and needed somewhere to go.

"I didn't think," he says. "I just said she could come here. Which was really dumb because obviously she thought I was someone else—but I didn't know what else to do. And then she was just *here*."

Far out, she looked so much like Mum standing there on the door-step; the resemblance was even stronger in real life than in her pictures. "Lucas isn't home right now," he'd said, trying not to stare. "But he should be back any minute. Come in if you like, he really won't be long."

But his friend didn't know him, didn't trust him. "That's okay," she said, "I'll wait outside."

Wyatt cringes as he remembers how he shrugged and turned away, pretended it was no big deal—and then his phone vibrated in his pocket with a call. Running straight out the back door and into the yard, he answered it just in time.

"Lucas here," he said, his heart rattling like a machine gun. "Oh, hi . . . shit, sorry, I'm still tied up with a job, but I'm only round the corner and finishing up now—can you wait ten minutes? . . . No, go on inside, Wyatt will look after you, he's a good kid. Grab a beer, make yourself at home, I'll literally be ten minutes. No, eight . . . Can't wait."

He hung up. And then he just kept running, past the garage and out the back gate, sprinting through the scrub, away from the house and into the dunes toward the sinkhole where he knew no one would find him. He lay down in the sand and hid for so long the light changed.

Eventually he went home, tail between his legs, unsure if his friend would still be there or not. She wasn't—but he found Lucas sipping a beer in the kitchen, back for a surprise visit, and Wyatt was so happy to see him that he forgot all about his friend and the shitty way he'd treated her. There was no evidence she'd ever been there anyway, and eventually he thought he might've dreamed the whole thing.

The next day he'd got sick, which he'd taken as karmic retribution.

Obviously he doesn't tell Dad any of that last part, but Dad seems to know anyway. He is literally shaking with rage, so disappointed in his son for conning an innocent girl and treating her with such disrespect. Wyatt feels so ashamed he could die.

"I'm sorry," he said. "But that's all. I promise. That's all that's on the tape."

Dad cuts him off. "When exactly was this? I mean, *exactly.*"

"Three weeks ago? June third?"

For several seconds, Dad is silent and still. "Do you have any idea," he says at last, "what you've fucking done?"

Then, with no warning at all, he bends his knees and flips the dining table. Cups and plates and sauce bottles go flying, and Wyatt barely has a second to jump out of the way before Dad has seized a chair and hurled it at the stove.

And while Wyatt knows that what he did was bad, this seems to him like such an overreaction—and so surreal—that for a long time afterward he yet again can't be certain it ever happened at all.

CHAPTER SIXTY-NINE

Katy

My body is a bag of spare parts that no longer work as a whole—but somehow my feet are already moving, taking charge as if they've done this before. I jog, the impact of each shaky step jolting from my heels to my skull and into my ears, *thud, thud, thud*. I stumble into a fence post and trip over a rock, I plunge into long grass and a snarl of something spiky. Shadows loom and I reach out, my fingers grasping at the suggestion of things. Bursting out onto some kind of path, I follow it up an incline and down again, weaving around bushes, ducking under branches, losing my step then finding it again, *thud, thud, thud,* breath burning, spit spilling from my lips, hanging from my chin in a long bowing string, *faster, faster.* The path widens and gives way to dunes, the ground under my feet softening like butter, the air salty and moist. I slow down to catch my breath only to speed up again when, under the distant roar of waves, I hear footfalls pounding the trail behind me. A sweep of light illuminates the dunes. *Go, go, go.*

Up ahead, a black boxy shape nestles between two sandbanks. A house, a hut, a kids' clubhouse? I hurtle toward it, my toes digging into the sand, dodging around a tangled mass of leaves and branches and stumbling sideways into a pothole. I cry out as the sand gives way, the ground opens up and something tries to swallow me—and I can't tell if it's just my imagination or if there really is something under the powdery grain: a cold slippery surface, jagged teeth and claws, a long buried beast grabbing at my heels and scratching at my flesh, sucking me down and down and down . . .

Somehow I push and pull and heave myself out of the hole and force myself on toward the shelter. I get closer, it gets bigger, and the flat moonlight reveals it to be two structures pushed together: an old burned-out Kombi with a corrugated lean-to built onto one side. Unoccupied, or it looks that way. Reaching out, my fingers meet metal, rust, peeling paint. I find a gap between the sheets of metal and drag myself through into the dank space beyond. I curl myself into a ball and wait.

Outside, someone approaches. I can hear them moving fast, panting hard. The footfalls get louder, then stop. I listen, trying not to breathe. The silence makes my skin crawl, like there's something moving beneath it. Seconds later, a bright beam sweeps through my hiding place, slashing through the cracks and lighting up the corners. I press myself deeper into the shadows, *get down, get low,* flinching every time the light swings near—

Darkness returns. Then the footsteps change tempo: slow, heavy, deliberate. On the other side of the metal, a swish of clothing. Then torchlight stabs through a different gap. The beam powers through the gloom, catching the edges of other things pressed into other corners, and . . .

I stop breathing. There's something in here with me. By the far wall of the lean-to: a stark outline, all angles and straight lines, strange but somehow familiar. Smaller objects are arranged on the ground beneath.

The light passes, the outline disappears, then the torchlight swings back again and I can see the objects more clearly.

Oh my god.

My body goes cold. My hand flies to my mouth. I stand, pressure building behind my eyes. I want to run, but my legs won't move; I want to scream, but I can't make a sound. All I can do is stare at the wall, into the corner, at the assortment of *things* before me.

Oh my god, oh my god, oh my—

CHAPTER SEVENTY

Wyatt

"I'm sorry," Wyatt moans. "I know I should've stayed, I just panicked. Is she okay? Did she tell you? Is she mad at me?"

Dad stands very still. He stares at the floor. And then he walks slowly and steadily to his bedroom. The door closes. Wyatt is left in the kitchen alone.

"Dad?" He shuffles cautiously down the hallway. "Dad, I'm sorry. I didn't mean to lie. I just wanted to be her friend." Crying, he stops outside the bedroom door. "I'm sorry, Dad, please don't hate me."

Seconds later, the door opens and Dad is striding past him, a blue backpack swinging from one hand.

"Dad?"

Ignoring him, Dad disappears into the kitchen. The screen door squeaks and slams. Wyatt goes to the window in time to see Dad pushing open the back gate and taking off into the night.

CHAPTER SEVENTY-ONE

Beth

Beth races over the sand, brandishing the torch. She can just about see Katy up ahead, the weak beam catching her in pieces: the kick of a foot, a streak of bare shoulder, a flash of thigh. She appears and disappears like a ghost, here one minute, gone the next, a trail of messy footprints and swaying branches the only hard evidence she even exists.

She's not fast though—her injuries are slowing her down—so Beth catches up quicker than she expects. At one point she rounds a corner to find Katy bent double in the middle of the pale sandy track. "Hey," Beth calls, just meters away. "Katy, stop, it's just me!" But Katy flinches like a cat and takes off again, gaining some ground before stumbling sideways into a clump of bushes.

Beth waves the torch around, even though the lightning flashes are now so frequent that it's barely necessary. No rain, though—not yet. Ahead, Katy has slipped into some kind of hole and is struggling to pull herself out again. Beth powers toward her but trips over a creeper and falls on her face, and by the time she's righted herself Katy is off again, free of the hole and staggering away.

Beth gives chase—but stops when her attention is caught on something right where Katy had slipped: a glint of silver under the sand and bushes. She slows down, takes a closer look. It looks like a sheet of metal, not old or rusty but fairly new. Breathless, Beth reaches down to wipe some of the sand away. It's a pane of glass. She shines the torch down and in the dark cavity beyond she sees a blanket, a pillow, curtains.

Jesus Christ.

Beth grabs a branch and pulls hard, but it comes away easily in her hand. She tugs on another. The bushes aren't attached to anything, they're not growing in the sand, they've been placed there deliberately. The thing beneath has been buried.

Clearing away as much as she can, she finds blue paintwork. A door handle. A registration plate. Partially submerged in sand and covered by tree cuttings and hedge trimmings is a car. No, a camper. The make and model read TRAKKA Akuna A2M-E. The registration is 1HF 1VG.

Vivi Green.

Hollow with terror, Beth looks up into the night. "Katy?" she yells. Her voice is swallowed by the distant roar of waves. Getting up, she runs once more over the dunes and climbs the next rise. When she reaches the crest, she can see a structure down below. Another van. She points the torch and catches a flap of movement, hears a very faint *clack* of metal on metal.

Panting hard, she keeps going. Close up, the second van is much older than the first. Rusty, wind-worn, and dust-blown, Beth can hardly tell what color it used to be but she recognizes a classic Volkswagen T2 when she sees one. Someone has used sheets of corrugated metal to build a lean-to against the side, like a garden shed.

Beth approaches the shelter. She can hear a shuffling sound from inside, ragged breaths, and whimpers like an animal in a trap.

"Katy," she says gently. "Come out. It's just me. It's Beth." She goes right up to the metal sheets and shines the torch through the gaps. Sees slivers of a dark, messy space. Objects litter the floor. A garden chair, a lopsided camping side table. A plastic sheet, a small suitcase. She can't see Katy, though.

Running her fingers over the metal, she finds a larger gap and shines the torch again. This time the light finds three mugs and a plate, two wineglasses and a bottle, all standing right way up on a dirty-looking towel as if ready for a picnic. And countless piles of stones, stacked one on top of the other and placed around the edges of the shelter, just like the ones left outside the van on the way to Shark Bay, right before they discovered the lock of hair.

Oh, god. The realization is harsh and stark. The hair, the notes, all the "clues" . . . Katy hadn't just found them. They'd all been inside the van all along. She'd been following her own breadcrumbs.

And then Beth sees the cross.

She points the torch directly at it. In one corner, two planks of wood have been crudely hammered together and propped up against the wall. Beneath are two separate clusters of objects. One cluster consists of a handbag, a three-inch vinyl record, a neatly folded cardigan with a daisy pattern, and a silver necklace with a pendant in the shape of a star. The other comprises a denim jacket, a beaded bracelet, a crystal rearview mirror charm, and a crochet throw blanket. A small gold hoop sits on the blanket, and Beth can't be sure but the first place her mind goes is: *septum ring.* Both clusters are surrounded by silk flowers.

Horrified, Beth raises the torch back to the cross. There's writing on the horizontal plank: two names. On the right side, VIVI. On the left, NOVA.

"Oh my god," she whispers. "Oh shit. Katy, we have to get out of here, we have to leave."

No answer.

"Please, Katy. God, I'm so sorry. I should've seen it coming, I should've known."

A breeze eddies around her like the currents of a stream, bringing with it strange unfamiliar sounds. *This is a bad, bad place.*

"Please, Katy, come on, we have to go—"

And then there's a crash at her back and she's knocked to the ground.

CHAPTER SEVENTY-TWO

Katy

BANG.

A loud noise paralyzes my brain. Someone is trying to break their way inside the shelter. I swing around, lose my balance, and stagger into the corrugated walls, knocking them over. The night rushes in, along with bodies, two of them, a tangle of arms and legs. The pressure in my head becomes real pain, blooming and bleeding down the length of my spine and I start to fall—but right before I hit the ground, several things become clear all at once: suddenly I know where I am, what's happening, and what kind of place this is. Deep in my mind, something clicks and I understand everything.

My heart clamors.

I should've seen it coming.

The ground rushes up.

I should've known.

My last thoughts, before everything goes black, are of Phoebe.

CHAPTER SEVENTY-THREE

Wyatt

Wyatt runs, following the track from the back gate into the dunes, following Dad who marches on ahead with his backpack on, following his nose in the dark. It's not cold but he's shivering. He's deeply afraid—mainly that he has done something so terrible that Dad can't even speak of it, but also that suddenly nothing in his life is what he thought it was, almost like he and his family have stepped into some kind of ghost realm.

The farther into the dunes they go, the less familiar the surroundings. Lightning punctuates the darkness, the flashes weirdly silent, the air eerily still, but even with the brief illumination Wyatt doesn't recognize where they are, he's never thought to come this way, strike out off the trails, but Dad seems to know exactly where he's going. And then somewhere under the roar of the ocean, a voice calls out. He slows to listen. There it is again. A female cry.

Dad seems to speed up, marching faster and faster through the night. *Lucas,* he thinks, *where are you, help me, Dad's gone mad, he's running around outside, what do I do?* He considers calling, but he has no phone and the memory of his brother's face as he left the house would've stopped him anyway. *I'm going to fucking kill her.*

He presses on, following Dad. Grass becomes creeper becomes shrub becomes bush. Dad winds his way around the tangled clumps, climbs a rise and stands on the crest looking down into a natural bowl. Wyatt follows his gaze. In the bowl is an old fishing shack or a shelter of some sort. Lightning flares and everything is bright for just a few seconds, but it's long enough to see that it's not actually a shack, it's a camper, a VW Kombi. Someone must've tried to drive it to the beach and got stuck. But the shape of it, the color . . .

Wyatt watches as down below a figure with the torch reaches the Kombi. Dad descends into the bowl and Wyatt follows. Reaching the camper, Wyatt circles around the other side and the feeling of recognition grows even stronger. Sheets of metal have been stacked against it to form a shelter. He inches closer, near enough to see the figure more clearly. The stranger is standing right up against the metal as if spying on someone inside. Electricity lights up the sky again and he sees a face, and it's *her,* the girl who was in his house. If he charged at her right now, could he wrestle her to the ground, grab the black bag, and take it home? Then he'd *really* be a hero . . . But the moment the thought enters his head, three things happen at the same time. First, he realizes the girl doesn't have the bag, or she's not carrying it anyway. Second, he catches sight of something on the back window of the van, a looping pattern that makes his insides slide around. Third, Dad comes bolting out of the dark and launches himself at the girl.

Wyatt sees the whole thing play out before it happens. He sees Dad pulling the girl onto the ground, watches them writhe around, the girl screams, Dad grunts and huffs, restraining her, overpowering her, crushing her, because he isn't a big man but he can do these things, has done them for a long time—and suddenly Wyatt is back inside the dream, the demon in the girl's bedroom, the movie with the forgotten name, but this time he recognizes it for what it is, not a dream or a movie but a memory.

Rory, don't. Not in front of the boys.

The Noises in the walls. Snarls and shouts, thumps and scuffles, muffled cries behind closed doors, all heard while curled up under his bed or beneath the blankets or in the linen closet.

Don't, Rory. Stop, calm down, please, we don't—

Wyatt in the linen closet with a towel over his head. Lucas in the bathroom with the door locked. The dream demon stalking the hallway, banging on the walls, heading for the bedroom.

Bang.

Everyone sitting at the dinner table afterward and pretending nothing had happened.

Thud.

Waking up at night and pretending they couldn't hear.

Slam.

Watching Mum's make-up get thicker and thicker, her sleeves longer, and her necklines higher.

Don't touch the kids, Rory. Don't you ever, ever hurt my boys.

The house getting quieter and quieter until every room contained a black hole where she once was.

I can hear things, Mum. I see them, too.

Oh little man, you and your active imagination. You'll be a storyteller one day, you see if you don't.

Then one day, she was gone.

It got too much for her. She wasn't well. She wasn't the settling kind. She wasn't a natural mother. It was hard for her. You kids were too much. She couldn't handle it. She wanted different things. One day you'll understand.

A gut-wrenching noise drags Wyatt back to the present, back to the dunes and the dark and the ghost-girl who was in his house, now on the ground and screaming because Dad is crushing her, pinning her to the ground with a knee to the back just like the cops on TV. The girl resists, kicking and thrashing, and—

It's a movie, Wyatt thinks. *I'm in a movie.* In a story, what would the hero do? He would run forward—*lights, camera*—and knock the villain off the girl's body—*action*—which he'd find to be harder and more painful in real life but effective nonetheless. They would all fall down together, crash into the corrugated sheets—*thunder*—and open up a hole in the side of the makeshift shelter. The villain would then try to get up but the hero would grab his ankle and down they'd go again in a tumble of Foley sound effects, a chicken carcass smashed by a bat, walnuts

pounded into slabs of meat, and the shelter would collapse completely—
lightning—revealing the secrets within, the final clues needed to solve
the mystery. Still screaming, the girl would wriggle away while the villain remained writhing on the ground making weird noises because, un-
beknownst to both hero and audience, he is wounded, perhaps fatally,
and then it's over, the fight is done—*cut, that's a wrap.*

But that's not where it ends and nothing fades to black. Wyatt the
not-hero stands bruised and bewildered in the real-life mess, shining the
torch of his phone at Dad the not-villain who is now lying on the ground
covered not in corn syrup but in real-life blood.

"Dad?"

The torchlight moves as if by itself, caressing the spread of objects
now exposed to the elements, and Wyatt silently names each one.

Picnic blanket. Wineglass. Beer bottle. Plates.

Silk flowers. Star pendant. Wooden cross.

A vinyl record, "Hotel California."

Nova. The creation of a star.

A cry trips from Wyatt's mouth. He lifts the beam and points it at
the decrepit VW, at the looping pattern on the windshield. A sticker,
bearing the van's moniker. *Lola.*

He drops to his knees. *Mum?*

Lightning flash. Everything bright. A tableau: Dad on the ground,
eyes bulging, torso twisted—*not real, it's a movie, I'm in a*—and he's
gasping and grunting and gulping, and the crystal-clear stem of a wineglass is sticking out of his neck, and the base is still intact so it looks like
one of those plastic suction cups you use to stick things onto walls and
windows, and blood is gushing from the wound, pouring over Dad's skin
and soaking into his shirt, and pooling on the sand beneath his back.

Darkness returns.

Wyatt reaches out, not for Dad but for the daisy-print cardigan. He
picks it up gently, like one might handle a newborn kitten, and brings the
material close to his face until the print blurs and the daisies dance as if
coming to life.

CHAPTER SEVENTY-FOUR

Beth

Shingle on her tongue, grit between her teeth, Beth lies on her back watching the rainclouds bubble and bulge. The gentle roar of the ocean is everywhere, a lullaby of white noise, a mother's shush. A breeze breaks the calm, swooping low over the dunes, and the seagrass sighs in unison.

Reaching out with both arms, she sweeps her hands up and over her head, a sand angel sifting through grain, until her wrist hits something solid and her fingers close around the reassuring flat rectangle of a phone. She grips it tight, brings it to her heart, slides it into her pocket, curls onto her side. Her whole body hurts from crust to core.

She can move though, so she does, sits up, grounds herself. Just meters away, the shelter lies in pieces. The copper-haired boy, also fragmented, stands amid the destruction, staring at nothing. A silk flower rolls past him like a tumbleweed.

Slowly, Beth becomes aware of a wet choking sound coming from somewhere near the VW, but rather than approach or call out or try to help, she turns away, blocks out the noise, doesn't want to know. She gets to her knees and scans the dunes until she locates a lumpy bundle that could easily be a pile of washing or a collapsed tent or a sleeping child. She crawls close. "Hey," she whispers. "Can you hear me?"

Katy doesn't respond. She's on her side, facing away, but her eyes are open and blinking.

Kneeling, Beth activates the torch. Katy's T-shirt is almost completely torn, exposing her lower back. Beth points the beam at her knobbly vertebrae and the sacral area where black lines, swirls, and curves are etched into the skin. Katy had never removed her clothes in front of Beth, never swam or sunbaked, never uncovered her body except to shower in private. If she had, all if this might've been solved much sooner.

Beth reaches out, her fingertips almost brushing the compass. *It symbolizes adventure, and always knowing the right way to go.* She studies Katy's cropped hair, the dark whorls sticking up in untidy clumps; her bony, malnourished frame, and sunken cheeks. The missing tooth, the hypervigilance and simmering anxiety, the flyers and the business cards, the cleaning company, the Instagram account, *William, that's where she's telling me to go,* and suddenly all the holes in her story make sense.

If a man has lost a leg or an eye.

Gently, she places a hand on Katy's shoulder. "It's okay," she says. "I see you. I know who you are."

But if he has lost a self, he cannot know it.

And for the first time, she uses Katy's real name. "Pleased to meet you, Phoebe."

Finally, the storm breaks and it starts to rain.

CHAPTER SEVENTY-FIVE

Phoebe

I wake up in hospital. Beige walls, white sheets. Curtains hang from a circular rail, a monitor beeps in a corner. The air smells of vanilla sponge cake and disinfectant.

Every single part of my body hurts. I wait for my brain to supply the reason why, but nothing comes. Where memory should be, there's just a gaping blank space.

I wait and wait. Images come to me in pieces. A winding road. A steel sculpture. Me, smiling wide in mirrored sunglasses, taking a picture to capture a lie: *I am not where you think I am.*

I close my eyes. Something is coming, rising up from out of the fog . . . a hazy recollection of driving, of sitting in a café with sunny yellow chairs. As if watching from above, I see myself posting on Insta then continuing on to an address written in Biro on my hand. I'm rolling down the windows, cranking up my favorite song and singing along with Kate Bush about rain and yo-yos and all the good things about to happen.

I see a front yard, porch steps, a blue door opened by a short boy with red hair. *Lucas isn't home right now but he should be back any minute. Come in if you like, he really shouldn't be long . . .* Then nothing.

The next memory, when it comes, is starkly different. Darkness. Pain. My cheekbone pressed into gravel, my palms grazed. Glittering splinters of glass, and a voice just as sharp. *Who are you? Answer me.* A second voice, higher in pitch. *Hey. Hey, motherfucker. Don't ever ignore me.* Had I been in an accident? Maybe I'd crashed the van, or been hit by another vehicle. I feel terrible. I hope the other driver is okay.

I try to sit up but my body doesn't feel like mine, it doesn't work the way I expect. Slowly and with a great deal of clumsy negotiation, I prop myself up, slide my butt to the pillow, and rest my back against the headboard. My abdomen burns like someone has taken a hot poker to my rib cage.

Looking around, I catch my reflection in a mirror . . . but with a sense of growing horror I realize that the face is not mine. Instead, I'm looking at a monster, a wild thing.

I coax my legs out from under the sheets, persuade my feet to meet the floor. More bargaining and I'm up and swaying. The thing in the mirror sways too. It stares at me until I'm forced to accept that it *is* me, but not as I know myself. My hair is scraped back in a ponytail, one of my eyes is swollen shut, my nose is bandaged, and my lip is split. One of my teeth is even missing. There are marks around my neck too, little purple smudges like I've been smeared with ink.

I cry out. My head throbs. I touch the back of my skull—and my stomach drops. My long wavy hair. It isn't tied back. It isn't there at all. Someone has cut it all off.

I double over and vomit onto the floor.

A nurse pushes through the curtains, helps me back into bed like I'm a child, cleans up the mess on the floor.

"Why am I here?" I say. "I don't know what's happening."

"A doctor will be in to see you shortly. For now, let's just check you over."

The nurse palpates my stomach, ribs, and clavicles. He takes my blood pressure and temperature, listens to my heart. His fingers feel like cutlery.

"Do you know where you are?"

"Hospital."

"Whereabouts?"

"I don't know."

"Which state?"

"I don't know."

"What's your name?"

"Phoebe."

"What day is it?"

"I don't know. June. June third."

"It's July ninth."

"No, that's wrong. You're wrong."

But *I* am the one who has it wrong.

I'm told I have two fractured ribs, a sternoclavicular subluxation, significant bruising but no internal bleeding, and one of my teeth has been knocked out. I also have a head injury, the extent of which is yet to be determined.

I ask where my hair is. The doctor seems confused.

I ask about my van, the damage, the crash? "You weren't in a crash," he says.

My phone turns up beside my bed, the charger coiled neatly by its side. A change of clothes, my toothbrush, and facewash. License and credit cards sealed in a plastic sandwich bag. An endless parade of medical staff glides past my bed as if on a conveyor belt, asking their own questions but answering none of mine.

"Where's my van?" I say, over and over. "Where are the keys? When can I go?"

No one will tell me. Instead they ask about a makeshift grave, human remains, and a man found bleeding from his neck. I have no idea what they're talking about. I've fallen into a Lynchian nightmare. I am living in Twin Peaks.

"I don't know anything," I insist. "None of this makes any sense. Please, can *you* tell *me* something? What am I doing here? What happened? What's wrong with me?"

Glances are uneasily exchanged.

"All we can say for sure," says someone eventually, "is that, other than a few rather opaque texts to your mother, you were missing for five weeks. And, it seems, under the impression that you were someone else."

"Missing?" Pins and needles ravage my limbs. "Someone else? I don't . . . I can't . . ."

"Okay, let's take some deep breaths. Why don't we continue this conversation when your mum arrives?"

At the mention of Mum, I break down. "Where is she?"

"On her way." A faceless, nameless nurse pats me with a hand that feels like an empty glove.

I expect Mum to crumble, to be the outward manifestation of my inner chaos, but she appears at my bedside like a rescue ship at sea and somehow manages to be the anchor, rudder, and sail I'd been missing.

Still, as soon as she arrives I start apologizing. "I'm sorry, so sorry that you're hurting because I'm hurt, sorry I didn't take better care of myself, sorry that you have to take time off work and spend money on an airfare and fly to the other side of the country to live out your worst nightmare just because I'm stupid enough to let something happen to me, sorry, sorry, sorry."

"Stop," she says, cutting me off. "You have nothing to be sorry for. None of this is your fault. I'm here now. I've got you."

She's brisk but gentle, efficient but kind. She takes over, and I am so grateful.

My face is on the news. People know about me. Reporters camp outside the hospital. The whole country wants me to tell them what happened.

As a result people come forward, witnesses who claim they saw me on the road, even spoke to me, but I don't know them, I've never seen them before. One family insists I was traveling with a friend, a woman called Lily, but I don't remember anyone by that name. A gray nomad couple say they had troubling conversations with me on two separate occasions, first at a beach camp near Jurien Bay and then at a roadhouse north of

Kalbarri. They all say my name is Katy and I'm a high school teacher. Some even know the name of the school I work at because it was printed on my shirt.

"Shirt? What shirt?"

I am shown a grubby polo shirt. I recognize it. A family gave it to me in Carnarvon, the day my clothes were stolen. I put it in a drawer, thinking I might return it one day, then forgot all about it.

Now I hold it out in front of me, pinching each sleeve between my finger and thumb, and stare at the school emblem. *Marita Heights Primary.* I've never been a schoolteacher, never even considered it, and the one time I visited a classroom as an adult was during the four months I dated an assistant principal. It was not fun; he'd showed me around his school after hours, complaining incessantly about all the extra work involved.

I ball up the shirt that is not mine, and I throw it across the room.

At first my behavior is attributed to psychosis, my memory loss to the head injury. A specialist flies up from Perth and suggests I might be schizophrenic, possibly bipolar. Another joins him who leans more toward dissociative identity disorder.

I sit in my room, frozen and terrified, while my mum sits by my bed, endlessly checking my bank account and sifting through "evidence"—receipts and shopping bags and food packaging and paperwork—found inside my van.

"I don't get it," she mutters, her brow in a permanent knot. "I don't get it, I don't get it."

"So, to be clear," I hear her whisper outside my door one night. "People actually saw my daughter in this state? They spent time with her?"

"Correct," says a second voice, much deeper but equally hushed.

"Well, why didn't they do anything? Couldn't they tell she wasn't . . . herself?"

"Witness statements suggest she was pretty lucid."

"But what about those missing weeks between June third and when she turned up again at Sandy Cape. How do we find out what happened then?"

"I'm afraid we might not ever know."

"But how did she survive? What did she eat? What did she do?"

"She had an emergency supply of water and canned goods in the van, but her intake would've been minimal. Which makes sense, given her apparent weight loss and nutritional deficiencies."

"Yes. And her hair . . ."

"That's interesting, and not diet related. It appears she cut it all off and put it in a plastic bag. It's undergoing tests, along with the clothes."

"Why would she do that?"

"So far, it's unclear."

A pause.

"With your permission, Mrs. Sweeney," says the low voice, "I'd like to set up a proper study. We have little to no information about certain aspects of this disorder and cases don't crop up all that often, so it'd be extremely helpful if—"

"Wait, slow down, I can't . . . Are you saying it's over now? Finished? She's definitely Phoebe again?"

"As far as we can tell."

Another pause.

"What brought it on?"

"Well, as we've already discussed there's currently no proven physical or medical cause, but the most common trigger is severe stress or trauma."

"Trauma? Like what?"

"Lunchtime."

A tray is placed by my bed. I smell gravy and mashed potato. I turn onto my side, draw the sheets up to my neck. I don't want to eat, or drink, or see anyone, or for anyone else to see me. I lie on the bed and stare at the wall. I watch thin strips of light travel the room, willing the sun to move faster, stop shining, disappear altogether so I can drift away into darkness and feel nothing at all.

CHAPTER SEVENTY-SIX

Beth

Beneath a tree a little way back from the street, Beth stands shrouded in shadow, staring at a single lit window on the east façade of the hospital. She's considered sneaking in but can't think of a way to slip in unnoticed. The hospital is a modest building but brand-new, all sharp angles and block colors, so security is unlikely to be lax or outdated, and Phoebe's story is gaining traction now, so staff will be on the lookout for unapproved visitors.

Never mind. She hugs the paper pharmacy bag to her chest. Plenty of alternatives. There always are.

She stares at the window for so long the light stamps a dazzling square shape onto her retina. What would be going on in that room right now? What must Phoebe Sweeney be thinking and feeling? All Beth knows is what she's heard on the news, and tidbits from Jesse, which is that Phoebe has suffered severe memory loss. Which means what? Does she know anything of what happened? Does she remember being Katy?

Does she remember me?

But she can't dwell on that thought for long. Instead, she checks up and down the street, watching for cars, people, shadows that shouldn't be there. The gaze feeling is constant now, she carries it everywhere she goes, a monkey forever on her back. And it's not just the reporters that have flown in to lurk outside the hospital doors. It's Lucas, and the last time she saw him: the dull thunk as the rock connected with his head, the way he fell, that slow keel all the way to the ground. The movement of his chest, up and down, faint but perceptible, and the empty patch of dirt the police must've driven right over when they arrived. *Where are you*, she thinks. *When are you going to show up?*

Her eyes drift back to the lit window just in time to see it go dark. She sighs, a slow deep inhalation. Then, clutching the bag even tighter, she hurries away.

The hostel receptionist waves as she hurries through the scrappy lobby to the stairwell. "Hey, Jess," he says, waving a padded envelope in the air. "Package for you."

And she only remembers at the last minute that this is her new name— for the time being anyway. *Jesse Anderson.* The name on the booking, and the credit card that paid for it. *Jesse. Jess.* That's who she is now, or at least until she gets back to Perth. After that, she won't ever use the card again or any more of the real Jesse's money. She'll pay everything back too, no excuses. She'll never again put herself in a man's debt, never again relinquish control.

"Thanks," she says, taking the envelope without meeting the receptionist's eye, then climbs the stairs two at a time to the second floor and locks herself inside her room. Private, thank god; Jesse had been kind enough to shell out for that. Deadbolting the door, she tosses the envelope on the bed and takes the pharmacy bag and its contents straight to the bathroom.

Twenty messy minutes later she's sitting on the bed with her hair wrapped in plastic and her nose full of bleach. She opens a packet of chips and turns on the TV, flicking straight to the local news. Phoebe's story is snowballing: the girl who disappeared and became someone else. The entire country is invested. All the outlets and stations are gagging for an exclusive but so far no one has got close; someone in Phoebe's camp is working hard to keep them at bay, but Beth knows it won't be long before the whole thing blows up.

She watches reporter after mike-wielding reporter wring the story dry against a background of sliding emergency room doors, thinking not of what they know but all the things they don't. Like, how Beth stayed with Phoebe until she heard the sound of sirens followed shortly by the distant whirr of a chopper, how she promised they'd see each other soon before getting to her feet and running as fast as she could. How, as the first of the officers arrived, scurrying over the crest of the dunes with their flashlights held aloft like swords, she was but a few hundred meters to the south, half buried under dry sand and foliage, and how from her hiding place she risked using the stolen phone to call Jesse. "Don't mention anything to the police about me," she hissed. "I can't tell you why, but it's important."

Jesse agreed. Not only that, he offered to pick her up from Gracious Bay, if she could get herself there, and to help keep her under the radar.

"Is Lucas alive?" she asked before hanging up. But Jesse couldn't tell her anything about Lucas at all. William Wilson had been empty when he'd arrived: no other cars, no inert bodies on the ground. Which meant that either Lucas had at least been conscious enough to drive himself out of there, or someone had come to get him—which in turn meant that he was still out there. Furthermore, she hadn't since heard anything on the news about a bag full of cash found inside the HiAce, which strongly suggested he'd taken it before escaping.

Beth waited until Phoebe and Lucas's kid brother were helped by police officers back to the rest stop, and Lucas's father was airlifted out of the dunes. Then, choosing her moment, she crawled out from under the sand before they could start any kind of search, managed to find her way to the beach unseen, then walked back to Gracious Bay where Jesse made good on his word. The next day, Phoebe was all over the news.

Beth, thankfully, was not. In the days that followed, police interviewed Jesse due to the fact that he was found close to the rest stop but couldn't prove he was anything but a passing traveler in the wrong place at the wrong time, which in many ways was entirely accurate, and he kept his promise not to mention her. The kid brother, whose name Beth had quickly discovered was Wyatt, seems not to have said anything either, possibly because he doesn't want to make the situation worse, possibly because he has much bigger things to worry about. A couple of witnesses have spoken of a friend traveling with Phoebe, dark haired, goes by the name of Lily, but so far Beth hasn't come up.

And she won't. Because Beth Randall no longer exists.

She removes the plastic wrapping from her hair, bends over the tub, and rinses out the bleach. Crossing to the sink, she plants herself in front of the mirror and meets the eyes of Jess, drama student, who has short platinum hair, wears glasses, and is in WA for a two-week holiday only.

And after that, who knows? Maybe for a while she will be nothing and no one. Just thin air and no traces.

Back in the bedroom, she retrieves the envelope from where she discarded it and, with one eye still on the TV, carefully opens the seal. The real Jesse Anderson is a dick, there's no two ways about it, but without him she's not sure what she would've done or how she'd ever get out of Gracious Bay. And even though he must be dying to write his own version of events—she can practically hear his internal monologue: it's *his* story, he was first to arrive on the scene, *he* knows more about the involved parties than any of those hack reporters, *he* should be the one to tell the whole thing—he isn't even trying. Which says something.

As the news cycles back around to aerial shots of Gracious Bay, William Wilson, the crime scene on the dunes and the nearby sinkhole, Beth reaches inside the envelope expecting to find the last wad of cash from Jesse, which she will use to get back to Perth and which she will definitely, *definitely* pay back. But instead of money, she pulls out a letter. Handwritten, on plain paper. She opens it out. *Dear Phoebe,* the first line reads.

And then Lucas's face fills the TV screen and Beth's world explodes.

"A man has been found dead," says a glossy-faced reporter, "at the wheel of a white Troop Carrier on the road to Carnarvon. Police have confirmed that a bag containing a large amount of money was discovered inside the vehicle, as well as a hoard of stolen goods. Cause of death appears to be a significant head injury. Police are investigating connections with local crime gangs, as well as the grisly discovery of human remains at the long-abandoned William Wilson Rest Stop not far from peaceful fishing town Gracious Bay. They're asking anyone with any related information to please step forward."

The mysterious letter falls forgotten from Beth's hand. The gaze feeling drops away. Lucas is not coming for her. Lucas is gone. That lost little boy, that vicious man, is dead. And she is a murderer.

Slowly, she sits down on the edge of the mattress. Her father was right: she really is a monster.

CHAPTER SEVENTY-SEVEN

Phoebe

Dissociative fugue.

That's the final diagnosis. A rare state of amnesia coupled with unexpected travel, or so I'm told. Which at first sounds rather cheerful to my ears, like a top prize in a game show or a positive astrology reading, until I realize that it is in fact the opposite.

"The sufferer," a doctor explains to my mother in a flat tone as if said sufferer is not sitting in the same room and does not have ears, "typically loses all sense of who they are and assumes an entirely new and sometimes unrelated identity. Simultaneously they travel somewhere brand new, a compounded behavior often referred to as "bewildered wandering."

"I don't understand," I say eventually.

"On many levels, neither do we," says the doctor. "Fugue is probably the least understood of all dissociative disorders, mainly because most patients don't present for treatment until *after* they have resumed their original identities. I've personally never seen it myself, though I've been fascinated for years."

They list the few known case studies. A Vietnam war vet who went missing from his home and turned up six months later at a homeless shelter almost 1300 kilometers away living under a completely different name. An American teacher who went missing three times over nine years, whose fugue state was caught on camera and who remains missing to this day. A Nigerian medical student, a New York City nurse, an entire Australian family. They refer my mum to certain academic papers, articles, and websites, and reassure me that a full recovery is more than possible.

"You'll be back to normal in no time," the doctor says.

I tune him out. I have no idea what normal is anymore.

It takes a long time to unpack everything and even then no one seems entirely sure of the facts, but from a combination of witness statements, bank and phone records, GPS tracking, campsite check-ins, and occasional security footage, plus evidence found both at the scene and collected from my van, a reasonable sequence of events is cobbled together.

I, Phoebe, arrived in Perth on Wednesday May fifteenth. I picked up my van, prepurchased online from a guy in Scarborough, and set off on my trip the following day, stopping en route for food and supplies. I then traveled north along the Coral Coast, via various campsites and beauty spots as detailed in my Insta posts, all the way until just after Quobba when I announced my decision to go to Karijini. I remember writing that post, secretly gleeful that I was throwing my weirdo stalker off the scent and spending a few invisible days on the Ningaloo reef instead.

After June third though, I seemed to vanish. And, according to the police, I wasn't seen again until three weeks later when I popped up back at the first campground I'd originally stayed at: Sandy Cape near Jurien Bay. The staff there provided witness accounts of having spoken to me, along with a gray nomad couple who insisted we'd met and had a conversation. Not only that, they said I'd been with a man who'd claimed to be my boyfriend. However, several days later when they apparently saw me again at Red Gum roadhouse, I was on my own and seemed not to know who the man was.

Equally confusing are the statements of other witnesses—a couple who'd seen me at Plains Ranch, a waitress at a Carnarvon café, and a Big Lapper family who'd apparently stayed on the neighboring pitch at Quobba blowholes—who mention a dark-haired female companion. My phone records also show that I'd made repeated calls to a cleaning service right here in Exmouth after having apparently mistaken them for the police.

It's all impossible to process, even with the smattering of recordings gathered from servos and road cameras—not that I can bear to watch many of them. The handful from what I'm starting to think of as my "first" trip aren't so bad; I'm quite clearly me, Phoebe, long hair, short shorts, big smile. But in all images captured between June 24 and July 8 I am scrawny, hunched, and unsmiling. My hair is cut right down to my dark roots, I have a gap in my teeth where one is missing—even my posture, gait, and mannerisms are completely different. It's not surprising no one realized we were the same person. If I hadn't seen my reflection for myself, I would never have believed it either.

Ultimately though, there appears to be little doubt that three weeks after I dropped off the face of the planet I somehow found my way back to Plains Ranch and for the next fourteen days retraced my itinerary to the letter. However, no one can tell me why. Neither can they confirm where I was or what I was doing in the gap between disappearance and reappearance.

Even so, they come at me again and again with question after question about Vivi Green and Nova Cleary and the Kombi and the graves. They show me photos of the crime scene but nothing is familiar.

Then they ask about my Insta relationship with Lucas Cleary, how well I knew him, if I'd ever met him in person, and I draw a different kind of blank. I remember our friendship but don't know how to explain it. Is it possible to know someone better than you know anyone else in the world and at the same time not know them at all? Is it normal to feel so close to someone you've never actually met?

I scroll through our messages and contemplate reaching out, but he hasn't been active for weeks, not since I called him from his own doorstep. "Hey," I said, after the dorky red-haired kid had informed me Lucas wasn't home. "Funny story—I just knocked on your door but apparently you're not here. Some kid answered, says he's your brother. Where are you?"

"Shit, sorry," he said, sounding out of breath. "I'm still tied up with a job, but I'm only round the corner and finishing up now—can you wait ten minutes?"

"Um . . ." I bit my lip. "Sure, okay. I'll wait in the van."

"No, go on inside, Wyatt will look after you, he's a good kid. Grab a beer, make yourself at home, I'll literally be ten minutes. No, eight."

"I'll give you seven."

"Can't wait."

Smiling ruefully—I'd forgive him—I climbed the steps back onto the porch, pushed the blue door open and stepped inside. And that's the last I remember.

I've asked; of course I've asked. But no one will tell me anything about Lucas or his brother. *Soon,* they keep saying. *When we know more.*

Instagram waits. The cursor blinks, but like an insect caught and wrapped in a spiderweb, I am paralyzed.

Turning off my phone, I shove it deep under my pillow.

"What about this other identity?" Mum says. "Who was she for a whole month if she wasn't Phoebe?"

The psychologist checks his notes. "Usually with fugue the new persona is unconnected to the old identity, but it seems Phoebe's was very much related. Literally, in fact." He looks at me. "You told people Phoebe was missing, and that you were looking for her. You said you were her sister."

Mum and I exchange puzzled glances.

"According to statements you asked fellow travelers if they'd seen you, showed them your own photo. You said you were following Phoebe's itinerary using an Instagram account that also turned out to be yours. Fascinating really—it's as if some part of you was aware of the fugue while it was happening and was trying to find both a reason for it and a way out."

Oh yes, fascinating. But somewhere among all the nonsense there's a vague tug of recognition, like catching the scent of home in an unexpected place. "When I was this other person," I ask hesitantly, "did I have a name?"

The doc checks his notes. "Katy."

"Katy?" Mum exclaims, turning to me. "As in *Katy,* Katy?"

Another sudden dump of mind pictures. Summer days and ice cream. Mum all dressed up, ready to go out. My hands cupped around a small green insect. *Katy.*

"Does the name mean something to you?" says the doc.

"When Phoebe was little," Mum explains, "she had an imaginary friend. It was like her shadow side, a naughty little sister, someone she blamed when she got into trouble."

I remember. My quiet friend whom nobody else could see. She lived in the dark places under the bed, the space at the back of the closet. But she was kind and comforting and she loved me. No, she *was* me—and I was her, but somehow we were also separate. It made sense at the time but now it's hard to parse.

"How old was Phoebe when it started?"

"I'd say five," says Mum. "The first time I remember it happening was . . . well, it was summer and Pheebs was out in the garden. I was on my way out to meet a friend for dinner, late as usual. The neighbors were babysitting, they'd already arrived and I guess I was a little stressed. Phoebe kept running around the garden, chasing crickets and showing them to me. I remember she picked one up and asked me what its name was, I told her it was a katydid—that's what we called them when I was a kid—and Phoebe thought that was great, she kept asking 'Katy did what, Katy did what?' And y'know, it was funny at first, but of course then she wanted to bring the damn thing inside and keep it as a pet—and I just lost it."

Mum's cheeks burn pink and she looks down at her hands. "It wasn't my finest parenting moment. I was probably rougher with her than was appropriate but she'd been whingeing all afternoon, her father and I were going through a hard time—you know how it is. Anyway, I left her hiding under the bed bawling her eyes out. The poor neighbors, god knows what they thought of me."

I stare at her, the emotional honesty so out of character she might as well have turned into a donkey.

She looks up, right into my eyes. "You never let me forget it. For months afterward, anything you did wrong was Katy's fault. Any sign of trouble at all, and it was all 'Katy did it, Katy did it.'"

And I can see it, *her,* my shadowy friend who looked like me but not as pretty (obviously), who was shy and always worrying, always telling me to be more careful, more wary of potential danger. I never was, of course, and always blamed my bad behavior on her because I was so frightened of getting in trouble. Mum and Dad were scary in those days.

But Katy wasn't real. I knew that then and I know that now.

"Am I insane?" I ask, eyes brimming. "Am I some kind of psycho?"

The psychologist shakes his head. "Imaginary friends are healthy. They can protect young kids' minds from things they don't understand, help them process things that frighten or worry them. It's rare in adult-hood, but no different." He gives me a kind smile. "Dissociation is the brain's way of shielding itself from things it can't process. It's actually a strength, not a weakness."

I nod, even though I don't agree. The very last thing I feel is strong.

For days I pick over the puzzle pieces, trying to make them fit.

What happened at Lucas's house? Can't they just ask the kid brother? Perhaps they can't find him. Maybe he's dead.

With my memory still MIA, I sift through possible scenarios. Did I go for a walk and stumble across the old Kombi, the discovery of which was so traumatic that my mind fractured? Or did something else happen to me? Was I bitten by a spider or a snake? Did I fall down a cliff? Was I attacked? Did Lucas do something terrible to me? I don't want to believe it, but what do I really know about him? What had I ever known?

I go back through my DMs in search of some clue and show the mes-sages from lonewanderer66 to the police. They doubt it's connected. "We see that kind of stuff all the time," one officer says. "Most trolls use fake accounts and they're usually just out for a reaction. You can report it to eSafety if you're concerned."

Whatever the trigger, the fugue had caused me to wander back to the house, get back in my van, and drive 1,200 kilometers back toward Perth.

I cut off all my hair with the scissors in the first aid kit and stashed it in a plastic bag with my clothes and driver's license. I threw away all my bikinis, crop tops, short skirts, and instead wore a polo shirt borrowed from a teacher. I disappeared inside myself and became someone else.

If it hadn't happened to me, I would never believe it.

Then again so many things still don't add up. Doctors keep telling me that fugue sufferers don't tend to remember what happened during the state, but I feel like I do recall some things. Little stones. A shiny resort. Dolphins. When I close my eyes I see a vast body of water. I hear a warm female voice, a peal of infectious laughter. I feel a warm presence at my side, a swell of trust and comfort, and a rising sense of freedom. Other times I see awful things, images and feelings that could just be nightmares but which feel terrifyingly real. Blood and screams. Nails in my flesh. An indistinct face close to my own. But there's no one who can confirm that the pictures in my head are real, so who the hell knows what any of it means.

One morning I am told that my sweet friend Lucas is dead. He was found slumped behind the wheel of his car on the nearby highway, having apparently suffered an injury-related brain hemorrhage. And my DNA was all over him. Which feels impossible because I'm certain I never met him in person, only his brother.

I wish harder than I've ever wished before that I could remember, or that someone would come along and tell me they saw the whole thing.

And then, on my last day in hospital, someone does exactly that.

It's a young woman with elfin features, heavy-framed glasses, and short bleach-blond hair poking out from under a trucker cap that says EXMOUTH TAVERN. She hovers in my doorway with an expectant look on her face, and for a second I experience a kind of *mal de debarquement*, that feeling of still being on a boat even hours after returning to shore. But it disappears quick. She doesn't look like she works for the hospital or the police, so I assume she's a reporter.

"Are you lost?" I say frostily. "Can I help you?"

The woman's expression falters. "No," she says. "I'm pretty sure I can help you, though. My name's Jess. And I have something for you."

CHAPTER SEVENTY-EIGHT

Beth

Phoebe sits up on her bed, propped against a stack of pillows, head bowed, hands in her lap. She's been sitting like that for a long time, listening without question or comment, just occasionally shifting position and rubbing her eyes. "Wow," she says when Beth finally stops speaking. "That is . . . a lot."

Beth nods. "It is." She began her story perched at the very end of the mattress but now she's leaning back against the end frame, legs outstretched on the stiff, crunchy sheets. "I'm sorry."

"No, *I'm* sorry," Phoebe says. "I can't believe I don't remember you."

"That's okay."

There's a pause.

"They say I have dissociative fugue," Phoebe says.

"I heard. How's that going?"

"Shit. I feel like a monster. Tyler fucking Durden. I don't want to be like that."

"You're not Tyler Durden. *Fight Club* was about dissociative identity disorder. Like that other one, what's it called?" Beth snaps her fingers. "*Split.* James McAvoy. That's not what you have. Fugue is different."

"How?"

"Well, DID can be a lifelong condition, whereas fugue is typically a few days to a few months. Also there's only one alternate identity, not multiple, and usually not interchangeable with the original. As soon as the episode is over the new persona is forgotten along with everything that happened during the state, and then the sufferer goes back to being who they were."

"And then it never happens again?"

"Sometimes it does, sometimes it doesn't."

"So how is that better?"

"I don't know. Not better, I guess, just different."

Phoebe pauses to bite a nail. "How do you know all that? Are you a doctor?"

Beth smiles grimly. "I once wanted to be, but no. I never finished my psych degree." Then her heart plummets as she realizes how much of Phoebe's situation is her fault. "I'm so sorry I didn't see it earlier. None of the really bad stuff would've happened if I had; we could've got you to a hospital weeks ago. You just seemed so . . . normal. But from what I've read patients *do* tend to appear normal to the average person. It's standard fugue fare—if "standard" is possible with something that hardly ever happens. Apparently in some cases it looks a lot like sleepwalking, which FYI is something you did." She pauses, thinking about Phoebe wandering around at night, collecting rocks and stacking them outside the van. Even in sleep her subconscious had kept her busy, reenacting her trauma and dropping the clues she would need to solve the puzzle.

"Sometimes water is a thing," she continues. "Like, sufferers are repeatedly drawn to it. But otherwise it's just another human walking around doing ordinary human things." She takes a breath. "Sorry. I'm babbling. This is a lot for me too."

Phoebe looks down at her hands again. "Am I crazy?" she murmurs. "Like, clinically insane?"

Beth's heart aches for her. "I don't think so. You've got—"

"They're going to lock me up, aren't they? I'm never going home."

"Phoebe, listen, you're okay. You're going home. And you will be fine."

"I don't know if I believe that."

Beth can sympathize.

"It's like I'm not even a real person," Phoebe continues. "There's all this lost time where my body was running around without me so I don't trust it. It's like we don't belong to each other anymore. Also . . ."

"What?"

Phoebe swallows. "What if I'm stuck like this forever? They've scheduled all this therapy once I'm back in Sydney, but the more I think and talk about everything the more confused I get. The harder I try to remember, the less sure I am of who I was before, who I *am*. Does that make sense?"

"It makes perfect sense," said Beth. She thinks for a moment. "Have you written any of it down?"

"What do you mean?"

"I don't know, I'm just wondering . . . you wrote about your experiences before, maybe you should do it again. Not so publicly this time, but in a journal or something." She catches herself and rolls her eyes. She sounds like some teenager's out-of-touch mother. *Journaling. Ugh.* "Sorry, that's super basic advice. But I once read that the opposite of trauma is order, everything in its right place. Working through your thoughts on paper might help."

Phoebe makes a face. "What's the point? I spent five whole weeks with no idea who I was and I still can't remember any of it. I might *never* remember. If I wrote it down I'd just be making it up."

"Identity is constructed in part by the things we tell ourselves; even in normal circumstances we reshape our own selves every day. By writing your own story you wouldn't be making it up, you'd be *remaking* it."

Phoebe seems to think about that. "Far out," she says at last. "You sure you didn't finish uni?"

Beth smiled wryly. "I definitely did not. But who knows, maybe one day I will."

They sit quietly, listening to the tick of the clock on the wall and the hum of the hospital building. A staff member walks by on the corridor outside, their shoes clacking on the vinyl floor.

"I still don't understand how," Phoebe says, breaking the silence.

"Like, neurologically. I just want to understand where this other person came from."

Beth purses her lips and looks at the ceiling. "I don't know the science. But I guess it tracks that Katy was drawn out by the collision with your original itinerary. So, fugue Phoebe was somehow driving herself home, reversing your trip, but then the route intersected with your original starting point and, I don't know, caused some kind of mental disruption? Your subconscious remembered but not in a way that the fugue could process. So it created a new identity, fleshed out with your immediate surroundings: the van, its contents—even me. I gave you a story and you sort of co-opted it. You showed me a photo—of yourself, as it turns out—and I assumed it was your sister. I can't say at what point you conjured your imaginary friend, probably just a childhood memory that slipped through the gate, but she bubbled up from somewhere and that's who you became."

Enter Katy Sweeney, a lost soul trying to find her way back to the truth. A woman who never existed, but without whom Phoebe might've died.

Phoebe nods. "Yeah. I kind of get that. I just wish I knew what caused it in the first place. The blank spaces are killing me."

Beth sighs. It's time. This is why she's really here. Heart heavy, she stands up and pulls the letter from her pocket, the one that was left for her at the backpackers. *Dear Phoebe.* "I don't know if you're going to want to read this or not," she says, holding it out. "Maybe I should've just taken it straight to the cops but it didn't feel like my decision to make."

Phoebe looks at the envelope but doesn't take it. "What is it?"

"It's for you. And so is this." She reaches into her other pocket for the phone she took from the Cleary house. *Wyatt's* phone. She lays it on the bed with the letter.

Phoebe stares at them both as if they might explode.

At the door, Beth looks back. "I'll stay for a bit. Just outside. In case you need me."

Then she slips out into the corridor, pulls the door quietly shut behind her, and waits.

CHAPTER SEVENTY-NINE

Beth

A little while later, Beth leaves the hospital and makes her way to a black Jeep Wrangler at the rear of the car park. She opens the door and climbs into the passenger seat.

"How did it go?" says Jesse, turning the radio down.

Beth shrugs. "It was okay, I guess." She waited a long time, but Phoebe didn't call her back in. Probably for the best. There isn't anything she could possibly have said or done to make it better.

The radio babbles quietly. Phoebe's name is mentioned. Jesse switches it off—not that it'll do much good. The story is everywhere, they can't escape it.

"So, that's it then," he says, tapping his fingers lightly on the steering wheel. "Mission accomplished."

"I guess so." Beth sighs. "Thank you, Jesse. For all your help that night, and in the days since. I really appreciate it."

"Oh, please. It's the least I could do after, you know, everything."

Beth can't argue with that.

"Your hair looks good," he says.

Cringing, she touches the blond tufts.

"And listen, I'd totally let you keep the glasses but I literally can't see a thing without them, so . . ."

"Oh. Of course, sorry." Beth takes his black-rimmed glasses from her face and hands them back.

Taking them, Jesse polishes the lenses on his T-shirt. "So, what are you going to do now?"

"Good question." Beth puffs out her cheeks and exhales through pursed lips. "I think I have to go home, for a little while anyway. There's some stuff I need to figure out."

She thinks of the fish tank, the clock, the blood in her undies for days after the abortion. What happened to her was categorically not her fault, she sees that now; shitty things, and shitty people, sometimes just happen and choices are made based on how best to survive. But after a few days alone in a hostel room to think, she now understands that she's always tried to numb her feelings, has always been drawn to men who hurt her, and has always met problems with a mixture of flight and denial. And she'll never stop doing those things unless she understands the reasons why.

"You know what I still can't get over?" Jesse says. "How wild it is that you and Phoebe ever met in the first place. It seems like a pretty big coincidence, all things considered, that your paths crossed as closely as they did."

Beth shakes her head. "I don't think so." She remembers the way Lucas's gaze had been fixed on the HiAce that night, clearly recalls thinking he was chasing it for some reason. "I think he recognized Phoebe's van and was purposely tailing it, trying to get a look at the driver."

"Why?"

"There's something on Wyatt's surveillance tape that suggests Lucas saw Phoebe's van parked outside his dad's house on June third, or maybe pulling out of the driveway. I think he thought the driver might've been his mother—or had something to do with her anyway."

"How come?"

Beth chews her lip. "Lucas never got over losing her. After she disappeared he spent every day wondering what had happened; it's the main reason he lived on the road in the first place. He knew she'd been a traveler, had been told that she'd preferred the road to being a mum. I think he was obsessed with the idea of being closer to her, maybe even finding her one day. So then when he arrived home on the night of June third and found a camper pulling away from his house he assumed—or hoped—it might've been her. Or something like that, anyway."

Another pause. Jesse fidgets in his seat, clearly piqued by the mention of the recording. Beth can practically smell his frustration, can feel the questions coming. *Three, two, one . . .*

"So what *is* on the tape?" Jesse says. "I'm dying to know."

There it is. "You're kidding, right?"

"What? We're cool now, aren't we? You know I'm not going to write about it, I just want to know how it ends."

Beth rubs her forehead. "You know what, Jesse? I want to like you, I really do. I think essentially you're a good guy, and I really am grateful for your help this last week. But no, we're not *cool*. You put a tracker on a woman's van. You followed her without her knowledge, you *watched* her *sleep*. You wanted something from her, and you weren't prepared to stop until you got it. I just don't think there's any coming back from that."

Jesse's face falls. "But I explained. I said sorry. I never meant to scare her, or you."

"Maybe not. But you did. You saw an easy target, and you—"

"*Easy?*"

"Okay, fine, maybe the word is *acceptable*. You saw an acceptable target. Justified, because it was something *you* wanted."

Jesse looks like he's about to argue the point, then decides against it.

Beth turns away, thinking about Lucas and all the things that had made him who he was, how scared he must've been growing up with all that violence and entitlement. How desensitized he would've been to the sight of a man physically overpowering a woman. She's starting to understand that so much of his rage was in fact shame and fear. In his own way, he too was trying to survive. And while it's definitely not an excuse for the way he treated her, it is a reason. She wishes she could tell Jesse some of that. *Forget ghosts and an anesthetic gas and mutilation,* she wants to say. *Write about* this.

But then she'd have to tell him the whole story. She'd have to share what she saw on the tape.

And maybe she will one day; it's an important piece of the puzzle. Then again, maybe she won't. After all, the story isn't Jesse's to tell. It's not even Beth's. In the end, what's on that recording belongs to Phoebe and Phoebe alone.

CHAPTER EIGHTY

Wyatt

July 14

Dear Phoebe,

I heard you've got amnesia like Jason Bourne so I don't know if you remember me or not but I'm so sorry for the damage I've caused. I know you won't believe me when I say I didn't mean it, but I really didn't. I would never have hurt you on purpose, and I ~~promise I never~~ didn't know what would happen, and I just want you to know because even now after everything I still feel like we're friends, even though I'm not who you thought I was, and I'm really sorry for that too. I just saw ~~your face~~ you and I wanted to be friends so badly but I didn't think you'd want to be friends with someone like me so I used my brother's name and photo, and I posted pictures and videos of him, sometimes things he sent me, sometimes things from when he still lived with us, and of course that did it because he's hot and confident and interesting and also your age, but I didn't expect that we would get on so well, which we did. And then I felt like we were really friends and you felt the same I think, and sometimes I thought maybe you knew me better than anyone in the world, that no one understood me on the level that you seem to. So ~~once you~~ then when

*you needed help I ~~knew I could~~ knew you'd be safe with me but
then when you got here you didn't know me, which was fair enough
since I'd been pretending to be someone else but still. Anyway, I just
wanted to say that this is all my fault and that nothing will ever
make up for it but I hope you know I'm sorry, and that I'm not like
them. Dad, and Lucas. At least I ~~hope I'm not~~ don't want to be.
Anyway all of this is shit and weird and I don't know what's going to
happen but I wanted you to have ~~this~~ the phone before the police get
it, just because I think that's what I would want if it were me, which
in a way I guess it kind of is. So when you get the phone the passcode
is 237237, go to the MyGarrison app and click on my recordings.
Whatever happens from here, I'm sorry and goodbye I guess, because
I'm sure you don't want to be my friend now but for what it's worth
I'm still yours.*

~~Love~~

From Wyatt.

CHAPTER EIGHTY-ONE

Phoebe

As the recording starts, it's like there are two separate people inside me, layered one on top of the other like two sheets of tracing paper. I see a living room. A tattered couch and a front door. To the left is a wide entryway through which I can see a kitchen. I hear a knock, then Wyatt walks into frame, padding slowly over the threadbare carpet and wiping his palms against his T-shirt. He pauses before opening the door, then as he does something happens to his body, a kind of expansion as though he's suddenly been pumped full of air. He starts to speak, and even though the microphone isn't quite strong enough to pick up the words it's clear that he's inviting his guest inside. But the person on the porch (me) does not accept, so Wyatt shrugs and retreats back into the living room, leaving the front door wide open. As he passes the camera, he speeds up, hurrying toward the kitchen and out of frame.

There's a two-and-a-half-minute pause during which nothing happens. And then I appear in the doorway. This, I vaguely remember. My body recalls stepping over the threshold, my throat still holds the words I called out. "Hello? Sorry, do you mind if I come in after all? Lucas says to wait." I remember standing alone in the middle of the house, waiting for the kid brother to return from wherever he went. But that's where my memory runs out. As the recording continues and I step forward, right up close to the camera, and pluck a photo frame from somewhere out of shot, I feel my mind shut down.

This is it, I think. *This is the moment.*

While the me I don't remember pulls more photos from the bookshelf and studies each in turn, something happens behind me. A shape appears in the entryway, a dark silhouette backlit by the kitchen window. It glides into view so slowly and silently, and stands so still for so long that at first I think it's a cardboard cutout. But then it moves forward and takes the shape of a man, much older than the boy.

He edges quietly into the room like someone trying not to wake a sleeping dog, staring in disbelief at my turned back. His puffy face is stubble-speckled and his shoulders are hunched. Then he speaks; it sounds like "Nova?"

The me on the screen jumps and spins around. "Oh my god," I say, my voice clear. "I'm so sorry, I was just—"

Still staring, the man tilts his head. There's something not quite right about him, something slow and disconnected about his movements. His eyes are like two black holes. "Wyatt?"

"Sorry," Screen Me says again. "I'm not sure where he is. He answered the door and invited me in but now he's gone. Anyway, sorry, I'm Phoebe. I'm here to see Lucas?"

The man looks around again as if not quite sure where he is.

"I just spoke to him, he told me to—"

"Nova," the man says again. "Is it you?" And then suddenly he lumbers forward and in three strong strides he has me, both hands clasped around my arms. I cry out in shock, but the sound is cut off as the man pulls me toward him. Shaking, he strokes my face. Then he wraps his arms right around me and presses his face into my hair. He starts to cry, rocking back and forth and moaning. At first I am still and stiff in his arms, clearly waiting it out, hoping it'll be over soon. But when he doesn't release me, I begin to struggle. "Stop," I say. "Please, get off." The man doesn't stop. He sobs loudly. And then he presses his big hand over my mouth and forces my head back.

If the forced intimacy wasn't shocking enough, the ensuing violence is like the smash of a train through a bedroom wall, an unexpected explosion. It arrives with little forewarning and escalates like a bushfire. Watching it is the strangest, most intensely awful moment of my life.

Screen Me puts up a decent fight; I kick and thrash but it's like watching a tree try to hold back a flood. I go down. The man punches me in the face. A tooth goes flying. There's blood everywhere, but he doesn't stop. It's so distressing that I have to stop watching to throw up a little bit onto the uncollected lunch tray at the end of my bed.

After an immeasurable pause, I return to the phone and skip forward to where the ordeal ends. The girl that is me but also not me goes still. The man cries again. Then he cleans up. Then he gathers me in his arms and carries me out of the house.

There's a short gap of nothing.

Then a faint rumble of an engine. The swing of headlights across the wallpaper.

And then the front door opens and my friend Lucas walks in, a real-life walking-talking version, glancing back over his shoulder to the street outside with a puzzled frown on his face. The recording captures the roar of a van outside taking off at speed, and Lucas lingers in the doorway, staring out into the fading light. Then he closes the door and stands biting his nails for several seconds before ambling into the kitchen and out of shot.

Thirteen minutes and forty seconds later, the door opens again and Wyatt arrives.

"Hey, bud," says Lucas, stepping back through the entryway with a beer in his hand. "How's my favorite bro?"

"Lucas. What are you doing here?"

"Just thought I'd drop in and say hi."

When the recording ends, I exit the app and turn off the phone. Slowly, as if my bones are about to break, I lie down and stare at the ceiling, thinking of the moment Rory Cleary had carried me from his house. Dangling in his arms, I looked like a corpse. Small wonder then that my subconscious had presumed me dead.

CHAPTER EIGHTY-TWO

Wyatt

There are noises in Wyatt's house. No longer in the walls, but voices in the living room, footsteps on the porch. The chime of phones, the clang of plates, and the hiss of the kettle. This is because there are people here now, lots of them, always in and out, asking questions, taking notes, delivering news. And Mrs. Creeping in the middle of it all, making coffee and baking things, banana bread, zucchini slice, and Anzac biscuits even though Anzac Day was months ago.

Everyone wants to talk to her. They all want to talk to Wyatt too, but the stream of visitors to his room seems now to be dropping off a little, either because all the questions have been answered or because Mrs. Creeping is starting to send them all away. "Leave him alone," he's heard her say. "That's quite enough now. The poor boy needs space."

Somewhere inside, Wyatt is grateful for this but it's a feeling he can't quite access. It's the medication, a prescribed SSRI, a buffer between him and the raging typhoon that is somehow now his life. He's aware of what's happening, can hear the clamor of his emotions and all his own stampeding questions, but it's like they're all zombies banging on a bulletproof window that he's happy to keep shut. He spends most days lying in bed watching Netflix on his iPad, comfortably numb and paddling in the shallow end of his consciousness. Today it's some show about a remote island community and the arrival of a mysterious new priest. He's only on episode two but he can tell already it's a good one. Lucas would love it.

"Wyatt?" Mrs. Creeping's voice drifts in through his open bedroom door, along with the smell of home cooking. Lasagna or something. "Can I come in?"

Wyatt pulls down his headphones and eyeballs her. She's wearing an apron over a man's shirt and jeans. The apron is smeared with tomato sauce.

"How are you doing?" she says, pulling out his desk chair and sitting down. Standing here in his house, in his room, she looks a lot less witchy than she used to. She actually looks pretty normal.

He shrugs. "I don't know."

She smiles like he's just said something wise. "I've just been speaking with Child Protection about next steps for you, and it sounds like it'll be a while before we know anything for sure. There are a lot of different processes and assessments, and Rory needs to decide a few things with his lawyers. But I just wanted to let you know that the conversations are happening, and in the meantime you'll stay here, at home, unless you choose otherwise."

Wyatt nods. He has no idea where else he would go, but he doesn't want to be alone. No Lucas and no Dad? He doesn't even understand how that would work. "Will anyone stay here with me?" he says.

Mrs. Creeping purses her lips. "Well, there are few options. A caseworker will look for existing family members, perhaps on Nova's side, but unless you want to consider foster care or a group home, I was thinking maybe I could stay. Not in the house if you don't want, I can sleep next door. But I could take care of you, for as long as you like. How would you feel about that?"

Wyatt's fuzzy head spins. If Mrs. Creeping is the only option then he really is alone.

Funnily enough, his thoughts go straight to Phoebe. Is she alone, too? What will happen to her? What is she doing right now at this very second? Has she read his letter yet? According to some guy with glasses who cornered him on the driveway one morning, the girl who'd broken into the shed was Lucas's ex-girlfriend and a close friend of Phoebe's. The guy had begged Wyatt on her behalf not to mention her involvement or even existence to the police—and Wyatt agreed (no need to get himself into even more trouble) on the condition that his phone be delivered to her along with a private message for Phoebe. *Tell her to take it to the hospital,* he told the guy, *and swear on your life you won't read it yourself.* Because Phoebe never would've been at his house in the first place if it wasn't for him. Everything, *everything,* is his fault. And he's so deeply sorry. Does she know that?

From within the medicated bomb shelter that is now his mind, Wyatt can imagine how it all went down. Mum and Dad got married, had Lucas, and moved in with Nan and Pop. When Nan and Pop died, the mortgage fell to them. Dad worked hard to support his family, but it wasn't enough. And then Wyatt came along. Dad worked harder, started to drink. Mum and Dad fought. Wyatt was a difficult baby, a Bad Kid; he never slept, demanded too much. Mum was alone, needed help, couldn't cope. Dad turned to drugs: antidepressants, sedatives, and tranquilizers. They fought some more. And then . . .

And then.

And then.

It wasn't really Dad, Wyatt knows that. It was like he'd been bitten or infected or possessed. He still looked the same but underneath he was different: a subhuman creature with an insatiable, uncontrollable thirst for darkness. A Dream Demon. The real Dad had been gone for a long time.

He understands now that on the night Wyatt had abandoned Phoebe in his house, the Dad-creature had returned home from the pub and found her in the living room. Seeing her through a narcotic veil, he'd thought she was Mum. The recording from the phone, or what little Wyatt had managed to watch, reminded him of Macbeth. *Avaunt and quit my sight. . . . Never shake thy gory locks. . . . Blood will have blood.*

He's not sure exactly what had happened with the crab spaghetti woman—Vivi—but he supposes it had been pretty much the same. If he'd had the stomach for it, he could've checked the surveillance footage, discovered the reason she too had ended up in the dunes. But he couldn't face it. And in the end, he supposes, there doesn't actually have to be a reason because most monsters don't do logic. If the movies have taught him anything, they've taught him that.

Wyatt wonders if Phoebe would agree. He also wonders why, after what the Dad-creature had done to her, she'd come back? Wyatt thinks about that a lot, tries to picture the sequence of events. Dad-creature had driven Phoebe's campervan and taken her to William Wilson. He'd planned to hide the van in the dunes, in the forbidden sinkhole wastelands, and add Phoebe's body to his makeshift graveyard. But somehow Phoebe had escaped. And then five weeks later, she returned. Wyatt doesn't quite understand it. It has something to do with Phoebe also being sick, but he's not sure of the details. He half hopes she might've come back for him.

What he *does* understand is this: he was right. There had been something evil in his house, in the walls. It just wasn't what he thought.

Mrs. Creeping had known though. Wyatt overheard her telling police that she always suspected Nova hadn't left of her own accord. She grew up next door, she said, she'd known Rory since he was a child. The whole neighborhood had known about his father, how he beat his wife and kids with a metal rod, how he chained Rory to a pole in the garage when he misbehaved and left him there for hours. Which at the time, she said, wasn't so weird, it was just discipline. But as she grew older, Mrs. Creeping started to see things differently. She saw Rory change from beaten boy into hardened man. She saw how he began to treat his new bride, free-spirited vanlifer Nova. And then she saw how he handled his own children, his two beautiful boys.

Mrs. Creeping said she spoke to Mum, tried to intervene, get her to admit what was happening. When that didn't work she hung around, offered to watch the kids, popped over when things sounded like they were heating up, and it seemed like it was working. Things calmed down. But then one day Mum just wasn't there anymore. Dad told everyone she'd abandoned them—which for the record Mrs. Creeping did *not* believe for a second, Nova would *never* have abandoned those boys—and then he started behaving oddly.

He'd asked Mrs. Creeping if she'd like him to take care of her garden, and she'd accepted because that had always been Keith's job and she had no idea how to maintain it now that he'd passed. She'd said he could use her side of the garage too, if he needed more space for his tools—which he had, and bought a new padlock, which was smart and also fine by her because she never went in there anyway. But then she saw him slipping in and out at night, sometimes staying there until sunrise. She'd been confused—*what on earth could he be doing in there all night?*—but then she'd heard things that reminded her of the old days when Rory was punished as a boy and wondered if he might be putting himself back in there again, chaining himself up, atoning for his crime the only way he knew how. And she'd been right—but she hadn't known he'd also been storing stolen goods as part of a father–son theft ring.

She tried to tell a few people, even reported him to the police, but no one listened. She was just a loopy old lady, a known crackpot. All she could do was watch the house, she said. Keep an eye on the boys, visit the house when they were alone, try her best to make sure they were okay. Let them know that if they needed help, she was there. Lucas, she'd quickly realized, was long gone. But for Wyatt, maybe there was still hope.

Wyatt doesn't fully understand exactly what she'd meant by that, but he keeps thinking about it, especially at night. Because among all the muted fear and blunted grief, the fever dreams and endless dark hours, there is a tiny glimmer of peace. When he can't sleep, he looks out the window, up to where the same pinprick of light seems always to shine unusually bright against the velvety black sky. The creation of a star.

I love you, Mum.

She loves him, too. He knows that now. He also knows she's never coming back. But it's some comfort to know that she did not leave him.

She did not choose to go. And maybe she never did. Maybe, even after everything, she stayed.

This is all, of course, a lot for him to process. As is the more immediate prospect of being looked after by Mrs. Creeping. Or Jill, as she keeps asking him to call her. And how *does* he feel about that?

"Do I have to decide now?" he says.

Jill smiles and shakes her head. "Of course not," she says. "Little by little. One step at a time."

Turns out, she's not so creepy after all.

After dinner, Wyatt draws the blinds, sits on the couch, and selects another horror movie, one of his new favorites. He presses play and the film begins.

A young woman pulls up outside the Airbnb she has booked, but the house is already occupied by a man who says he too has booked the property but through a different rental site. What a mix-up. The young woman grapples with the decision to stay or leave. The man pours her a drink, offers her the bedroom while he sleeps on the couch, persuades her to stay. Wyatt feels a ripple of anticipation; he knows what's coming, the whole film is about to be turned on its head—but just as things are about to get interesting he surprises himself by pressing pause. The scene freezes on the actress's face.

Wyatt loves these movies. They've kept him company for years, validated his fear, and taught him how to survive. (Top tips: never poke around in the haunted house, never go into the basement alone, never return to the killer once you've escaped, never leave your phone behind, never pick up a hitchhiker or get into a stranger's car). They've showed him that the monster *can* be vanquished, that there *is* life after terror, that the girl often *does* get away. They've also been the perfect distraction— because watching someone get chopped to pieces on screen is scary but not nearly as horrific as what's inside his own heart and mind. But now maybe it's time for something different.

He turns off the TV and stands up. He thinks about how oblivious he's been, how much he's missed, almost as if he's been living on the other side of a mirror. He feels around the edges of the mammoth journey ahead, and all the ways in which his world must be rebuilt if he is to keep living in it.

Crossing to the window, he opens the blinds and lets the sunshine in. He closes his eyes and accepts it like a gift.

Five minutes later, he shuts them again, returns to the movie, and presses play—because you can't build a new world in a single go.

Little by little, he thinks. *One step at a time.*

EPILOGUE
ONE YEAR LATER

CHAPTER EIGHTY-THREE

Phoebe

Mum and I begin the fifty-or-so kilometer drive from Learmonth Airport in apprehensive silence, but a little music lightens the mood, and despite the shadow that sits on both our hearts we're soon cracking a packet of chips and rolling down the windows to let the desert air in.

Our rental, a sleek Mitsubishi Outlander, cuts through the red dirt on a road that twists and winds before us like something trying to get away. I gaze through the window at the breathtaking spread of Nyinggulu, yet again simultaneously intimidated and awestruck by the sheer expanse of wide open space. The gulf glitters on our right; to the left is the rugged rise of Cape Range. The light is just as extraordinary as I remember, the sky just as vast.

Forty minutes pass in a blink and we're there: climbing the hill to Vlamingh Head Lighthouse as the sun hangs low over the ocean. The sunset crowds have already begun to gather: dozens of cars and vans line both sides of the road, their occupants busy unpacking picnics.

Mum pulls up in a space up the front and we sit together, staring out at the panoramic ocean view. She squeezes my hand. "If it gets too much, I'll be right here."

I get out of the car and walk toward the lighthouse and the two figures standing at the base. "Hello," I say as I approach.

"Phoebe!" says Beth, throwing her arms around me. "You made it." She's looking smart and fresh in linen shorts and a crisp shirt. Her hair has grown out and the blond dye with it, and now sits dark and glossy on her shoulders.

"Hi," says Wyatt. He's wearing boardshorts and a T-shirt that reads BLUE NINGALOO TOURS and carries a black backpack. His eyes are brighter than they used to be, his pallor healthier. At sixteen, he's a little taller too, the angles of his adult face beginning to take shape under a speckle of teenage acne, and his hair has grown. He's actually starting to look a lot like Lucas, a fact that Beth and I have acknowledged several times over email.

Sensing immediately that he's not up for a hug—and fair enough, this is the first time we've properly met in person—I offer a toothy smile. "Hey." It's awkward, but not as excruciating as it could've been had we not been laying the groundwork over WhatsApp for the past few months.

We've all kept in touch as best we can, or as much as the ongoing criminal proceedings have allowed: tentatively at first, none of us really knowing what we wanted or needed from one another, but then with increasing frequency. It feels important. Me, him, and her. The living ripples of Rory Cleary's actions. Our connection is painful but undeniable—and wholly necessary.

"So what do you think of the location?" Wyatt says, gesturing north toward a spot almost right at the tip of the headland where the monument is said to be going. "She'll look right out over the reef. And the gulf too. She'll be able to see the whales migrating."

"I love it," I say truthfully. A brand-new sculpture, created especially for Nova Cleary, Vivi Green, and every other Australian life lost to gendered violence. A woman made of stone and steel, standing watch over her sisters. *I see you,* she'll say to anyone who tries to hurt them. *This is your problem to solve, not theirs.*

We talk like regular people about lives, our jobs. Wyatt is working for a whale shark tour company and training to be a dive instructor. Beth's back in Melbourne and finishing her psychology degree. After a prolonged period of sick leave, I've resumed my student support role at the college. I tell them about my new apartment in Sydney, already cluttered with piles of unsorted clothes and half-drunk glasses of water, until it's clear that the time has come to do the thing we've come to do. Walking three abreast, we make our way down a little track to a viewing platform and stand together watching the ocean ripple and surge, and again I feel both enchanted and exposed by the shock of blue water and the oil-painting sky—as well as more than a little gauche, like an uninvited guest. For the first time it occurs to me that this land is not and has never been ours to explore. That in fact we're not even guests upon it but recipients, vessels, here simply to accept what's offered.

Usually this kind of thinking would freak me out; I hate feeling out of control. But instead it generates a little bubble of wonder that rises inside my chest, a giddy feeling that takes me back to the days of sandpits and forts and imaginary castles.

Wyatt reaches into his backpack and pulls out a beautiful blue mosaic pot. Beth and I hold hands as he lifts the lid and scoops out a handful of tiny shells and white sand, tossing them over the water in place of ashes since Nova's remains are still being treated as evidence, and we all watch as the wind picks up at exactly the right moment and carries the grains up and away, into the technicolor sky. When they fall back down to earth they make a sound like fine rain.

"The most beautiful place on the planet," Wyatt murmurs. "The last wild place on earth."

Afterward we hug, and Wyatt says he has to go. "Maybe see you for breakfast tomorrow, before you fly home?"

"Sure," I say. "I'd like that."

Beth and I wave as he trudges slowly up the hill, back to his life, and then we're alone.

"Have you heard Jesse's podcast yet?"

I shake my head. "Not part of my mental health plan."

"Fair call. It's pretty good though, all about the truth behind so-called hauntings and exploring the real people behind the myths. He just did an episode on Eleanor Flannery actually."

"Yeah?" The name sends an unpleasant chill slithering down my spine. The ghost of Gracious Bay.

"He dug around, contacted a few museums, and unearthed old documents that suggest she was abused on that ship. Letters from some of the wreck survivors, journal entries from a Flannery family member, things like that. Also some correspondence from a medical practitioner that show Alexander Flannery had Eleanor committed to an asylum against her will, then forced her release so he could take her on his trade voyage to Fremantle. Sounds like she might've been kept on the ship as a kind of toy. No wonder she torched it, huh?"

We both stare down at the water. Beneath the surface, dark shapes are dancing, weaving, flying with wings outstretched. Manta rays. Ocean angels.

"What about you?" Beth asks. "How are you really?"

"What, *really* really?"

"Uh-huh."

"Ugh." I run my hands through my hair. "It's like . . . I feel stuck. I'm functioning better day to day, but I still feel broken inside. I just . . . I don't feel like anyone's going to move on until we know for sure what's the matter with me, what a fugue actually is or why it happened."

"That's understandable," Beth says, nodding. "I've actually been thinking a lot about it and I might have a theory if you're interested?" She says this shyly as if her opinion wouldn't be worth salt to me.

"Please," I say.

"Bear in mind I'm still not qualified."

"Go on, tell me."

"Right. So I've been learning at uni about this new model of psychotherapy that is based on the idea that our identities are made up of many different subpersonalities or 'parts.' And each 'part' is like a real sentient being with its own functions and opinions; kind of like organs if they could talk."

"O-kaaay. And how is that different from dissociative identity disorder?"

"Well, in some ways it's not. The model says that we *all* have multiple personalities, but in a healthy person they all function smoothly as one system. These 'parts' of the self are like a family, and each member of the family plays a different role. But certain life challenges and traumatic events can force these parts out of their healthy roles and into unhealthy roles. For example, in an extreme situation a part responsible for protection might be pushed into becoming what's called a 'firefighter' and use a behavior-like substance abuse to put out the 'fire' of the pain. A part responsible for executive function might be pushed into becoming a 'manager' and use obsessive or controlling behaviors to avoid experiencing the pain. With me so far?"

"I think so."

"Right, so in this hypothetical extreme situation the whole purpose of these parts becomes to bury or fight anything that might cause pain to the core self; so like shameful memories, bad thoughts, fears, harmful beliefs, stuff like that. But the ways in which they often choose to do that—substance abuse or eating disorders or self-harm—is obviously unhealthy. So then the therapy is about getting the unhealthy part to become healthy again by attempting to understand and validate its experience. Basically talk it down from the ledge. See?"

I grimace. "Kind of."

"The bad things that are being pushed away—the memories and fears and so on—are also parts, and they're called 'exiles,' mostly generated when we're young. And when an exile loses faith in the ability of the system to protect the self, it can rise up and sort of take over. Like a coup d'état."

"Sounds more like demonic possession."

Beth makes a face. "No, no, it's . . . look, the point is—what if your dissociative fugue was actually an exiled part, triggered to believe your survival was threatened. In order to protect you, the exile then rose up and took the wheel, overwhelming all identity and decision-making systems. Sounds crazy, but the therapy model does acknowledge that it can happen."

"Wow." I look up at the sky, then back down at the ocean. "Bloody hell," I say. "Okay."

"Good news is that, if that *is* the explanation, it confirms that there's nothing wrong with you. You just need to find your exile—Katy—and bring her back. Talk to her. Because she's not a sickness. She's just part of you."

I don't know what to say; my mind can't keep up with Beth's. But something does occur to me, something Wyatt told me while he was pretending to be Lucas. Whales, apparently, have hemispheric brains. When the mother whale falls asleep with her calf, her mind cleaves itself in two so one half can rest while the other keeps watch for danger. Maybe we're not so different.

I feel like I can "see" her, my exile, standing between me and Beth on the viewing platform, her hand on my shoulder. She's still scared, still paranoid. *Can we please go home now?* she says. *We shouldn't be here. Coming back was a mistake. It's dangerous.*

It's okay, I want to tell her. *We're safe.*

But I don't know if I can. Is healing possible after total destruction? How does anyone put their life back together when their whole world has been crushed? I don't know the answer. Perhaps there isn't one. All I know is I'm here, still breathing, still me. All the parts of me. And for now, that's enough.

Instead, I thank her. *Thank you for finding me. For not giving up until you did.*

I feel her smile.

I look over my shoulder, up at the lighthouse to where Mum is now out of the car and waiting for me. She waves. I wave back. Then I turn to Beth. "Listen," I say, taking her hand. "I just want to say that—"

"Oh my god, look!" she says, cutting me off and pointing at the water.

I turn to follow her gaze and my breath catches.

We stand together, fingers entwined, gasping with wonder and delight.

Out to sea, just off the headland, two whales are breaching.

Liked by **life_and_beth_situations** and **others**

pheebsinwonderland Hi everyone. It's been a while huh? I just wanted to reach out and say thank you for all the kind messages of support over the past year, and hello to all the new followers. It's been a tough journey, as I'm sure you're aware, but I'm doing really well now and even starting to consider traveling again. I know that might be hard to believe after what I went through, but I always said the world was full of magic and I still think it's true. I miss the freedom of travel. I miss the adventure. I miss vanlife. And I won't let what happened to me dictate the rest of my life. The man who hurt me doesn't get to take the magic away.

Anyway, thank you again for sticking with me and for all the love. Please, if you have any tips or suggestions on where and how a girl might start falling back in love with the road, drop a comment below, I'd love to hear from you! Until then, take care out there. Love and light, Pheebs xx

> (Image descriptions: 1. Two women stand together on a platform overlooking a turquoise blue ocean and a glorious sunset. 2. The proposed design for the new West Star statue at Lighthouse Bay, WA: a silver woman gazing out to sea, keeping watch over her free-spirited sisters.)

#solofemaletravel #thosewhowander #vanlife #vijasolo #travelgirls #wanderlust #roadtrippin

View all 2,735 comments

annabellas_fella Omg Pheebs, what you've been through. Thank you for sharing, your story is so powerful ♡

marinbrowning1872 You're so brave. I could never do what you're doing, it must be so scary. Praying for you and your family.

lovelifelaughtahlia This post made me cry. Sending love. Oh, and try Canada. Or Thailand.

AroundtheWorldwithStacyMays: Good to have you back! Defs swim with the whale sharks if you go back to Ningaloo, and Broome is off the hook, and you'll hate yourself if you don't make it to Kari-jini one day, it's a MUST DO!

lonewanderer66 Well, well. I knew you wouldn't stay away for long. I've been waiting for you. And I still have questions. Check your DMs.

28 September

ACKNOWLEDGMENTS

I've said it before and I'll say it again: it's a real wonder that there's only ever one name on the cover of a book. (Yes, I know, sometimes two if a book has been cowritten or translated, but you get what I mean.) Truly, if it weren't for the following people this book would not exist. My deepest love and gratitude to each and every one.

Top of the list as ever are Hillary Jacobson Creative Artists Agency (CAA) and Tara Wynne (Curtis Brown Australia) without whose tireless championship, guidance, and support I would surely spend every working day in the fetal position. Thank you both for being my friends as well as my agents.

Also Caitlan Cooper-Trent at CB Australia; Emma Finn at C&W; and my magnificent film and TV agents, Josie Freedman and Berni Vann, at CAA.

Thank you to Catherine Richards, my extraordinary US editor, who understood this book from the word go and helped me see what it could be at a point when I had lost faith. Catherine, working with you just the once was a dream come true, never mind a second and third time. Your enthusiasm and belief in me continues to mean the whole world.

I'm also indebted to the whole Minotaur team, especially Kelley Ragland, Kelly Stone, and Steve Erickson; thank you so much for all that you do. And a very special shout out to David Rotstein for the beautiful cover.

Martin Hughes, my Australian publisher, whose insight and story instincts always make such a huge difference. And to the wider team at Affirm Press, you're all bright and shining diamonds, thank you for all your hard work.

Ruby Ashby-Orr. You are a game changer. When The Cranberries sing about "a totally amazing mind, so understanding and so kind," I swear they're singing about you. I hope you know how much I appreciate every bit of your editorial brilliance.

Nikki Lusk, the greatest copy editor on Earth. Your eye for detail rocks my world.

I will be forever grateful to Lucy Kilgannon (@aswetravel_au), on whose excellent suggestion this book is set on the Coral Coast of WA. When I called you out of the blue asking to pick your brain about vanlife and the Big Lap, I could never have dreamed where it would take me. So much of what you said that day shaped my initial ideas for this story.

Sara Foster was the very next person I called, who gave me a Perth local's perspective, as well as great advice on potential routes and itineraries. That chat was so helpful, thank you so much.

Special thanks to digital creator and solo traveler Rebekah Hamilton (@beckkyhamilton, www.trekwithbeck.blog), who gave me the most generous and uplifting interview from the road, and who provided crucial inspiration for the character of Phoebe.

Also Nina Burakowski (@waexplorer, www.westaustralianexplorer .com), whose intimate knowledge of WA and extensive solo travel experience were invaluable. Thank you for sharing your expertise with me.

My descriptions of the HiAce are largely based on the ten days I spent traveling between Perth and Exmouth in Lola the Love Bus, the most delightful campervan that ever did exist. A massive shout-out to her owner and maker, John Williams in Scarborough, Perth: thank you, and please give Lola a kiss from me.

Dr. Shen Lin Koo. Any therapist who does not work with a bird on their head is of no interest to me. Thank you for the epic journey, and for showing me the entrance to the rabbit hole.

My writer friends. You know who you are, and I hope you know how much you mean to me. You ought to, I tell you all the time, but still: I honestly don't know what I'd do without you.

Also my non-writer friends, who never fail to get excited. I'm so lucky to have such good people in my life.

Thank you to the wildly talented and very busy authors who read early copies and provided endorsements. Sally Hepworth, Candice Fox, Hayley Scrivenor, Christian White, Gabriel Bergmoser, Sarah Bailey, Hannah Richell, and Allie Reynolds. The drinks are all on me.

I acknowledge Aboriginal people as the Traditional Owners and Custodians of the lands on which this story is set and was written. I recognize that sovereignty was never ceded, and unreservedly support the Uluru Statement from the Heart.

I'd like to pay tribute to Tim Winton's awe-inspiring ABC documentary *Ningaloo Nyinggulu*. Tim is not only one of our finest living writers but also a fierce defender of "the last wild place on earth," and his advocacy for this astonishing part of the world is unrivaled. Please watch the documentary if you can, and then check out the preservation campaigns of charity organization Protect Ningaloo (@protectningaloo, www.protect-ningaloo.org.au), which is fighting to defend Exmouth Gulf from mass industrialization.

I drew thematic inspiration from Doon Mackichan's radio documentary *Body Count Rising* (Radio 4) and Gavin de Becker's book *The Gift of Fear*. The therapy model referenced by Beth in the epilogue is Internal Family Systems, developed by Richard C. Schwartz; for more information, you can read his book *No Bad Parts*. And when Beth mentions the idea that "the opposite of trauma is order, everything in its right place," the book she's thinking of is *The Trauma Cleaner* by Sarah Krasnostein.

None of what I do would be possible without the support of my family. I love you all, especially you over there in England.

Extra love and adoration to my sisters: Lucy, to whom this book is dedicated; Jessie Eliza; and Lotte Beth. Team Tommo forever.

Daisy and Jack. You are both exceptional humans and my very favorite people to spend time with. Thank you for all that you give and teach me.

Matt Downes. You know how when I'm on a boat I sometimes get seasick and have to look at the horizon to stay steady? That's you. You're the horizon. Thank you, among many, *many* other things, for always bringing me snacks when you know I need them.

Finally, thank you to the readers. As I've said before, my books are never complete without you. May we make many more stories together in the future.

AUTHOR'S NOTE

As a storyteller, I am constantly collecting ideas. I listen. I read. I watch. I scroll. And when something sparks my interest, I make a note. But for a whole year in 2021, I couldn't read or listen or collect anything at all, because all I could think about was travel.

Perhaps you were the same. During that time, even those of us who'd never before experienced wanderlust were daydreaming from behind our locked-down doors about far-flung beaches, natural wonders, and the open road. My husband and I found ourselves having the same conversation over and over again: Let's get out of here. Rent out the house, grab a van, pull the kids out of school, and head off on the Big Lap around Australia. And we weren't the only ones. It seemed everyone we spoke to had vanlife on the brain.

Unfortunately, there were a number of factors standing in our way that made the trip impossible. *It's not fair,* I'd whine at times of peak claustrophobia. *If we can't all go, I'll just go on my own.* To which the reply, no matter who it came from, was always: *Please don't do that. And if you do, be careful. Anything could happen.*

Meanwhile, the pitch for my next book was due and I was struggling to settle on an idea—that is until, one morning, my husband suggested that instead of actually going on a road trip, I could write about one. And: *light bulb*. A novel about the Big Lap . . . a family in a campervan . . . a travel thriller, fraught with danger and tension. Yes. My husband was a genius. Immediately, I set about brainstorming ideas. I thought about campfire tales and horror stories, and all the serial killers, psychos, and ghosts in every scary movie ever made.

Then, in August of 2021, twenty-two-year-old Gabby Petito was killed while traveling with her fiancé on a vanlife journey across the US. As the story made global headlines, I tried not to engage with it. I was writing a novel about a family, not a couple, and besides, I was done with dead women in crime fiction. Those narratives were overdone, often mishandled, and I suspected their ubiquity only served to reinforce the idea that the world is unsafe for women. But Gabby's name followed me around until I couldn't help but pay attention. And what I found was a profoundly upsetting tragedy, very far from exciting: the story of a young woman killed not, as it turned out, by a marauding axe murderer or even an unknown opportunist, but by her intimate partner. A man she loved and with whom she was "living the dream."

I looked into other women who had been attacked while traveling solo. Grace Millane, strangled in New Zealand. Mia Ayliffe-Chung, stabbed in Queensland. Hannah Gavios, attacked in Thailand. And on the surface these stories seemed to support the warnings—anything can, and does, happen on the road. But who exactly were the perpetrators? A sexual partner. A roommate. The security guard at a resort hotel, whose job it was to keep guests safe. All of them known to the victims. All of them men.

Falling further down the rabbit hole, I discovered that while women more than ever are traveling solo, there are huge differences in how we treat female and male travelers: itinerant men are celebrated as "adventurous," whereas women spark debates about safety (for example, see the hashtag #viajosola, meaning "I travel alone," which went viral on social media after the brutal murders of two backpackers in Ecuador). I learned that a huge proportion of violent crimes against female travelers in certain countries are not reported, or even considered noteworthy. I also found countless travel blogs, articles, and websites geared wholly toward safety tips for women but not one that exclusively spoke to men, which not only suggested that women were wholly responsible for what might potentially befall them but also that men need not join the conversation at all. Not their problem, nothing to do with them.

Around the same time, guided by a great therapist, I began to interrogate myself, digging deep into why I was prone to certain thought patterns and emotional hamster wheels. I found the process not just helpful, but fascinating. I became obsessed with attachment theory, reparenting, and the behavioral blueprints we receive when we're young. Then one day, while I was listening to *We Can Do Hard Things*—the superlative podcast hosted by Glennon Doyle, Abby Wambach, and Amanda Doyle—something lit a fire in my mind. Glennon said, "I just keep thinking about how hard it is to be the detective of your life, and also the mystery of your life."

Yes, that's exactly it, I thought. In therapy, you are both the mystery and the detective. Sometimes the crime scene too.

And that made me think of something else, a story I'd once heard. I went back to my notebooks, read through my scribbles, and the final ingredient of what became *Red River Road* dropped into place.

Let me tell you about Hannah Upp.

In August 2008, a twenty-three-year-old teacher disappeared into thin air after leaving her Manhattan home to go for a run. After what felt to her like mere minutes, she woke up in hospital with no idea how she got there. She was told that she'd just been pulled out of the Hudson River after deckhands on the Staten Island Ferry spotted her floating face down in the water. What's more, she'd been missing for three weeks. From her sick bed, Hannah searched her memory but drew a blank; despite having been caught on CCTV at a handful of locations around New York City, she had no recollection of anything she'd done during that time. Eventually, she was diagnosed with dissociative fugue, a form of amnesia so rare that few psychiatrists ever see it in their career. Fugue, Hannah was told, is triggered by a traumatic event—but she was not aware of any such incident.

Five years later, Hannah was gone again: her wallet and phone had been found on a footpath in Maryland, but she was nowhere to be seen. Unlike in New York City, though, Hannah exited her fugue state without help, "coming to" while standing in a creek with a two-day hole in her memory.

Another four years after that, she went missing for a third time, vanishing in 2017 from her new home in the US Virgin Islands, where she'd moved for a teaching job. Her clothes and car keys were found on a local beach, and her car was parked nearby, but once more, Hannah Upp had vanished. At the time of this writing, she remains missing.

Reading that story again, I marveled at the fragility of both memory and identity. What is the "self"? Do we have just one mind—or many? Who are we without memory? What really happened to Hannah? And how is it that we still know so little about disorders such as dissociative fugue? I reflected on those horror stories in a different light, all the movies and TV shows that fetishize and desensitize. Where do those stories come from and what is their value? How does what we imagine will happen to women on the road compare with what actually does?

I also thought hard about those who have fallen victim to male-perpetrated and intimate-partner violence. Many survivors mention dissociation as a coping mechanism, both in the moment and during the aftermath: *"I'm not here, it's not happening to me."* Their minds fly away while their bodies remain. I couldn't stop thinking how such a violation would decimate a woman's identity to the extent that, post-trauma, she might have to learn a new way to be in the world: how to move, how to speak, how to think. I tried to imagine the lived experience of that.

In the midst of all that thinking, Phoebe and Katy Sweeney were born. And their story is of course designed to entertain—I love a bit of adrenaline—but at its heart, *Red River Road* is about the joy of travel and the right of all women to move through the world without harassment, judgement, or constraint. It explores perceptions of safety, personal responsibility, and gendered violence. It's a story about stories, those we tell one another and those we tell ourselves, and the power we each carry within us to break a particular cycle. More than anything, it's about compassion—for ourselves and others. Because we're all dealing with something. Whatever our actions and behavior, we're only ever trying to survive the best way we know how, based on what we've been taught, and digging deep is how we change.

So, dear reader, thanks for sticking with me and for choosing to spend time with this book; I sincerely hope it was a positive experience. And I hope it made you want to see Western Australia and the awe-inspiring Coral Coast for yourself! Gracious Bay, Red Gum Roadhouse, Willowfield, Plains Ranch, William Wilson, and the café in Carnarvon are all fictional creations; however, all other places and locations along Phoebe's itinerary are real. Ningaloo truly is one of the most wildly astonishing places on Earth, and a road trip is a wonderful and (generally speaking) very safe way to see it. Trust me, I've driven the route myself and it's incredible. For more information check out www.australiascoralcoast.com or www.westernaustralia.com, or any of the travel 'grammers mentioned in my acknowledgments.

Please do drop me a line if you enjoyed this or any of my books: you can reach me at www.anna-downes.com, and on Instagram @anna_downes_writer. And in the meantime, I'll get working on the next one! I hope to see you there.

ABOUT THE AUTHOR

Ona Janzen

Anna Downes (she/her) was born and raised in Sheffield, United Kingdom, but now lives just north of Sydney, Australia, with her husband and two children. She worked as an actress before turning her attention to writing. She has degrees from both Manchester University (drama) and the Royal Academy of Dramatic Art (acting). Her previous novels include *The Safe Place* and *The Shadow House*.